A TIME OF QUESTIONS, A TIME OF QUESTS

Was it worth destroying her marriage just because her husband was unfaithful—time and time again? Ann had to make that decision as she saw her perfect Grosse Point life falling apart.

Could she pretend to be a pure bride of Christ when her mind was filled with forbidden images and her body stirred by unbidden urges? Louise had to face her fear of life and love beyond convent walls.

How could she want the man she loved to marry her, when it violated her liberated ideals . . . or shrink from doing the "sensible thing" for the new life growing in her womb? Tina found that freedom's path had led her to a cruel crossroads.

The Marcassa sisters. They could only depend on themselves—and each other

THE RESTLESS YEARS

THE RESTLESS YEARS

by

Lucy Taylor

A SIGNET BOOK

SIGNET
Published by the Penguin Group
Penguin Books USA Inc., 375 Hudson Street,
New York, New York 10014, U.S.A.
Penguin Books Ltd, 27 Wrights Lane,
London W8 5TZ, England
Penguin Books Australia Ltd, Ringwood,
Victoria, Australia
Penguin Books Canada Ltd, 10 Alcorn Avenue,
Toronto, Ontario, Canada M4V 3B2
Penguin Books (N.Z.) Ltd, 182–190 Wairau Road,
Auckland 10, New Zealand

Penguin Books Ltd, Registered Offices:
Harmondsworth, Middlesex, England

First published by Signet, an imprint of New American Library,
a division of Penguin Books USA Inc.

First Printing, November, 1992
10 9 8 7 6 5 4 3 2 1

 REGISTERED TRADEMARK—MARCA REGISTRADA

Printed in the United States of America

PUBLISHER'S NOTE
This is a work of fiction. Names, characters, places, and incidents either are
the product of the author's imagination or are used fictitiously, and any resemblance to actual persons, living or dead, events, or locales is entirely coinci-
dental.

For my loving family.

Special thanks to
Alicia, Joyce, Linda, Kathy, Phyllis, and Veronica

Prologue

Chiara's face was lined but serene, her eyes still a brilliant aquamarine, an echo of her beloved Adriatic Sea. One silver streak issued from her left temple in hair darkened by too many years and too little sun, one stubborn strand giving in to age, although at sixty-one she felt as energetic as ever and still handled the housework and occasionally filled in at one of the bridal shops when Ann needed her.

Chiara thought about her three daughters. All she had ever wanted for each of them was a good marriage, a happy life. She sighed. Only Ann had wedded. Luisa, her middle daughter, seemed happy with her choice of the convent, though Chiara had had misgivings at first about that. Luisa had been so young when she decided she had a vocation. Fifteen years old! Her youngest, Tina, was still finding her way.

Life was so different now in 1970. Women were bursting the chains that bound them. Some of the new ideals were acceptable, even laudable, but others— well, the feminists were moving too fast and too far in her opinion. She had to smile at the contradiction of her own life. Hadn't she faced opposition to realize a dream of having her own bridal shop? That was before women took up the standard for "equality." In the old days women were still feminine, and hid any strengths with coquetry, got their way with wiles.

The new feminism was confusing. This talk of "free

love," for instance. Love was never free. Not for women, at least. Men—well, that was a different story. Men had a careless attitude toward love, had more insistent urges. She blushed again at her duplicitous thinking. Mike, she was almost positive, had never strayed, while she, in a moment of need and weakness, had buckled, giving in to her sensual nature. But she had paid a price. And she was convinced women always paid, one way or another.

Not that *her* girls were the sort to give themselves easily to men. Ann was safely married. Luisa was sheltered in a convent. And Tina—well, Tina was another story entirely. Chiara purposely avoided thinking of Tina, her rebel. Tina reminded Chiara of herself. Stubborn. Too stubborn for her own good.

Chiara had reluctantly given up the bridal business when Mike retired. He wanted her company at home, and she was tired. So she'd given up the reins to Ann, who thrived on the business. But Ann didn't seem happy lately. Oh, she hadn't said so, but Chiara could tell there were tensions between Ann and her husband, Martin. Whatever the problems were, Chiara was sure her daughter could work them out.

Yes, she'd done her best to raise her girls properly, though she'd made many mistakes along the way. Truthfully, they had been somewhat pampered. What did they know of life? They hadn't known of poverty and defeat, hadn't had to leave their home and country, hadn't faced the death of a beloved child.

They would eventually taste all of life, the good and the bad, and learn from it. That was the way of life, and what could you do? Nothing.

Chiara dusted her hands with flour and proceeded to knead the dough for pizza.

1

$\mathbf{A}$nn Norbert hardly noticed the blooming lilacs and brilliant forsythia that bordered the manicured lawns of her Grosse Pointe Park neighborhood that lay just east of industrial Detroit along the Detroit River. Her husband guided the Lincoln Town Car past stately homes, Tudors with leaded glass, Georgians with stern facades, Greek revivals with tall-columned porches.

They moved onto Lake Shore Drive, past the Grosse Pointe Yacht Club with its landmark tower. On Lake St. Clair the sun cast a glittery spangle of diamonds across the water, where sailboats glided serenely. At one time the sight had brought Ann a smug sort of comfort; she used to bask, self-satisfied with her happy, complacent existence. But lately her life felt chaotic. She pressed her temples, determined to ignore the headache that threatened. The thought of work left undone—bridal-gown sketches she should go over before tomorrow morning and the laundry piling up in the basement—nagged at her.

Ann eased her head back against the car's headrest and decided, once again, that she would slow down her life. Today's birthday celebration at her parents' home would be a pleasant diversion, a chance for relaxation. She smiled in anticipation of the wonderful foods her mother would prepare. The dinners had once been a ritual. Now, as Ann's mother often lamented, it was increasingly difficult to gather all the family together.

Martin grumbled at the traffic on Jefferson and twisted sporadically in his seat to yell at their three boys, who squabbled and giggled in the back seat.

"Let them be, they're just being kids," Ann said.

"I could be at home watching the Tigers play the White Sox." Martin's tone implied Ann was at fault for disturbing his Sunday routine.

"You can watch the game there. It won't kill you to give up one Sunday."

"It's not the same as being in the comfort of your own home."

Ann sighed, explaining again, "We have to show up. It's Dad's seventieth birthday."

Martin shrugged and mumbled under his breath. He'd get over his sulk. He usually did. Martin had a grudging respect for her father despite the fact that they never agreed in their ongoing debate of labor versus management. Her father, Mike Marcassa, had been an early union organizer for the United Auto Workers. Because Martin was in management at Ford, the two men argued endlessly for their respective positions and made a game of baiting one another. Although Mike had retired, not willingly, four years ago, he still maintained the fervor of a religious convert.

Ann rubbed her forehead.

"Something wrong?" Martin asked, sounding annoyed rather than solicitous.

"Just a headache." She smoothed back a strand of short dark hair.

"You're working too hard. When are you going to give up the rat race?"

Ann knew the old refrain was just so much rhetoric. Martin wasn't serious about her giving up her income from the bridal salons. Their life-style required two salaries. "Let's not discuss it now." She glanced at the children in the back seat. "Spare them another argument."

Minutes later they pulled into the drive of the Marcassa home. The roomy Tudor-style house was in a settled, well-tended community on the Detroit side of the Eight Mile Road barrier between the city and the suburbs. Ann was forever fearful of the encroachment of what she referred to as "a lower element," and tried to convince her parents to move. Though they could well afford to upgrade, they resisted change. This was their home, for better or worse. Ann felt sure the neighborhood would become worse. The street looked strangely barren without the shady canopy of elms that had succumbed to Dutch elm disease. New trees had been planted, but were still young and inadequate imitations of those they replaced.

Her mother, Chiara, an apron covering her generous bosom and hips, met them at the door. She enveloped the boys in her arms, then kissed Ann. "You look tired, Ann. You're working too hard."

"That's what Martin says." Despite her fatigue, Ann's spirits lifted when she walked into the house. The sights and smells were echoes of her childhood; the easy chair, recovered twice, that she'd cuddled into, the garlic-and-parsley aroma that had greeted her on her return from school, the slightly crooked crucifix in the dining room where the family had recited their daily rosary. Home.

Martin settled in front of the television, gathering scattered sections of the Detroit *News* from the coffee table while Chiara urged seven-year-old Theodore and the twelve-year-old twins, Brian and Matthew, into the kitchen with promises of culinary samplings from her stove.

In a large skillet golf-ball-size meatballs sizzled. Chiara expertly culled several tiny ones that nestled in the oily bubbles and placed them on a plate for the boys.

"Yummy," Theodore said.

Ann laughed and speared a meatball with her fork. "Me too," she said, savoring the food and the memory of her own childhood and the dime-size meatballs that her mother served to stave off hunger pangs. It was pleasant, this feeling of continuity. Would her own children have that? Did she foster rituals and traditions they would cherish? Regretfully, she was so involved with her work, there was little time for the small touches. Yet it seemed now that her most vivid memories of childhood involved just those small rites and ceremonies. She would have to remember to make the miniature meatballs for her boys. Or at least ask Cousin Flora, who acted as babysitter-cum-housekeeper, to do so.

"Sit," her mother commanded, pouring coffee into a mug while the boys scampered to the basement rumpus room.

"No, let me help."

"There's nothing to do. Tina set the table before she left."

"There must be something."

"Finish the antipasto, then." Her mother slid a silver tray across the table.

Ann took a can of anchovies, slid a key into the slot, and slowly rolled the top away. "Darn. It always rolls crooked about halfway." She gingerly forked the small slippery delicacies onto the tray. "Where is Tina, anyway?"

"She went to a meeting. I warned her to be on time for dinner, but that one . . ." Chiara's eyes rolled heavenward.

Tina seemed always at loggerheads with their parents.

"What sort of meeting?" Ann asked.

Chiara lowered her voice. "I don't want to talk about it. Let Tina tell you."

Ann studied her mother. Her tight-lipped frown indicated something serious. Tina had always been somewhat rebellious. Their father had restrained her from joining the civil-rights movement when she was a teenager. The last time Ann talked to Tina, she was quoting feminist Betty Friedan. On the other hand, their parents, especially her father, maintained a rigid old-world belief. The new feminism was beyond Mike Marcassa's comprehension.

"Times change, Ma. This isn't the world you were brought up in."

"Ah, *that* world, *Italia.*" Her eyes glazed. "My own sainted mother would turn in her grave if she could see some of the things her grandchildren are doing. I just want to see Tina settled, like you, like Luisa. At her age she should be married. What's wrong with her?"

"Maybe she hasn't found Mr. Right. Who knows, maybe she doesn't want to get married. Marriage isn't always pure heaven." Ann dipped Italian bread into the simmering red sauce and popped it into her mouth with an appreciative "umm, good."

"You kids want too much. Tina wants *independence,*" Chiara said in a mocking tone. "She wants to 'do her own thing.' But she never had to work hard, struggle, like we did. Ahh, I can understand a little how she feels, but your father . . ." Chiara's eyebrows lifted, the implication clear.

"Where is Dad?"

"He's out for a walk. You know he likes to keep in shape. Not like me. I'm getting fat, eh?"

Ann laughed, hugging her mother around the waist. "You're perfect." The years, though adding a bit of padding, had only slightly dimmed her mother's beauty.

"No, I used to be like you. Pretty and thin. Ah . . ." She waved her hand airily, a characteristic gesture that meant: *so what can you do?* "But, Ann, you're looking *too* thin." Her eyes narrowed. "Is something wrong?"

"I'm just tired. It seems I'm never finished."

"It's not easy for women these days." Chiara stroked Ann's cheek. "I know. Remember, I worked way before it was fashionable for women, and I had to fight your father to do it. I worked to put food on the table back in the Depression. But back then there weren't all the other things going on, the PTA, the clubs, the social things. Maybe it's too much. Maybe you should give up some of that."

"I hate to. I need the socializing. I need to talk with other women who . . . who understand the problems. Martin certainly doesn't. He thinks his job is going to work every day and my job is everything else in addition to managing the salons."

"You and Martin are fighting?"

Ann gave a short laugh, avoiding her mother's studied gaze. "No, not really. We don't fight. We hardly even talk. You know Martin. He hates a confrontation and just clams up or leaves the house."

Chimes sounded and Ann hurried to answer the door. "Lou!" She hugged her sister for several seconds. "It's been so long . . . what, five months? Last Christmas, right?"

"Yes. Such busy lives we lead." Louise grasped Ann's hand. "But you're always in my thoughts and prayers, along with Martin and the boys."

Louise was dressed conservatively in a blue suit and white blouse, so typical of a nun's garments and in contrast to Ann's crisp white piqué dress. Surprisingly, Louise had admitted that in some ways she missed the habit that she used to wear; it was the definitive stamp that she was a "woman of God."

When they passed through the living room, Martin roused himself from his absorption in George Kell's television pregame talk long enough to give his sister-in-law a perfunctory hug. Though he never admitted it, Ann sensed he was somewhat uncomfortable in Lou's presence. He'd often said he couldn't understand someone giving up her life for "God's work," as Lou called it.

"Come into the kitchen, Lou," Ann said. "Ma's cooking."

"Of course. Ah, that aroma. We never get this in the convent."

"Luisa! You're too thin." Chiara shook her head, then wiped her hands on her apron and kissed Lou several times. "You're not eating enough, are you?"

Lou's answer was forestalled by the slamming side door and heavy footfalls signaling Mike's return. At seventy, Mike Marcassa still looked virile, his slight paunch hardly detracting from a lean physique and erect bearing. He had . . . *presence*, Ann thought.

"My best girls," he said, kissing the two sisters in turn. "Where are the little guys?"

"Downstairs." Ann sampled a wrinkled salty olive.

"We'll talk at dinner." Mike charged down the steps, calling out, "Hey, boys, Grandpa's here."

"Mike!" Chiara yelled after him. "Don't run, you'll have a heart attack!" To the girls she said, exasperated, "That man!"

The women finished the dinner preparations and in a half-hour they trooped into the dining room laden with platters of food: roast chicken, golden brown and juicy; pasta glutted with red sauce; meatballs; an array of vegetables; and the ever-present *insalata*, slick with oil and wine vinegar.

Ann smiled as she set down a basket of thick-sliced Italian bread. "Ma, why do you cook so much? You could feed Lou's entire sixth grade."

Chiara waved away Ann's remark. "You can all take some home."

Mike looked stern as they took their places. "Where's Tina?"

"She's at a meeting. She may be late," Chiara said.

"This is a family day. She should manage her time so that we can all eat together once in a while." Mike shook his head. "We've spoiled the youngest."

Chiara said, "She'll be here soon. Let's say grace."

Dinner conversation hopped from discussion of the boys' grades in school to the "grandiose" (Martin's term) union demands and "dirty tactics" (Mike's term) of management, to Ann's opening of the newest Rochester branch of Chiara's Bridal Salons, to Louise's lively sixth-grade adolescents. Dinner was almost over when Tina rushed in. She still looks like a teenager, Ann thought, noting her suede vest over a tie-dyed T-shirt and snug jeans. She stopped to calculate. Tina was ten years younger than herself—good Lord, twenty-six already.

Tina went around the table kissing all and ruffling her nephews' hair.

"Well, what's the big secret?" Ann asked. "Where were you?" Glancing at their parents, she sensed the tension. Chiara looked grim, Mike angry.

Tina took her place next to Martin. "I was at a meeting with my political-action group." She waited, as though for a reaction. When no one responded, she said passionately, "No one likes to talk about the war. They'd rather bury their heads in the sand." Her voice rose. "Does anyone know why we're fighting in Vietnam? Does anyone care? Cambodia! We're fighting in *Cambodia*, for God's sake. We should pull out of Southeast Asia entirely."

"Tina, I told you before." Mike pointed his fork at her. "I don't want to hear any more of that unpatriotic talk."

"Well, just because you don't want to hear about dissension doesn't mean it will go away." She piled pasta on her plate. "They're planning a peaceful demonstration in Washington. I'm thinking of going."

"You're not going anywhere," Mike said, his face turning red. "Next thing we know you'll be burning the American flag. Who do you think you are, saying our country shouldn't be in this war?"

"All war is wrong and this one is an atrocity. We have no business in Vietnam."

"And you want to demonstrate against it. That's close to treason! Do you understand that?" her father shouted.

"Pa, it's *not* treason. It's facing up to the truth."

"Whatever happened to 'my country, right or wrong'? What happened to loyalty, to integrity?" Mike's fork clattered against the china. "What happened to wanting to fight for your country? In World War Two the soldiers were proud to fight for the United States of America."

"That's bull. Propaganda. You think those soldiers wanted to die? Besides, World War Two was different. This war is totally—"

"I'm telling you," Mike said, leaning forward, pointing at Tina, "no daughter of mine is going to march against this country!"

Tina's eyes narrowed with anger. "And I'm telling you, I'm old enough to do what I think is right." She pushed away from the table, toppling her wineglass, and ran up the stairs.

An uneasy silence followed as Lou mopped up the spilled wine.

"I don't understand that girl," Mike muttered. "Why can't she be like you two? You, Ann, you've settled down with a good man and have a nice family. You have a good life. And you, Luisa. You knew you had a call from God and you answered that call. You're satisfied, happy. But Tina? I don't know how we went wrong with her."

"Pa, she's young . . ." Ann began.

"Young? She's twenty-six. She should have four or five bambinos by now." Mike shook his head ruefully and pushed away from the table.

Later, after Mike had blown out the birthday candles and they'd eaten the cake, Ann said, "I've got an awful headache. I'm going to lie down for a bit."

"It was all that arguing at the table," her mother said.

"No, my head ached before I came. I'm feeling so tense. Granted, Tina's outburst didn't help."

"Go lie down," her mother said, motioning upstairs with a damp dishcloth. "Luisa and I will finish cleaning up."

Ann's old bedroom was intact, as if waiting for her return. A flowered chintz bedspread with matching curtains, a faded slipper satin chair, a cerulean dressing table with bottles of cologne, all seemed undisturbed since she left home. She sat at the dressing table and pressed the tiny wrinkle between her brows. The years hadn't done too much damage, she thought, forcing a smile to her lips. She was her father's daughter; thick dark hair, defined arched brows, a nose she wished were a trifle shorter. Only her mouth was different; vulnerable somehow.

She picked up a cologne bottle. Lily of the valley. It must have turned to something vile after so many years. The cap was stuck tight, but came loose with a little pressure. She put her nose to the opening and sniffed. Pretty awful. Yet for some reason she couldn't throw the bottle away. She felt a need to preserve the essence of what she had been. Had she ever really been seventeen, eighteen? A sweet young innocent? She could hardly remember. She'd been only twenty-one when she returned from her honeymoon to find her mother ill and in need of surgery. While Chiara underwent a hysterectomy, Ann, without hesitation, had picked up the reins of the bridal business and supervised the opening of the third salon. When her mother resumed her position after a year-long recuperation, Ann happily assisted her mother as business manager. She'd given it up reluctantly when the twins were born. Ann adored her children, loved being a wife and mother, but the pure drudgery of being a housewife frustrated her. When the twins were three, Ann hired a housekeeper and began to work part-time. By the time the boys were in school, Theodore was born. It was several more years before she could devote full time to the bridal business. When her mother retired, Ann became the sole manager. From the beginning, Martin discouraged her working, though he was more than pleased with her paycheck. He couldn't understand why she wasn't fulfilled and happy in her housewife role. But Ann loved working. At least, she used to love it. What was wrong with her? Why the current dissatisfaction, the unease? She moved to the bed and with supple grace stretched onto the smooth spread.

After several minutes the door inched open and Louise whispered, "Are you asleep?"

"No, come on in. What's Ma doing?"

"She's *prewashing* the dishes. She still doesn't trust the dishwasher. Can you believe her?"

Ann nodded. "Yeah."

Louise studied her sister. "You have circles under your eyes. Are you overworking?"

"Of course. Don't I always?"

Louise's face was kind, her blue eyes, their mother's eyes, were concerned. "You should slow down, you know. All this overwork isn't good for you. Or your family."

"I know. I try to do it all. Supermom, super-businesswoman. How do I slow down?"

"There must be ways, if you really want to do it. Delegate more at work, make Martin take on some of the school projects and extra activities for the boys."

"Martin's not very cooperative." Ann sighed. "The trouble is, I don't know what I want. I only know I'm dog-tired. All the time."

Louise sat on the edge of the bed. "Have you had a physical lately?"

"It's nothing physical. But, yes, I did see the doctor recently and he tried to put me on a tranquilizer. The instant and universal cure. Of course I refused."

"What does Martin say?"

"He's hardly aware of my misery. When I complain, he says if I can't handle the business I should give it up."

Louise said nothing, but her look said that it was an idea worth considering.

Ann said, "Think about it, Lou. Ma built the business up from nothing. I couldn't sell it. It would kill her."

"Have you talked to Ma about it?"

"No. Besides, I really don't want to sell. I love the work."

"Look at the alternatives. You could put someone else in charge."

"Like who? There's no one with the experience and expertise. The managers of the six stores are all good, but none of them has what it takes to oversee the entire operation."

"Then look elsewhere."

Ann was silent for a moment. "I guess I don't want to give up the reins. I want to have my cake and eat it too."

Louise sighed and asked softly, "Then what are we talking about? There's something else, isn't there? Martin?"

"I suppose he's part of it." Ann's laugh was ironic. "I envy you, Lou. Your life is so simple. You knew what you wanted from the time you were fifteen."

Lou gave a wry grin. "Oh, yes. My life is so simple."

The doorknob rattled and Tina entered. "Girl talk?"

"Sort of. Come in," Ann said. "What's going on with you?"

"Look, if this is going to be a lecture . . ."

Ann lifted her hands in a gesture of peace. "No lectures."

"Pa's livid," Tina said. "I'm sorry I moved back home. I should have kept that apartment near Wayne State."

"Why did you move back?" Louise asked, patting a spot beside her on the bed.

Tina sat, crossing her legs Indian-style, the fringe of her vest swaying. "Money, of course. When I quit my job and started grad school, I was flat broke."

"It's tough being on your own. You have to cut a lot of corners," Ann said.

"Well, I tried," Tina said defensively, her arms crossed over her chest. "Unfortunately, I didn't save any money when I was working, and I know I made some bad decisions job-wise. I'm earning a little teaching night-school classes, but that just covers my university expenses."

"If it's money you need, Tina, you know Martin and I—"

"No. No handouts. I can handle it." Tina was adamant. "I have enough to get to Washington for the peace march. I really want to go. I feel so strongly about it. I suppose you both think I'm crazy too."

Louise touched Tina's shoulder. "I don't. I think you're very courageous."

"You may not be crazy, but this march is ill-advised," Ann said. "What do you hope to accomplish? You could get thrown into jail. And ultimately, nothing's going to change."

"That's the sort of head-in-the-sand attitude I'd expect from you, Ann." Tina sighed with exasperation. "I guess we just don't see eye-to-eye."

Ann's mouth tightened. "I don't pretend to be politically minded. I hardly keep up with the news at all. But, Tina, I just don't want to see you hurt."

"Don't you see if everyone had that attitude, changes would never occur? We 'doves' have to take a stand against Nixon and the rest of the 'hawks.' "

Louise broke in. "I agree with you, Tina. You must have the courage of your convictions. I *hate* war—all that senseless killing."

Ann rearranged a pillow behind her head. "When did all this political activism take hold, Tina? You weren't always this way."

"I don't know. I guess it's been gradual. 'The times they are a-changin'.' Civilization should have progressed to where we can settle differences without bloodshed." Tina turned passionate eyes to Ann, pleading for understanding. "Surely you agree with that!"

Louise said, "Bravo. If I had the nerve, I'd join you."

Ann reached over and grabbed Tina's hand. "Tina, stop and think of what you're doing to Ma and Pa, the worry you're causing them."

"Oh, please! That's all I hear from them. They'll get over it. They should know me by now."

Ann held her ground. "They should be considered. Stop being so self-centered."

"Self-centered! Ann, there's a whole different world out there that you are completely ignorant of."

"Stop it!" Louise said. "Ann, you know you can't change her mind. You'd both better agree to disagree and leave it at that."

Ann glared at Tina for a moment, then relented. "Okay, little sister. It's your life. If you definitely decide to go ahead with this peace demonstration, let me know, okay?"

Tina gave a conciliatory nod. "Sure."

From downstairs their mother's high-pitched voice rang out: "Girls!"

The sisters snapped to attention, much as they'd done when they were small. At the door they hugged for a long heartfelt moment. Friends. No, more. Family.

2

That night sleep eluded Tina as she tossed, replaying her sisters' words in her mind. She wondered if Ann were right, that protests did nothing more than anger the authorities, that they were the actions of teenagers and immature college students. Was she acting immaturely? She thought not. Though she was well past her teens, she shared their idealistic passion for peace and justice. Yet she was uneasy about her parents' disapproval.

The events of the next day, May 4, decided the issue for Tina. During a nonviolent antiwar demonstration on the campus of Kent State University in Ohio, shots rang out for thirteen seconds. Thirteen students were struck by National Guardsmen's bullets. Four of them died. The entire nation was shocked and horrified. Seething with anger and revulsion, Tina strengthened her resolve and prepared to join the peace march.

She bore her parents' recriminations stoically and called Ann to tell her she was coming over, with the vague hope of moral support. When she arrived at Ann's house, the kids were in bed and Martin was asleep in front of the television. Ann hugged Tina and beckoned her to the kitchen.

"So, what's going on?" Ann turned on the gas under a kettle and arranged chocolate-chip cookies on a plate.

Tina rummaged through a tin of herbal teas. "I just

wanted you to know that I'm going to Washington. The Kent State massacre clinched it for me."

"I can't say I'm surprised, knowing how you feel. It was an atrocity." Ann poured steaming water into mugs. "But what bothers me is . . . well, it seems like you've rejected all our standards, the family standards. This is going to upset the folks."

"Do you imagine I haven't thought about that? My God, I've spent most of my life with my conscience whispering that phrase: What would my parents think? It's a bad way to live, Ann. It restricts my freedom of choice. At some point I *have* to say: What does *Tina* think? At some point I have to follow my own beliefs, not my parents', not my church's, not yours or Lou's."

"Oh, so all our values are worthless."

"I didn't say that." Tina, frustrated at Ann's opposition, her unwillingness to understand, raised her voice. "Look, I don't tell you how to live your normal father-knows-best life, so don't tell me how to live mine."

Ann bristled. "I'm not trying to tell you how to live your life. And my life is not normal. Not all women juggle a business and a family."

"Well, nearly normal. The point is, I can't see myself living your sort of life. Not now, anyway." Tina dropped a tea bag into her cup. "I feel I have to take a stand, make my small statement. Can you understand any of this at all?"

"Not really." Ann's expression softened. "But it's your life, Tina. Don't squander it. Go ahead and do what you must." She put her arm around her younger sister. "Listen, write my phone number inside your hand just in case you need it."

Tina shook her head ruefully. "The big-sister/baby-sister routine."

"You never know what'll happen. And if you ever need anything . . . Well, Tina, you know I love you."

Tina's pent-up tears suddenly broke loose. "It's just

like you to end up being so nice." She started laughing through her weeping. "You never did play fair. I love you too." She snuffled into a tissue Ann handed her, and stuffed a few more into the pocket of her parka before she left.

Tina bobbed her head to the music of the Who, blaring "My Generation" from the radio. They'd left late at night, May 6, bound for Washington, and Max had been driving steadily, unwilling to stop except for a quick cup of coffee.

"I'm getting hungry." Tina consulted her map. "You need a break, Max. Let's stop at Breezewood."

Max, humming along with the radio, didn't respond. His sandy hair, shoulder-length and parted in the middle, kept sliding over his eyes. His fingers drummed constantly on the steering wheel. He switched to a news station. President Nixon had ordered his staff to compile a thorough report on what had occurred at Kent State. The Washington police were expecting huge crowds at the pending demonstration. Students were filtering in by car, bus, train, plane, and thumb.

"We're in on a historic event," Max remarked.

Tina agreed, then fell silent. In a few moments she said, "Let's stop for something to eat, then I'll drive awhile."

Max shook his head. "Unh-unh. I've seen you drive."

"What's that supposed to mean?"

"Nothing."

"I'm a good driver."

"Okay, you're a good driver." He smiled condescendingly. "It's just that I'm nervous whenever someone else drives. Especially women."

"Is that stupid remark supposed to placate me?" Max's grin widened and Tina dropped the matter. They were both on edge from weariness. At one time she'd thought she and Max could have a relationship, but the more she saw him, the more certain she felt that they had no future together. He had a reputation as a ladies' man. Besides, he was too much a drifter. His once-appealing laid-back attitude now often irked her. Still, she knew the carefree facade hid a strong intelligence.

Now, with a conciliatory nod, Max turned in to a diner. "Lots of trucks. That's a good sign."

Tina hopped out of the car. "Yeah, it means we'll get lots of greasy food for a reasonable price."

"Bitch, bitch, bitch." Max gave her a sidewise glance. "I'm surprised you came along. You have a strong conservative streak."

Tina was ready to make an angry retort, then decided he had a point. "I thought of backing out after my family, all but Louise, voiced their opposition. The slayings at Kent State convinced me."

Max nodded. "That's got everybody fired up."

Inside the diner, Tina flicked back long dark hair that trailed over her shoulders and slid into a booth, her tight jeans binding at the worn-white creases.

Max glanced at the menu a moment before he heeded the waitress's impatient tapping. He ordered an omelet with hash browns, and pie à la mode. "I thought you were hungry," he said when Tina ordered soup and salad.

She shrugged. "Have you figured out where we're going to stay?" Before they'd left Detroit he'd convinced her to buy a sleeping bag.

Max's glance roved approvingly over her loose gauzy Indian shirt.

"I told you not to worry about it. I'll take care of you." He gave her a sly sidewise look.

"I'm not worried. Just curious." She supposed he expected her to sleep with him. But she wasn't into easy love, despite its general acceptance. For her there had to be a stronger basis for sex than mere physical attraction.

"Live in the here and now, that's my motto," Max said.

"I try to be spontaneous."

"That's the point. You can't *try*. You can just *be*.

"Okay, so I'm a worrier. You said you'd make all the plans. But it seems there aren't any plans at all. I heard they're expecting over one hundred thousand protesters in Washington."

"That's the beauty of it all." Max smiled benignly. "We don't need plans. Everything works out."

To him this trip was an adventure; to her it was a statement, a commitment.

"Max . . ."

"Shit! You worry about all the small crap. Hang loose, baby."

His theory that everything works out was still a fairly new concept to Tina, and one she had a hard time accepting. Up to now her life hadn't worked all that well. Then again, she hadn't expected it would. Aye, there's the rub, she thought. Expectations.

While waiting for the pie, Max tapped a cadence on the table with his spoon and smiled at her, coaxing a reciprocal grin. He could be charming, especially when he smiled, his forthright gray eyes crinkling almost shut.

Maybe his theory was right. Be like the lilies of the field. Oh, sure, a lily. Of all the flowers she could think of, a lily was the least she resembled. A morning glory perhaps, or a wildflower.

Max took a bite of the pie, cream dripping off his fork. "I'd like to burn my draft card, you know? Just stand on the Capitol steps and—poof—up in smoke."

"You're 4-F."

Max glowered. "Okay, so I've got a slight heart murmur. They don't need to know that. I could be burning my library card or something. It's just a gesture.''

Tina decided not to pursue a discussion of Max's illogical thought processes.

They finished their meal and were soon on the road again. Tina closed her eyes and wondered what had brought two such unlikely personalities as she and Max together. Peace and a quest for justice, she decided, was the reason. She'd known Max since they were both students at Wayne State. When they were reintroduced at a party six months ago, they'd begun seeing each other casually. It was Max who had sparked her latent interest in the peace movement. He would have liked a more romantic involvement, but although she couldn't deny he had a certain charisma, she wasn't really interested in him as a lover.

Dozing, Tina heard Max singing off-key along with Bob Dylan. He turned again to a news station and she heard another report about the upcoming peace rally in Washington. The newscaster quoted Ronald Reagan, governor of California, who had said about student protests even before the Kent State incident, ''If it takes a bloodbath, then let's get it over with.''

''That swine,'' Tina said, while Max muttered obscenities.

It was dawn when they stopped for takeout coffee. Tina marveled at Max's energy. In the capital there was a steady stream of beltway traffic, even at this early hour.

''It's always congested in Washington,'' Max said. ''But don't worry, I always find a parking spot.''

Tina rolled her eyes at his abiding confidence. When the Capitol came into view she drew in her breath. A sense of pride welled up in her at the sight of the gleaming dome. ''Max, it's awesome, isn't it?''

''Yeah, it sure is.''

''Think of all the power in that building. But we

have power too. Do you think we can really make a difference?'' she asked urgently.

"If nothing else, they'll notice us.''

Several minutes later they slowed in front of the office of the New Mobilization Committee to End the War in Vietnam and a car pulled out of a spot directly in front of them. Max eased the Pinto in with a self-satisfied smirk, saying, "Hey, what did I tell you?''

Inside, the place was jammed with enthusiastic protesters, talking, singing, shouting greetings. A tall thin man grinned at Tina beneath a bushy mustache and gave a peace sign, which she returned. The group was as one, exuding an energy that was almost palpable. The leader, wearing a fringed vest and leather headband, shouted for quiet.

"All right, here's the plan,'' the man said. In an authoritative voice he gave instructions. Each group was assigned an area. Tina and Max went with the Massachusetts Avenue group. As Tina loaded her arms with leaflets, she wondered how these people knew what to do. Until now she hadn't realized there was a methodology behind the operation. She'd imagined it was an almost spontaneous happening. Did the organizers go to protester school or take night classes in peaceful demonstrating?

Max steered Tina out the door. "Shit, I was hoping we'd have Pennsylvania Avenue. Well, let's get going. Anybody need a ride?''

Several people scrambled into the car with them. The little Pinto strained under the weight of six high-spirited, singing passengers. As they unloaded at Massachusetts Avenue, Tina pulled up the hood of her blue sweatshirt against the light breeze. Though the sun shone high and bright, the air was cool.

"Tina,'' someone shouted. She turned to see a former student from a remedial English class she'd taught at a community college.

"What are *you* doing here?" the girl asked, her eyes widening in surprise.

"The same thing you're doing. Juliet, isn't it?"

"Yes. This is great. Did you come alone?"

"No, with Max. Max Ardry." Tina nudged Max's unresponding back with her thumb.

"Do you have someplace to stay?"

"Um, no, we're winging it." Tina cast a glance at Max, who'd turned their way by then.

"Look, if you need a spot to lay your head, my cousin has a place not far from here." Juliet found a tattered pad in her backpack and scribbled an address on it. "Don't be surprised at the house. It's not the Ritz."

"Thanks, I may just need this."

"Did you bring a mask?" Juliet asked, twirling a white surgical mask around her finger.

Tina was puzzled. "What for?"

"In case we're gassed."

"Gassed!"

"Yeah, tear gas. This is no Sunday-school picnic. It's a demonstration."

"But it's supposed to be *peaceful*," Tina said emphatically, suddenly wondering if she were getting in over her head. "Well, if they can shoot students at Kent, I guess I shouldn't be surprised at a little gassing."

A boy joined them and hung his arm loosely around Juliet's shoulder. His stringy black hair fell forward, hiding part of his face, which was covered with acne. "We *could* get gassed," he said with assurance. "But that little thing won't be much help, Jul."

"This is Tod. Tina Marcassa," Juliet said.

"Tod, have you ever done anything like this before?" Tina asked.

"Nope. It's my virgin voyage."

Tina nodded. "Mine too. I wish I knew the area

better. But what good would it do? I get lost a block from my own house."

"It's easy to get lost in Washington," Juliet said. "Do you have a street map?"

"No." Tina realized she was woefully unprepared. Maybe she *had* been expecting a sort of Sunday-school picnic.

"Take mine." Juliet reached again into her backpack. "I know my way around from spending time at my cousin's."

Max had tuned in to the last of the conversation and placed a hand on Tina's shoulder. "Don't worry about getting lost. Just stay with the group. We're cool."

Nevertheless, Tina gratefully accepted the map and Juliet and Tod moved to the other side of the street. Stopping traffic was amazingly simple. The protesters linked arms and spanned the road while others pushed leaflets through open windows or under windshield wipers. The drivers came to a halt with a variety of expressions: some looked angry, others frightened, others simply annoyed. When the demonstrators got a receptive ear, they gave their peace spiel. Tina experienced an awareness of power, a sort of high, with the knowledge that this small band of peace marchers could effect such responses as fear and anger. Yet the group was actually harmless. She wanted to say: Don't be afraid, we're just making a statement here. Just trying to get you to think.

After all, they were after *peace*.

A man with a thin mustache rolled down his window and shouted obscenities at the "goddamn hippies."

"Look, this will get you nowhere," said a frowning elderly woman. "Let me through. I have important work at the Pentagon."

An angry naval officer yelled, "You've got no business doing this. What are you trying to prove?"

A woman about Tina's age, obviously going to some office job, got out of her car and approached the protesters.

"We don't want to hurt anyone," Tina said. "We have no weapons. This is just our way to draw attention to a war that we had no business being in to begin with—"

"Look, kid, it's okay with me. I wish I could join you, but I'm too chicken. I was supposed to go to a bitch of a meeting this morning. Now I've got an excuse to postpone it. Go for it!" She turned back to her car, whistling.

Horns blared, drivers craned their necks to see what was causing the holdup, and the marchers, in a festive mood, broke into song—"Where Have All the Flowers Gone?" and "This Land Is Your Land."

After they'd been at it almost two hours, Tina said, "I'm beat. My feet hurt, my head hurts, and I'm hungry."

Her companion, a black girl, her hair dyed red, agreed amiably.

"Hey, Tina," Max yelled over a few heads. "Looks like we've worn out our welcome."

She turned to see several police cars parking on an adjacent street. The police, in full riot gear, streamed from their cars and raced toward the protesters.

Absurdly, Tina felt the urge to yell: Wait a minute. We didn't mean any harm! Instead she said, "Let's make tracks."

"Right on," said the black girl.

Max joined them. "We've accomplished our mission. Traffic's bottled up so bad it won't get back to normal till tomorrow. Get a move on."

Tina sprinted after Max toward the area where they'd parked the Pinto, while the other marchers scattered in all directions. Venturing a glance over her shoulder, she saw a burly cop tailing her.

"Oh, God, why me?" she muttered, the adrenaline pumping furiously through her veins. A stiff breeze twisted her hair across her face. Though the air was warm, she felt a distinct chill. She turned for another quick look. The cop was gaining on her. Rather than fear, she felt indignation and anger. She stopped and turned to confront him.

When they were face-to-face, she said through gritted teeth and panting breaths, "This is absurd. I'm only five-feet-four. You're bigger, faster and, I'm sure, tougher." Dramatically she thrust her wrists out toward him. "Go ahead, arrest me."

He gave a short derisive laugh. "I don't want to arrest you, kid. I just want you to go home like a good little girl and quit playing dangerous games."

"Were you in the war, officer?"

"Yeah, Korea, if it's any of your business."

"Do you agree with this war?"

"Look, kid, I'm just doing my job. Now, scram before I *have* to arrest you."

Tina gave him a level look before hurrying on. She reached the Pinto just as it was about to screech away. Her heart pumping furiously, she squeezed in on someone's lap.

"Thanks for rescuing me, Max," she said sarcastically. "I almost got arrested back there."

"I looked for you but couldn't see you in the crowd. I was going to drive around until I found you."

Later that day Tina and Max joined a large group gathered at the Lincoln Memorial. The adrenaline high had worn away and Tina was exhausted. She gazed upon the bronze Lincoln with reverence. Erect, stately, kindly, he embodied the American ideal.

She leaned her head on Max's shoulder and whispered, "I think I'm going to cry."

He hugged her, brushing his cheek against hers in unaccustomed sentiment. "Yeah, baby, I know how you feel."

The evening sky soon turned pink, then gray, and the air turned cooler. The music grew mellower. Judy Collins sang sweet songs of peace and love, and people spread sleeping bags on the grass, preparing to settle in for the night. The sickly-sweet smell of hash filled the air.

"We should go to Juliet's cousin's place. It's bound to be more comfortable," Tina said.

"And miss this?" Max replied. "Not a chance. You go on if you want to."

"I would if I could find Juliet again. But I haven't been able to spot her in this crowd."

"Go on your own. You have the address."

"I'd never find it. I don't have a compass built in my head like you."

"Things work out."

"Okay, Mr. Cool." Tina unrolled her sleeping bag. "I guess we're in this together."

"Right on."

Cold and dampness from the ground under her sleeping bag seeped into her very bones. She was painfully uncomfortable no matter which way she positioned herself. She wondered fleetingly what events had gotten her in this particular place in her life. Though she wore the regulation long hair, used little makeup, and sported the tattered-blue-jean standard of the counterculture, she'd never thought of herself as a "hippie." It was a shame, she thought, that they had to be lumped under a label, that she couldn't just be a citizen against war.

She scrunched up against Max's sleeping form for the scant warmth it provided and thought of her comfortable bed at home. Home. Her parents were clearly disappointed in her. At the moment she was jobless. "Security!" her father hammered at her. "Get a job with the government." A staid conservative, he had no perception of her mind-set. It was hard to believe that he'd been a firebrand in his younger days, at the forefront of the union movement.

"When will you grow up?" her mother often wondered aloud, with a mixture of affection and perplexity.

Tina felt she'd been floating, directionless, waiting for some wave of inspiration to wash over her, or a heavenly finger to point out the path of her future. Her future was not in teaching, she knew. After graduation she had taught in the Detroit public-school system. She'd endured it for two miserable years; she was no Louise, patient and long-suffering. The high-school students alternately irked and terrified her. The only benefit she received from her experience was meeting Richard. He'd been a teacher; a bearded, jean-clad free spirit before it became commonplace. "You're still living at home?" he'd asked in derision. That remark had prompted her to move to an apartment near his, to the dismay of her parents. Richard's place was spare but messy, with books and papers scattered on every flat surface and an alleycat who answered to "Uncle Milty." Richard had been her first lover and she shivered again in the cold, remembering his furry chest and lean limbs, his passion, and sadly, his distance.

"I'm not the marrying kind," he said.

"Neither am I," she lied.

Their breakup was shattering. She had thought he'd marry her to keep from losing her. Since then she was restless, unable to find with other men the spark she'd had with Richard.

On impulse she resigned from the school system. After many weeks of freedom and boredom, she took the first secretarial job that presented itself. She endured several months of a pompous and portly chain-smoking boss before deciding office work was even less satisfying than teaching. She entered a master's program in English literature at Wayne State and, because of finances, reluctantly moved back home, to her parents' delight. She'd just completed a part-time teaching stint at a community college, which suited her somewhat better than teaching high school.

Reflecting on it, she thought that after her relationship with Richard she'd simply jumped track, moved in a different direction, and was still uncertain of where her journey would lead. Was she, after all, simply immature as her family seemed to believe? It was a disturbing thought.

Now scattered loud laughter jarred her from her reverie. She twisted to avoid an uncomfortable lump beneath her spine, and peeked over the covering of her sleeping bag to see the Milky Way in its glittering splendor. If she weren't so numb, she would get her pad and pen out and write something inspirational.

She wasn't sure when she fell asleep. Several times during the night she awakened shivering and miserable. Something jarred her into consciousness. Her lids lifted to the opening edge of daylight.

She felt it again. A kick in the small of her back.

"Hey, cut it out!" Springing to a sitting position, she turned her head.

A National Guardsman, a rifle slung over his shoulder, glared at her. She caught her breath.

"Get outta here," the soldier said, his thumb jerking upward.

Outrage sparked in Tina. "What? You can't—"

"Out!" he yelled, reaching for his rifle.

That gesture spoke volumes. Tina looked around. The makeshift camp was ringed with guardsmen, rifles at the ready. All around her, protesters were rousing and collecting their gear, grousing all the while. This, Tina thought sensibly, is no time to demand my rights.

Max had stirred also, swearing under his breath. "Shit. I guess we gotta go."

"What now?" Tina asked.

"Let's find someplace to eat. Then we'll go to Washington University. There'll be students meeting there."

During the following days Tina met all sorts of people: altruistic, dedicated people with love in their hearts, determined radicals with fire in their eyes. She and Max found refuge at night in the home of a senatorial aide named Waters, a man who remained outwardly neutral but who was clearly on the side of peace. In his carpeted basement, six protesters watched President Nixon's press conference. At the end of the conference, as the President walked out of the East Room, the protesters, sprawled on the sleeping bags, chanted "oink-oink-oink" in cadence with his steps. Tina felt as though she were watching history being made. But still, when she thought of the upcoming march, she felt a slight stir of apprehension.

The next day the President met with candle-carrying youths outside the White House and listened to their pleas, but refused to back down on keeping troops in Cambodia. Thursday and Friday went by in a swift blur with Senator Percy chatting with students on the Capitol grounds and Senator Edward Kennedy addressing a group on the steps of the Senate wing of the Capitol.

Saturday, May 9, the day of the major protest, dawned bright and clear. Tina's heart thrummed as she and Max neared the huge grassy oval of the Elipse just south of the White House.

"What a crowd. I've never seen so many people in one place!"

Most of the assemblage were teenagers, long-haired flower children, but many were in their early twenties and a few were older. She and Max must be the oldest protesters around. Delayed adolescence? she wondered. No, she decided, delayed commitment.

With flags flying, signs waving, and loudspeakers droning, Tina thought the scene resembled a country fair. Police directed oncoming traffic, blowing their whistles and waving their arms.

A long-haired white youth offered a peace button to a black police officer, who accepted it with a smile and fastened it on his gun belt. A band of young people snaked through the crowd chanting, "Peace now," while they raised signs that said, "Remember Kent." There were other somber reminders of the recent Kent State incident. One group carried four symbolic coffins with a banner declaring, "Thou shalt not kill." Someone wore a shroud and bore a sickle with the notation "41,733 plus four," representing those killed in Nam and the Kent slayings. But mostly the protesters were in a jubilant mood. Tina and Max, caught up in the festival spirit, mingled with the crowd.

Tina turned her attention to the platform. Phil Ochs was singing, "All we are saying, is give revolution a chance." A stranger flashed Tina the peace sign and hugged her in a gesture of camaraderie. Exhilarated, filled with a spirit of empathy, Tina hugged back.

From the loudspeaker came an introduction followed by applause and shouts. Dr. Benjamin Spock took the platform. Tina remembered seeing his childcare book, dog-eared and coffee-stained, at Ann's house. Her bible, Ann called it. Tina wondered how Ann felt about her honored doctor being a war protester. Dr. Spock told the crowd, "We salute the students of Kent State University, the GI's fighting in Vietnam, and we salute the black militants, particularly those who died. We're not here just to demonstrate, we're here to plan where we go from here. We're here to demand an end to the war, not in seventy-two, not in seventy-one, but in 1970!''

Tina cheered along with the others. She mopped the line of sweat that had gathered on her brow from the climbing temperature.

Jane Fonda took her turn, saluting them with, ''Greetings, fellow bums,'' alluding to President Nixon's earlier referral to the protesters.

Her speech urged them to demand a stop to the war. Other speakers followed, calling for a move to action. But among the crowd and even among the speakers, there seemed to be a division between love and hate, reform and revolution, liberalism and radicalism, violence and nonviolence. Yet Tina felt that violence seemed foreign to the spirit of the occasion.

A representative of the New Mobilization Committee took the stand and pleaded with the mob to remain nonviolent. Thousands of leaflets were circulated through the crowd warning that any violence would mean suicide for the movement and delay in ending the war.

David Dallinger, radical publisher and Chicago conspiracy-trial defendant, said, ''This is not just a picnic on a lawn, no more fun and games. We're here to get energized, to build a head of steam, to get a focus.''

The leader of the Black Panthers, Det Miranda, taking another tack, chided, ''We're concerned with a war thousands of miles away, while oppression and murder of blacks is happening a few feet from your noses.''

''One problem at a time,'' muttered Max.

In the escalating heat, the crowd's attention slowly wandered away from the speakers. Several youths, giving in to the temptation of the cool reflecting pool, tore off their clothes and rushed in nude. Soon hundreds joined, and Tina blushed to see bare-breasted girls and white-bottomed males splash into the water, unheeding of the stares and hoots.

A lucky few had found refuge under the cooling branches of the scattered elm trees, while across the way sprinklers arced their cool silvery sprays on the emerald White House lawn.

The march began in earnest as the group advanced to the White House, chanting, "Peace Now," and "Remember Kent."

At the White House the assemblage continued shouting their protests. After a while Tina and Max broke away from the group and headed toward Lafayette Park. North of the park, on H Street, demonstrators began rocking one of the buses that offered a barricade between the protesters and the White House.

"Max," Tina screamed. "They're going to tip it over!"

"Shit! They'll get arrested for sure."

Several students rushed forward in an attempt to stop the first group, yelling, "Hey, this is nonviolent. Stop it!"

Max and Tina joined the peacemakers, and attempted to push the rowdy students away from the tilting bus. One of them took a swing at Max and he swung back. Others intervened to stop the fighting. Meanwhile, the bus teetered dangerously.

"Lock arms," Max instructed, grabbing Tina's hand. Others clasped hands and they formed a human wall around the buses to keep the unruly faction from the bus and to protect the spectators who milled about.

From the corner of her eye Tina spotted several policemen in riot helmets running toward them.

Suddenly the air filled with acrid smoke. "Tear gas!" someone rasped through a coughing spasm. Tina's eyes and throat began burning and she gagged violently. The protesters, coughing and retching, sprayed out in all directions, screaming in raspy voices.

A short distance away Tina leaned against a tree, her eyes tearing so she could hardly see. As she wiped her watery eyes, someone took hold of her arm. When she looked up, a grim-faced policeman was standing over her.

"You're coming with me, girl," he said.

3

Tina gasped, blinking through burning eyes.

The young pink-faced cop jerked her arm and said, "You're under arrest."

For a moment Tina sputtered in disbelief. "No! What for?"

"Just shut up and you won't get hurt."

"But I haven't done anything," she protested through a cough. This could not be happening to her. "I . . . I was just standing here trying to recover from your gas bomb. You're being totally unfair!"

"You're disturbing the peace."

She wheezed. "I'm trying to *make* peace."

Tina circled her free arm around the tree and tightened her grip, but the officer yanked her away and dragged her, resisting and screaming, toward the street, where he shoved her into a half-filled paddy wagon.

"This is an illegal arrest," she yelled to the unheeding officer. In minutes the wagon was filled with other prisoners, all objecting vehemently. Tina viewed the motley group, shabby protesters with plastered-on knee-ripped jeans, all sporting long straggly hair. It occurred to her that she probably looked as seedy as they. The great unwashed, someone had dubbed them.

The vehicle lurched once, then sped away. The smell of perspiration, dirt, and the residue of tear gas that lingered on her clothing made Tina nauseous. She swallowed hard, determined not to vomit, or worse yet, cry. Scrunched on the bench next to her, a frightened young girl barely in her teens started crying, tears streaming down her freckled cheeks.

"My mother'll kill me," she burbled. "I'll be grounded forever."

Tina, sorry for the girl, suppressed her own discomfort and placed her arm around the youngster. "It's okay. They can't keep us for very long."

The girl sniffed and wiped her nose with the back of her hand. "I wasn't even doing anything!"

"Neither was I. They have no reason to arrest us."

"They're doing it," the girl answered reasonably.

So they are, Tina thought. This is unreal. I feel like I'm acting in a stupid B movie. How could this happen to a nice girl like me?

She handed the kid a tissue from her pocket and tried to soothe her, but somehow the words she uttered sounded insincere. How could she be reassuring in the face of her own apprehension?

The vehicle swerved around a corner, throwing the passengers against one another. After a while Tina asked, "What's your name?"

"Karen." The girl sniffled. "What's going to happen?"

"I'm Tina, Karen. And I've no idea. This is my first arrest." As if it were a commonplace happening, as if everyone had a first arrest, as in "first date" or "first kiss."

The vehicle came to a screeching halt, jostling the passengers, who responded with curses and complaints.

The disgruntled group was herded from the wagon and through double doors, then directly into already crowded holding cells, men in one, women in another. Tina craned her neck in search of Max or another familiar face, and finding none, felt deserted. Outrageous, Tina thought, being shoved and prodded like animals. She kept an arm about Karen, shepherding her, sharing her fright, her pain.

This is infuriating, she thought angrily. Here we are, citizens who want to be heard—demonstrating peacefully, for the most part—and for expressing our beliefs, we're incarcerated. Granted, some might be guilty of misdemeanors, but she certainly was not.

Before long the cells were unlocked and the throng of prisoners was allowed to mill and mingle. Two women smiled at Tina, placid, reassuring smiles in open, unwrinkled faces that God gives only to nuns. They wore polyester slacks and neat white blouses and that unmistakable look of goodness. One carried a book by the philosopher Teilhard de Chardin. But what were nuns doing here, in jail? Before Tina could strike up a conversation, an authoritative voice thundered over the din.

"To be arrested for a peaceful demonstration is a violation of the Bill of Rights," the man's voice boomed. "You don't have to answer any questions or give your name if you don't want to. Just give any name. John or Jane Doe. That's all. Your rights are being violated. This is America, the land of the free, the home of the brave!"

"Hardly," Tina muttered as she scanned the crowd for the man who owned the commanding voice.

When she spotted him, she grabbed Karen's arm and said under her breath, "Jesus Christ."

"Huh?" Karen's eyebrows lifted.

"That man." Tina, fascinated, couldn't take her eyes off him. She lowered her voice to a whisper. "He looks like Jesus Christ. Look at those eyes. Electrifying."

His chocolate-brown eyes matched shoulder-length hair; his mouth, surrounded by a mustache that joined a thick beard, looked sensual.

"I'll find out what's going on, Karen," Tina said, and began weaving her way through the crowd.

She managed to slip up next to the man who'd just spoken. "You seem to know what to expect. Have you been arrested before?"

His eyes slid down to hers. His smile sent a shiver down her arms. "Yes."

"How long will they keep us?"

"I don't know. Not long, probably. The ACLU will get us released, you can be sure of that."

Tina's eyes fastened on the several rows of beads of every conceivable shade—cobalt and garnet, emerald and opal—strung around his neck.

"Just glass," he said, noting her appraisal. "You like?"

A smile lit her face. "I like."

He slid the brightly colored necklace from around his neck and eased it over her head. "It's yours."

Had he offered her diamonds and rubies, she couldn't have been more enthralled. His eyes, soft and smiling, reassuring, rested on hers. She wanted to say more, but she felt tongue-tied. Others vied for his attention and he turned away.

Several harried police officers returned and made vain attempts to organize matters. Eventually two officers began ushering the prisoners one by one into a small office.

A burly officer, overweight and with a porky face, pressed Tina's thumb on an ink pad for fingerprints and asked questions in a hostile voice. She decided to go along and give her name. "At least you're not another Jane Doe," the officer said. "Do you take drugs?"

Is this a legal question? she wondered; is occasional pot use considered drug-taking? She remained mute on several questions. Her own queries—When will we be let out? Can I make a phone call? Will I need bail?—remained unanswered.

She spent an uncomfortable and sleepless night cuddled on a cot with Karen, who kept saying, "I just want to be home in my own bed."

I'm with you, kid, Tina thought. Home sounded terrific at that moment: a comfy bedroom full of her precious books and mementos, loving (despite their anger) parents, caring sisters.

Early the next morning the prisoners were unceremoniously released.

"The ACLU arranged it," someone declared knowingly. "There'll be a lawsuit for illegal arrest."

Tina searched the departing crowd for a glimpse of the man who'd given her the beads, but he wasn't in sight. She headed through the metal doors, relieved that she wouldn't have to call home for bail. She could just imagine her father's horror at that ultimate humiliation.

On the street, Tina bade Karen good-bye and watched her walk disconsolately away, obviously unprepared to make the necessary explanations to her parents.

Now what? Tina wondered, feeling confused. She rubbed a sore shoulder. She must find Max. He had apparently escaped arrest. Where was the Pinto with her clothes? Where would she go? Back to the Waters home? She was uncertain exactly where that was, unable to remember even a street name. To Washington University? Hopefully she could hook up with some student protesters there. But she wanted, more than anything, a hot shower, clean clothes, a real rest on a real bed, and something to eat. The peanut-butter-and-jelly sandwiches (from a sympathetic community group) she'd eaten last night hardly comprised a real meal. She stuffed her hand in a back pocket and came away with the scrap of paper on which Juliet had scribbled an address. Her cousin's place, Juliet had said. Consulting the map, now creased and smeared almost to illegibility, she decided she could manage to find the street.

After several wrong turns Tina eventually found McArthur Boulevard and the street she was looking for. The house, though in need of a coat of paint, was a solid-looking three-story brick structure with gables and gingerbread.

A teenage boy answered the door, his wise and weary eyes belying his youthful acne-punctured face. Without a word he led Tina inside, as though he were expecting her. She glanced about the large foyer, from which several rooms opened. The style was decidedly Victorian, with a dark carved staircase and high ceilings. The boy silently preceded her to the living room, where a stained braided rug covered the center of the wood floor and worn comfortable furniture lined the walls. Clearly not *House Beautiful*, Tina thought, but at least a haven. The boy stopped uncertainly by a bookcase overflowing with books, both hardcover and paperback.

Tina broke the silence. "My name is Tina Marcassa."

The boy just nodded and shrugged, as though it didn't matter to him. He pointed. "The kitchen's that way. Help yourself to whatever. Just clean up when you're finished."

He turned and loped up the stairs, leaving Tina bewildered. Twilight Zone, she thought as she moved toward what he had indicated was the kitchen. A huge rectangular table with a potted philodendron on its center dominated the room. Tina strode to a bulletin board next to the back door and scanned the sheets of lists. "Kitchen Duty," "Shopping," "Gardening," were some of the headings, with days and names underneath. This is one huge family, Tina thought, turning her attention to the oversize stove, where a large copper teakettle stood in welcome. Strange herbs hung from strings in front of a window, and pungent smells permeated the large room. Feeling like an interloper, she added water to the kettle and turned on the gas, then searched for tea. Inside a cupboard overhead were clearly marked tins with an assortment of foods, and glass jars of grains and dried beans—navy, soy, kidney. She chose chamomile tea and several soda crackers. In the refrigerator she rummaged through a bin and found cheese.

At the sound of footsteps she turned somewhat guiltily.

Tina drew in her breath. It was him! The man in jail, the one who'd given her the beads.

"Welcome," he said in his resonant baritone. Then, frowning, "Have we met?"

When Tina found her voice, it was shaky. "Yes, in jail." She fingered the beads.

"Of course," he said, as if all his acquaintances were former prisoners. "What brings you here?"

"Juliet Firestone. Is she here? She gave me this address and said I could find a place to sleep."

"Ah, Cousin Julie. Yes, she should be back anytime." He moved to the stove and turned the gas off under the whistling kettle. "She went along with the shopping crew today."

"Where am I? I mean, what kind of place is this?"

"It's the Beehive. A sort of sanctuary for runaways and, on occasion, for kids released from jail."

Tina smiled and nodded. "That explains a lot. I'm Tina Marcassa. From Michigan."

"Adam Thornberry." He reached for two mugs on hooks under the counter and poured water from the steaming kettle into them. "Sit down. I'll have some tea with you. You must be hungry. We have all sorts of leftovers in the refrigerator."

"The cheese is fine."

"I could use a sandwich myself." He opened the refrigerator and proceeded to load his arms with tomatoes, sliced cheese, lettuce, and an enormous jar of peanut butter. "The bread is in that box on the end of the counter."

Tina chose a dark rye from the assortment and followed Adam's lead in assembling a sandwich.

"Now, Tina Marcassa, tell me about yourself."

"You know two important things," she said after swallowing a mouthful. "I'm from Michigan and I've spent the night in jail. Not an auspicious beginning."

"No, but it gives us a common ground; we're both jailbirds." His smile mesmerized her. "What do you do in Michigan?"

Her hand went involuntarily to the beads. "I'm in grad school and I teach night classes. I took a few days off."

The back door opened and Juliet strode in with two large grocery bags. Following on her heels were two other girls, similarly loaded down.

"Tina! You found us. Terrific!" Juliet said.

"I needed a haven. Luckily I didn't lose the address you gave me."

"I ran into Max," Juliet said. "He said he'd heard you were arrested. He's staying at the Waters place. He's ready to leave for Michigan."

"He'd better not leave me stranded. I'll call him. May I use your phone?" Juliet led Tina to the dining room to make the call. Max wasn't there, so she left a message for him to call her at the Beehive. When they returned to the kitchen, Adam was gone. As she helped Juliet store the supplies, Tina prodded her for information about her cousin.

"Adam was always looking for causes, as far back as I can remember. Where he gets the bread to run this place is beyond me. But somehow he manages. It's weird; when he's spent his last dime, some kind soul comes up with a donation. Hand me the tomato soup, will you?" Juliet stretched her arms to the top shelf to make room among the dozen large cans of soup. "You're spending the night, right? There's always room for one more."

'I'd love that. I need a shower desperately."

"I'll show you where everything is as soon as we finish here."

"I don't have anything with me. Do you have a razor I can borrow? I feel like a Greek peasant."

Juliet's disdain was apparent. "Why would you want to scrape your underarms and legs? It's not natural."

The remark gave Tina pause. Maybe Juliet was right. Maybe it wasn't natural. But was she willing to give that up to the feminist movement? Not yet, she decided. She was sure Juliet would have something to say about her bra, but with Tina's healthy endowment in that department, she had already made the decision to remain bra-clad despite any criticism. "To each her own," she said lightly.

Juliet gave Tina a tour of the upstairs rooms. Handmade printed signs over the doors stated "Cherokee Room," "Ottawa Room," "Seneca Room," "Iroquois Room." At the end of the hall was the "Chief's Room." Juliet explained, "The first batch of kids named the rooms. Of course, Adam's the chief."

"Of course."

That night more kids wandered into the living room and a huge bowl of popcorn appeared. Someone probably had popcorn duty, Tina thought. A young boy, shoulder blades and Adam's apple prominent on a thin frame, sat at the scarred upright and began picking out "Blackbird." In a wavery, unsure voice he sang the Beatles' ballad of freedom. One of the girls sat beside him and put her arm around his shoulder, joining her high soprano to his baritone. They seemed themselves like two wandering birds. It touched a chord in Tina, a chord of inner harmony.

Where was Adam? she wondered, her gaze straying often toward the door. After an hour of jokes and stories, Adam, wearing jeans and a blue T-shirt, strode into the room with a guitar. When he spotted Tina, a smile lit his face. He wandered toward her, then settled on the floor next to her chair. Strumming randomly at first, he soon selected a key and began playing silly songs: "My Old Man's a Sailor" and "Madelina Catalina." The kids knew the words and sang along. Then he played tunes more familiar. Tina, fondly remembering her glee-club days, harmonized with Adam's rich baritone on "Don't Think Twice, It's All Right."

After a heartfelt rendition of "Me and Bobby McGee," he turned to her and smiled. "We're a good team."

Her face suffused in a heated blush. How decidedly unfeminist, she thought, blushing because of attention from this virtual stranger. Still, there was no way to stop the warm and pleasurable rush. His back, resting against her legs, rippled with his strumming and felt like a caress.

When the group started breaking up after eleven, Juliet said, "Adam, with the two new girls coming in this afternoon, the rooms are all full."

"You and Tina can sleep in my bed," Adam said. "I'll bunk in with the boys."

Most of the group left for bed, but Tina lagged behind, reluctant to leave the presence of their lanky leader. Adam picked up a bowl containing a few salty corn kernels and headed toward the kitchen. Tina followed with empty glasses. Adam filled a dishpan with sudsy water and washed the accumulated bowls and glasses, making small talk all the while. Tina dried, absorbing his every word.

"What are you really doing in Washington? Looking for adventure?" His voice was teasing.

"No! Looking for justice!" She desperately wanted him to think well of her. "This war is a crime. All those soldiers losing their lives needlessly, it makes me sick."

"Right on."

After washing the last glass Adam swished suds around the sink. "Did you enjoy the song fest?"

"I loved it. It's been ages since I did much singing—not since high school."

Adam's face brightened. "I have a great idea. I have a few free hours tomorrow afternoon. Let's go on a picnic."

"Just us?"

"Of course. I need a day off."

She was as pleased as if he'd asked her to a ball, but she hesitated. Max's original plan was to leave tomorrow. She should think about tracking him down. Oh, well, Max always said to go with the flow. "I'd love it."

"Great. We'll fix some sandwiches and I've got a bottle of wine stashed away." He picked up his guitar. "See you tomorrow morning, then." Still he didn't move away.

Tina stood there, her hip against the counter, a damp cloth still in her hands, reluctant to end the evening, reluctant to surrender the cloak of warmth that enveloped her whenever Adam was close.

"Um . . . well, it's time to do bed check." Adam shifted his guitar to his other hand.

Tina remained silent, smiling. Her eyes locked with his and he touched her cheek with his index finger. Spellbound, she stood perfectly still, hardly breathing.

Adam moved away in slow motion with a pleased, easy grin. "Tomorrow, then." He took her shoulder and steered her through the swinging door and toward the stairs. At the bottom of the staircase he whispered, "Good night, Tina."

She put her fingers to her cheek, preserving the feel of Adam's touch. How had this man so enthralled her in so short a time?

"There you are." Juliet, coming from the bathroom, intruded on Tina's reverie. "Come on, I'll show you Adam's room. You could easily get lost in this place. Hold on while I do bed check.''

She knocked lightly on a door, then opened it. The pungent odor of burning incense assailed Tina's nose. Four girls sat on the floor between two double bunks, chattering and giggling, a breeze from the open window stirring the curtains and their long hair. A dark-skinned girl with sad Oriental eyes and a downturned mouth stubbed out a cigarette.

"Lights out, girls," Juliet called in a pleasant tone.

" 'Night, Julie," they called out, scattering to their beds.

The same sort of scene was repeated in another room. "We're pretty lenient about smoking, but drugs of any kind are a no-no. They know we'll make a search if we're suspicious. Anyone caught gets one warning, then they're out." Juliet smiled. "They're basically good kids, but we do get some losers."

Moments later they were in Adam's bedroom, which contained overlarge old furniture full of character and charm, mostly oak, none of it matching. The braided rug on the floor was obviously handmade. Tina slipped into a worn T-shirt of Adam's that Juliet gave her, and passed her hand over her chest. The sharp bleach smell of it was somehow not objectionable. She snuggled into Adam's bed and hugged his pillow to her. It held the vague residue of a male essence; a scent peculiar to Adam, a mixture of outdoors and perspiration and spice.

"Tell me about Adam," Tina said.

Juliet gave her a sidewise lifted-brow glance. "I think you have the hots for him."

Tina smiled. "I think he's very nice."

"You're right. He's nice, as in good. He concerns himself with the 'common good.' Has always been that way. We used to get together summers when we were kids, and he was always the organizer, the peacemaker during fights, the inventor of new and clever games.''

"I can imagine him that way.''

"Yeah, we had good times.'' Juliet yawned loudly. "Did Max call you back?''

"No.'' And Tina hoped sincerely he wouldn't call to insist they return to Michigan immediately. She wanted this time with Adam. She wanted to know more of this man who could thrill her with a touch. She wanted to know what made him tick. So okay, Juliet was right. She had *the hots* for Adam Thornberry.

The next morning, refreshed and showered, she went to the shrub-enshrouded yard to gather the clothes she'd laundered the day before. She basked for several moments in the warm sun, breathing in the rich earth smell. A row of marigolds at the edge of a garden patch raised cheery faces toward the sun while two doves teased each other on a fencepost. Her jail experience was all but forgotten in the glory of the sunlit morning. In a while, she donned her clean clothing and went to the kitchen to join Juliet for coffee and hard rolls.

"In case Max calls, tell him I'm out and to please leave a message,'' Tina said, slathering butter on her roll.

"Are you avoiding him?''

"Not exactly. I just want one more day in Washington.'' Tina was reluctant to give away any more than she had to.

Juliet nodded. "I'm going to work for a while in the garden. Want to join me?''

"In a bit.'' Picking up a day-old newspaper, Tina was shocked at the headlines. Walter and May Reuther had been killed in a plane crash. Hurriedly she scanned the sparse details. She remembered the Reuthers well. Her father had been a tireless worker for Walter in the days when being a union member meant placing yourself in mortal danger. Her father, she knew, must be grieving.

Distractedly she busied herself with assembling a lunch of cheese and bread, grapes, apples, and cookies. Then she joined Juliet in the garden. She helped herself to dirt-stained gardening gloves in a bucket on the porch and began weeding a row of tomato plants.

Adam's whistling brought her out of her crouch.

"Hi." She pressed her hand against the small of her aching back.

"Hi. I see Juliet's got you working."

"Yes. I'm just beginning to realize how out-of-shape I am."

"Your shape looks fine to me."

Juliet groaned but Tina smiled.

"Where were you?" Juliet asked.

"At an MOB meeting."

"Well, I think I'll wash up and get some lunch. Want some?" Juliet asked.

"No," Adam answered. "Tina and I are going on a picnic."

"Oh-kay. Alone. Just you two."

"You got it." He turned away from the garden and headed toward the kitchen door, calling behind him, "I'll be ready in a few minutes."

When he'd gone, Juliet frowned. "He's not one to get emotionally involved with an overnight guest."

"It's only a picnic," Tina said. But her pitching heart belied her carefree words.

Adam's vintage Volkswagen got them to Rock Creek Park, which separated Georgetown from the rest of the city. Holding hands, they strolled down a neglected path, Adam with his guitar slung over his shoulder and the picnic basket in his other hand. He found a choice peaceful spot beneath a weeping-willow tree and spread a blanket. He lowered himself to the blanket, and taking Tina's hand, pulled her down next to him. The willow's ribbons of bright green fanned across her face and she laughed at the pure joy of the day, at the chattering of birds overhead, at the pale blue sky dotted with an occasional puffy cloud.

"A perfect day," Tina said with a sigh as a blue jay circled their heads, then lit noisily on a hickory branch.

"Perfect," Adam repeated. "A good beginning."

"A prediction?"

"Why not? A pronouncement. I declare it, therefore it must be so."

Adam produced a bottle of Mateus rosé and poured it ceremoniously. "To this day and to our friendship," he toasted, lifting the glass high.

"To friendship," Tina agreed. She spread out the lunch. "How did you get involved in the Beehive?"

"Oh, I met up with some kids that needed a place to stay. Got some influential friends of my father's to set it up with an agency. It took a lot of meetings, a lot of organization."

"So a city agency refers the kids to you?"

"Yes. I do have credentials. I'm a psychologist." Adam munched on a chunk of Muenster cheese. "I get the kids back to school, sometimes back to their parents, though often that's a bad scene. I let them know someone cares, try to keep them on the straight and narrow. Unfortunately, I'm on shaky ground, what with the protests and my arrests."

"The agency supports you?"

"Yes, with city funds—not nearly enough. A few other benefactors come through: churches, community groups." He took her hand and rocked it in his.

His hand was warm, pulsing with energy. Tina, flustered, tried to keep the conversation going. "Are you from Washington originally?"

He shook his head. "I'm from everywhere. My father was in the service. I spent some time in Michigan. In fact I stayed over a month one summer with my aunt and uncle, Juliet's parents. They had a cottage at Higgins Lake. It was one of the best summers of my life.''

''I've hardly been out of Michigan. Living in different places sounds exciting.''

''It wasn't exciting to me, but I guess it *was* an education. I hated hopping all over the world—England, Germany, Alaska. I longed to stay put in one place and have real friends.''

Together they put away the lunch remains and wandered along the edge of the bubbling creek in companionable silence. Moving past the giant ferns, they crossed the water on a half-submerged log. On the other side Tina put her hand out to stop Adam and pointed to a pair of squirrels playfully chasing one another up a tree. It was somehow a touching and peaceful moment.

Adam broke into the solitude. ''So, Tina, what do you teach?''

''English. At a community college.''

''Do you like it, teaching?''

''I don't hate it.''

''But you're not very enthusiastic. Maybe you need to do something else.''

''Probably. But I don't know what.'' Tina stooped to admire a trillium flowering under a butternut tree. ''And meanwhile, I need to support myself.''

''Yes, that's usually the case.''

''If I wasn't so close to getting my master's degree, I'd chuck it all, stay in Washington for a while.'' It was almost a question.

''You don't want to disrupt your life on a whim. But if you decide to come back, I could help you find a job.'' Adam looked at her closely, studying her. ''I'd like to get to know you.''

Her heart soared. That was the encouragement she wanted.

They made their way back to the picnic spot and Adam played a romantic ballad, an unfamiliar old English tune, while they emptied the wine bottle. He stood and returned the guitar to its battered case. As they walked back to the car, he hung his arm over her shoulder. It felt right. *He* felt right, special. The day had been an interlude of peace in her chaotic life. She couldn't just go back to Michigan and dismiss this man.

Adam fit the key into the ignition, then turned to Tina. His gaze stirred her, made her go all soft inside. Slowly he bent his head until his mouth was an inch from hers. She made the slight movement upward that linked their lips in a kiss that went on and on and seemed to melt her bones. Stunned by the powerful emotions Adam evoked, she finally broke away.

He shook his head, emitted a low whistle, and eased the car onto the road. Tina felt vibrations from the warmth of Adam's body, felt his strength.

They didn't speak for a while; then Adam said quietly, "I've been on my own since I was eighteen. I'm a free spirit, like the wind, like the sea."

"So am I."

"I have things I need to do with my life. The Beehive is just the starting place."

Keep it light, Tina. "Ah, dedication. I like that in a man."

He was giving her mixed signals. He said she shouldn't disrupt her life on a whim, yet he wanted to get to know her. And the kiss spoke volumes. She was sure it had affected him as it did her. She was sure he felt the electricity between them just as she did; that was why he had arranged the picnic. He'd given her a few kernels of hope that they could be more than friends, yet he seemed to be telling her he wasn't ready for an involvement. He was an enigma.

Though she'd only just begun to know him, she was falling in love with this man. And if she played her cards right, he would fall in love with her too.

It seemed she always led with her heart.

When the Volkswagen churned up the driveway, Tina saw a familiar figure sitting on the porch steps. Max.

" 'Bout time,'' he said by way of greeting, eyeing Adam.

"Max, where've you been? I languished in jail, waiting in vain for your cake with the file.''

"Jail, eh? You have all the fun.''

She suspected he was only half-joking. He would have loved telling that tale to his Michigan buddies.

She introduced Adam and Max and went into the house to say good-bye to Juliet. In the kitchen she and Juliet hugged with promises to keep in touch.

At the front door Adam enclosed her in his arms. "I'm sorry you're leaving so soon.''

"I may be back.''

"I hope so.'' He brushed his lips on hers in a brief, heart-catching kiss.

She left feeling weightless and breathless. Her thoughts on the long drive home were filled with Adam.

4

On a warm July afternoon, Tina called Ann. "I talked to Louise and she can get away tonight. It's been ages since we talked. Are you free?"

"Why don't you have dinner here. I hate being away from the boys any more than necessary, and they'd love to see you too."

"Well, don't fuss. I'll pick up a pizza."

"Nonsense," Ann said. "Flora would love to make something Italian. She's anxious to see you. She won't stay late, though. Hates to drive after dark."

Their mother's cousin Flora had been caregiver to the three sisters when their mother worked in the bridal shop, and still thought of them as "her girls." Flora had learned to drive when she was fifty-five years old and now terrorized the streets by driving a maximum of thirty miles an hour even on main highways. Still, her spunk drew the girls' admiration.

Ann was anxious to hear all about Tina's experience in Washington. She had hinted at meeting "someone special." Ann thought of her sister as a product of another generation: free-wheeling, carefree, and careless. Tina had eschewed her Catholic upbringing, denied her church. Ann thought her younger sister had somehow gotten derailed.

Yet she realized that at some level she envied Tina her lack of responsibilities, her freedom, her faculty

for making decisions based on her own needs. Ann
had never had that. Life happened to her, as though
she had no choice in the matter. Some people be-
lieved there really *were* choices, but given Ann's
background, her environment, maybe even her
genes, had she ever really had choices? It was only
lately that regret had reared its Medusa head, and
she wondered if she'd made the right decision when
she married Martin. He had changed. But hadn't she
changed also? Those thoughts generated others that
were too complicated to pursue, and she hadn't the
time for philosophical musings.

Louise, ever the nun, Ann thought, arrived wearing a plaid blouse over a simple gray skirt. Her light
brown hair, blunt-cut and chin-length, still managed
to wave softly around her face.

Corralling the boys, she questioned them about
their schoolwork, making comparisons between their
school and hers. When Tina breezed in wearing hip-
hugging jeans and dangling feather earrings, all
attention was riveted on her. Ann was a bit discon-
certed to see that Tina was a heroine of sorts in her
sons' eyes.

"What was jail like?"

"Did they handcuff you?"

"Were you scared?"

Tina said, "It was the worst experience of my life,"
and told them briefly of her adventure.

After Martin arrived they had dinner, chattering
noisily and exchanging gossip with Flora, who knew
all the personal data of the longtime family friends.
Flora fussed over her "girls," urging more helpings,
basking in their compliments. These get-togethers were
all too rare, Ann thought, trying to absorb all the
channels of conversation.

Afterward the boys left for their own activities, and
Martin excused himself. The sisters settled in the large
and comfortable family room. Outside, the last rays of

sun lingered on the patio, touching and brightening the clay pots overflowing with red geraniums. Lou sat on the sofa, tucking her legs beneath her, and Tina lounged on the floor, her back against the sofa, her snug jeans straining at the seams.

Louise leaned down to touch Tina's gauzy Indian-print shirt. "I like that colorful design. Sometimes I wish I could wear things like that."

Ann poured and served wine in tall stemmed glasses and sat in the easy chair next to the fireplace.

After Martin called in a good-bye and departed, Ann said, "Tina, we're dying to hear details."

"I was thrown in jail for no reason whatsoever," Tina said, and began recounting her experience as a prisoner. "It was the most humiliating, dehumanizing thing that ever happened to me," she said vehemently.

Ann began, "Not one to *ever* say I told you so . . ."

"Ha!" Tina said, while Louise laughed.

". . . but the thought that there could be problems had entered my mind," Ann finished.

Tina ignored the remark and leaned forward, her body tense. "Aside from jail, being in Washington with all those dedicated people . . . well, you can't believe how *inspiring* it was. All united, with one purpose: peace. When we marched to the Capitol, I felt— I think we all felt—*empowered* somehow. Like we *could* make a difference. If only we could get more politicians to see the light." She relaxed and smiled, remembering.

"Something happened in Washington besides your arrest, Tina," Louise said. "I can see it in your face. What?"

"Oh, Lou, you're psychic." Tina picked absently at a thread in the rug. "I met a guy."

"A guy?" Louise exchanged glances with Ann.

"A guy." Tina looked as smug as a cat on a sunny windowsill. "He's a director in a home for run-aways."

After a moment Ann said, "So, what's he like?"

"Like no one else I've ever met." Tina closed her eyes dreamily.

Ann observed Tina closely. Her sister was obviously infatuated. "Well. Details, please."

"Kind, selfless, talented . . . and sexy. Dark hair, dark penetrating eyes. Handsome."

"This happened awfully fast, didn't it?" Louise asked.

Tina nodded, looking at each sister. "Yes."

Ann felt she should offer some counsel, some words of wisdom. She was, after all, the elder stateswoman, sage and insightful, the one with the answers . . . for everyone but herself. "What about logistics? Washington's a long way. Have you been in touch with him?"

"I've called him a couple of times and he's called me. We write. I write long, he writes short."

"Do you think something will come of this? Is that what you want?"

She pondered a moment. "I think so. But I'm willing to just try things out, see what happens. I feel a little confused."

Louise slipped to the floor next to Tina and put her arm around her sister. "How can we help unconfuse you?"

Tina laid her head on Lou's shoulder and said solemnly, "I think this is a do-it-yourself project. But I feel like I'm making progress. I think I want to go to Washington and get a job. I have my master's now."

Lou said, "Oh, Tina, I'd hate to see you leave."

"Have you said anything to Ma and Pa?" Ann asked.

"Not yet. We're not communicating well lately. I'd like to sneak away like a thief in the night, leave a note, something cute like, 'So long, it's been good to know ya.' "

"You're too old for that kind of rebelliousness," Ann said. "You don't want to hurt them."

"No, of course not. But they'll never understand."

"It's not easy to find love," Louise said. "Follow your heart, Tina. But maybe you shouldn't expect moonlight and roses."

"I expect wine and guitars."

"It's almost the same thing. You know what I mean. Guard your heart a little."

"Oh, Louise, easier said than done. I think I'm in love."

"Wait a minute," Ann said. "Shouldn't you think about this a bit first? I mean, it seems awfully sudden. Are you sure this . . . what's his name, anyway?"

"Adam."

"Are you sure Adam shares your feelings? Does he want you to make this drastic change to be near him?"

Tina uncrossed her legs and stretched them out. "He's not the only reason I'm leaving. I need a change of scenery. I feel stifled here. Washington's where the action is."

Ann almost said: *Grow up, Tina,* but wisely reconsidered.

Louise patted Tina's hand. "If it doesn't work out, you can always come back home."

"Something should work out in my life. It's time."

"Well, a lot's happened to you in the span of a few short days. And with the exception of the jail incident, no real damage was done."

"Except to my psyche," Tina said, sipping her wine.

Louise said, "And that's always undergoing change. Not only for you. It seems life is a series of phases."

"And that's the truth!" Ann said emphatically.

"You too?" Louise raised her eyebrows in Ann's direction.

"I was thinking more of Martin."

Louise nodded in agreement. "I noticed. He's become a latter-day hippie: gold chains, a vest—our conservative Martin. Where was he off to tonight?"

"A card game."

"I didn't think Martin was much of a card player. How long has this been going on?" Louise asked.

"Just the past few months. Some new people in his department got it going. He says he needs to get away once in a while. Lately he's been . . ." Ann searched for the word. ". . . distant." She shook her head ruefully, then mumbled, mostly to herself, "I don't know."

"Mid-life crisis?" Louise asked.

"Maybe." Ann rose and poured more wine.

"Be patient. He'll come around." Louise looked at her watch. "I can't stay much longer. I have papers to check, and Mother Serena's strict about late hours."

Tina said, "Don't you ever get tired of it, Lou? Don't you ever want to chuck the whole thing?"

"Not really." Louise sipped her wine. "Oh, I suppose we all have second thoughts. I have this picture in my mind of Ann and Martin after the twins were born, harried, overworked, exhausted with trying to get them both fed and taken care of, but still so happy, so in love. It seemed almost idyllic."

"That seems like a century ago. Martin's changed. We don't seem to have that unity of purpose any longer."

When Ann finally ushered her sisters out, it was almost midnight. As she prepared for bed, she mused over her sisters' lives. Tina's life, so undirected, was a far cry from her own, yet she could almost envy her the adventure that led to a new infatuation. Ann remembered the deep heartfelt stirrings that cried out for gratification when she had first met Martin. She longed to experience that intensity again.

Louise's life, on the other hand, was enviable for a different reason. She had a peaceful existence. The convent suited her, fulfilled her; the church community provided for her needs. Unless she allowed it, the outside world needn't intrude. Ann used to wonder if the convent was an escape, but now she thought of it as a haven. She almost wished she could retreat there for a few days, just to recharge. She creamed her face and slipped into bed. Martin should have been home by now. Again she felt the gnawing worry, the discontent. Was she being foolish?

What did she want from this marriage, anyway? Fireworks, at her age? Marriages couldn't retain the passion and excitement of the first years. It was silly to expect that. She thought of her parents' arranged marriage. They had been strangers to one another. Had there been excitement for them? No, her mother had said their love grew slowly. But even now they had a sense of devotion to one another, the sense of harmony that was missing in her own marriage. Maybe she should search inside herself. Had she been taking Martin for granted? She should appreciate his good qualities. But right now it was difficult, because she needed so much more from him than he was giving. She needed nurturing, love, attention. Was that unreasonable? A gnawing hurt grew inside her and tears sprang forth.

She was still awake when the door opened and Martin tiptoed in. Craning her neck, she read the luminous dial on the clock. Ten past one.

"I'm awake," she said.

"Sorry. Didn't mean to make noise."

"I was waiting for you."

"You shouldn't do that. It's late." A shoe dropped to the floor, then another.

"Very late."

He paused. "Don't start." His tone was querulous. Ann held her tongue. When he slipped into bed she fitted herself against his back and brushed her fingers against the sparse hair on his chest.

"I'm tired, Ann. It's been a long day."

She moved away to her side of the bed feeling lonely and rejected. Again.·

A vague smell of some sweetish cologne lingered in the air. Was it his after-shave? It wasn't familiar. He usually wore the same one. An unnamed fear wiggled in her abdomen. She'd have to make a point of sniffing some of the various bottles on his shelf tomorrow.

Inside the door of her parents' home, Tina removed her shoes by habit and quietly trod the stairs. Observing her clothing-strewn room, books piled on every horizontal surface, she promised herself a good cleanup tomorrow. As she snuggled into bed, his face floated before her. Adam. His hair, long but neatly trimmed; his hands, long-fingered, an artist's hands; his smile, slow and brilliant. There had been so little contact between them, yet she needed his touch, the warmth of his smile that seemed like a benediction. She cherished the memory of their stirring kiss. Almost embarrassed at her longing, she silently reaffirmed her decision. She must see him again. She would go to Washington.

The community house was asleep when Louise entered. She liked this house. It reflected her life: quiet, well-ordered, predictable.

Sister Perpetua was in the living room, reading in a wooden straight-backed chair, when Louise entered.

Perpetua closed the book on her finger. "You're late tonight."

Louise's back stiffened. It seemed a chastisement. Perpetua hadn't many "outside" friends, and her family had moved to Florida. She seemed a lonely soul, but wouldn't let Louise get close the few times she'd tried.

"You know how it is when you start talking. Especially sisters. We always have a lot of catching up to do." Louise locked the door behind her.

"I don't have any sisters. Just one brother, and he's much older than I."

"I hope you don't feel you must stay up and greet me, Sister. I'm perfectly capable of letting myself in."

"It's quite all right." Perpetua seemed to feel it was her duty to keep tabs on the comings and goings of all the sisters. "Tomorrow's a workday, you know."

Louise drew her breath in. "I'm well aware of that. Good night, Sister." She hurried to the staircase, not wanting any further discussion.

Perpetua switched out the light and followed her up the stairs. "Well, I'm only thinking of your welfare. I hope you won't be too tired in the morning."

"If I'm tired, I'm tired. I can handle it." Louise tried to keep the irritation from her voice. She wanted to say: *Just mind your own business,* but of course, that would be unkind.

There was something annoying about Perpetua. She was not someone Louise would have chosen for a friend, yet here she had no choice but to interact with her on an almost daily basis. Louise prepared for bed and knelt beside her narrow cot with its thin mattress and plain cotton spread. She prayed for patience and tolerance. Perpetua is one of the crosses I must bear, she thought.

Her vocation, as Ann had reminded her, had been chosen when she was fifteen years old, and she hadn't regretted it.

"You're too young to make such a big decision," her mother had said. But Louise was *sure.* She'd had the "calling," as clear as if it were a voice from heaven. She remembered it clearly, the grotto along a

dirt road in rural southern Italy, a respite for farmers
and travelers, an unlikely Madonna in faded robes
with soulful sky-raised eyes. Had she been simply an
impressionable child, carried away by the romanti-
cism of dedicating her life to Christ? Before entering
the convent she had searched her soul and determined
that there was nothing else she really wanted. She
felt an urgency to live in imitation of Christ and accomplish something in her life; something good,
worthwhile.

And now, the reckoning. What had she accomplished, really? Teaching children the three R's, sometimes successfully, sometimes not.

No, she didn't regret her decision. Not really. It was
just lately that she'd felt disquieted, uneasy about many
things, and her attitude toward Perpetua was one of
those things. Another was a vague feeling of unfulfill-
ment.

Tina's predicament, her confusion, was understandable to Louise. In her youth Louise had had no doubts,
had followed the church blindly. But lately she questioned more and more, and often heard dissenting
views from her superiors. Father Vernan had casti-
gated the Berrigan brothers for their part in fighting
for peace. She and Father had heated discussions about
the incidents which he called insurrection. Tina had
argued that if war was worth dying for, wasn't peace
even more worth the sacrifice? Father Vernan had
called her misguided. That hurt. They'd had such a
good rapport before. She was disappointed in his
narrow-minded viewpoint.

But that wasn't the only burr of discontent. The feminist movement surely had contributed, though she
discounted the more ludicrous manifestations of
the movement like bra-burning, easy sex, and such. The
deeper restlessness of women she could understand,
the lack of opportunity, of self-respect, of self-
attainment.

Her prayers ended with a plea for understanding, for contentment. "Thy will be done," she said aloud just before slipping into bed.

She had too many questions and too few answers.

5

Ann heard the alarm and waited for Martin to silence it with a tap. He groaned and yawned, then, instantly awake, hopped out of bed and headed toward the bathroom. Unlike her husband, Ann needed a few moments to reorient herself to the waking world. She tried to grasp the wisp of a dream that slipped further and further away, something about a mansion with secret rooms. Sliding her feet into the slippers beside the bed, she remembered she'd wanted to talk to Martin. But mornings, filled with rushing, with movement, were never a good time for talking.

She slipped into a robe and hurried downstairs. In the kitchen she opened the drapes to the morning sun. As she filled the electric coffee pot she could hear Martin's muttered complaints.

From the top of the stairs he yelled, "I can't find a towel. And where are my clean shirts?"

Ann, annoyed, envisioned him dripping onto the new stair carpeting. "Your shirts are in the closet. Where else would they be? Under the bed?" She had picked up his shirts from the cleaners yesterday, a chore she resented, one more errand on her way home. But at least she no longer laundered them herself, though it had taken a battle. Martin didn't like the way the cleaners did them, often losing buttons. On that issue, however, Ann had stood her ground.

She stirred scrambled eggs in the skillet, shoved

bread into the toaster, and poured orange juice from a carton.

Whipping up the stairs, she gathered a pile of articles she'd stacked on the bottom steps. The rule was that anyone heading upstairs would bring up anything lying there. Of course, she was the only one who heeded the rule.

She dumped the armload in the bedroom, where Martin, damp from his shower, towel skirted around his waist, picked through his sock drawer. He still looked good, she thought, taut stomach muscles, sprinkling of dark hair over tight pectorals. In a sudden moment of tenderness she touched the nape of his neck, where tendrils of wet hair stuck tight.

He shook her hand away, mumbling, "Whatever monster devours the socks could at least do it in pairs."

Ann nudged him out of the way and rifled through the mess. She came up with a pair of navy socks and tossed them in his direction with a rueful glare. He resented that she wouldn't take the time to match socks, and she resented his resentment. "I've got scrambled eggs for you. Almost ready?"

"Yeah." Martin drew a tie end through the knot and straightened it. "I'm running a little late."

Back downstairs, Ann poured coffee, black for herself, one teaspoon of sugar and a splash of cream for Martin.

While Martin ate, he scanned a report from his briefcase, a frown creasing his brow. "This is due today and it's full of inaccuracies. Damn."

Ann settled in a chair across from him and wet her lips. "Martin, we need to talk."

He looked up from his report, frowning. "What?"

The phone's shrill ring curtailed her reply. It was the treasurer from the PTA asking, "When are you going to schedule a meeting about fund-raising? The treasury is almost depleted."

"Oh, Lord, I forgot." She checked the calendar on the bulletin board next to the phone. "How about next Tuesday? Oh, no, the boys have a game." Softball games dictated their summer activities. "Make it Wednesday, seven-thirty." She scribbled a reminder on the calendar.

Martin arranged papers in his briefcase. With a quick snap he closed the case and took a last swig of coffee. "I might be a little late. I'll call you."

Ann sighed. No time, no time, no time, said a chorus in her head.

As the door slammed behind Martin, Matthew stumbled into the kitchen, yawning, his hair awry. "We have practice this morning. What's for breakfast?"

Ann kissed her son, ruffling his tousled hair. "What's your pleasure?"

"I think I'll just have some Cheerios." He poured himself into a chair and downed his orange juice.

"Better get Brian up, if you both have practice."

"I tried. You know Bri." Matthew rested his head on his hand, his eyelids half-closed.

Ann's heart squeezed. Her boys had their father's height and fair complexion, her own brown, probing Italian eyes. They were good, loving sons. Being twins was both a joy and a burden for them. She used to worry that they seemed a world unto themselves, needing no others. Their connectedness was sometimes eerier. Yet, since puberty, they seemed to have made a tacit decision to separate their interests. Brian was involved in art and photography, while Matthew focused on aeronautics. Planes fascinated him. The boys' diversity didn't extend to softball. They were on the same team. Ann was concerned about competition between them, but it didn't seem to be a problem.

They had a few mutual friends, but lately they each seemed to gravitate more toward other friendships.

Ann supposed it was best they become less interdependent. Ultimately they would always be best friends.

Lately, to Ann's dismay, girls had begun calling them. When she was a teenager, only brazen boy-crazy girls would dare call a boy. Now it seemed commonplace. Martin had agreed, early on, to talk to the boys, man to man, but he procrastinated. It wasn't something he was comfortable with, and certainly Ann couldn't do more than drop hints to her easily embarrassed sons, now thirteen years old and tottering clumsily on the brink of manhood. The school had some sort of "health class" that dealt with sex, but it was oblique and minimal at best. She wanted Martin to encourage the boys' questions and try to draw them out. Somehow, he never found the "right" time.

Tonight when she talked to Martin, she'd again mention the boys' needs. She took her cooled coffee and a slice of toast upstairs. She'd eat while she finished dressing.

As she passed Brian's door she knocked loudly, then went in. His tousled head emerged from under the sheet.

"Up and at 'em, sleepyhead. You have practice this morning." Ann smiled in empathy as Brian forced his eyelids upward and boosted himself to a sitting position. He was so much like herself, a night owl who liked to slumber in the morning.

"Up, up. Put your feet on the floor," she called, waiting for his compliance before moving on.

She took a quick peek at seven-year-old Theodore, who slept peacefully. Good-natured and amenable, he was the least of her problems. He would awaken later, after Flora had arrived.

At her mirror Ann picked up her hairbrush. The no-nonsense short (and expertly, expensively cut) hair needed only a quick brush-through. She made her face up automatically, a quick smear of foundation over smooth unblemished skin. Her large velvety brown eyes lined with thick lashes required little more than mascara. If only she could transform her marriage as easily as she did her face. But her marriage needed more than cosmetics; it needed a major facelift. She'd talk to Martin tonight, rationally, calmly. Her dissatisfactions were many, but often they seemed trivial when she tried to discuss them. This time she wouldn't simply whine, "I'm unhappy." She'd tried that before and Martin became first defensive, then depressed, and she'd ended up consoling *him*. Exactly how the tables had turned was a mystery. Frequently their discussions became arguments and got twisted up in misunderstandings and power plays. Sometimes he remained rigidly unbending, sometimes purposely misunderstanding. Ultimately, she was still dissatisfied, still carrying all the burdens.

When Ann returned from work earlier than usual, the house was quiet and relatively neat.

Flora sat forward in her seat in front of the television. "You'll get paid back one of these days, wait and see!" she was saying with a wagging forefinger.

She spent much of her time now watching the soaps, clucking her tongue, admonishing her "friends" on the screen, advising them, warning them.

Unperturbed at being caught talking to the television, Flora greeted Ann with, "David better watch out; they're out to get him."

Ann clucked in sympathy.

"Dinner's just about ready," Flora said. "Linguine with clam sauce."

"Ah, great."

"I'm going early," she said, removing her apron. "It's my bingo night."

When Martin entered shortly after Ann, she greeted him and followed him up the stairs.

"Martin, I want to talk."

Martin sighed resignedly.

In the bedroom he loosened his tie. "So talk."

Ann took a deep breath. How to begin? She wished she had rehearsed. "Things aren't right between us. You've changed. We don't do things together anymore." She sat on the edge of the bed, clasping her hands together in her lap. "I have the feeling that you're . . . you're hardly part of the family. You're just a figurehead."

"That's bull. I'm here, aren't I? I'm home more nights than you are."

"In the flesh maybe, but not in spirit."

Martin hung his suit neatly on a hanger and yanked on his jeans.

"I do my share. I take care of yardwork. I pay the bills."

"And so do I."

He stiffened. "If you were home all day, we wouldn't have so many bills—Flora, for one."

Oh, his male ego surfacing again. He always tried to discount her "work" as unnecessary, unimportant. The old attitude of men as the traditional breadwinners, demanding respect and subservience. And, as usual, she would tiptoe around his ego, act as though her income wasn't important to the family, to their life-style; their winter vacations in Florida; Martin's country-club membership; the ski weekends. She took a deep breath. "What I'm trying to say is, it would be nice if you would pitch in on other jobs once in a while, take over some of the chauffeuring chores, help with laundry . . ." She realized she wasn't attacking the main problem. "What I *really* want is some of your time, your attention." Her voice was pleading.

Martin ignored her last remark. "Can't Flora do the laundry?" He examined his slightly receding hairline in the mirror, then drew a brush over his long sideburns and hair that skimmed his collar top.

"No, all she'll do anymore is watch the kids and cook. You forget, Martin, she's getting old."

"Maybe we should get someone else . . ." Martin began.

"Martin! She's practically part of the family. And she needs the income."

"All right! Get someone in addition to Flora. We can afford it."

"You know money's a little tight." The bridal business was in a decline. Young people were living together without benefit of a ceremony, and when there was a ceremony, it was often a simple one. Ann had had to lay off sales staff. "But the point is, if we *all* pitched in, we could manage fine. And I'm not talking about just your help, I'm talking about the way we're not connecting."

Again Martin chose to ignore her meaning. "You wouldn't need extra help if you weren't so damn busy with this league and that society. You could drop some of that."

"No! I need to participate, to contribute! And it's good practice, business-wise. You just won't understand what I'm getting at, or you just don't care. We're not a team anymore, Martin. You never pay any attention to me, you never even touch me except in bed, you—"

"Bull. We're not newlyweds, for God's sake. I can't be your Romeo, I can't constantly stroke your ego."

Ann jumped from the bed. "Stroke my ego!"

"Keep your voice down—the boys."

"You're missing the point entirely; you're not trying to understand what I'm saying."

"I understand what you're saying. You want an adoring slave."

"No! I want a helpmeet, a companion."

Martin shook his head in a disdainful gesture.

Ann's voice rose to a crescendo. "You're not even listening to me." It was an annoying whine, what she'd hoped to avoid.

"You're right about that! I've heard all I want to

hear.'' Martin grabbed his leather vest and went to the door.

''Where are you going?''

''Out.'' The door slammed behind him. Ann crumbled to the bed and dropped her head to her hands, allowing the tears to escape. Why couldn't they discuss instead of argue? Why did their talks degenerate into recriminations, attacks, and counterattacks? Why couldn't she say what was really on her mind? That she feared she was losing his love. There. That was it. In a nutshell. It wasn't the lack of help and support, it was his disinterest, his . . . She swallowed hard. Lack of love. Tears stung her eyelids.

She remembered their early days, when they painted their small apartment together, glorying in the shared accomplishment, stopping to make love, hardly taking time to shed their paint-stained clothing, laughing at their own intensity. And now? Hasty exchanges in the morning, disinterested comments at dinner, perfunctory lovemaking on nights when they were not totally exhausted.

Was she expecting too much? Was this the sort of evolution most marriages went through? Maybe this was a normal phase, a rocky passage that must be traversed before the smooth sun-lightened path was found again.

And maybe not. Maybe they were in trouble. Maybe they needed a marriage counselor. She discounted *that* idea almost before it was formulated. Martin would never agree to counseling. He was too private, too repressed to share his real feelings with a stranger, when he hardly shared them with his own wife.

Ann was in the family room reading through a financial report when she heard Martin return. She hoped he would be, if not penitent, at least open to her concerns. She would be forgiving if he would. By the time Ann put the report in her briefcase and went to their bedroom, Martin was asleep, oblivious of the television newscaster's report of Mayor Roman S. Gribbs's latest pronouncement, of the doom covering the city, the accidents, the murders, the dope-peddling. Ann waited for the weather forecast, then punched the dial and flopped into bed, weary to the point of tears.

Weary. The story of my life, my runaway life, she thought before sleep overtook her.

6

Ann steered her Thunderbird onto Grand River Avenue toward the Redford branch of Chiara's Bridal Salon. On a whim she passed the store and drove to Rouge Park, where she found a parking spot. Rolling down her window, she breathed in the warm autumn air and basked in nature's almost sensual beauty. The Michigan *grande dame* of autumn began her triumphant parade toward winter with a palette of rich oranges and muted russets, brilliant golds and earthy tans. Leaves from a maple tree, mottled with color, sailed onto the car's hood and settled. She left the car, locked it, and, leaves crunching pleasantly underfoot, walked toward the muddy river. Her heels sank into the loamy soil at the river's edge. Beneath a shady maple she found tissues in her purse and spread them on the ground, then sat gingerly. If only she could carry the peace of this moment with her for a few hours. She closed her eyes and inhaled deeply for several moments, then remained still, in an impromptu meditation. She was moved to whisper a hurried prayer to a God she'd been (as Louise gently chided) increasingly neglecting. *God grant me serenity, give me strength.*

Serenity had been missing a long time. Her life should be more satisfying; she took pleasure in her work, in her children, in her home, if not in her marriage. The wrinkle in the fabric of her life was Martin. The problems that had been gradually surfacing during the past years seemed somehow to have been exacerbated in the past several months. Since her attempt a week ago, she had given up trying to talk to Martin, who was more taciturn than ever.

She thought of their early days. They'd had an apartment in Detroit, later a small Cape Cod-style house. She'd loved that house, enjoyed making curtains, papering walls. In those years she and Martin had had more time for each other and for their family.

They used to be a tight-knit unit: taking camping trips throughout Michigan—the Thumb, the Upper Peninsula—and venturing to Kentucky and Tennessee. Martin spent time with the boys, teaching them the finer points of fly-fishing. But it had been many years since they'd done that sort of thing. Something was missing now. And when she tried to articulate her concerns, Martin said little. He rarely argued. In a confrontation, he backed down and left the room.

A squirrel scampered past her and up a graceful white birch. She checked her watch. Better not tarry any longer. She had work to do. Reluctantly she returned to her car, started the engine, and moved on.

At the salon, Janet, a salesclerk, hung frothy discounted gowns on a revolving rack. She looked like a teenager, though she was over thirty. When Ann hired her, she'd seen past the ponytail and tight jeans to her potential. "You're on if you'll get rid of the kiddy hairdo and wear regular clothes," Ann had challenged. Janet readily agreed and soon became a first-rate worker, manager material.

Ann approached her now. "How's it going, Janet?"

Janet, startled, turned. "Slow," she said, shifting her attention back to her work.

"How about you?" Ann persisted. "You doing all right?" She'd heard Janet was having personal problems.

"Sure, okay." Avoiding Ann's gaze, she jostled a

gown from the rack and replaced it in its proper section.

The manager, Frieda, joined them and greeted Ann with a worried frown. "Not much business going on, Ann. Janet, we'll be in the office. Take over for a while."

She led Ann to the back office and poured coffee into two mugs. Ann insisted on hiring women with a sleek, sophisticated look. Frieda had that, as well as professional competence. She carried her long, solid frame with grace.

"Let's hear the bad news," Ann said, slipping her large bag from her shoulder to the desk.

"Well, you know the story." Frieda took a page with figures from a folder. "Young people, if they decide to get married at all, opt for a simple ceremony in the park. They barely wear shoes, let alone a bridal gown. It's playing havoc with the business."

Ann scanned the figures. She had already considered closing this salon, but couldn't bear the thought of putting her people out of work. By now several workers had been discharged from each branch and Ann herself had taken a pay cut.

"We can hang on for a while. It's not as bad as I thought." She placed the paper back in its folder. "What's wrong with Janet? She hardly spoke to me."

"She's going through a rather messy divorce. I've been walking on eggshells around her." Frieda rolled her eyes.

"Oh, yes, I remember. She talked to me about it. Or rather, she mentioned it to Martin. It was at the staff party I had last spring. She was just thinking about a divorce then." Ann recalled noticing Martin and Janet in what looked like a serious discussion. They were isolated in a corner of the garden surrounded by peony bushes, away from the noisy crowd on the patio and in the gazebo. Janet's legs were long, tanned in short shorts and white boots, and her fawnlike eyes looked sad.

When Ann remarked about it later, Martin said that Janet sought out his advice on some financial matter. She was thinking of suing for divorce. "I feel sorry for her; she's very confused," he'd said. Divorce. It was becoming a rampant epidemic, Ann had thought. "I promised to mail Janet information," Martin had continued. It was kind of him, Ann remembered thinking.

When Ann returned home that evening, Flora was on the sofa, head back, snoring slightly, embroidery in her lap. Ann snapped off the television and Flora jerked upright.

She fingered a gray strand of hair behind her ear. "I was watching that."

Ann, feeling almost motherly toward Flora, turned the set back on.

"I've got a stew on the stove," Flora said. "The twins are upstairs and Theodore is at his friend Jimmy's."

"The stew smells good."

"We're out of milk." Flora wiggled her bulky body to the end of the sofa and lumbered upright.

"I'll have Martin stop on his way home. He's working late again tonight."

Flora was a godsend, though at sixty-four she wasn't as energetic as she'd once been. Whenever the family needed a housekeeper/babysitter, Flora, a widowed second cousin, was there. After the twins were born she'd offered her services and had remained ever since. Rather than stay with them, Flora insisted on preserving a bit of independence by keeping a small apartment in Detroit.

Ann went upstairs and slipped into age-softened blue jeans, then called Martin's office. The phone rang many times before someone answered. Finally a disinterested voice said, "No one's here. They quit at five."

"I wanted to catch Mr. Norbert. He's working late."

"I'm cleanin' and no one's here," the now-impatient voice said before the line was disconnected.

Ann held the receiver for a moment until the familiar impersonal dial tone sounded. Martin had obviously changed his mind. He'd be home shortly.

Downstairs Ann looked around appraisingly. It was time to replace the Swedish modern furniture that had been Martin's choice. Now it seemed too plain, too functional. Ann preferred traditional. As soon as business picked up, she'd shop for furnishings more to her taste; a Persian rug perhaps, an oil painting or two.

Everything changed with time—tastes, pastimes, mores. It wasn't only Martin who had changed. *She'd changed*. She knew that. Women's lib, Martin occasionally sneered, was the culprit. And it was true that she had gained a growing awareness that the system was unfavorable toward women. Slowly, imperceptibly, the women's movement was making inroads on her perspective. She'd always felt there was no glory in washing diapers or scrubbing toilets. Yet the media still touted just such an attitude. Television shows portrayed mindless women whose only thought was how to trick or outwit men. The magazines emphasized the joys of domesticity, the beauty of a white-white wash, the glory of gleaming tile. Ann was baffled when she heard a woman television hostess say, "What better thing can we do with our lives than to do the dishes for the ones we love?" Did doing dishes strengthen her children's character? Advance her husband's career? Bring her fulfillment?

The word "fulfillment" sounded so . . . so self-serving. And shouldn't she be *fulfilled* as wife/mother? Demeaning words and phrases were heaped on women, such as "penis envy" and Philip Wylie's "momism." In his *Generation of Vipers* Wylie concluded that mothers were intent on destroying their children. *I have an education, I have a mind,* she wanted to shout, *let me use it to benefit myself and my family.*

Yet she had little support, especially from Martin, who hardly noticed such questionable accomplishments as no wax buildup on the tile and super-white sheets (before colors became fashionable in linens), and she'd felt guilty at her lack of pride in baking a flaky pie crust, an art which she had never quite mastered. She loved her home, her family, but the lure of business, of being in the mainstream, of making money, called to her. And *still* the guilt followed her. Was she all that she should be to her boys, to Martin? In desiring more for herself, was she giving less to them? In working outside, was she in some way failing them? To prove her worth, her floors had to be immaculate, her bed always made, her drawers tidy; in short, she must be supermom, superwife.

Yes, she wanted Martin to open doors, to take her arm, to offer his strength, his masculinity. No, she had no urge to enter exclusive men's bars, to smoke cigars, to change a tire. She still wanted to be cherished and admired for the person she was, aside from being mother, wife, and housekeeper.

She was everything to everyone, but where was the sustenance, the support she so desperately needed? Where was the love? Was any of it, in the end, worth the struggle?

Ah, but the heady sense of pride in a successful managers' meeting, in a well-bargained price from a vendor. *That* was instant gratification.

It was after seven when Martin wandered in. Ann took his plate from the oven and set it on the table. "Where were you?"

"I told you I was working late."

"I called your office. You weren't there." Ann

poured coffee and heaped in a generous teaspoon of sugar.

"Maybe I was in the rest room."

Ann frowned. "Someone answered. A cleaning person. She said everyone was gone."

Martin mashed peas with his fork, concentrating on the task. "A couple of the guys stopped at the Respite after work."

Ann stopped her vigorous polishing of the stove and looked at Martin squarely. "Well, why didn't you just say so?"

Martin sighed. "I changed my mind about working late at the last minute and didn't bother to call you, all right?" He pushed his half-eaten dinner away and moved from the table.

"At least clear away your mess," Ann said through a tight mouth.

Martin ignored her and went to the living room.

Ann followed him. "Theodore needs help with his homework. He needs drilling in math and spelling."

"I don't have the patience."

"Force yourself!"

Reluctantly Martin sat Teddy at the dining table and began a disinterested quizzing. When Teddy poked at the flower centerpiece with his pencil, his father shouted at him to concentrate. Ann, finishing the kitchen work, tried to ignore the scene as Martin became irritable at wrong answers and gave the child that familiar look of vexation. Teddy became quieter, less forthcoming with answers.

Afterward Ann said, "How can he learn when you put him down like you do? That certainly doesn't foster confidence."

"I can't help it." Martin flipped the paper to the business section. "I always think he should be smarter than he is."

"He's only seven. He's just learning. We all start out from ignorance."

"Look, I've had a hard day. I'd just like to relax. *You* help him if you can do it better."

"He needs some time with his father. Besides, I have other things to do. Tonight there's a PTA meeting, not to mention marketing plans I have to go over. And don't forget, *I* work too."

"Let Matthew or Brian help him."

"They're just kids. Besides, they have their own lives. Anyway, they usually end up teasing him or fighting."

Martin retreated behind the newspaper and Ann knew better than to pursue the argument. She looked at her watch. If she didn't leave now, she'd be late for her PTA meeting.

The meeting eventually degenerated into a squabble over whether to hold a fair annually or biannually. They disbanded earlier than usual without having reached an agreement. By the time Ann returned, she had rehashed the meeting in her mind and decided she should have been more forceful. The familiar tattoo at the back of her head heralded the beginning of a headache. She let herself into the house quietly, not wanting to disturb anyone. By the television sounds coming from the family room, she knew Martin must still be up. The phone was ringing as she hung her coat in the hall closet.

Someone must have picked up the receiver a split second before Ann. A soft voice was saying, "It's me."

Before Ann could answer, Martin said, sounding annoyed, "I told you never to call here."

Ann drew in a sharp breath and covered the receiver with her hand.

The soft voice sounded vaguely familiar. "I just needed to talk to you. We still have things to talk about."

"I'll call you tomorrow."

"Promise?"

"Yes, promise." Martin's voice was soft, tender. The way it used to be with her so many years ago.

After she heard the click, she returned the phone to its cradle and slumped against the wall. Fear clutched at Ann's stomach and her heart thudded against her ribs.

Who was this woman? What did it mean? Her mind shrank from formulating the words. But there they were anyway.

Martin was having an affair.

She buried her face in her hands. No, it couldn't be. Not Martin. There had to be an explanation.

Her stomach heaved suddenly and she ran up the stairs to the bathroom. Placing a wet cloth over her forehead, she sat on the edge of the tub and observed her stricken, pain-filled face in the mirror. Not an affair, not Martin, not her husband, father of her children.

Fool. The evidence couldn't be more overwhelming. She thought about the past months. The signs were unmistakable, classic. The phone calls with a hasty click when she answered, the late nights with unreasonable explanations, the disinterested lovemaking. How could she be so blind?

Think, think. What to do, how to handle this. But she couldn't think. Her mind swirled and blurred. The woman. Who was she? Was she young? Beautiful? Someone he worked with?

She must go to him now, confront him. But she felt paralyzed. It occurred to her that she should pray. But the only words forthcoming were, "Jesus, Mary, help me."

Martin. You bastard. What have I done or not done to deserve this? Have I been too much mother, not enough wife? Have I been too much professional woman, not enough helpmate?

She wasn't sure how long she'd sat in a half-crouch

on the edge of the tub when she heard Martin's footfall on the thickly carpeted stairs.

"Ann," he said, glimpsing her through the half-closed door. "I didn't hear you come in."

With a great effort she stood and gripped the edge of the pink marbleized sink. Her face expressionless, staring wide-eyed, she said, "I heard. I picked up the phone and you were talking to a woman. I heard."

His eyes widened and darted to hers, then to the floor. "What? You heard? What do you mean?"

"I mean I know you're having an affair."

He shifted uneasily, then gave a short laugh. "It's a joke. A game. This girl . . . a girl at work . . . she's . . . it's a silly infatuation on her part . . . it's . . . nothing."

Ann screamed, "Don't lie, Martin. Don't make it worse by lying."

He put a hand up, warding off her words. "Ssh. The kids." Turning abruptly, he went to the bedroom. Ann followed, closing the door softly behind her. The boys shouldn't bear witness to their troubles, shouldn't be drawn into their problems.

"Martin, I want to believe it's nothing."

He seemed more composed now. "Then just believe it."

"How can I? You've been so distant, so uncaring for a long time . . ."

Martin lowered his head and shook it. "You want too much from me."

"Too much! I only want your love. Is that too much? Don't I deserve that?"

"I do love you. It's just . . . I don't know what it is." Martin dropped heavily to the bed, his fingertips supporting his head as though it was inordinately heavy.

"Are you so unhappy with me?" Her hands spread out imploringly.

"No, it's not that. It's that everything's changing.

Young people have time to enjoy their lives now. I never had that, never had a chance to . . . be young.''

"So you're recapturing your youth? Is that it? You're falling for the 'free-love' crap?'' Her voice sounded shrewish in her ears.

Martin got up abruptly and took clean pajamas from a drawer. "I'm sleeping in the guest room.''

Ann stood against the door. "No! We have to talk!''

Taking her arm, Martin moved her aside easily. "I can't talk now. Tomorrow. We'll talk tomorrow.'' The door closed behind him.

She fell to the bed and cried. Dawn's first gray hues covered the sky before she dropped off to sleep.

The next morning he was gone before she got up. After a torturous day during which her mind refused to fasten on anything other than the stunning phone call, she was determined to insist Martin make a decision between her and the *woman*.

He didn't come home that night until the boys were in bed. Ann sat in the darkened family room waiting, a constant stream of incoherent and disconnected thoughts drifting through her mind.

He sat heavily in a chair across from her, not speaking for several minutes. Finally he said, "I'm going to end it.''

"When?''

"Soon.''

"Tomorrow. End it tomorrow.'' She took a deep breath. "Who is she?''

He shook his head.

"Martin, talk to me, please talk to me about it.''

"There's nothing to talk about. I said I'll end it. Isn't that enough?''

"No! There were reasons for this to happen. How do I know it won't happen again?''

"You'll just have to trust me.''

"Trust? How can I, ever again?''

"Just shut up, Ann. Don't say anything. This isn't easy for me. I . . . I don't want anything to happen to our marriage."

"How can you say that? You're destroying our marriage!"

He rose abruptly and left the room. She couldn't force herself to follow. Trying to communicate was useless anyway.

She muffled her sobs in a pillow, miserable, angry, hurt.

Alone.

7

Tina was the first to arrive at Dino's on the Lake. She asked for a table overlooking the water and sat, tucking her short skirt under her thighs, crossing her white-booted legs. Having decided to move to Washington, she wondered how to break the news to her sisters. She hoped, probably unrealistically, for their support. Her gaze went to the scene outside the window, where the late-summer sun glinted on the water and giant waves crashed to the shore below. Her resolve was somehow buoyed by the sight of nature's unrelenting force. She had vacillated long enough.

Neither Ann nor Louise would be happy about her decision initially, but she would convince them it was for the best.

The manager appeared beside her. "Tina! Good to see you." He pulled out a chair and sat sidewise. "So, how's the old man?"

Tina searched her brain for the manager's name, but could only recall that he was a friend of her father's. All the local old-timers knew Mike Marcassa from his firebrand days as a union organizer.

"He's fine. Misses the old days. He hated being put out to pasture."

"Yeah, that's the way it goes when you get old. But Mike still has it"—he tapped his forehead—"up here."

"He sure does," Tina agreed.

The manager moved to his feet and saluted. "Give Mike my regards. Tell 'im to stop in and I'll buy him a drink."

Tina, relieved to be left alone, resumed her introspection, planned the words she would use. She'd barely gathered her thoughts when Ann and Lou walked toward the table.

They all hugged, then settled into their seats while a waiter poured from a complimentary bottle of Chianti.

"I almost didn't make it," Louise said. "Mother Superior had the car and I had to borrow—beg, really —a car from one of the parishioners. Mrs. Darnell is so sweet usually, but this time she seemed a bit reluctant and asked that I have it back by ten."

"I wonder how you stand it, Lou, with nothing to your name." Tina laughed suddenly at her words. "Imagine me saying that! I haven't much either. But I *do* have my freedom; that's something."

"I have a lot more freedom than I did when I first entered the order," Louise said defensively.

Ann lifted her glass. *"Salute.* To the three muscatels." They all laughed at the playful appellation Ann had given them when they were children. Ann sipped, nodding appreciatively. "Pretty good. How's the job-hunting going, Tina?"

"Not good. I did go so far as to put my application in several school districts."

"That's a start," Louise said.

"But even if one of them calls me, I don't think I'll accept."

Ann looked at Tina, assessing, waiting for more.

Louise blurted, "Why ever not?"

A lake breeze wafted in through the open window, lifting and settling Tina's long dark hair on her shoulder. "I've made a decision. I'm going to Washington." She forced a smile, looking from one to the other for a hint of approval.

"Washington?" Ann looked incredulous. "It's that guy, isn't it? What's his name?"

"Adam."

"And he's encouraging you to move?"

"He's not against it." Tina split a roll in two and began buttering it. "He says it's my life. But I know he'd like me there."

Ann frowned. "Tina, it doesn't sound like a whole-hearted endorsement."

"Oh, it is." Tina had expected she'd have to defend her position. "It's just, well, he's so involved in his work. And he's fiercely independent."

A waitress in nautical garb interrupted to take their orders. When she left, Louise touched Tina's hand. "This plan seems so . . . so impetuous. Have you thought this through? What if things don't work out? What if you can't get a job?"

"Things will work out. But if they don't, they don't. There are always choices, alternatives. Listen, how often in your life do you meet the man of your dreams? Adam is everything I've ever wanted."

"You sound like an old movie heroine," Ann said, leaning forward with an intense expression. "You've met him only once!"

"We were together quite a bit. And we've been talking. A lot. We're on the same wavelength."

"From what planet?" Ann asked.

Tina removed her hand from underneath Louise's. "Can't you trust me? Can't you take something on faith for once?"

"Faith. *There's* an old-fashioned word." Ann shook her head. "I guess if I ever had any, it's gone now."

Louise turned to her sister and said sharply, "Ann, that's not like you."

Tina went on, "What's the sense of plodding along, waiting for life to happen to you? Adam's come into my life and I want to be a part of his."

Louise looked back at Tina with a frown. "What do you hope for? Marriage?"

"Whatever." Tina felt a stab of irritation. "Just a relationship, if that's how it turns out."

"You're acting like an adolescent," Ann said.

"Wait, Ann," Louise interrupted. "Maybe she's right. Maybe you need to seize the day, the moment. It *is* rare to feel so passionate about something or someone."

Ann looked astonished. "Louise, I can't believe it's you talking. Conservative, straitlaced, nunnish you."

Louise shrugged. "Maybe I'm a romantic at heart. From what you've said, Adam sounds like an upright, humanistic sort of a man. Who knows? He and Tina may be meant for one another. He may be ready to marry." She smiled benignly. "He may even settle Tina down."

Tina rolled her eyes. "Thanks a lot. Like I'm a wild mustang."

"Doesn't anyone have any common sense around here?" Ann asked.

"It's my life, Ann." Tina set her mouth in a grim line.

Ann sighed, lowering her head. "So it is. And who am I to argue? I haven't done so well with my own life."

"How can you say that?" Tina looked bewildered. "You have everything you've ever wanted."

"Not quite."

"What do you mean? What are you lacking?"

Ann shook her head as if warding off questions.

Louise said quietly, "It's Martin, isn't it?"

Ann was silent for a moment while her sisters stared at her. "Yes. Things have happened. Things I don't think I can forgive."

It was unthinkable that Ann's life wasn't working out. "What things?" Tina prompted. "Tell us."

"I don't want to talk about it."

Tina asked, "Is he running around on you?"

Ann looked away as the waitress brought salads and more rolls. The others waited for her answer, but she remained silent.

"That's it, then, he's having an affair," Tina said, her brow furrowing in anger.

"You can talk to us," Louise said. When Ann didn't respond, she continued, "If you and Martin have problems, you must try to work them out. You can't just toss away the past years. And what about your children? Think of them."

"God, don't you think I've told myself all that?"

"Your marriage is sanctified. People make mistakes. You must find it in your heart to forgive. Jesus' message was of love and forgiveness." Louise leaned forward earnestly. "Find it in your heart."

"Right now I can't forgive. I'm hurt. Angry."

"Maybe he's been foolish," Louise said. "Martin's not a bad person. He's probably going through—to use the pop psych term—a mid-life crisis."

Tina said, "Lou! How can you defend him? He's a jerk, an ass, scum. For Chrissake, Ann, leave him. How can you love him after this?"

"I don't know what to do." Ann's face crumbled, and tears escaped her cloudy eyes.

Louise handed Ann a tissue from her purse. "You must pray. Pray for guidance."

"You two are really no help." Ann snuffled into the tissue.

Tina said, "How can we help you when you won't tell us what happened?"

"I can't talk about it. I just can't." She grabbed her bag, stuffing the tissue inside. "Look, I'm not hungry and I feel rotten. I'm leaving. I'll call you both later, maybe next week." She pushed her chair back and hurried from the room.

Louise whispered, "This is a time for compassion."

"I have no compassion for Martin," Tina said.

"You're young. Maybe it's one of the lessons you need to learn."

"Louise, you've been out of the mainstream for so long. The world isn't a kind place. It's a mean place."

"It's what you make it. I hope you make it a kind place in Washington."

'Am I doing the right thing?" Tina looked imploringly at her sister. "Put yourself in my place. Would you go?"

Louise's eyes closed. "I don't know. I used to have all the answers, but now I just don't know."

The waitress interrupted with steaming plates, and the two ate in silence. Tina stared out the window. The lake seemed to have calmed somewhat and gulls wheeled gracefully, landing on a cluster of gleaming rocks. The tranquil scene seemed to wash away her frustration, leaving her with a sense of the rightness of her decision. "I think I'm doing the right thing, Lou. I hope you'll support me."

"This is just a small event in your life, Tina," Louise said. "There's only one who can see the entire picture. Only he knows what's right and what isn't. Go where your heart leads you. I'll pray for you. For Ann too."

When they left the restaurant, Tina breathed deeply of the tangy air that drifted across the parking lot on a breeze. Lou could save her prayers. Tina didn't need them. She was doing the right thing.

Tears gathered in Ann's eyes, blinding her. She reached the Thunderbird and yanked the door open. Inside, she dropped her head on the wheel and gasped for breath. It had been a mistake, telling her sisters. She'd wanted to keep it secret; had hoped matters would be resolved and no one would ever know. But obviously her misery was all too evident, and Lou, as always, was so perceptive.

After Martin had promised to end his affair a week ago, he refused to discuss the matter and ignored Ann's pleas for communication. Now there was an icy wall between them that she feared would never melt. She must try to forgive, Lou had said. But how? She felt raw, her heart torn and bleeding.

Ann barely remembered the ride home. The garage door squealed as it swung upward, and she eased the car into the garage and entered through the kitchen door.

Martin was pouring a cup of coffee at the counter. A bottle of Scotch stood nearby. ''Want coffee?'' he offered. His voice was slow, the way it was on the rare occasions when he drank.

Was this an opening? A peace offering? ''Yes, I could use a cup.''

He poured for Ann, then sat at the kitchen counter, intent on stirring sugar and cream into his coffee.

Ann leaned on the counter across from him. ''Have you done it? Ended it?''

He continued stirring as if that task required all his attention. ''No.''

Ann closed her eyes slowly, painfully. ''Martin . . .''

''I've no defense. Try to understand, Ann. It's hard . . . hard to just finish, just say good-bye.''

Ann gripped the edge of the counter. ''Then this is such a grand passion?''

Martin didn't answer.

''Who is it? What's her name? Is it some . . . some bimbo you picked up somewhere?''

Again silence.

''What about me, Martin? Do I mean nothing to you? Don't you care about me at all?''

''Of course I do.''

''Do you love me?'' Her words were a whisper.

His eyes downcast, he hesitated for a moment. ''Yes, I love you. I'll always love you. This is . . . it's different. I can't explain it.''

"Martin. You have got to end it."

He shook his head. "Annie, please try to understand. You don't really know what my life has been like, my childhood, what my parents—"

"Of course I know." She'd learned to get along with his stern, unbending parents, but she'd never managed to feel a bond between them. They had pushed Martin, demanded the best from him. More, perhaps, than Martin was capable of achieving.

"No, you don't know my life. Nose to the grindstone since I was thirteen. I had to get all A's. I had to work and save for college. Then, as soon as I graduated, it was marriage." He slid off the stool and leaned against it. "That's what I thought I wanted— marriage, you, just a happy-ever-after life." His shoulders drooped and he dropped his trembling hands loosely between his knees. "It's not what I thought it was, marriage. It's still nose to the grindstone. I . . . I was never a kid, never carefree, never a rebellious teenager. I was scared all my life."

"Oh, spare me, Martin. That's a reason for this? For adultery?"

"No . . . I know how stupid this sounds. I'm not trying to make excuses. But it's true. Or at least it's the way I feel, rightly or wrongly."

He dropped his head into his hands and shook it from side to side.

Ann was unmoved. If she wasn't so devastated, she supposed she could summon a bit of pity. But at this moment she hated him. How had this happened? She had loved him. He had loved her. He had fathered her children. They had a history, and, she'd thought, a future.

She grasped for answers. *Am I at fault? Am I lacking? No! It isn't me. It's him. Him! He discarded the love I offered, disdained my efforts to work out solutions, ignored my overtures. It's him! Damn him!*

She felt a tremor, a low thunder in her brain; a gathering storm. "You don't love me," she said in an agonized whisper.

He lifted his tearstained, pathetic face. "Yes. No." He covered his face with his hands. "Oh, God."

"You love this . . . this person?"

He said nothing.

"Martin?"

He shook his head. Not emphatically. Not sincerely.

"I hate you!" she screamed. "You son of a bitch, I hate you."

"Shh, the kids." He made a move toward her, but she wrenched away.

"Yes, the kids," she said. "Have you thought about them? Either end it tomorrow or get out of this house and say good-bye to your kids forever!"

She ran from the kitchen and to the bathroom, where she stripped and turned the shower on full force. Hot water beat on her, drowning out her anguished sobs. Would she ever feel whole again? The water ran cold before she finally dried off and went to bed, where her thoughts continued to badger her consciousness.

Some marriages stayed glued together, the mucilage being children, even after ruptures such as this one. But there must be at least the willingness to forgive, and try as she might, she could not summon the necessary absolution. And what of other bonds, the physical ones? Could she bear to have Martin touch her ever again? Wasn't that important to a marriage? Whenever he touched her, would his thoughts be with *that* woman? Whether they were or not, could she believe otherwise?

And there was *still*, in this enlightened era of the seventies, a subtle stigma on divorced people, on children from broken homes. That old saw—keep it together for the sake of the children—had some small validity.

What of other considerations, like respect and communication? She couldn't live in a state of distrust, of resentment, of repressed anger. Perhaps, after all, the best solution was to dissolve the marriage and make the best of things.

Tina's trip to Washington began on a sour note with dire predictions from her parents. "You have no business running all over the country, without a job or a place to live," her father had ranted. She hadn't elaborated on her relationship, slight as it was, with Adam, just that she was staying temporarily with a friend. If only she wasn't so beholden to her parents. In spite of his misgivings, her father had sold her his "old" car for a minimum down payment and promises of monthly installments, and at the last minute tucked a hundred-dollar bill into her pocket.

"It's dangerous for a young girl in a strange city," her mother said. "And you won't know your way around."

"Ma, did you forget that you left your home permanently at twenty-two and traveled across an ocean?" Tina said.

"That was different," her mother sniffed. "I was married."

Tina was hours into her trip before she could put aside thoughts of her tearful mother and angry father and begin imagining the reunion with Adam. Her daydreams of Adam had carried her through the Ohio farmlands and green Pennsylvania mountains. Finally, early that evening, tired and hungry, Tina parked the four-year-old Buick in front of the Beehive and glanced at her reflection in the rearview mirror. Definitely a candidate for a shower and a nap. She hoisted one of her smaller bags to her shoulder. However anxious she was to see Adam, right now she longed for a bed and pillow.

The Victorian structure looked welcoming with its fringe of newly painted gingerbread and wide embracing porch. Tina was disappointed when a young girl with stringy hair and a sullen mouth greeted her at the door, saying, "Adam had a meeting. He said to settle in the Cherokee Room and he'd see you later. There's a roll-away bed in there. If you're hungry, there's plenty of food in the kitchen. I'm Carla." The merest trace of a southern-belle drawl crept into her voice.

Tina showered, then joined the young, somewhat familiar group for a dinner of macaroni with cheese and salad. She was helping with the cleanup afterward when Adam appeared. Tina was struck again by his powerful aura, his open good looks, the shoulder-length chestnut hair that matched forthright dark eyes.

"Tina!" He gave her a wide smile and a hug, then moved her an arm's length away. "You look terrific. It's great to see you."

He looked more imposing than she'd remembered, in a gray suit, his beard neatly trimmed. "I hardly recognize you."

"Had a funding meeting this afternoon." Adam loosened his tie. "I somehow feel like an impostor when I wear a suit. Come on, let's sit down and catch up."

He took two colas from the refrigerator and led her to the living room. When they'd small-talked for a while, he said, "I've circled some apartments listed in last Sunday's paper, the ones that are in a suitable neighborhood. Of course, you can stay here for a few days, until you find something. Are you okay for cash?"

"Yes, I've managed to save a little."

"What about a job? Will you go back to teaching?"

"I suppose it's a place to start."

"I know the school superintendent. I can get you an interview, then it's up to you."

"I was thinking of volunteering at the MOB office too."

He smiled approvingly. "Good idea."

He seemed anxious to get her "settled," almost as if he were afraid of her dependency.

Through a yawn, Tina said, "I guess I'm still wiped out from the long drive. I think I'll turn in."

"Okay, I'll see you in the morning." He placed a chaste and disappointing kiss on her forehead, then, as if thinking better of it, brushed a kiss on her lips. Much too quickly.

The bedroom was large but crowded, with three beds, three chests, and the roll-away, which Tina proceeded to make up with the mismatched sheets that lay across it. Berating herself, she privately admitted a fondness for the accustomed amenities at her parents' house: the private room, the large closet, the matching drapes and spread. Perhaps she wasn't so liberated after all. The letdown she was experiencing was partly due, she was sure, to the long trip, but besides that, Adam's welcome left something to be desired. Still, what had she expected, wine and flowers? After all, it was she who had instigated the move, not Adam, and they were still practically strangers, despite the warm feelings engendered in their brief meetings and talks. As she slipped into bed, the feeling of exuberance and certitude with which she had started out from Detroit were replaced by a vague uncertainty.

At the first jarring sounding of an alarm clock, Tina sprang upright in her bed. One of the two other inhabitants of the room stirred and, fumbling for the culprit clock, stilled its annoying clamor with an expletive. The other girl flopped a pillow over her head and yelled, "Keep it down!"

The two who finally arose were teenagers who whispered and stumbled about, obviously readying themselves for school. Through slitted lids Tina observed, remembering her own teen years. Kids wore jeans to classes now, she noted, the more tattered, the better. Such attire had been unthinkable when she was in high school; now it was commonplace. Her bothersome puritanical streak emerged to question if such clothing were conducive to proper learning. The nuns would never have approved. In a few short years, she mused, she would be thirty and one of the suspect generation.

When the girls departed, Tina arose and dressed quickly in a Wayne State sweatshirt and jeans with fabric still intact at the knees. In the kitchen Adam stood at the counter drinking coffee while jotting in a notebook and calling out instructions to several youngsters grouped around the table. A lanky boy scooped dry and lumpy scrambled eggs onto a few plates.

"Want some?" he asked Tina.

"No, thanks," she said, preferring one of an assortment of cereals lined up on the table. The enticing aroma of bacon, however, was more than she could resist.

Adam flashed her a smile. "Good morning. You look rested." He automatically reached for the toast that had popped noisily from a toaster and dealt out the four slices around the table. Someone tossed more bread into the toaster, another poured milk into an earthenware pitcher.

"Ten minutes, kids. You snooze, you lose." Adam passed a huge jar of jam to the nearest girl.

Tina smiled in appreciation of the expertly orchestrated scene.

Adam slipped the notebook into his pocket. "This is my friend Tina. She'll be bunking here for a while."

"Far-out," said a lanky youngster who eyed her from head to toe to head.

One of her roommates said, "Hey, put her on KP, man."

Tina laughed. "I don't mind KP."

"Nice welcome, kids," Adam said, hefting the coffeepot. "Coffee, Tina?"

"Thanks."

"Come on, let's go out on the porch."

Tina sat on the glider, balancing her mug. "I'm duly impressed by this operation. How do you keep order?"

"You didn't notice the whip?"

"Seriously."

"Different methods." He perched on the porch rail and swung his leg back and forth. "It's trial and error mostly. What works with one doesn't necessarily work for others. But they all know they have to abide by the basic rules."

"Can't they find foster homes for these kids?"

He shook his head sadly. "Too many kids, too few homes. Besides, who wants problem kids? It takes special people to deal with them."

Tina's smile was full of admiration. "You're special people."

He seemed a little embarrassed. "Just doing my job, ma'am," he parodied. "I'm going to hole up in my office for a while; paperwork. I'll call the superintendent first thing. Maybe you'll want to call some of the rentals. Then this afternoon I'll take you to lunch and we can look at any good possibilities. Sound okay?"

"Sounds fine. You're so organized."

"Got to be. Without organization my life would be pure chaos." He checked his watch. "I'd better get started. Marina should be here a little later on. She's my helper, second mate, chief cook and bottle washer, et cetera. You know to help yourself if you need anything, right?"

'Right." She felt dismissed and once again disappointed. She'd hoped he would be as glad to see her as she was him.

Then Adam redeemed himself. He reached out and touched her cheek, then gave her a light hug.

After helping in the kitchen, Tina made her phone calls. Back in the bedroom she debated whether to bother with makeup, opting finally for only a touch of lip gloss. Her lustrous, newly brushed hair waved and curled on her shoulders. She had given up setting it on frozen orange juice cans to achieve the current pipe-straight style.

As she descended the stairs, the front door opened and a young book-laden woman entered, kicking the door closed behind her. She eyed Tina warily, then repositioned her books to free her right hand.

"Hi. I'm Marina, head flunky around here."

"Hello. I'm Tina Marcassa."

"Oh. Yeah. Adam told me." Her assessment was thorough.

Adam emerged from the first-floor room that served as his office/study and clapped Marina on the shoulder. "You've met? Tina, I told you about Marina. Couldn't run this place without her."

Marina turned adoring eyes on Adam. Major crush here, Tina thought, her heart squeezing in a sudden alert. Did Adam share Marina's feelings? She was young—not much past twenty—and willowy, with her curves all too evident in the skintight jeans.

"I've got several rentals we can look at, Adam," Tina said, suddenly in a hurry to leave. "When do you want to go?"

"Now's fine. Going out for a while, Marina. Hold down the fort, okay?"

When they'd settled in the car, Adam explained, "Marina's a college student, doing this for training. She wants to be a social worker, more's the pity."

He checked Tina's notes and separated the listing into an A, B, and C list according to area. They headed first just a few blocks away to a large old house that had been divided into three apartments. The rental had a tiny kitchen and few windows, yet the high ceilings and polished wood moldings were attractive. The landlady, in a pouffed red wig, waved long curving nails and warned, "This'll go fast, dearie." Tina put it on her maybe list.

Their other searches proved fruitless. The apartments were either too small, or too large, or too expensive, or in a marginal neighborhood. Getting an apartment wasn't going to be as easy as she had thought.

"Don't get discouraged," Adam said as they left a flat with peeling wallpaper and mildewed carpeting. "Let's stop for lunch and finish up afterward."

She made an effort to raise the dejected slump of her shoulders.

At a small Chinese restaurant Tina hungrily tossed down rice and pepper steak she'd laced liberally with soy sauce.

"By the way," Adam said, "forgot to tell you, I talked to Langley, the superintendent, this morning. You have an appointment with the personnel office at ten o'clock tomorrow morning. You may need a DC certificate, but I think you could at least substitute with your Michigan credentials."

Tina pursed her lips and nodded. "Good."

"You seem less than ecstatic."

"It's just that . . . well, I've never been really totally hooked on teaching. I can't help feeling there's something else I'd prefer doing."

"Like what?"

She lifted her brows with a woebegone look. "That's just it. I don't know. Does that make me seem like a total flake?"

"No, it makes you normal. Lots of people live out their lives and never find out what they really want to do. As a matter of fact, I'm rethinking my career, even as we speak."

"You too?"

"Yep. In fact, I'm taking night classes." He toyed with the chopsticks. "Law school."

She tipped the teacup to her lips. "What led you to that?"

"Believe it or not, I want to go into politics. That's the place to make changes, big ones, not little ones, like I'm doing now."

Tina paused with a forkful of rice. "Adam, you never cease to amaze me. Somehow, I rather thought you'd be the type to, say, take a walking tour through the United States. Or backpack through Europe."

Adam laughed. "Looks can be deceiving." He pointed his finger at her. "But those aren't bad ideas."

"How long will it take you to get a degree?"

"With luck, another three years. Less if I go full-time."

"You ought to go full-time, then. Get it over with."

"Cash is the problem. I need to work, even with loans. Besides, I'm reluctant to give up the Beehive. They need me." His smile was rueful. "Inflated ego, eh? I'm sure someone else could do it, but I'm just attached to the kids, as you know, and for the most part it's gratifying work." He looked at his watch. "We'd better look at the last two listings. I don't want to get back too late. Marina leaves about five and I can't leave the place unsupervised."

The last apartment they viewed, available in a week, was adequate: clean, in a decent neighborhood, and close to transportation and shops. The drawback was that it was unfurnished and Tina preferred a furnished place. She mentally totted up her meager savings and decided buying furniture would be a problem. But Adam assured her his basement held some odds and ends and he knew of a great flea market. Tina could imagine what assortment of "leftovers" he had, judging from the worn and ancient furnishings already in place at the Beehive.

"I think you should take it," Adam said as they drove back to his place, his arm slung casually over her shoulder. "You need your own space."

Obviously he wasn't anxious to share his space with her. And even more obviously, she couldn't bunk on a roll-away in a room with three or more kids. Dormitory living wasn't her style, but she'd vaguely hoped there might be an empty bedroom she could occupy for a short time. And become one more of his family of strays? No, definitely, she needed a place of her own. It would be better all around.

"I'll take it, then," Tina said with conviction. "Let's go back and I'll leave a deposit."

"Atta girl. I think you're doing the right thing."

On the trip back the radio played "Bridge over Troubled Waters," and Adam began singing along. Tina joined in harmony, thinking of the last time they had sung together.

"Remember our picnic, Adam?"

He cast a quick sidewise glance at her and said softly, "How could I forget?" He ran an index finger from her cheek to her chin, then took her hand in his, resting it on his thigh.

That's when I knew I was in love with you, she wanted to say as she basked in the warmth of his touch.

Back at the Beehive, Marina greeted them with a smile for Adam. She touched his arm. "How'd it go?"

"I found a place," Tina said. "Not furnished, but in a nice area, and the price is right."

"Great!" Marina's enthusiasm was genuine. She probably didn't want Tina hanging around permanently.

Gathering her books, Marina said, "I'll see you tomorrow."

Adam gave her a quick hug. "Thanks, Marina."

There seemed to be an easy camaraderie between the two and Marina was emerging in Tina's mind as an adversary. Tina wanted to get close to Adam, but sensed that he was close to many, intimate with few. He kept a certain reserve, a distance.

But she could change that.

8

Tina worked beside Adam in companionable silence while gray doves spread their white-tipped wings and sailed about the gnarled apple trees in the corner of the yard. Wearing oversize yellow rubber gloves, she scraped old paint from a cherrywood sideboard, circa 1920. Her eyes teared up as she applied a fresh coating of paint remover. The Beehive's back porch was covered with newspapers to catch the scrapings, and the creaky glider was moved out of range. Enchanted by Adam's closeness, Tina longed to touch his sun-browned arm. During the past several days, as they worked side by side, Tina had tentatively probed for clues to his persona. She was slowly gaining a perspective on Adam Thornberry, while he, she was sure, was conducting an assessment of his own.

In a tube top and cutoff jeans that displayed slender, curvy legs, she sat back on her haunches and wiped her forehead with her arm. "Whew, I need a break. This odor is getting to me. Want a pop?"

"You mean a soda?" he teased. "Sure." Adam attacked an obscure corner of a table with a solvent-laden toothbrush. "This'll be a nice piece of furniture when it's done."

Tina wasn't looking forward to the completion of their project. Soon she would be teaching and that would end their halcyon days. Adam had helped move her into her new apartment a week ago. Since then she had spent most evenings, when Adam wasn't in class or otherwise occupied, at the Beehive. She loved working beside him, liked being part of his "family." The kids were used to her by now, and she occasionally took time with the girls, giving a little advice, a little direction, disguised as aimless chatter. Many nights she'd make popcorn or bring in special treats.

When she returned with two colas, the sun was disappearing overhead in a rosy glow. Autumn was definitely in the air, beguiling them with a piny scent, a pale rising moon. Tina shuddered. Another summer gone. Another winter on its way. The passage of time taunted her with a message: procrastinate no longer, get on with your life.

After the kids were settled for the night, she sat in Adam's study, reading while he studied and made notes, sometimes talking softly to himself. She wished the study of law wouldn't take so much of his time and concentration. She stretched and yawned loudly. "It's past my bedtime, Adam."

He looked up distractedly, then frowned. "Already? We haven't had a chance to talk."

"So what else is new?" Tina said reproachfully, her hand on the doorknob.

"Sorry. How about tomorrow, then?" Adam said, walking toward her. "No, wait. I have class tomorrow. Let's make it Friday. You'll have my undivided attention." He kissed the tip of her nose. "Hey," he said, suddenly solicitous, "Monday's your first day of work. Are you ready for the challenge?"

"As ready as I'll ever be. I have my shield and my sword." She'd secured a position as a substitute for a teacher on maternity leave. With any luck it would take her to January.

"All you need is your big smile along with that big heart."

"I only wish that were sufficient armor."

"Nervous?"

"Not really. I've done it before and I can do it again. I just wish I could muster more enthusiasm."

"You'll do fine. Let's celebrate Friday. Maybe we can go to a movie or something."

"Okay. 'Night, Adam."

He gave a little salute and was back immediately in his world of lawbooks.

A few days later, Tina sat at the kitchen table of her freshly painted apartment and stacked books and notes into her briefcase for tomorrow's class. The garage-sale table wobbled, and in desperation she'd taped a wad of paper to the bottom of the short leg. Suddenly homesick, she pulled a pad of foolscap toward her and jotted a short note to Louise, ending with a plaintive, "How I've always envied your stability, your dedication, your sense of purpose, especially in these days when sometimes the world seems to be churning. Someday you must tell me how you do it."

On Friday a movie was out of the question. Adam had Beehive reports to finish, as well as cramming for an exam.

Tina put down her book, *The Feminine Mystique,* and, feeling a sudden cool draft, closed the window behind Adam's desk. She wandered into the kitchen and made cocoa, then brought it, along with a plate of chocolate-chip cookies that Marina and Carla had made, to the study. Adam nodded his thanks and went doggedly back to his books.

Tina sat patiently reading while he worked, then finally stood, saying, "I'm going now, Adam."

He looked up, startled. "Wait, darlin', don't go yet." He rose and stretched. "I need some air. Let's take a walk."

Outside, he tucked her hand into his and whistled a melancholy tune that resembled "Greensleeves." The notes lingered in the cool, silent air as if waiting to be plucked.

"Smell that air," he said. "It's the fragrance of autumn."

She squeezed his fingers, filled with an aching for him that reached from the top of her head to her toenails.

He stopped walking suddenly and brought her around to him. "I'm sorry if I've been remote lately."

"You have been that."

He ran nervous fingers through long hair, pushing it off his forehead. "I had no idea the study of law would be so consuming."

Tina patted his cheek. "I know how it is." It was enough to be near Adam, to be part of his life.

"You're so understanding. No one else would put up with me."

Their eyes locked for a long moment; then he bent to her and kissed each corner of her mouth and nipped at her lower lip. In languid slow motion he enveloped her mouth with his, while she savored the growing passion. They stood against a sycamore tree, locked in a warm embrace, lost in a star-spangled world of their own. Tina finally moved away for air. Adam's warm breath tickled her ear.

"Tina, I want you . . . but not tonight, not tonight."

Disappointed, Tina nodded. His studies and the Beehive came first. She was beginning to understand that. But how long could she be patient? "Soon, Adam."

"Soon. God, yes, soon."

Tina's junior-high class in turn delighted and exasperated her. The work load was heavy and she found herself busy each night correcting papers. Although she talked to Adam on the phone every few days, two weeks went by before they were able to go on a "real" date to the movies. Tina offered to make dinner and dredged up her mother's *sugo*-and-meatballs recipe.

The garlic-and-basil aroma brought up such a pang of homesickness that she called her mother, then was immediately sorry. Her father got on the line and said, "When will you come to your senses and come home?"

During dinner Adam heaped praise on Tina and her culinary artistry. They talked about the kids at the Beehive and she told him about her junior-high class. "It's like walking into a mine field, but I like most of the kids, even the delinquents."

Adam helped her clear the table, then dried dishes while Tina washed. A lovely intimate domestic scene, Tina thought, smiling to herself. The folks at home.

Adam must have been thinking the same thing. "Do we have to go to the movie?"

"Yes. I haven't been out in ages. I'm in danger of becoming a hermit."

During the movie, *Love Story*, they held hands and on the way home they discussed the film.

"I noticed you wiping away a tear or two," Adam said, laughing.

"I admit it. I'm a sucker for a love story, especially a sad one. Did you like it?"

"It was okay. I like MacGraw."

"I like O'Neal."

"Do you really think he's handsome?" Adam asked.

"Um, yes. Very. Did you think MacGraw was pretty?"

"Adorable." At her put-on pout, he gave her shoulder a hug. "But not nearly as adorable as you."

"And you're adorabler than O'Neal."

When they reached her apartment, she invited Adam in for a glass of wine. He readily assented. Earlier he'd told Marina he'd be late and she agreed to spend the night at the Beehive.

Tina's small living room contained one well-worn but comfortable chair with an ottoman, one vintage floor lamp, one end table. Adam took the chair at her insistence, and she poured wine into two goblets from a set of six she'd found at her new haunt, the flea market.

Tina carried the wine, cheese, and crackers in on a tray. "At least the wineglasses are elegant, even if they are secondhand."

Sitting on the ottoman, she rested her back against Adam's knees. They sipped silently, listening to teenagers who passed by outside, laughing and shouting in youthful exuberance.

"Seems far removed, the teenage silliness," Adam said.

"Not so far. Seems like yesterday." Tina poured more wine and spread cheese on a cracker. She popped the tidbit into Adam's mouth.

He lifted her long hair from her neck and twisted it around his finger. "Pretty hair. Silky. That's a good name for you, Silky."

A rush of emotion engulfed her, a sensation that had been lurking under the surface of her awareness all evening.

He put his goblet on the tray and stood. "I suppose I should go, Silky Tina."

"No, stay. We should talk."

"There's nothing much to say. We understand each other." He took the glass from her hand and set it down, then pulled her roughly to him. His kiss was insistent, pulsing, and she pressed closer, feeling the hardness of him.

"Ah, Tina, I've wanted to do this all night." He pulled the shirt loose from her jeans and ran gentle fingertips over her flesh, then wiggled his hands under her bra.

She eased away. "Let me get into something more comfortable," she parodied, "like a bed." She lifted her hand to him and they went to the bedroom.

He undressed her, openly admiring the white smoothness of her skin, the gentle curve of her hips, the dark, tightly curled hair below the swell of her belly. She undressed him, easing the jeans over taut hips and a sturdy erection. He lifted her easily and deposited her gently on the bed. His kisses were probing, electric, and in between the kisses he murmured loving words, "You're so sweet, so beautiful."

Tina's breath came in small pants, her hands stroked and urged. Adam's lovemaking was practiced; at first gentle, then excruciatingly sensual. Tina moaned with delight until finally, knowing she was ready, he entered her.

Afterward he held her for a long time, only their breathing and the ticking of a Kmart clock disturbing the intimate silence.

Adam shifted and observed her with his chin propped in his hand. "It was good, huh?"

"Exceptional." She teased the curling hair of his chest with thumb and forefinger.

He kissed her shoulder. "I've wanted you for a long time."

"Me too."

"You're special."

"You're special. We're two special people." Engulfed in a sense of peace, of fulfillment, Tina traced her finger along his collarbone.

Adam turned on his back and stared at the ceiling. "I care about you so much. Too much. With sex it gets complicated."

"It doesn't have to."

"But it does. People get entangled emotionally."

Tina frowned. "Love shouldn't be complicated." He hadn't used the word "love," she reflected.

"It always is."

She arched an eyebrow. "You talk like a man with lots of experience."

"I'm thirty years old. I haven't exactly been a monk. And I assume you haven't been a nun."

"No, I left that to my sister." Tina rolled to her

stomach and nuzzled her head on Adam's chest. "Adam, have you ever been in love with anyone, I mean serious stuff?"

Adam toyed with her hand, gently separating the fingers. "I've had my share of girls. There was one, a few years back." He looked contemplative, a bittersweet smile on his lips.

Tina felt a stab of jealousy. "What happened?"

"She wanted to get married."

"And you?"

"Marriage isn't for me. She had a job offer in LA and wanted me to move there with her. I didn't want to go. She would have declined the job if I'd given her hope of a future together. But I don't want to be responsible for directing someone's life, her career. Maybe it was her way of pulling out of the relationship, I don't know." He dropped her hand and gently moved her head from his chest. Crossing his arms, he said, "Besides, I need to feel free to do the things I need to do."

"You could have a committed relationship and still be free."

He raised his eyebrows. "I'm not so sure about that."

Tina squeezed her eyes shut. Was he warning her? She wanted this man, needed him. "Adam, this is 1970. We have expanded horizons. Anything is possible. Everything is possible."

He leaned over and nuzzled her neck. "Sweets, you have got a lot to learn."

She wanted to object, to argue, but his lips moved to her mouth, obliterating her next words. His hands roved, exploring, fondling.

"You're insatiable," she said with a feline smile.

"I'm afraid I'm going to have to spend the night," he murmured.

As it turned out, he did.

* * *

Louise returned the car she'd borrowed from Mrs. Darnell, making a mental note to postpone buying new shoes (worn though her old ones were) until next month in order to save something for a small present for her accommodating friend. Mrs. Darnell's kindness allowed Louise to get into the "outside world" now and then, which hadn't been the case a few short years ago. She was grateful to Pope John and Vatican Council II, which had dragged the religious orders (some of them recalcitrantly) into the twentieth century, although, God knew, there was more work to be done, more advances to be made. The antiquated system of poverty and obedience left little to the concept of free will.

Vatican II had opened wide the doors, letting out the musty air, welcoming in the fresh ideas suited to a modern world. And yet there was still the suppression of free thinking, still the reliance on the old ways, on blind faith. In many ways there was confusion, especially in the older members of the community, who deemed guitar playing at Mass close to an evil, who disdained the banishment of Latin, and, prim-lipped, repeated the liturgy in their own stubborn way, in the Latin of their novice days. Change was never easy.

Louise had met the Darnells at a Chryssalio meeting. The Chryssalios—meetings with parishioners to strengthen their faith and share their problems—was another concept born of Vatican II. Louise had been greatly impressed with the strong faith she'd encountered in the parishioners, and found it increasingly difficult to counsel women who wanted to follow the dicta of the church but didn't feel strong enough to continue having five, six, seven, and more children. How could she say, "God will provide," when, in some cases, he clearly wasn't providing, when the males, confounded by too much debt, too much noise, too little money, left their women? Or when women, frazzled by the same problems, fell apart? She realized some of the women had a holiness far surpassing her own, for the crosses they bore were exceedingly heavier.

At the convent door Louise's key rattled in the lock and she let herself in as quietly as possible. Fortunately Sister Perpetua was not about. Louise was in no mood for Sister's subtle remonstrations, her acerbic tongue camouflaged in a tone of concern. If only Sister Theresa were still awake, perhaps she could talk to her. Theresa always seemed a sympathetic soul, although they had never spoken at length. Indeed, there was neither time for nor encouragement of "rapping," as the children called it. They couldn't talk during supper except on Sundays and holidays. The sisters' days were filled and scheduled and there was scant time for friendship. Mother Superior often warned against "particular friendships." Thank God for her times with Ann and Tina, but even those meetings must be humbly solicited. She had stretched the truth recently when she told Mother she was meeting her sisters for an "urgent" family meeting. As it turned out, the meeting *had* been rather urgent. Ann seemed at a crisis point in her life and Tina had decided to follow a dream. Louise was thankful to see her family occasionally. A few short years ago she couldn't have even considered that.

In the bathroom there was a note on the empty toilet-paper holder. "Sister Louise, you forgot to replace the paper," the note read. There was no doubt who the writer was. Perpetua. Louise snatched a fresh roll from the cabinet below the sink and pushed it into place. Although that task was Louise's charge, it was a particular annoyance to her that no one else would perform the mean little chore whenever it became necessary.

She splashed her face and brushed her teeth, determined to banish the aggravating thoughts. Her mind was filled with more urgent problems. She tiptoed quietly to the chapel, dipped her fingers in the holy-water font, and made the sign of the cross.

Kneeling at the altar, she folded her hands beneath her chin. For the first time in her life she could not pray. She was somehow filled with an ineffable sadness for Ann and Tina. Although Ann wouldn't speak openly, there were obviously major problems in her marriage and she seemed unwilling to forgive Martin. Tina admitted that she hardly went to church anymore and now was going off to be with a man. Tina had never admitted to having sexual relations with men she had loved, but by her attitude, Louise suspected that was the case. She had admonished Tina, at the same time that she had tried to understand her physical needs.

Yet when Tina had divulged her plan to go to Washington, Louise had actually *encouraged* her, almost as if she could live her own hidden desire for independence through her younger sister. Oh, God, was it a sin to want a bit of freedom? Had she sinned in encouraging Tina?

Louise was beset with doubts. She was sure the "free-love" orientation of the sixties had sinfully invaded Tina's soul. An image of Tina and Adam, whom she had described at length, sprang to life in Louise's mind, a powerful image that she tried heroically to dismiss. She dropped her face into her hands. *Jesus, take this temptation from me*, she pleaded silently. But the picture remained, warming her insides, flushing her skin. Finally, unable to quiet the images that filled her with forbidden emotions, she rushed from the chapel, her rosary beads clutched in her fingers, reciting Hail Marys by rote, one after the other, in quiet anguish.

The next day, after chapel, Louise knocked tentatively on Mother Superior's door.

"May I speak with you, Mother?"

"Come in, Sister." The older woman held a book

in long tapered fingers. She could have been a concert pianist, Louise thought, recalling that Mother played the piano expertly for their festive occasions. Her face was plain, thin-lipped with a long nose and pale eyes, but hardly wrinkled, though Louise was sure she had passed her sixtieth year.

Louise took the leather chair opposite the desk and folded her hands neatly on her lap.

Mother Serena said, "You look troubled, Sister."

How to begin? "I am troubled, Mother. I . . . I often feel irritable. I don't always have compassion for my sisters, and feel angered by small incidents of thoughtlessness. Then, even when I pray, I can't shake the feeling."

Mother tipped her head and shook it in compassion. "Daughter, you must learn to overlook thoughtless behavior in others. We are all, though in God's special graces, still human in our feelings. But Jesus preached forgiveness. And he forgives us all. Can you do less? Can you learn to forgive?"

Louise nodded silently, staring down at her tightly gripped fingers. "Mother, I feel great unrest. Sometimes . . . sometimes I think of men and women together—for instance, my younger sister and her male friend, I think of them . . . loving one another, and . . ."

Mother Serena rose regally and came to Louise's side. Laying her hand on Louise's head, she said sadly, "The devil is tempting you, my child. You must do penance. You must give yourself over to prayer and good works. I promise you, your troubles will ease with the passage of time."

Time. How much time? Mother Serena was not young. Perhaps she had never had these thoughts, or if she had, perhaps she had forgotten them. "Yes, Mother," Louise murmured.

"For penance, you must kiss the chapel floor on entering each day for the next two weeks."

"Yes, Mother." The small worm of annoyance returned. Would God forgive her more readily if she demeaned herself in that way? Mother Serena's words did nothing to alleviate her uneasiness. Perhaps she would talk to Father Vernan.

The following Saturday, at the weekly confession, Louise felt, as she always did, calmed by the ambience of the church. A vague incense smell permeated the dim interior, and the familiar icons seemed like old friends. Late-afternoon sun filtered in through cathedral-shaped stained-glass windows, warming Louise's back. Her palms were damp as she opened the polished oak door of the confessional. Inside, the door separating her from Father Vernan slid open and she bowed her head toward the screen. In a faltering voice Louise confessed her failings. She could sense the priest's unease. In the dim light she saw him stretch his neck and run his finger beneath his collar.

"The world, the flesh, and the devil are always with us," he intoned. "You're a young woman, with a young woman's . . . ah . . . feelings. You must pray and ask for guidance."

"Yes, Father. I *have* asked for guidance. I've done penance. But I still feel so confused."

"It's a temptation that will pass. You were called to this vocation. That means that God considers you special, holy."

"Father, I see people in my Chrysallio meetings who I think are far holier than I. Mrs. McGuire has ten children and she's raising them with kindness and compassion and with very little money. Isn't she as holy? Isn't her role in life far more demanding than mine?"

"Child, she has her role, you have yours. Yes, she's holy, but never denigrate your job. By teaching, by spreading God's word, you are doing God's work. For that you will be rewarded, never doubt it."

Tears prickled behind Louise's eyelids. He didn't

understand. No one understood. If only she could talk to Sister Theresa. There was something in her eyes, some sympathetic recognition, that told Louise that here was a kindred spirit. It showed in the way she slowly closed her eyes when Sister Perpetua said something obliquely critical, in the pained look about Sister Theresa's eyes when Mother Superior demanded a penance such as eating her meal kneeling on the floor, with her plate on the chair, for some trivial omission or error. Was God so demanding, so vindictive?

Yet Louise loved her work, she loved her God. She would leave her questions and her problems with him. He wouldn't fail her.

9

Ann forced papers into her briefcase and snapped it shut. She and her manager had been selecting designs for the 1971 summer bridal catalog. Outside her small office in the Detroit store the cold air was a welcome refresher; the crunch of crusty snow, hardened by many feet, brought a comforting remembrance of childhood play. In the gathering dusk the silently falling flakes glittered like tiny stars. She whisked away snow that had accumulated on the windshield of her Lincoln. Eschewing the I-94 freeway, Ann drove down East Warren and the old neighborhoods of Detroit. There used to be something stirring and nostalgic about going past the tattered street where she'd spent the first several years of her life, where her character had been molded, where she'd forged strong friendships. Now the homes were run-down, with boarded-up windows and peeling paint. Empty lots stood deserted and cluttered with debris where houses had been razed during the riots that plagued the city in 1967. In the street, the playing children were mostly black. They wore joyful expressions as they frolicked, forming "angels" and rolling huge balls of snow for snowmen.

She should hurry home. She'd agreed to go with Martin to a retirement party, at first reluctantly because she had last-minute shopping and all the Christmas presents to wrap. On reflection, she decided that the retirement party might afford her an opportunity to see *her*, Martin's paramour. Though he steadfastly refused to tell Ann the woman's name, she felt sure she was someone he worked with.

They lived now in an uneasy peace, considerate of one another *(Can I get you more coffee, dear?)*, forcing bright chatter in front of the children.

Martin had said, "It's over," meaning his affair, but she had read the anguish on his face, knew it had been a wrench. And the questions continued to plague her. Who was the woman? How could Martin do this to her and the children? What had gone awry? What had she done wrong? She searched her memory for obscure incidents that might display her inadequacies, her disinterest, her lack of passion. Then, contrarily, she singled out all of Martin's sins, parading his transgressions in her mind, remembering his remoteness, his negligence with the boys.

Still, as each day went by, she was better able to cope and more capable of putting her resentments and fears behind her. Christmas, she decided, would be the terminus. By Christmas she would put all this torment to rest. The holidays would be as nice as she could make them. She would buy a special gift for Martin. New golf clubs, perhaps.

Her mother would have Christmas dinner, as usual. Tina promised to be home. And of course, Louise. They would be reunited.

She needed to talk to Louise, wanted her support and encouragement. Louise could always be counted upon for compassion and an uplifting word. But her sister was busier than ever and Ann made do with short phone calls.

Her contacts with Tina, too, had been unsatisfactory, reduced to terse notes and a few hurried calls. But at least Tina was happy. Her last letter revealed that she had finally found a "meaningful relationship." Ann suspected that meant an *intimate* relationship. She wanted the best for Tina, but was always in dread that she'd make a poor choice in a man. Still, Adam appeared to be a nice-enough person—at least in Tina's unrestrained and probably overblown descriptions—a man both altruistic and ambitious. Ann smiled ruefully to herself. Was her own choice in men so astute? Was it so clever to hold out your virginity for marriage?

She sighed, thinking: *There I go again.* Difficult as it was, she must force herself to end these destructive thoughts. Indeed, she needed to talk to her sisters.

Louise awakened at dawn on Christmas morning and, wrapped in comforting silence, crept from her room to the chapel. She loved the feeling of aloneness in the wee hours of the morning and often went to chapel at that time to seek peace and solace. Blessing herself, she knelt before the statue of the Blessed Virgin. Tears tumbled forth, and it was several moments before she could utter a prayer. Her prayers, like her thoughts, were fragmented and tortured.

"I'm lost . . . I'm confused. . . . Show me the way. . . . I have faith you will guide me. . . . Send me the wisdom of the Holy Spirit." She repeated those phrases for several minutes, then covered her face with her hands and waited in the eerie quiet.

If she expected a miraculous answer from the lips of the Virgin, she was disappointed. Yet gradually her tears dissipated and she was filled with a tranquillity such as she hadn't known for a long time. "Thy will be done," she whispered.

When at last she arose, the sun was shining through the single stained-glass window. She stood in its warmth, basking in the rosy glow, feeling lightened and somehow blessed.

As she returned down the dimly lit hall, she encountered Sister Perpetua.

"Are you all right, Sister?" asked Perpetua, peering at her with a frown.

Louise hugged the surprised Sister. "I'm wonderful. Merry Christmas, Sister."

Ann asked Brian to give the blessing at breakfast on Christmas morning. He mumbled, but the words were discernible. "May God bring peace on earth, and also to this family." Ann worried about Brian, and had mentioned it earlier to Martin, but he dismissed the boy's behavior as adolescent moodiness. The slighter twin was more sensitive than his brother Matt, seemed more tuned in to family politics. Ann was sure he perceived the problems between his parents, had noticed her own unhappiness, her frequent tears. His large eyes would grow sad in his thin longish face when he observed her cheerfulness, though she and Martin were oh-so-heedful of letting no hint of their unhappiness escape. But of course, one so sensitive as Brian would notice something askew. Possibly Theodore and Matthew noticed as well, but perhaps were better able to dismiss it.

After they opened their presents, Ann gave Brian a quick hug and lifted the thick sandy hair from his temple to plant a kiss there. He moved away, embarrassed, then gave her a forgiving lopsided smile. She understood his adolescent vacillation between accepting and rejecting her shows of affection.

Martin raved over the golf clubs and Ann was surprised when she unwrapped the small package to find that her conservative husband had given her an obviously expensive necklace of emeralds and diamonds. *Guilty gift,* she thought fleetingly, then as quickly banished the ugly thought.

Later, at the Marcassa home, the mingled holiday smells assaulted Ann—turkey trimmings and *sugo* along with pine. After the effusive greetings, she placed gifts under the ceiling-high tree. In the kitchen her mother and Flora chattered while they put the finishing touches on the Christmas dinner.

"No, things are not so good at that house," Flora was saying. "I'm not one to bring bad tidings, but . . ." When Ann walked in, she stopped abruptly and busied herself slicing celery into neat sticks.

Had they been talking about her? She didn't want her mother upset. "Not so good where?" Ann pinioned Flora with a piercing look as she poured coffee into a cup decorated with holly wreaths.

"Oh, a paisano you wouldn't remember." Chiara wrapped an apron around Ann's waist. "Here, put this on or you'll get that beautiful dress dirty." She tied it with a flourish in the back. "You can put ice in the glasses," she added.

Ann decided not to pursue the subject. Christmas was not the time for squabbling. "Where's Dad?"

"He's at the airport, picking up Tina. I thought she'd come home earlier, but she wanted to spend Christmas Eve with her friend." Chiara rolled her eyes upward disparagingly on the last word.

"Adam seems like a nice person, Ma."

"What kind of a future does he have?" Chiara sat at the table cutting X's into the shells of shiny dark chestnuts. "Tina says he doesn't make much money."

"Since when has money been so important to you?"

Chiara shrugged. "Since I was a poor girl in Italy. That's the trouble with your generation. You never knew want."

Ann took the ice bucket to the dining room. She'd heard that particular lecture before. Perhaps it was true. Perhaps that was what had fomented a generation of hippies. But there were dissenters in every age, called by different names—bohemians, flappers, beatniks. She laughed to herself. Even her own mother had been somewhat of a dilettante when she opened her first bridal salon. The ice made chink-chink crackles as she dropped it in the glasses.

Back in the kitchen she filled the ice-cube trays with water. "I'm dying to see Tina. I got her the nicest outfit, the latest style, a polyester pantsuit. Louise was harder to shop for. The choices are limited." The convent allowed only plain clothing, conservative and colorless. And personal items like perfume were out. "I finally settled on a warm robe, properly ladylike."

She heard the front door closing and Louise burst into the room with a flurry of cold kisses.

"Look at you!" Ann exclaimed. Louise was wearing the merest hint of lipstick and blusher. "Is the convent entering the twentieth century at last?"

"No, but I am," Louise said with a laugh.

"Well, I like it."

Mike opened the back door with a merry shout. "We're here, ho, ho, ho!" Apparently he'd decided on a truce for Christmas, Ann thought, hoping he wouldn't harp on Tina's "defection" to Washington during dinner. Tina hustled in, her arms laden with holiday-wrapped parcels, looking radiant. She's in love, Ann realized a bit enviously.

The boys, who adored their aunts, and especially Tina, who always had exciting tales to tell, crowded into the kitchen, where they all talked and laughed at once.

When the dinner was over at last, all sat back patting their full tummies and complaining that they'd overeaten. Louise refilled her wineglass and said, "I have an announcement to make."

Only Ann, who was sitting next to her, heard over the burble of conversations, and she stared at her sister, perplexed. "What?"

Louder, Louise said, "Everyone. Listen. I have an announcement."

Ann noticed that her lower lip quivered somewhat.

When they all turned to her, she said very quietly, "I'm leaving the convent."

The silence wrapped around them in a cold glaze while all eyes stared at Louise. Finally Louise herself broke the silence. She raised her wineglass and said brightly, "Here's to me."

Mike shook his head slowly from side to side. "What's happening to my family?"

Flora made the sign of the cross and the boys tittered nervously.

"Why? Luisa, what happened?" Chiara pleaded, using her Italian name.

Louise closed her eyes. "I just don't want to be a nun any longer. I think I can have a more satisfying life out of the convent."

Ann and Tina looked at each other. Louise had been the family's mainstay, the crusader, the bearer of the standard. Especially, she had been the pacifier, the conciliator, the one with solid advice, with kind and soothing words. She had been their own link to God, their nun.

Something must have happened.

"I thought you were so happy," Ann said. "You seemed so happy."

"I am. I mean, I was." Louise looked down at her hands, folded in her lap in typical nun fashion. She unfolded them and placed them on the table. "I'd like to try to explain it. But I don't know if I can. I don't understand it all myself."

Chiara murmured, "I don't know, I just don't know. I think it's a mistake."

Louise expelled a burst of air and a tear escaped down her cheek.

Tina rushed out of her seat to her sister's side and hugged her tightly, then poured herself more wine and lifted her glass high. "Here's to you, Lou. Here's to freedom."

They all drank amid self-conscious murmurs.

Mike, to break the tension, said, "Isn't it time to open gifts? I can't wait to see what sort of ridiculous tie I get this year."

Forced laughter rang out, and they moved from the table to the living room, where the tree lights cast a cheery aura over them.

Later, in her old room, Ann said, "I can always exchange the robe for a miniskirt or lacy underwear." She flopped down on the bed. "What's happened to us? We're all going through changes."

Tina said, "My life's falling nicely into place."

"I think mine's just beginning," Louise said, "even though I'm still feeling a bit confused."

"When are you leaving, Lou?" Ann asked.

"Next week. I want to start the new year fresh."

"What about work?"

"I'll stay until they get a replacement. I've already sent résumés to several school districts. I'm sure I'll get in somewhere. We still have plenty of baby boomers to educate."

"Have you said anything yet to Mother Superior?"

"Nothing definite. She knows I'm not happy."

"So, let's make plans," Tina said. "Will you get an apartment? How about furniture and stuff? And clothes? God knows you can't enter the real world in those drab Salvation Army rejects." She clapped her hands. "I know! We'll go shopping together, all three of us. Won't that be fun?"

Louise laughed. "I won't let you talk me into miniskirts, Tina. I'm not one of those who'll dye my hair blond and grab the first man who makes a pass." All three giggled at that improbable image.

Ann grew sober. "What led you to this decision, Lou?"

"Lots of things. When I first entered the convent I found what I was looking for—the peace, the oneness with God. But slowly I discovered the convent was not perfect; or rather we mortals are not perfect. Little things bothered me—petty annoyances among us, small jealousies, uncharitable remarks, unhappiness. Oh, I'm guilty as well. But mostly it was the . . . the *unlovingness*. God *is* love, isn't he? We who have devoted ourselves to God, shouldn't *we* love unconditionally, shouldn't *we* forgive? Isn't that what Christ taught us?''

"But couldn't you get past that stuff, ignore it?'' Tina asked.

"Perhaps in this day and age the world is too much with us. We've been let out of our cages, so to speak, since Vatican II, and maybe we see things with a clearer eye. I feel that I can evolve as a spiritual being better on the outside. I have things to accomplish on the outside.''

"Like what?'' Tina asked softly.

"I'm not exactly sure just yet. But the spiritual aspect isn't all of it. There's more. There's the growing hurt''—Louise touched her fist to her heart in a *mea culpa* gesture—"right here. Right now. The need to fulfill myself as a woman. The need to have physical love, a family, a child.'' Louise stopped suddenly and lowered her eyes. "Surely you can understand that?''

Ann touched her arm. "Of course.''

"I was too young, too impressionable to make the decision to enter the convent when I did. I was totally unaware of what my options were.''

All three fell silent. Then Ann broke the silence. "What does anyone know at fifteen years old? You don't know that living means changing, accepting new ideas, discarding old ones, broadening your horizons.'' Ann rested her head against the headboard. "Life is very confusing, isn't it?''

Tina said, "Amen.''

Ann was introspective for several moments, then said, "What about you, Tina? How's your job?''

"The job's fine. I'm beginning to understand the kids and I like seeing them grow and learn. Some of them, at least."

"What's going on with you and Adam?"

Tina picked at the red polish on her thumbnail. "I think you could say I'm in love with Adam."

"Does he love you?" Louise asked.

"Yes, though he hasn't said so. Now, don't lecture me, you two. I know what I'm doing."

"Oh, Tina, I'm not in the mood to lecture anyone," Ann said. "Peace and goodwill."

Tina said, "So what's up with Martin?"

"Everything's fine," Ann said, too brightly.

Tina observed her through lowered lashes. "Sure it is."

"It is. Martin's back into the bosom of the family and I'm slowly but surely giving up blame and recrimination."

"Sure."

"Well, I'm trying. It takes time. Or so says my therapist."

"Well, we've entered the seventies for sure," Tina laughed. "A shrink, no less." She leaned forward. "I've been thinking of going to one myself."

"Let's all go," Louise said. "Maybe we'll get a family rate. And I used to think the three of us were so well-adjusted."

"No one's well-adjusted," Ann said. "Least of all us."

Mother Superior steepled her fingers and leveled a steely gaze at Louise. "You're making a big mistake, Sister Louise. I'm afraid you're falling from grace."

"I don't think so." Louise's eyes strayed to the crucifix on the wall above Mother's head, then down to the polished wood floor. It had been difficult to tell her superior of her decision, and she'd hoped for a smidgen of understanding, a blessing perhaps. There'd been none of that. She'd endured Mother's homily, barely listening, but certain words caught her, disparaging words like "severely disappointed," "wavering faith," "worldliness," "passing cloud of unhappiness."

"I think you'll regret this decision, Sister."

"I've thought long and hard." Louise met Mother's gaze steadfastly. "I've prayed. I feel God's grace. For the first time in a long while I feel at peace."

Mother shook her head slowly, sadly. "Then there's nothing more to say. You'll leave all your belongings behind. Go as you came to us, with nothing." She rose, terminating the meeting, her mouth drawn in a disapproving knot.

Louise struggled to keep the threatening tears from falling. "I would like your blessing, at least."

Mother silently bowed her head.

Louise swallowed. "All right, then. Good-bye." As an afterthought she added, "And God bless you."

Sister Theresa, waiting outside the office, whispered, "Well, how did it go?"

"Not well. She made me feel like I was guilty of a terrible sin."

Theresa grabbed Louise's hand. "I'll miss you, Sister. I always thought, given half a chance, we could have had a warm friendship."

"Friendships aren't allowed," Louise said with an ironic smile. She put her arms around Theresa in an impulsive hug. "I'll miss you too."

"Please stay in touch." Theresa tucked a small package into Louise's hand.

An hour later, a small satchel filled with a few personal items clutched in her hand, Louise closed the door of the convent behind her. She was curiously dry-eyed as she marched to Ann's car, in wait at the curb.

Inside the Lincoln, Ann smiled and reached over to squeeze Louise's hand.

She reached into the satchel for Theresa's gift. Inside the white tissue was a packet of notepaper. Tiny whimsical clowns were hand-painted in pastel watercolors across the heading, with Theresa's initials almost undetected in a corner. Louise had never known Sister Theresa was so talented.

For some reason that she couldn't explain, that was the catalyst that brought tears, fast and furious.

The next day the twins helped load a borrowed pickup truck with discards from their grandmother's basement. Louise directed them, wearing her newly purchased stiff, not-quite-form-fitting blue jeans. "Do I look like an ordinary person?" she asked the boys.

"Sure, Aunt Lou, like one of the guys." Matthew laughed and slapped the thigh of his own tattered jeans.

Chiara was strangely silent as she helped Louise fill a box with cans of soup and vegetables and boxes of dried foods from her cupboard.

"It's going to be fine, Mother, I promise," Louise said when their fingers touched.

"I know, *cara,* but it seems so strange."

"This is good," Mike said firmly. "Now we'll get to see you often. It's good."

Back at Ann's house, there were more boxes and odds and ends of furniture.

"I want to replace this old chair in Martin's study anyway," Ann said as she directed the boys' movements. "Do you want this end table? It's a relic from someone's attic."

"Of course." Louise passed her hand over the surface. "It just needs a little polish."

Ann handed Louise a carton. "These towels may

not match your bathroom, but they're getting a bit frayed and I need new ones.''

Louise peeked inside. "Oh, Ann, they're perfectly good.''

"Just take them," Ann said impatiently.

"I've got lots of kitchen furnishings from the 'shower' Mrs. Darnell gave me. I wish you could have been there, Ann.'' Louise shoved the box into the truck. "There were ten women there and we laughed and played games. The parishioners were so kind. They gave me the support the sisters couldn't—or wouldn't.''

"Those are the friendships you'll keep. Well, I guess we're loaded,'' Ann said, slipping behind the wheel. "Oh, did you get to the bank?''

"Yes, I've opened a checking account,'' Louise said with delight. "I've always wanted a checking account. It marks my passage into the real world.'' Her father had "lent" her a thousand dollars. "Next stop is Art Van's for my one major splurge, a sofa.''

At the furniture store Louise made her purchase and stood at the desk, pen in hand, checkbook before her. She had never written a check before. Date. That one was easy. She chewed the end of the pen. The little box must be for the amount. She bit the corner of her lower lip. What about the next line? Did the payee's name go there? She supposed so. Where was Ann when she needed her? The clerk across the counter waited patiently, a puzzled expression on her face. She had string-straight hair to her waist and wore a miniskirt and shell beads. In her stiff jeans and plaid shirt, Louise felt very circumspect indeed. Leaning over, the clerk peered at the check and stabbed at it with a pink-daggered finger, saying, "No. The amount goes there. Art Van's goes here.'' She looked annoyed.

"Oh, of course.'' Louise, blushing, ripped the check out and began again.

She had so much to learn.

* * *

Louise finished arranging family photographs on the wall in her dining area. The past week had been pure joy for her. In the convent she'd longed to simply rearrange a chair or table in the tidy, conservative living room. Or to buy a colorful throw pillow or two. Or to hang an inexpensive print—a vivid Renoir or Gauguin, perhaps. But none of that was allowed and she had restrained herself regretfully. Now she tossed several bright red and orange pillows onto the sofa with gleeful abandon.

She'd asked her parents to visit and was as nervous as a teenager let loose. Indeed, she felt as though she were going through adolescence. When she let her parents in, her usually volatile father seemed tentative, shy around her. Chiara hugged her for several moments; then Mike took her hand.

"It feels like I have my daughter back," he said.

In response she squeezed his hand. "Want a tour of the apartment? That should take about thirty seconds."

After the walk-through, during which her mother straightened her bedspread and moved a vase, her father said, "Now, what about a job? If you want to leave teaching, I still have a few friends in high places."

"Thanks, but I love teaching. I sent my résumé to several districts and I have an interview next week at one of them. I thought I'd be able to stay longer at St. Margaret's, but Mother Superior thought it best that I leave immediately. I'm the black sheep."

Chiara looked concerned. "Are you sure you did the right thing, Luisa?"

"Absolutely. Do *you* think I did the right thing?"

"I don't know." Chiara frowned. "It seemed like you had a real calling. I'll always remember you kneeling at the grotto in Italy. The statue of the Madonna wasn't even very pretty—it was faded and chipped, remember? But you looked like you saw a vision." Her hands, palms out, split the air. "A vision."

"Chiara!" Mike said. "Of course she's doing the right thing."

"Mother, try to understand. I was so young. The polio that kept me bedridden for so long also made me look inward, and I found a sense of peace in praying and thoughts of God. Other things pushed me in that direction—the daily Masses, the rosaries said after dinner each day."

"We don't do that anymore." Chiara looked reproachfully at Mike.

"Living means changing," Louise said softly. "What fulfilled me ten years ago no longer fulfills me."

"I still can't understand it," Chiara said.

"There were so many things." Louise rubbed her brow. "The convent was too restricting. You don't know how badly I felt that I couldn't even afford to buy you much of a Christmas present, or when you'd come to visit and I couldn't even offer you a glass of pop or a few cookies. That may seem trivial, but it bothered me."

Chiara clucked, then sighed. "It was such a mark of honor, having my daughter in the convent."

"I hope you love me for what I am, not for what I do. I'm the same person inside."

The three were silent for a few moments, deep into their own thoughts.

"It won't be easy for you," Mike said. "Everything's different from when you went in fifteen years ago."

"I've found that out already. I didn't even know how to write a check!" She told them of her dilemma in the furniture store, and the ensuing laughter broke the tension.

Louise said, "Let's have coffee. At least I learned how to make that."

Mike rose and headed for the tiny kitchen. "Now, *that's* an important first step!"

10

Tina spent the early part of the evening at the George McGovern campaign headquarters, helping with organizational work. She'd volunteered her services in early 1971, soon after McGovern had announced his candidacy for president in the next year's election.

Her father was pleased to hear she was working for the Democrats, but lamented the fact that McGovern hadn't inaugurated his campaign with a Labor Day speech in Detroit's Cadillac Square, the way his predecessors had done since 1948.

She was glad to get away from the noisy office and into the cold brisk air. Her spare time was split among various causes and now she looked forward to dinner with Adam.

She flicked damp snow from her hair and headed down the stairs to Paul Young's Restaurant, where government personnel converged and plaques commemorating certain senators were placed above "their" tables. She wondered how many of the distinguished men engaged in muted earnest conversations actually *were* senators.

It had been a week since she'd seen Adam, though they'd had phone conversations almost every day. "I miss you, sweets," he always said. Did he miss her or the physical satisfaction that came of their lovemaking? To be truthful, no matter how enjoyable their other time together, she, too, couldn't wait for the evenings' end and their passionate coupling. It was sometimes sweet, sometimes urgent, always gratifying, and for her, filled with peace and love. But for Adam? She couldn't quite fathom his real feelings. He seemed sometimes to hold back. But for now she was perfectly willing to overlook her apprehensions and just bask in the wonder of their love.

When Adam had bemoaned their lack of time together, she'd said in earnest playfulness, "We could always live together."

"At the Beehive? That wouldn't go over too well. It would really throw the board."

There was an alternative which Tina wouldn't bring herself to mention. They could get married. Even as she thought it, she rejected the idea. She was doubtful marriage was what she wanted at this time, and even more doubtful about Adam's position.

When Tina spotted Adam seated at a leather booth behind a tall pillar, a proprietary feeling of pleasure swept through her. He looked up and smiled. A catch at her heart stopped her momentarily. He was so handsome in a tweed sport coat over jeans and an open-necked shirt. As soon as she was seated, old Mrs. Young, the owner's mother, greeted them with a fresh loaf of bread.

Adam leaned over to kiss Tina. "You look great."

"You look tired."

"My normal condition lately. What's happening at campaign headquarters?"

"We're just getting organized." Tina sliced warm bread and handed Adam a piece. "There's lots of work ahead of us."

"I wish I could be a part of it, but there's no time. How's the job going?"

"I have a few battle scars, but I'm surviving," Tina said.

"Tough, eh?"

"I like the class, basically. There are some problem kids."

"Tell me."

She scanned the menu, then set it down. "Omer is the worst. Darn good-looking, chocolate complexion and hair out to here." She spread her hands to a foot from either side of her head. "And I suspect intelligent, too, despite the fact that he does absolutely nothing. Does stupid things like spitballs, then he's defiant when I confront him. Disrupts the entire class, not that it's so hard to do. Finally, the other day I wanted to sit down and cry. I said, 'Okay, Omer, you win. I lose. I've lost control.' I just sat there in a staring contest with him; then I said, almost in a whisper, 'Come up here, Omer.'

"He swaggered up in that slinky, insolent walk, you know what I mean. And I looked in his eyes and I saw a kid—a wiseacre, nasty kid, but a kid. And I remembered reading his file. Five kids in a fatherless home, mother on welfare, the usual situation. Here was a mixed-up kid trying to make it in a hostile world. And suddenly I wasn't angry anymore. I felt this sort of empathy—love, really. I guess my eyes teared up." Her eyes welled up at the memory and she swiped away a tear with a knuckle.

Adam took her hand and rubbed it gently. "What happened then?"

"I said, 'What am I doing wrong, Omer? If you were the teacher, how would you handle a kid like you? How would you handle the class? You're a born leader. Show me.'

"He tried to read me, with that cocky smirk, tried to figure what game I was playing. We stared at each other while the class got quieter. I kept my gaze forthright and . . . well, *kind*, you know? His insolent look slowly dissolved. He tried to turn his eyes away, but couldn't seem to. 'I'll just sit in the corner while you take over the class,' I said. I walked to the back of the room and sat in an empty seat. He just stood there, confused. Some of the kids tittered and guffawed, but Omer didn't laugh. He gave the class a stern look and said primly, 'Quiet, class.' They roared. I just closed my eyes and shook my head. He saw that, then had this defiant look. He hollered, 'Shut up!' Finally, in desperation, he yelled, 'I'll cream anybody who don't shut up!' and the class slowly cooled down. He looked at my desk and said, very controlled, 'Class, read page forty-nine and keep your mouths shut until the bell rings.' There were a few self-conscious giggles, but Omer's steely glare shut them up. Whenever anyone started up, he'd point a threatening finger at them.''

Adam nodded encouragingly.

"Anyway, when the bell rang, I grabbed his arm before he could dash away. I said, 'That's great, Omer. You think I should threaten the class with violence to get them to behave? Believe me, sometimes that would be very gratifying, but how long do you think I'd last here if I did that?' I told him he was bright, a leader, and he could use that talent for good or for evil, not a new thought, I know. 'I think you're smart enough to make the right choice.' He still wore that cocky expression, but it was softened and he dropped his eyes.''

The waitress hovered, waiting for their order. When they'd made up their minds, Adam said, "Tina, you keep saying you don't want to teach. But you have a real gift for it, and that major important ingredient, love.''

"I don't know if I can make a difference. Given Omer's environment and all the rest, I don't have a lot of hope. He's probably not into drugs now, but he'll be up against it soon. He's thirteen. It's so enticing for the kids. But I'll keep trying with him. And the others as well. Even though most days I know I'm beating my head against the wall.''

"You're bound to make a difference.''

"Maybe. Since that day, he's quit his antics, and the

kids have settled down. I've managed to tutor him occasionally after school. He's really bright.''

Adam reached over and touched her hand. ''You're terrific, you know.''

''I know. What about you? How was the test you were cramming for?''

''I aced it.'' Their food arrived and Adam said, ''C'mon, let's eat. I'm famished.''

After dinner they went to her place rather than to the Beehive, where the excessive activity discouraged any hope of intimacy. With silent mutual agreement they went straight to her bedroom and undressed each other in sensual slow motion. In Adam's arms all Tina's perceptions were heightened. The ceiling light, shaded in a cobweb patterned fixture, seemed a work of art, the Indian-print bedspread a colorful sunburst, the burled wood of her dresser a cabinetmaker's crowning achievement. She closed her eyes and gave herself up to the moment, letting Adam work his magic with hands, with lips, with words. Afterward she lay quietly in his arms.

''What did I ever do without you?'' he asked.

''I don't know. Tell me.''

''I don't remember. I guess I was dead.''

Tina rolled away and sat on the edge of the bed. ''Adam, I have to know something.''

He slid over to her, one hand lifting to cup her breast. ''What?''

She moved his hand away gently, to quench her immediate arousal. ''Do you love me?'' There. She'd finally uttered the words.

''Ah, Tina. You know how I feel.''

She said, ''Don't equivocate!''

He swung around and sat next to her. Taking her hand, he kissed the fingers one by one.

''Adam. You're trying to seduce me into silence. Why won't you say it?''

''I can't.''

"Yes you can. It's easy. Watch my lips . . ."

"I'll do better than that. I'll kiss your lips."

"Stop it. I'm serious."

He sighed. "All right. I can't say it. Because. Because love means a commitment."

"We *are* committed, aren't we?"

"Sort of. But I don't want to think of permanency."

"I haven't asked you for that."

"No, but you're thinking it."

"Well, what's wrong with permanency?"

"Nothing. For some folks."

"Adam . . ."

"Look, Tina, let's talk about it later, okay? I feel a sudden urge coming over me." He drew her back on the bed and nuzzled her neck.

She pushed away. "No, I want to talk."

"I have a better idea." He nibbled her ear.

Tina sat upright. "No. We're going to talk."

"I don't want to talk." Adam looked at his watch. "Marina leaves at eleven. I'd better get going." He bounded from the bed. Grabbing his shirt, he punched his arms through the sleeves.

"Adam, don't go." Tina drew herself to her knees. "Why can't we just have a discussion?"

He yanked his jeans up and zipped them with finality. "I don't like where this is leading."

"Well, dammit, go then!" Reaching down, she grabbed his shoe and threw it, just missing his head. "Just go."

"I think she's good and mad," he said, swooping up his shoes. As he whizzed out the door, he said, "Don't call me; I'll call you."

She buried her head in the pillow. The jerk! She hated him!

No, she loved him and couldn't live without him. He would call tomorrow morning and apologize (sort of) and she would go running into his arms.

* * *

It was just a scent at first that alerted Ann, a particular scent from the shirt he'd discarded last night. A woman's cologne; too flowery for Martin's after-shave, which she usually recognized. Her stomach cramped, her throat closed. She clutched her middle and sagged to the floor next to the closet, dropping her face into the armload of crumpled shirts. *Oh, God, not again.*

They were planning a Caribbean cruise for their fifteenth anniversary. They were kind and considerate to one another. And she'd thought everything was wonderful.

No, everything was not wonderful. The kindness covered up a lack. A lack of caring, of passion, of unity. Their marriage was a sham, a display for the children, their parents, the public at large. They were actors in a true-life drama, playing out the devoted couple, the happy family. What had Tina said? Your father-knows-best life. Maybe that was it—life imitating art or at least life imitating an imitation of life.

Perhaps she'd been waiting for this. Perhaps she'd known all along it couldn't last. It had been several months since he'd vowed he had ended his affair. She stood and straightened her shoulders.

Who was it this time? Or was it the same one? She'd never known the name of her rival.

When had he been seeing her? Most of his time was accounted for. Not that she'd been playing warden. Not consciously, anyway. Who was she kidding? Each ten- or fifteen-minute lapse was cause for acute anxiety.

She wanted to cry, but was devoid of tears. She was cold, almost emotionless as she gathered the shirts into a bag. Her stomach clenched in pain. It had been bothering her for the past several months. After examinations and tests the doctor said, "You're getting an ulcer, Mrs. Norbert. Are you under undue stress?"

"Who, me? Ha, ha, of course not. I have a wonderful life." Denial, denial.

* * *

Later, at the Redford store, Ann closed the door behind her and waved at Frieda, who was helping a customer. Sales were picking up lately. Hopefully it was a trend toward big weddings again. She scanned the discount rack. It looked sparse, she thought, re-arranging several gowns by size. She made small talk with Janet and a new girl, Marge, then headed to the office.

Frieda's catalogs and files were stacked neatly on a table and her desk was cleared, orderly. Ann poured some coffee and sat on the swivel chair, resting her chin wearily on her fist. She thought again of Martin. There would be another confrontation.

Frieda walked in, hands clasped nervously at her waist.

"What's the problem, Frieda?"

Frieda seemed about to say something, then thought better of it. "Nothing."

"Well, let's go over this inventory list, shall we?"

When they'd checked lists and figures for a while, Janet stuck her head in the office and said, "I'm going for lunch now."

Ann closed her file and said, "I'm ready for lunch too. I'll pick up something from the Tulli's. Want a sandwich?"

"Sure, get me a Reuben."

Outside a cloud was slowly drifting past the sun, releasing a pleasant warmth in the drab March day. Ann decided to walk the three blocks. The exercise might clear her head. Ahead of her she saw Janet, her unmistakable long-legged stride taking her swiftly down the street. She was probably also headed toward Tulli's Deli. Ann was about to call out to her when she turned the corner. As Ann reached the spot, she saw Janet sliding into the passenger seat of a silver Corvette. Just like Martin's. A stab of fear rent through her. Janet leaned toward the driver, who turned his head to kiss her. It was Martin. Ann stifled a gasp. Her husband and Janet!

The car moved forward, away from her, and for several minutes Ann stayed rooted to the spot, not believing her eyes, unaware of life moving around her, of traffic noises, a bicycle whizzing past. Slowly she turned and headed back to the bridal shop on rubbery legs.

"That was quick," Frieda said.

"I didn't get the sandwiches." Ann turned toward the office.

Frieda called to Marge to take over and followed Ann, who had slumped into a chair.

"What's wrong? You're absolutely ashen."

Ann dropped her head into her hands and cried. "It's Martin. And Janet. I saw her getting into his car."

Frieda clenched her hands. "Ann, I knew. God help me, I knew. I wanted to tell you, but I just couldn't."

Ann turned even whiter. "How did you find out?"

"I happened to catch the end of a phone conversation a few weeks ago. She said his name."

"What, exactly, did she say?"

Frieda took a deep breath. "Oh, God, I hate doing this. I absolutely hate it. She said, 'Good-bye, Martin. I love you.' " Frieda's face puckered. "Oh, God, you don't know how I hate this. That's not all. I saw his car at lunchtime. He was parked over on the next block, but I'd walked down to Tulli's for a takeout sandwich and . . . well, it was Martin, all right, and I was going to yell out a hello, but something stopped me. He was reading a magazine and didn't see me. Then, when Janet left, I watched her. She went right to his car and they . . . they kissed and drove off."

"And you didn't tell me?"

"How could I? I've been getting up the nerve to talk to Janet."

"Now what, Frieda? What do I do now?" She rubbed her temples. "Dear Lord, what do I do now?"

* * *

Ann drove slowly, randomly. She could pretend none of this was happening. She and Martin could go on existing in an almost loveless marriage and play at being a stable, happy family. Some women did just that for the sake of family unity, of financial security. That would mean going through life as the pitiable "wronged" wife. No, she had too much pride for that.

Confused, bewildered, her mind blurred with images of Martin and Janet, she drove automatically, thinking she should cry, but feeling too numb for tears. Nothing made sense anymore. She couldn't think. St. Paul's Church on Lake Shore Drive seemed to beckon her, twin spires rising to the sky, white block structure brilliant in the early-afternoon sun. She'd been missing Mass lately. Blessedly, the door was open. Inside, the silence enveloped her and the vague smell of incense comforted her with its familiarity. Sitting quietly in a back pew, she tried to pray. *Mother of God, help me.* No flash, no enlightenment, no inspiration came. But she left with a sense of determination. This time there would be no tears, no begging, no pleading. She'd lived the last year in a fragile shell, knowing in a sub-liminal way that there were problems to confront, but afraid to delve too deeply; content to believe that "all's well that ends well." But this marriage was ending. And not well.

Still, it deserved one last-ditch effort.

Janet's house was one of those small shingled bun-galows in Royal Oak, built by the thousands after World War II, two bedrooms and a converted attic. When she opened the door, Janet drew in her breath at the sight of Ann. In bare feet, wearing jeans and an oversize shirt, Janet looked childlike. Her blond hair hung loose around her narrow shoulders. Two pale-haired little girls who looked startlingly like Janet stood shyly behind her, and another, visible through a kitchen archway, banged a spoon on the tray of her high chair.

"What are you doing here?" Janet asked.

Ann said, "I think you know. Can we talk alone?"

Janet sighed and shrugged, then turned to the two replicas. "Go on upstairs and play in your room for a while." She snatched a package of M&M's from a chipped teapot on a shelf separating the kitchen from the living room. "Here. Don't fight."

When they'd left, Ann said, "I want you to give Martin up."

The baby chortled in the background and beat a tattoo with her spoon.

"You have a colossal nerve, coming to my house—"

"*I* have nerve. You've had an affair with my husband for God knows how long, and you have the audacity—"

"All *right*. Let's try to be rational about this. Sit down, Ann." Janet indicated a kitchen chair. She slid the tray from the high chair and wiped the baby's mouth with a corner of her bib. "Go on upstairs with your sisters," she said, giving the child a pat on the bottom.

Ann noticed a slight tremor in Janet's hand when she lit a cigarette. She blew out the match and said, "What does Martin say?"

"We haven't talked yet."

Chin tilted, Janet exhaled a long stream of smoke. "I love him."

"He has a wife. He has three children."

"Sometimes things change in a marriage. I should know. My husband left me just before I had the baby." Janet's mouth turned bitter. "Why shouldn't I take what happiness I can from life?"

"At the expense of four other people?"

"Martin's found something with me he doesn't have with you. Don't deny us our chance at happiness."

We had that once, happiness, passion. What happened? Where did the love go? Ann closed her eyes and fought for control. "Did Martin say he wanted to marry you?"

"No. But he would. If he were free."

"Don't bet on it. Maybe soon he'll find someone to replace you."

"That won't happen."

"You're determined to hang on?"

"I told you, we're in love."

"So were we, once." Ann felt the tears stinging, heard the edge of a sob in her voice. She swallowed and regained control. "All right. That's it, then? You won't let him go?"

Janet averted her gaze. "I can't."

After the three boys were in bed Ann went to the family room. Martin, stretched out on the sofa, watched Flip Wilson on television. In her present frame of mind, it seemed inane. She wanted to scream at Martin. Instead she switched off the television and stood before him.

"I know about Janet."

He sat upright. "What?"

"You and Janet. I know."

Martin ran nervous fingers through his hair. "What are you talking about?"

"Don't evade or deny. I know. I talked to her. It was Janet all along, wasn't it?"

Martin hesitated, then took a deep breath. "Yes."

"I'm not asking you to break it off. I want you to leave. I'm filing for divorce."

"I don't want a divorce." Martin shot to his feet. "We can work this out."

"No, Martin. I'm not going through this again."

"What about the kids?"

"You should have thought about them long ago. I'll get custody. We'll work something out about visitation." She wanted him to beg, to promise fidelity, to declare his love. He did none of those. The strength she'd promised herself failed her now and tears streamed down her cheeks. She walked starchily from the room. Martin didn't follow.

A week later they assembled the boys. Martin made a feeble attempt to explain. "Your mother and I haven't been getting along. Sometimes marriages, for whatever reasons, don't work out . . ." He faltered.

Ann filled the breach. "Your father's leaving. He'll have an apartment close by and will see you often."

Teddy's mouth puckered. It was too much for an eight-year-old to absorb. Large tears formed, then dropped. He ran to Ann, sobbing, and buried his head in her lap while the twins looked bewildered.

Matthew bunched his fists at his side. "Dad, why are you doing this? Why are you ruining our family?"

Only Brian, quiet, sensitive Brian, said nothing, his face a mask of indifference.

"I'm not deserting the family. I'm still your father. Every week we'll—"

"Oh, sure, weekend father, going bowling or to the zoo. My friend James has one of those. He hates it! And he hates his father!" Matthew turned pleading eyes to his mother. "Mom, can't you make him stop this?"

"He's made his choice. I can't do anything more." Her heart was broken for her boys, but she didn't want to struggle any longer to save a marriage that seemed hardly worth the effort.

Matthew looked helplessly from one parent to the other, then ran from the room.

"Wait!" Martin shouted. "Come back here!"

"Fuck you, you son of a bitch!" Matthew said, stomping out the front door. Brian ran after him and Martin started for the door.

"Let them go." Ann grabbed his sleeve. "Do you have any idea how devastating this is for them?"

Teddy whimpered beside her and she smoothed his

hair with trembling hands. "Go on up to your room, son. I'll be up a little later."

"They hate me," Martin said helplessly as he sank to a chair. "You haven't helped. You've made me the heavy."

"You stupid man. You *are* the heavy."

"You've done your part. You have your faults, you know. You're not the perfect person you think you are."

"Oh, sure, try to exonerate yourself by blaming me. I've done my best. I may not be perfect, but I haven't committed adultery."

"Things happen, things I couldn't control. Maybe we're just not compatible anymore."

But we were compatible once. Maybe we could be again. If only . . . if only . . . Ann shook away the tears, the ever-present tears lingering just behind her eyelids. She must be strong for the children's sake. "I'll make some coffee. Do you want to go and talk to Teddy? You can bring him some oatmeal cookies." As though food would alleviate the pain.

"I don't know what I'd say."

For the next several months Ann went through the motions of living, until finally she had the decree in her hand, the decree that officially ended a marriage that had been slowly eroding for over a year. In a strange way, she felt a sense of relief. Now she must get on with her life.

11

Louise gulped the last of her morning coffee and looked out the window for a hint of sun. The early-spring weather in 1972 was as full of surprises as a witch's pot. Yesterday she'd had to dig out her winter coat again for the unseasonable snowfall, but the weatherman was predicting partial sun for today.

While the radio emitted the tiny sound of Tiny Tim's falsetto rendition of "Tiptoe Through the Tulips," Louise stuffed her briefcase with corrected papers. She had an early staff meeting and would have to speed to arrive at school on time. Smiling to herself, she gazed around the small apartment, delighting in the atmosphere she'd created during the past year, combining old and new with charm and whimsy. Like a new bride she'd shopped for throw pillows and inexpensive prints, and invited friends on whom to practice her newly acquired culinary prowess. After substituting for several months, she'd secured a position as third-grade teacher in Warren, a suburb north of Detroit. Leaving the convent had been the right decision. Making a sign of the cross, she thanked God for guiding her path.

Although Louise felt secure professionally, her entrance into the social mainstream hadn't been without its problems. After mingling with men at a singles dance, she realized she was virtually an adolescent in the secular milieu, unsure of what to do and say. She'd had two dates, both rather unsatisfactory, due, she was sure, to her unease and reserve. She took solace in her job and students, whom she adored, and in her new home.

Thank God for Ann, who, despite problems of her own, continued to be helpful and supportive. Louise whispered a prayer for her sister. Ann's divorce was final, and although she displayed a facade of strength, Louise knew she was suffering. They'd had several meetings during which Ann had, not surprisingly, broken down and cried, admitting her misery. She still vacillated between hate and understanding, between vindictiveness and forgiveness. Forgiveness, Louise told her, would take time. Louise thought her sister had been too hasty with the divorce. She should have given Martin more time to make amends. "You don't understand," Ann kept telling her.

On the ride to the suburban Warren school, Louise listened to Dick Purtan, whose put-on calls were often the topic of discussion in the staff lounge. She wanted desperately to be *normal,* to talk and act like everyone else. Yet she didn't want to lose her identity. In order to assimilate into "civilian life," Louise hadn't told anyone of her past, yet she was sure the rumor had circulated. In many ways she felt like a tourist in a strange land. So far she hadn't made any strong friendships.

At school, Louise was grateful that the staff meeting was blessedly short. She munched on a sugar doughnut, the principal's "reward" for attendance, and finished checking math papers. Mr. Blandy, the principal, stopped beside her and asked that she come to his office after the meeting.

"We've got a new student for you," Mr. Blandy said when she settled in a chair across from his desk.

"But I got the last new student," Louise protested. Her third-grade class was already overloaded with twenty-seven students.

"You also lost one last month. All three third grades

are even now. Also, I picked you purposely because this child needs special attention.'' Mr. Blandy steepled his fingers. "She has cerebral palsy. Rachel Wheatly's her name. She'll get picked up twice a week for therapy and the Social Services Department will be involved. I know you'll manage just fine.''

Louise sighed and began to rise.

Mr. Blandy stayed her with his hand. "There may not be much support from the family. Mother's divorced and . . . well, you'll meet her soon, no doubt.'' He handed Louise a CA-60 file.

Not an auspicious recommendation, Louise thought, glancing through the file. "She's been in three schools already and has missed a lot of classes.''

The bell rang, ending their conversation. "Sounds like a challenge. But I can handle it.'' She fell back on her lifelong habit of acceptance.

Heading back to her classroom, she realized she'd been lucky thus far. The class was interesting and interested and she had more flexibility than she'd had previously in the Catholic school. This would be her first real challenge since she'd left the convent.

After the other children had entered and settled down, Mr. Blandy appeared at the door with a frail child, her shoulders lifted above the weight of crutches. Behind them stood a woman who was obviously the child's mother. Louise went to the door to welcome them while the children whispered in the background. Mr. Blandy introduced Mrs. Wheatly and Rachel. The child entered the room slowly, her left leg dragging, while her mother stood at the door, eyes darting here and there about the room, taking in the colorful bulletin boards and the children's scrawls and drawings hanging from cork strips on each wall.

The resemblance between mother and child was astonishing, with identical dark violet eyes and ebony hair accentuating the white of their skin. Rachel's hair was pulled back into a ponytail with escaping wisps forming a charming frame for her elfin face.

" 'Bye, Rachel.'' Mrs. Wheatly blew a kiss and was off.

Louise introduced Rachel to the class and instructed the day's "helper" to show her where to hang her coat and hat. The children cast surreptitious glances at Rachel during the day, and at lunchtime Louise assigned two friendly girls to assist her.

After class, Louise thoroughly read Rachel's file. Not surprisingly, due to moving from school to school and absenteeism, she was behind in both reading and math. She would need remedial work. Yet she seemed a bright student, though a little shy, which was understandable given her background. Louise sat back and closed her eyes, remembering her own bout with polio as a child, recalling the loneliness, the fear, the pain. Rachel deserved the best that was in Louise to give.

During the next few weeks Louise worked with Rachel whenever time permitted, and was constantly astonished by her aptitude and unerring cheerfulness. With extra help at home, she would soon catch up to the class. Louise had written to Rachel's mother asking that she work with her, but the notes remained unanswered. The parent-teacher conference in early May would give Louise the chance to talk to Mrs. Wheatly.

Louise was disappointed when Rachel's mother didn't attend the conference, though Louise had made the effort to schedule it at the woman's convenience. When Louise called the Wheatly home the next day, a man answered. Mrs. Wheatly came to the phone, sounding curt and annoyed.

"I'm sorry you couldn't make it to the conference," Louise began. "Could we schedule another time?"

"Look, I'm a working mother, okay? The kid's all right, isn't she? She says she's doing fine."

"She's progressing, but she's still behind in both

math and reading. There are things you could do to help her at home.''

"Listen, I do enough as it is. I do therapy with her every day and take her to the hospital twice a month. Her father won't do it. He can't be bothered. Him with the fancy car and fancy wife.''

"I know it's a burden, but just twenty minutes of your time for a conference would really help Rachel.''

There was a pause and a sigh. "Okay, okay. Wednesday after school? I don't start at the bar until five.''

The school secretary, Marci, overheard the conversation. "Don't waste your time. That Mrs. Wheatly's a loser. Rachel owes lunch money, and when I call, I get a nasty response.''

"I don't give up easily, Marci. Rachel's such a lovely child. She deserves a break.''

"I know she is. But don't get attached,'' Marci warned. "She's not your responsibility.''

"I can't help it.''

"Good luck.''

Surprisingly, Mrs. Wheatly kept the appointment, though she was fifteen minutes late. She had a gamine expression, youthful except for weary violet eyes that looked wounded, guarded. Her hair was a dark halo of curls, her Cupid's-bow mouth overly glossed and pouty. The leather skirt clung to her curves.

"I'm sorry I'm late, Miss Marcassa. I was shopping, you know? I forget the time sometimes. She's okay, isn't she?'' She swooped over to Rachel, who was storing her papers in a backpack, and kissed the top of her head. "You're not mad at me, are you, baby?''

Rachel shook her head, eyes averted, then struggled to her feet and went to the back of the room for her coat.

"Wait in the activity area, Rachel,'' Louise said.

Mrs. Wheatly sat next to Louise's desk, crossing

shapely legs and tapping her foot nervously. Patiently Louise displayed sample papers and explained test scores, spoke of Rachel's strengths and weaknesses. "With fifteen minutes of help each day, she could easily catch up to the class."

"I don't have time for that stuff." Mrs. Wheatly picked nervously at her skirt. "I do the therapy on her legs every day, *every day!* Well, sometimes I miss. It's like I'm shackled to this kid. I love 'er, don't get me wrong. But somebody's always after me to do this for her, do that." She turned her face and stared at the floor.

"Mrs. Wheatly, I'm concerned about Rachel. I'd hate to see her repeat third grade, and with a little help, she won't have to."

"Well, don't be concerned. She's a tough kid; she can handle it."

"Not without our help."

"Help. The story of my life." Mrs. Wheatly hung her head and shook it slowly from side to side. "When do *I* get help? When is it my turn, huh? Don't I get a turn? When does somebody do something for me?" The last sentence was a desperate plea.

Louise hardly knew how to answer.

Mrs. Wheatly looked up suddenly. "Look, you got kids?"

"No, I . . ."

"Then you got no idea how tough it is. Especially with a kid like Rachel. I'm doing it on my own. Her father sends a few bucks when he feels generous. I don't have time for this crap." Mrs. Wheatly stabbed at the pile of papers. *"You're* the teacher. You help her."

"Our children are precious gifts from God. Rachel needs us." Louise leaned forward and touched Mrs. Wheatly's hand. "I know it's hard for you, but—"

"I don't need no lectures, Miss Marcassa." Her face turned hard.

Louise knew when she was defeated. "I can see you're overburdened. Maybe I can keep her for a half-hour after school twice a week. The problem is, she'd miss the bus ride home. You'd have to pick her up."

Mrs. Wheatly stared out the window and heaved a great sigh. "Okay. I'll pick her up."

"That's wonderful. I'm sure we'll see a great improvement in her work. Let's make it each Monday and Thursday."

The tutoring became routine, and week by week Louise was more drawn to the pixie-faced child with staggering burdens. That her spirit never seemed to falter was proof of her character.

By the end of May Louise knew she would miss the biweekly sessions when school let out. She swept an eraser across the green chalkboard, with one eye on Rachel, who waited patiently for her mother in the activity area just outside the classroom. Twice before Mrs. Wheatley had "forgotten" to call for her, and Louise ended up taking her home. When Mrs. Wheatly did show, Rachel would call out happily, "My mother's here, Miss Marcassa." She seemed to be adding silently: *You see, she does love me.* Sometimes Mrs. Wheatly would hop out of the car to help her daughter, fluttering her small ring-laden fingers around her, showering her with kisses, patting her arm while assisting her into the car. Then she would speed off, giggling with Rachel as if they were two school-age chums dreaming up some mischief. Other times she would stare at Rachel stonily and let her struggle to open the car door and maneuver her frail form into the seat. When Rachel leaned over to kiss her mother's cheek, Mrs. Wheatly stared straight ahead, not acknowledging the child's presence. An urge would overcome Louise to shake the woman's silly empty head; then she would tell herself to pray for tolerance. It wasn't her place to judge. At least most of the time, in her own way, the woman showed love for her daughter.

Louise gleaned Rachel's home situation from her chance remarks. Once she said, "Sally came home very late last night. I heard her tripping on furniture."

"Who's Sally?"

"My mother," Rachel said matter-of-factly.

What happened to the old-fashioned "Mom"? Louise wondered.

Another time she offered, "Sally has a new job. Her old boss was mean and fired her just because she was late sometimes. She can't help it if she's sick."

"What kind of sick?"

"I don't know. She cries a lot. When my Uncle Fred leaves, she cries."

Uncle Fred, indeed, Louise thought, wondering how many "uncles" Rachel had.

Louise knew things were not going well financially when Mrs. Wheatly sent in an application for free lunch.

Now Louise glanced at the large round clock on the wall. Four-fifteen and Mrs. Wheatly hadn't arrived. Louise would have to drop Rachel at home. She sighed and gathered up her papers. It wasn't much out of her way, after all.

At the large barrackslike apartment complex, Louise helped Rachel from the car and watched her totter up the walk. Failing to open the obviously locked door, she punched the bell. Noting the growing look of alarm on Rachel's face, Louise hustled from the car to assist her. When her knocks drew no response, Louise stretched to peer into the picture window, but partially drawn drapes obstructed her view.

"Sometimes she sleeps," Rachel said apologetically. "She works late. Sometimes my Uncle Fred is home."

"Maybe I can get a look inside through the slit in the drapes." Louise hopped from the porch and reluc-

tantly stepped into the loamy dirt. She felt a run zipper
up her leg as the scratchy shrubs attacked her calves.
Squinting an eye, she peered inside. When her vision
adjusted to the gloom, she saw Mrs. Wheatly's inert
form on the sofa, an empty gin bottle on its side on
the floor. On the coffee table stood several glasses and
an overflowing ashtray.

"She's in there. Asleep." Louise rapped on the
window with her car keys until Mrs. Wheatly groggily
raised her head. Cautiously she elevated herself to her
feet with a grimace, her lips moving in an epithet.
Slowly, frowning with effort, she pushed one foot before the other, making her way to the door. Louise
smiled encouragingly to Rachel as she made her way
back to the porch.

Mrs. Wheatly opened the door and, squinting
against the sun, focused on Rachel. She clutched the
neckline of her red satin robe and said thickly, "Rachel? Was the door locked?" Her eyes, heavy-lidded,
wandered to Louise. "Oh. The teacher." She wet her
lips. "I . . . I guess I fell asleep."

Rachel pushed herself on crutches past her mother,
obviously embarrassed and anxious to end the dis-
tressing episode. "Come on, Sally," she said, taking
her mother's arm. Before the door closed, Louise
caught a whiff of an unfamiliar musty odor like moldy,
burning leaves. Marijuana, she thought, remembering
the workshop on drugs she'd attended.

Rachel, poor child, hadn't much chance to make it
in life, Louise thought with a catch in her throat.

When Rachel was absent two days running, Louise
wasn't unduly alarmed; her absences were not unusual. She would return to school with a scribbled note
saying she hadn't been feeling well, but Louise was
sure the absences were due to a careless mother, too
unconcerned to make sure her child was up in time for
school. Yet Louise couldn't hate the woman, who was

probably doing the best she could. She needed help or counseling. Perhaps Louise could talk again to her and broach the subject, perhaps suggest agencies that might be helpful.

After a hurried lunch Louise headed to the office to call Rachel's home.

"Louise," Marci said, "I just saw this in the paper." She thrust the *Free Press* at Louise and pointed at an article. "WOMAN FOUND DEAD," read the headline. Oh, God, no. Sally Wheatly. Overdose of drugs. Daughter in custody of Social Services."

Louise slumped into a chair and dropped her head into her hands. She had recognized the woman's anguish. Why hadn't she offered a helping hand? Why hadn't she offered to pay for help? Why hadn't she prayed for Mrs. Wheatly? Rachel! Poor overburdened child. How would she handle this?

Marci thrust a glass of water in Louise's hand and hugged her.

"Marci, I could have helped her. I did nothing."

"Christ, Louise, you couldn't have done anything. That woman was on her way to self-destruction, and no one could help her."

"If I had only . . ."

"Face facts. Oh, I know how you felt about that kid, but—"

"What's to become of her? I'm going to call Social Services and see if I can talk to her. Oh, that poor child."

After being referred to several disinterested people at Social Services, Louise was finally put through to a businesslike but sympathetic male who explained that Rachel had been placed in the custody of her uncle, Jonathon Wheatly, and no, he couldn't give out that phone number. Louise hung up in disgust. If the uncle was anything like Rachel's father, whom she knew of from brief disparaging references by the child's mother, Rachel's prognosis was discouraging at the very least.

It had been almost two weeks since she'd read the awful news. Automatically she went through the motions of teaching, preoccupied with thoughts of Rachel. Was her uncle capable of caring for her? Were there kindly grandparents who would take her in, who would see to her myriad needs? Was Rachel tormented and miserable? Louise knew from her child-psychology classes that children tended to blame themselves for their parents' problems. Rachel was not her responsibility, she kept telling herself. Yet the vision of that dear gentle child in the throes of a most severe personal anguish, perhaps unwanted and unloved, haunted her.

School was finally, blessedly out for the summer. Louise piled Rachel's papers and belongings into a plastic bag and took them to the office. "In case someone bothers to come for them," she told Marci.

"Surprise. Someone called. Her uncle, apparently. He's coming in later, about four, to pick up her report card and whatever."

"That *is* a surprise. Maybe I've misjudged him. Maybe he *is* caring."

"With Rachel's luck, probably not."

"I hope you're wrong. She's had a rough go of it," Louise said.

Now that all the mundane year-end tasks were completed, she wanted to hurry home. She planned on grocery shopping, then a visit to Ann, who needed moral support, though Louise felt her own encouragement was minimal. She kept hoping for a reconciliation, even though the divorce was final. Their parents were even less help. Chiara and Mike did not approve of the divorce and alternately harangued and commiserated with Ann about it.

Consulting her watch, Louise decided she'd wait for Mr. Wheatly and call Ann to postpone the visit. Mentally she scolded herself for setting such great score by "schedules." Another throwback to convent conditioning she'd have to work on.

Settling in a plastic molded chair, she read the paper while Marci cleaned off bulletin boards and chattered about an upcoming trip.

When the office door opened, Louise wasn't prepared for the distinguished-looking man who strode in.

"I'm Jonathon Wheatly, Rachel's uncle," he said to Marci. "I'm here for her things."

After returning the greeting, Marci turned to Louise. "This is Rachel's teacher, Louise Marcassa."

Louise rose and extended her hand while Mr. Wheatly turned assessing eyes on her. He took her hand and smiled. "Mrs. Marcassa. I'm so pleased to meet you. Rachel speaks of you often."

Louise was momentarily flustered. She'd imagined Rachel's uncle as a blue-jeaned, long-haired hippie, and here was a stocky, powerfully built gentleman in a dark well-cut suit, hair cut stylishly with sideburns, a briefcase in his hand. Finally Louise found her voice. "If you have a few minutes, I'd like to talk to you about Rachel, Mr. Wheatly."

"Of course." His smile was warm.

"You can use the clinic office," Marci offered, giving Louise a smarmy smile and feigned whistle behind Mr. Wheatly's back.

The clinic had a faintly antiseptic smell. Louise settled in the chair behind the desk. Next to her was a poster of a huge tooth.

Mr. Wheatly smiled at the poster and sat across from Louise.

"I've been thinking about Rachel," Louise said. "I'd grown very fond of her. How is she doing?"

He ran nervous fingers through his hair. "Not well. She's a rather mature little girl and felt a responsibility toward her mother, and now she feels guilty." His laugh was rueful. "It's ironic. It should have been the other way around. But Sally was . . . well, Sally was Sally, and life happened to her before she was capable of handling it."

"Rachel's had a lot to contend with for an eight-year-old."

"When my brother and Sally got married they were barely out of their teens," Mr. Wheatley continued. "It was ill-advised from the beginning. They were both irresponsible, and Harry wasn't man enough to handle the problem of Rachel's illness. He left Sally with all the burdens. I do give her credit—she tried. And she loved Rachel. But . . . I suppose the situation was overwhelming for her."

"Where is Rachel now?"

"For the time being she's staying with my mother. Unfortunately, my mother's arthritis and her age prevent her from permanently taking on Rachel's care."

"What's to become of her?"

"I'm not sure at this point. She's been through so much in her short life, I can't think of letting her go to strangers. Yet—"

"No." Louise gripped his arm. This man seemed intelligent and insightful. "You can't send her to some sort of institution."

Mr. Wheatly shook his head sadly. "We haven't many options."

"As I said, I . . . I've become very fond of her. I know Rachel. It would break her spirit to be sent away. Please, I can see that you're a caring man, please try keeping her for a while."

"I'd like to. But I don't think—"

"Can't you hire a housekeeper, a helper for your mother?"

"That's a thought. But my mother . . . well, the mental burden alone would be too much for her. She's very fragile."

"Then you. You keep her." Louise was shocked by her own effrontery.

"Me?"

"Yes. Can't you take her?"

Jonathon looked at Louise dubiously. "I'm afraid not. I'm alone, you see, and my work takes me out of town often. Besides, my apartment isn't adequate. I'd like to take her, but she needs constant care and a sense of security. I couldn't give her that."

Louise felt an odd sense of relief that he was alone, then embarrassment at her wandering thoughts. "What about her father?"

"As I explained, my brother is . . . well, I guess you'd call him a black sheep. Totally negligent. I'm not even sure where he is right now; out of state, I think. He never could stand responsibility. He's remarried, but I don't expect this marriage will last either. I've made excuses for him in the past, but not now." His face hardened; his eyes were a cold, steely gray.

Mr. Wheatly rose abruptly. "I appreciate your concern, Mrs. Marcassa, but I'm sure we'll work things out for the best."

"Miss." It was suddenly important that he know she was unmarried.

"What?"

"It's *Miss* Marcassa." She blushed. She was acting like an adolescent again.

"Miss, then. I'll just take her things. Is there anything I should know about her schoolwork?"

Louise passed the parcel over, saying, "She's a bit behind, but should manage fine in fourth grade. Math is still a problem." She smiled with a sudden thought. "Perhaps I could tutor her this summer. I haven't made many plans as yet."

"I appreciate the offer. Let me think about it. If you'll give me your number, I'll get in touch with you."

She felt inordinately pleased that Rachel's uncle was so decent and caring. With any luck she would see this kind, attractive man again. She scribbled her number on a scrap of paper and handed it to Mr. Wheatly.

"Please give Rachel my regards, Mr. Wheatly. And perhaps I could have her number. I'd like to talk to her."

He fished a card from his wallet. "This is my business number, in case you should want to reach me for any reason." He turned the card and wrote on the back. "My mother's number."

Louise read the card. Jonathon. What a lovely name.

"Good-bye, *Miss* Marcassa." He reached for her hand and shook it, holding it as he continued, "I appreciate all your concern."

Louise swallowed hard, unable to break eye contact. She was sorry when he finally released her hand. "Good-bye, Mr. Wheatly." When he walked away, she noticed a slight limp.

"Well, quite a hunk," Marci said when Louise returned to the office. "Is he married?"

"Marci, I'm sure that's not important."

Marci looked dubious. "Sure."

12

Streams of psychedelic hues flickered from the spinning mirrored ball, washing Ann and Frieda in eerie colors. On this warm summer evening in 1972, Ann wondered what sort of insanity had prompted her to agree to attend a discotheque with her friend. She should be weeding her flower garden.

"Already I don't like it," Ann whispered.

"Relax. You'll love it."

The pounding, insistent beat of "Pinball Wizard" drummed right through Ann's flesh to her bones. "The noise. I can't stand the noise."

"What?"

"I rest my case."

"Oh, the noise. You'll get used to it."

"Like you get used to a wart?"

"Ha-ha."

Ann tugged at her leather skirt, trying to cover her thighs a bit. "Is my skirt too short?"

"With legs like yours? No way. Relax, will you?"

They found a small round table and Frieda ordered Harvey Wallbangers. "It's the 'in' drink," she said knowingly.

"I don't feel like drinking."

Frieda looked at Ann under lowered lids. Enunciating each word, she said, "We are here to have fun."

Ann pasted on a fake smile. "Fun it is."

When Frieda bopped her shoulders and snapped her

fingers in time to the music, Ann thought: I'm too old for this. A mustached man at the bar swept his eyes slowly, appraisingly over Ann, then moved his attention elsewhere.

"Just what is the price of beef?" she muttered.

A slightly drunk, blatantly leering man stopped at their table. "Mind?"

"Yes," Ann said.

"No," Frieda said, indicating the chair next to her.

Ignoring Ann's answer, the small dark man smiled an oily smile and sat. He wore a polyester leisure suit. His silk flowered shirt was open to display several thick gold chains. He extended a hand. "Hamilton Tripp. My friends call me Ham."

Ann forced a smile while Ham told them of his exploits in the courtroom.

"If he's a lawyer, I'm a truck driver," Ann said *sotto voce* to Frieda. She felt sure he was replaying an old Perry Mason episode.

". . . married three times, twice to the same woman," he was saying with a laugh.

"She had fortitude," Ann said.

He seemed to ignore the remark. "Dance?" he asked Ann. Frieda nudged her with an elbow.

They danced to a rock tune on the postage-stamp-size floor, not touching. The steady, roaring tempo released Ann's natural sense of rhythm and she improvised steps and movements, finding pleasure simply in expending energy. The song ended and a slow, mellow tune began. Ham's body moved against hers, despite her efforts to arch away. His eyes dreamy, he sang off-key, "The first time, ever I saw your face . . ." She hated being so close to a virtual stranger, a man to whom she felt a growing aversion. What was probably sensuous to him was disagreeable to her in the extreme. His cologne, cheap and heavy, gave her a headache.

"Could we sit this one out?" she pleaded.

"Sure, baby." He flashed a toothy grin.

At the table he ordered another round of drinks. While Ann sipped, he told her about his boat, his large condo, and his trips to exotic places. Frieda forced vacuous eyes on him, while Ann responded with vague "uh-huhs." He groped for Ann's knee under the table and squeezed. She twitched away. Suddenly the Wallbanger, on an empty stomach, rumbled around her abdomen, creating a small thunder.

She swallowed hard, then pushed away from the table. "Excuse me, but I'm going to be sick." Weaving between crowded tables, she made her way to the rest room.

Fifteen minutes later Frieda appeared in the ladies' room. "Are you okay?"

"I'm better." She dabbed a damp tissue on her face. "That's it, Frieda. No more bars."

"Oh, Ann, I admit Ham was not a good start. But one bad experience shouldn't spoil it for you. Give it another chance. Next weekend—"

"No. No next weekend."

"You're a snob, you know?"

"Maybe."

"Unadventurous."

"Definitely."

Frieda laughed. "You're also my boss, so I'd better watch myself, right?"

Ann joined weakly in the laughter. "You're lucky I can't get along without you."

Back home she tiptoed into each room to check on the boys. She felt uneasy about leaving them without supervision. The twins, at fourteen, should be responsible, but they often argued and teased Teddy unmercifully. Now she placed a quiet kiss on each and gently pulled Teddy's thumb from his mouth. Lately he'd returned to that old comfort.

In her own room she dropped to her bed, exhausted. So much for the singles scene. At least she was too miserable to think about Martin. Maybe this was a breakthrough. Thanks, Ham.

But her thoughts wandered despite her resolve. She stretched across the bed. It was all hers now. She patted the pillow beside her. It would be nice to cuddle up to a warm body. Whatever else Martin was, he was adequate as a lover; not inventive, but thoughtful. Although, she reminded herself, she had no means of comparison. Hugging the sheet to her neck, she recalled her complaint that Martin rolled away with all the covers. Now at least her sleep should be more restful, more comfortable.

Still, tonight the bed seemed big and empty.

Ann made a quick pasta-and-salad meal and thawed out strawberries to dish up on pound-cake slices, while Teddy set the table. Louise, she knew, would be prompt. She yelled at the boys to pick up their discarded clothing, then felt bad about yelling so much. Feeling harried and cross—Flora had the flu and hadn't come for two days—Ann retired to the bathroom to splash her face with cool water. Glancing in the mirror, she noticed how grim she looked and traced her finger on faint creases edging her eyes. Lately she felt unlovely, unloved. Her mind roamed unexpectedly to happier days, to premarriage days, to boys she had dated prior to Martin. Not so many dates, and with juvenile boys, really. All but Dante. And she hadn't actually dated him. Although she was only eleven when they met, he remained, for many years, her knight on a white stallion, her yardstick against whom all other men were measured.

Dante had been a prisoner of war, interred at the Michigan State Fair Grounds during World War II. Her mother had learned that a paisano, Franco, from her home town was imprisoned there, and so she'd requested his release for Sunday dinner. The authorities were very obliging. Franco brought along a friend,

Dante, and Ann was instantly smitten. Sunday dinner with the two soldiers became routine. Dante taught Ann to play chess and teased and joked with her. Although she knew he regarded her as a "little sister," she was enamored of this handsome and dashing man.

When, at war's end, the boys returned to Italy, Ann and Dante corresponded. Her teen years were filled with daydreams of Dante. Other boys paled by comparison. Now sudden nostalgia washed over Ann as she recalled the family's journey to their relatives in Italy and the subsequent visit to Dante's grand villa in the wine country. She had felt an instant kindling of her old ardor, and when he kissed her she knew the feeling was reciprocated. Even now, twenty-one years later, she flushed at the memory of that kiss.

But that was the extent of her romance. For some inexplicable reason her father had hustled them off two days early, and her castles in air evaporated. He'd never explained, though he'd been clearly agitated. Her letters to Dante had gone unanswered and eventually she stopped writing.

She felt a sudden need to recapture those halcyon days, to bask under the warming sun of an Italian sky. The desire came with such an urgency that it brought tears to her eyes. The memory of Dante captivated her until she longed to see him once more, to ask why he'd never answered her letters.

Ann's reminiscences dissipated when the doorbell rang. Louise. And right on time.

"How *are* you?" Louise said. "You look so thin. Or is that Mother's line?"

"I've lost a few pounds," Ann said, touching her waist.

"You look great, really. New pants?"

"Yes, Frieda went shopping with me." The bell-bottom hip-huggers did justice to her slim hips and thighs. "Bless Frieda, she's made me her project. She'll cure me or kill me."

Dinner was quiet. The boys had little to say and dispersed soon after dessert. They were always a bit tentative with Louise anyway, not like they were with Tina, who was more of a "pal."

Afterward the sisters sipped coffee in the family room. Ann said, "I saw the folks the other day. They're having a hard time accepting the divorce." Divorce was contrary to church laws and something Italians didn't do. No amount of explanation would convince them. "For better or worse," her father said. "Give him more time," her mother said, "sometimes men stray." Ann thought she knew her mother, but this accepting attitude toward infidelity was inconceivable.

Louise said, "It's understandable that they can't accept your divorce."

"I don't want to talk about the divorce or Martin anymore. It's no fun. I'm no fun. Louise, I've been thinking. I need a vacation, a change of scenery. What would you think about my going to Italy?"

"All alone?"

"Yes."

"What about the boys? Is it a good idea to leave them now?"

"It'll only be a week or ten days. I'm sure Flora will stay. She can handle it, though she can be so absentminded sometimes." Ann brushed her hand across her forehead. "I need to get away. I'll wait until October or November. The spring- and autumn-wedding rush will be over. I'll want you to look in on them every few days."

"Of course."

"Martin may want to keep them, but the boys are still angry with him. I just don't think that will work. Besides, I want them home. They need that continuity."

Louise nodded.

"I want to see Dante again. Does that seem silly?"

"Dante?"

"You remember him, don't you?'"

"Yes, I just haven't thought about him in a long time."

"Louise, don't you remember the major crush I had on him?"

"Oh, sure, when he was a prisoner of war. He'd come over every Sunday on a pass."

"Something happened when we visited him in Italy. Pa rushed us off so fast, we hardly had time to talk."

"I really don't remember it all that well, Ann. I was in a world of my own, on a spiritual high from visiting all those basilicas, I guess." Louise's laugh was self-deprecating.

"I asked Pa not long ago about that trip, why we had left so abruptly. He said, 'I don't remember, it was so long ago.' When I pushed him, he said we hadn't left abruptly—it was time to go and he was tired of traveling."

Louise nodded absentmindedly.

"Louise, what's with you? You're so distracted."

"Hm? Oh. No, I'm listening, Ann." She walked to the window, where a warm breeze wafted past the drapes. "You're right, I have had something on my mind." She told Ann about Rachel and her uncle. "There's something special about Jonathon Wheatly, Ann. He's strong yet gentle. He's concerned."

Ann put her cup on the table and went to her sister. "It sounds like you have a thing for this man."

Louise reddened. "Oh, no, nothing like that. It's just that I've never met anyone like him before." She turned and looked squarely at her sister. "Maybe you're right. Maybe I do have a 'thing' for him. I know I've never felt so attracted before." She smiled shyly. "I guess I have a crush. My adolescence is showing, isn't it?"

Ann laughed. "At your age, it's probably more than a crush. And about time, too."

"I feel like I'm in a time warp. I've lost those post-pubescent years of learning about the other sex and I'm not sure I'll ever catch up. I'm so afraid of being with a man and doing or saying the wrong thing. But I'd like to see him again. Maybe he'll call me. If he doesn't, do you think I could call him?"

"Why not? It's allowed these days. You could ask about Rachel."

Louise smiled, pleased to have permission. "I will. I'll call him."

That night Louise tried rehearsing what she would say. Could she ask Mr. Wheatly to bring Rachel for a visit or to come over and discuss her? Did that seem too forward?

She vacillated for a week, then, surprisingly, Mr. Wheatly called. His voice, though businesslike, excited her. "I talked to Rachel about your tutoring her, and she seemed receptive. It's rare to get any reaction from her these days. I'd like to take you up on your offer."

Louise's heart tripped. "I'm glad you've made that decision. I'm pretty free. Mornings would be best."

"Then how about twice a week, Tuesdays and Thursdays?"

"Perfect. Ten o'clock until noon?" She couldn't keep from smiling. "Can you bring her here, or will that interfere with your work?"

"No, I'm flexible. Miss Marcassa, I really appreciate this."

"I'm happy to do it. Please call me Louise." She gave him directions.

"Louise. Thanks. I'll be there next Tuesday."

She hung up the phone with a quick prayer of thanks. She'd be seeing Jonathon Wheatly again.

Tuesday morning Louise put on a pot of coffee and made cinnamon buns. She changed her outfit twice and applied a bit of makeup with inexpert shaky fingers, pale blue eye shadow and coral lipstick. Assessing herself in the mirror, she decided she liked it and might even make it a habit.

Unfortunately, Mr. Wheatly brought Rachel only as far as the apartment door, then excused himself before Louise could offer him a cup of coffee.

Disappointed, she stooped to hug Rachel. "I'm so very happy to see you, dear. How are you?"

"I'm fine," Rachel said, her pale face showing no emotion.

"How about some milk and a cinnamon bun to start off with?"

"Yes, please." This time she allowed herself a small wan smile.

Louise gave Rachel a present, a Dr. Suess book, which she accepted wordlessly.

"Let's read it together, then we'll do some math," Louise said encouragingly.

The child acquiesced, but didn't smile at the silly verses. Louise closed the book and settled her at the kitchen table to begin math-review work. After a while she progressed to more advanced problems. Rachel was easily distracted and would often look off into space and Louise would nudge her into attention. Louise tried drilling her on multiplication tables, using flash cards. She took frequent short breaks and tried unsuccessfully to draw the child out. Two hours, she decided, was too long.

"We need a break," Louise said after a while. "Would you like me to read to you?" At Rachel's assenting nod, Louise went to the bookcase and drew out *The Boxcar Children.*

Rachel sat stiffly beside her as she began reading about the orphaned children, then soon curled up, resting her head against Louise's shoulder. Louise felt pleased beyond measure. The remainder of the hour went more smoothly.

When Mr. Wheatly returned, Louise invited him in.

"Thanks, but I'm afraid I'm pressed for time."

Louise hid her disappointment behind a smile. "I understand. Maybe next time?"

During the next session Louise tried to keep Rachel occupied with math games she'd invented, but again the child's attention wandered and she often fell into introspection.

Poor child, Louise thought, it would take time and love to banish the awful memories that must accompany her always. Rachel had lost first her father, who, according to Mr. Wheatly, had not been totally without feeling in the early days, and now her mother, who, though flawed, at least loved her and had been a constant in her life. How long would it take for Rachel to become whole of heart again? Months, years, a lifetime?

It wasn't until the third session that Louise convinced Mr. Wheatly to stop in for coffee. Flustered, she settled Rachel in the living room with a puzzle and she and Mr. Wheatly sat at the kitchen table. As she fussed with cups and placed brownies on a doily-lined plate, she stilled her nerves by discussing Rachel's progress. "It's very slow going. I can't keep her attention for long. She stares off into the distance."

"We have to be patient with her."

"Yes, I agree. I don't intend to push her, Mr. Wheatly."

"Jonathon, please." His smile was electric.

"It's nice that your job gives you some time to spend with Rachel, Jonathon." She liked the way his name sounded. Jonathon. Jon.

"I really don't have much time. I've been neglecting my business, I'm afraid. I have a small tool plant in Mt. Clemens and another in Tennessee. I travel between the two." His large square hands, gripping the mug, looked powerful.

"That sounds like a great deal of responsibility."

"I love it." He reached for a brownie and took a bite. "I confess to being a workaholic."

"That's not the worst thing in the world."

"I'm going to have to make a decision about Rachel. My mother's health is deteriorating and I can't continue to be around. I'm often gone several days or a week at a time."

Louise pushed the plate of brownies closer. "Have you thought about hiring help for your mother?"

"She has a cleaning woman. But that isn't doing Rachel any good. Mother just doesn't have the patience."

"I wish there was something more I could do."

"You're doing great as it is. I've noticed a lightening up since you've been working with Rachel." He consulted his watch. "I have some business calls to make. I'd like to talk to you further when I have more time."

"Perhaps next Thursday, then."

The next time, he stayed a bit longer, and the time after that Louise prepared a simple lunch for the three of them. They ate at the umbrella table on her tiny patio. A stray cat found its way to the small yard beyond and Rachel coaxed it to her and petted its furry back.

Jonathon observed Rachel fondly. "She's getting better, isn't she?"

"Much. She's more responsive to me and her work is improving as well. I always knew she was a bright girl."

"We always talk about Rachel. Sometime I'd like to talk about you." His smile was slow and warm. "What are you doing for dinner?"

Though Louise's heart skidded, she hesitated for a moment, not wanting to appear too eager. "I'm free."

"Six o'clock, then?"

"Perfect."

She discarded one outfit after another, then con-

sulted Ann about what to wear, finally settling on a
simple pink cotton sheath. The sides of her fair hair,
grown longer now, she pulled back, and the rest fell
gently to her shoulders.

She dabbed Chanel perfume on her wrists and behind her ears and smiled in self-conscious pleasure at
the delicious scent. When Jonathon arrived, Louise's
heart surged at the sight of him. His well-cut dark suit
didn't quite hide the powerful build. She was pleased
when he held the door for her. So many men no longer
bothered because of women's lib, but for Louise it was
the mark of a gentleman.

They went to a quiet English pub-style restaurant
across the Detroit River in Windsor, where waiters
took orders with starched efficiency. With a background of old show tunes played on a piano, they eased
into conversation, at first talking in generalities. When
Louise asked about his family, Jonathon said he'd in-
herited the shop from his father, who'd started it
twenty-five years ago. The somewhat tyrannical senior
Wheatly had had a tight grip on both sons, but the
younger boy, Rachel's father, had, in a sense, escaped.
"I wanted to be a journalist, but my father discouraged college. He insisted I come into the business, so
I did, working every sort of job. Then Uncle Sam
called in 1966. I was drafted and spent time in Nam."
His face took on a blank look.

"Was that where you acquired the limp?"

He nodded and looked away.

"I suppose you don't want to talk about it."

He sighed. "I didn't want to go. Even considered
running to Canada. But I didn't want to disappoint my
parents. A matter of honor and all that crap."

"The political mind-set seems to be changing now."

"Not fast enough. Too late for me. I was in the Tet
offensive. That's where I got the bum knee. Suffice it
to say I was one of those poor suckers someone like
Hawkeye worked on."

"Hawkeye?"

"As in *MASH*. At least the medic was sober when he worked on me."

"Tell me about it."

"Nothing to tell. I was wounded. I got stitched up."

"There must be more. Where did it happen and how? How were you rescued?"

"You don't want to know, Louise. War is ugly." His gray eyes turned cold.

"I do want to know."

He was silent as a momentary look of pain crossed his eyes. He passed a hand over his face. "I saw two buddies die."

"I'm so sorry," Louise said quietly, placing her hand on his.

"I was in the hospital ten months. It wasn't only my leg, it was"—he tapped his head—"it was here. The worst of it was, when I came home, it wasn't in glory. People actually spit on me." He winced. "My father was so proud of me, but I was ashamed and miserable and felt like an outcast. I lay around the house for a while, then went back to work for my father, managing his new plant."

"The job seems to agree with you."

"I thrive on work. When my father had a stroke, the total responsibility for the business fell to me. I made improvements, then expanded; the plant flourished. My father had a second stroke last year and passed away. We'd grown close in the last couple of years."

"What about your interest in journalism?" Louise asked. "Do you ever write?"

He flushed slightly. "Promise you won't tell. I write poetry. Occasionally a short story. They're sealed away from prying eyes."

She smiled fondly. "How like you."

He buttered a hard roll. "You're the first person I've

ever told. It's my skeleton in the closet. Now you know my darkest secret.''

''Then I suppose you should know mine.'' Louise hesitated. If it scares him away, so be it. Oh, please, God, don't let it scare him away. ''I used to be a nun.''

''Well, I'll be damned. Excuse me; I'll be darned.''

Louise made a tight mouth. ''Don't do that. That's precisely the reason I don't tell people. It changes their attitude. I'm sorry I told you.''

He looked contrite and placed his hand on hers. ''Don't be sorry. I'll say 'damn' and even worse if you want. I know some great swear words.''

She laughed. ''Now you're going overboard. I just don't want my past to influence the way you treat me.''

''I'll let you open your own doors too.''

She laughed again. ''Are you making fun of me?''

''Not at all. I think you're delightful. You're sweet. If being a nun made you the way you are, then I'm all for it.''

Louise heaved a sigh of relief. ''You have no idea how I worry about telling people. I'm glad you know now. It puts us on an even footing.''

''Not really. I'm not religious at all. My family were Methodists, but I'm nothing at all.''

''You're a Christian, aren't you?''

''I suppose so.''

''That's enough for me. You're a good person. I knew that from the beginning by the way you treated Rachel.''

''Rachel.'' He ran his fingers across his brow. ''I've had to make a decision. Caring for her has become more than we can handle. I've been neglecting my work for her. As much as I hate to do it, I'm going to have to place her in a foster home.''

''No!''

''Mother can't manage her care, and I'm away too much. Besides, I can't be Rachel's everything. She needs mothering. I'm not good at that.''

Louise closed her eyes for a moment. In the past weeks she'd thought often of Rachel and her plight. It was obvious Jonathon and his mother couldn't go on as they were. Louise hadn't formulated any real plan when she blurted out, "Let me take her."

"What?"

"I can handle it," she said quickly, eager to convince him, and herself as well. "She can register at my school and we'll come and go together."

"You don't know what you're saying. It takes total commitment to handle a child with her problems."

"I'm committed. I love Rachel."

"Louise. Think about this."

"I have. I know I want to do this. I've always wanted a child to care for."

Jonathon sat back in his chair and observed Louise. "You're something. It would be perfect, just perfect. But you have to think about this very carefully."

Within a week Rachel came to stay. Rachel of the violet eyes and dark ringlets was hers; and so, in a sense, was Jonathon. Whenever he was in town he planned outings for the three of them—a trip to the zoo, a walk at Stony Creek Park, a special movie. When Rachel tired of the crutches, Jonathon would push her in her wheelchair, making a game of it. The therapy she received for her cerebral palsy seemed to strengthen her muscles, but she tired easily.

Rachel had been there a month when, after an enervating afternoon at the Cranbrook Gardens, Jonathon tucked her into bed. Louise heard him singing a silly song, heard Rachel's giggles.

As he walked into the living room, he stretched, filling the doorway. "My back is sore from pushing that wheelchair," he complained.

Louise set down a huge bowl of hot, heavily buttered popcorn. "Come on, lie on the sofa and I'll give you a back rub."

"That's the best offer I've had in years." He dutifully lay on the sofa and Louise knelt beside him and began kneading his muscles through the cotton of his shirt.

"Wait a minute. Let's do this right." Jonathon sat up and yanked his shirt off in a quick motion.

Louise hesitated a moment, awed by the sight of his muscular chest with fair furry hair funneling down the middle. When he turned over, she traced her finger down the ridge of his spine. Splaying both hands across the expanse of his back, she felt the warmth, the taut muscles, the sharp jutting bones. The soothing sensation of hands upon flesh brought a small smile of pleasure to her lips. Eyes closed, enjoying the intimacy, she let the energy seep through her hands. She massaged, pummeled, stroked.

"Ah, heaven," Jonathon murmured as she continued the massage.

She changed to fingertip strokes and he became so quiet she thought he was asleep, when suddenly he turned in a swift fluid movement and, grabbing a handful of her hair, pulled her head down to his. His lips touched hers with a hot urgency.

For a brief moment she thought of pushing away, but the need was too great. She returned his kiss with the same ardor, her pulse racing. His tongue pressed her lips apart and stroked against hers. She found herself sinking into a well of desire. When his hand fondled her breast, she stiffened.

"Oh, please, Jon, don't, please don't."

"Louise, let me. It's all right."

She struggled from his grasp and collapsed into a chair.

Jonathon let out a great sigh. "The nun's story."

She stared at a piece of lint on the carpet. "I can't help it."

"It's perfectly all right, you know. Teenage kids pet. And more."

"I know. But I can't."

He stood up and shook his head. "You're mired in preadolescence."

"I know. Try to understand."

"It's not easy."

"I know."

"Christ! Stop saying 'I know.' I hate that."

"I know."

He burst out in laughter and she joined him. He pulled her upright and enfolded her in his arms. "I'll try to understand if you will please discard that nun's habit you're wearing in your mind. You can't carry that around for the rest of your life."

She was about to say "I know," but checked herself. "I think you'd better go now, Jon."

"I'll go, but in the immortal words of MacArthur, I shall return."

After that, Jonathon called her almost every day. The summer melded into a golden autumn and they went to movies and plays at Meadowbrook and the Fisher and always there was talk, lots of talk. And there was warm affection, growing, growing to something more, something stronger. Jonathon, however, contented himself with little more than ardent kisses.

After a ride to the nearby town of Romeo for apples on a brightly spangled October Sunday, they spent the evening peeling apples for sauce. Later, when Rachel was asleep, Louise slipped off her shoes and lay on the couch, resting her head on Jonathon's lap.

His hands wandered over her body and under her blouse. His fingers wiggled under her bra. For a moment she gave in to the pleasurable rush, then pulled his hand away.

"Dammit, let me, Lou. You're a grown woman. We're allowed."

"No, not yet." She held his hand for a moment, then put it to her mouth and kissed it. It was strong, firm, a worker's hand, bristly hairs scattered along the knuckles.

"Then when?"

She shook her head, feeling confused.

He banged his fist on the arm of the sofa, blowing out air in exasperation. "You're a nut, you know that?"

She knew it. She was an enigma, a vestal virgin. An unloved (as far as sex was concerned) woman. It seemed almost un-American in this era of open, carefree love and flower children. A man, a wonderful man, wanted to love her, to enclose her in a cocoon of passion and feeling. Yet she couldn't do it, she couldn't succumb to that age-old siren call. Her convent past accompanied her; that small prim voice of conscience whispered, "Sin, sin; fornication is sin." Fornication. What a hard, ugly word for love, for *amore, passione.* She wanted to beat down the voice that denied her, but it wouldn't quiet. Sex outside of marriage was, in her mind, a sin. As simple as that.

"Please, Jon, I've tried to explain. I just can't give in. Can't you understand?" They'd had this discussion before, when her lips were bruised from kissing and her body limp from desire.

"You're a throwback to the fifties. You're holding me up. Blackmailing me. Into marriage. Me, the last of the carefree bachelors."

"No, no, it's not that way at all." She reached up and touched his cheek.

He arched a thick dark eyebrow. "You mean you don't want marriage?"

"Of course I do. But not if you don't."

"Uh-huh, sure. You've got me in a corner, and you know it."

She sat upright and straightened her shoulders. "Stop talking that way, as if this is a game. It's not a game. There are no winners and losers."

He sighed and gave her a lopsided smile. "You're

wrong. You win. Your irrational idealism or Catholicism, whatever, has beaten me. And I win. I win you.''

"What are you saying?" For a brief moment her heart stopped.

"Must I get on my knees?"

Louise giggled. "Yes."

He scrambled to his knees and took her hand. ''Fair lady, I desire your hand in marriage. Please don't make me ask your father.'' He kissed the back of her hand, then turned it and kissed the palm.

Louise rested her chin on his head. ''Kind knight, I accept with pleasure. And you must ask my father.''

"We'll tell him together. I'll get a ring."

"Jon, I'm so happy."

He regarded her through slitted eyes. ''Now can we?''

"What?"

"You know."

"Oh, Jon, we've gone this long . . .''

Jon pulled Louise upright and enclosed her in his arms. ''Dammit,'' he said, moving his taut arousal against her. ''Let's get married soon; the sooner, the better.''

Her joy overwhelmed her. A tear slipped from her eye. ''Right after Christmas would be perfect. Tina will be home then.''

13

Tina's sign read, "No mo' GI Joe." She chanted with the other marchers, "No toy guns!" Cold and tired, in the biting October air, she turned and handed the sign to the boy behind her. "You take it for a while. My hands are chilled." She stuffed her hands into the pockets of her parka as the small group circled the pavement in front of the toy store.

"No toy guns!" the chanting continued.

The owner glared at them from the front door and shook a fist. "I'll get the police," he yelled.

Tina shrugged. Although she'd helped organize this protest, for some reason her heart wasn't into demonstrating. She'd had a trying day at school and wanted some coffee and sympathy from Adam. Turning to her companion, a youthful mother of four, she said, "Look, Alma, I think I'll call it a day. A few more people should get here soon."

"Okay. See you later," the woman said agreeably. "No toy guns!"

Tina wondered how effective picketing was, anyway. Despite constant demonstrations, the Vietnam war dragged on. Last year, in 1971, a group of Vietnam Veterans Against the War threw their medals at the Capitol in vehement protest. President Nixon, away at Camp David, didn't even hear the message. Even the troops in the thick of the war, on at least one occasion, had refused to fight. Still, on the positive side, according to news reports, cease-fire talks were going on. With any luck, Senator McGovern, an avowed dove, would win the presidential election in a few weeks, though the polls were discouraging. Surely, if elected, he would put an end to the war.

Tina munched on an apple she'd stashed in her pocket against a hunger attack, then jogged down MacArthur Boulevard and turned toward the large rundown Victorian house that housed Adam's kids. The Beehive. Her second home.

"Hi, Tina," said Cricket, the slender redhead who opened the door. She was new at the Beehive and looked deceivingly about twelve. "Adam's in the kitchen."

Pushing through the swinging door, Tina saw Adam leaning over Marina, who sat at the table. His chest brushed her shoulder; his mouth was mere inches from her earlobe. The two were deep in a conversation. Marina's smile, as she looked up at Adam, was full of admiration, full of . . . longing?

Tina bit her lip and strolled in casually. "Well, I hope I'm not disturbing anything," she said, unable to keep the agitation from her voice. She pawed through the huge basket of colorful fruit centered on the table.

Adam smiled at her. "Hi, sweets, I was going to call you."

"I wasn't home."

"Talk to you later, Marina," he said, patting his aide's shoulder. It seemed to Tina that she wore a sort of smug look. "C'mon," he said, taking Tina's arm and steering her to his office. He closed the door and kissed her thoroughly. "Mmm, you smell like autumn. You taste good too, like apples."

Tina moved away.

"What's wrong?"

"That was a cozy scene."

"What, with Marina? Do I detect a note of jealousy?"

"No, just interest."

Adam tilted an eyebrow at her.

"Okay, I admit it. I'm jealous because she has a lot of time with you. I just get crumbs of your time. I saw the way she looked at you. Adam, she's in love with you."

He laughed. "She just broke up with her boyfriend. I was giving her some sound advice."

"Oh, as if you're such an authority on relationships!" An ugly thought occurred to Tina. "Adam. The truth. Have you and Marina been . . . have you gone to bed with her?"

"Of course not! She's a kid."

"She's a woman. And she loves you."

Adam frowned. "You're blowing this all out of proportion." His playful tone was gone.

"I'm telling you what I know. I have eyes." She held her shoulders stiffly, not looking at him.

"What's wrong with you? You've been acting weird lately."

Weird. That was so like a man. "How would you know? You rarely see me."

He sighed and shook his head. "I don't like it any more than you do. But it can't be helped."

Feeling very close to tears, Tina said, "Maybe it's time to rethink our relationship." God, what made her say such a thing? She loved this man!

Adam stared at her. "What's gotten into you, anyway?"

She could claim her period was due, but that was an easy out. No, it was more than that. It was a growing unhappiness with the status quo, it was an unnamed yearning.

"It's you! Us! Everything." She turned on her heel. "I'll see you later. Maybe."

She jogged several blocks, her mind a blur of conflicting thoughts. Okay, she knew she was acting irrationally. A Yorkie on a leash yapped at her and its owner, a fit thirtyish man, gave her an apologetic grin. "Sorry," he said, then smiled at her. He turned and jogged beside her for a while, trying for small talk. Her obvious disinterest finally discouraged him and he turned and ran in the opposite direction. Undoubtedly he was married, she thought. Everyone was. Everyone her age, anyway. She should go back to the Beehive and apologize. Probably she had overreacted. Damn! She hated every moment she was away from Adam. Her time with him was too short. If they lived together, it would be different. But that was out of the question in the Beehive. Unless . . . unless they were married. She stopped in her tracks and caught her breath. Marriage. That, she admitted finally, was what she really wanted. The big C. Commitment, total and forever. Matrimony, holy wedlock, a marriage license, that piece of paper (she'd been so sure it wasn't important) that legalized their love. She realized with a pang that she longed to be Adam's family, to have his child, to belong to the PTA, to be a room mother, to bake brownies and chocolate cookies, to read Little Golden books, to make Halloween costumes. Yes, she wanted all of it. Suddenly nothing else seemed important, not the war, not women's lib, not toy guns.

Was this normal? Was she going through some strange rite of passage? Had she finally graduated from idealistic youth to pragmatic adult? In two years she would be thirty, the suspect age. *Don't trust anyone over thirty,* Abby Hoffman said.

She leaned weakly against a lamppost, her breath coming in short pants. She had to go back, she had to straighten it all out with Adam.

At the Beehive she drank a full glass of water from the tap and wiped her forehead with a paper towel. Adam wasn't in his office.

"He's in his bedroom," Marina said, observing her from the hallway, a lean hip resting against the wall.

"Is that where you were, consoling each other?" Oh, God, how bitchy she sounded, how immature.

"Oh, come on, Tina," Marina said, neither acknowledging nor denying.

Tina burst in on Adam without even knocking. He was bent over his bookcase and looked as if he'd been expecting her.

"Hello again, sweets."

"Adam, I'm sorry. We need to talk." She drew him to the bed and with outspread palms pushed him down. "Why don't we get married?"

"Married!" He pulled her to his lap. "Just when we're having fun?"

"Don't joke. I'm serious."

His face grew solemn. "I like the way it is between us."

"So do I, but there's a natural progression to this sort of relationship. Dating, courting, marriage."

"We're still at dating."

"No, we're not."

"Sweet Tina." He nuzzled her behind the ear. "I'd like to get married. But not now, not yet."

"Then when?"

"I don't know. I have to get my law degree, then pass the bar, and—"

"You can still do all that." She moved her head. "Stop doing that to my ear."

He slid his hand all the way from her neck to her thigh, causing an immediate tingle. She took his hand, stilling it.

He said, "I just couldn't do justice to a career and a family."

"Lots of people do. Almost everyone."

"With me, it's different. I have to give my all to whatever I'm doing. I can't dish out a few minutes a day to a family. You'd want children. And so would I, ultimately. But not yet, not while I have—I know this sounds altruistic and clichéd—a destiny to fulfill.'' His small laugh was self-deprecating.

"From anyone else it would sound corny, but not from you, not you, Adam. I've always known you were special. But dammit, I want all of you, not bits and pieces.'' Oh, God. The tears pushed against her lids. And she had thought she was so together. Her head dropped and the tears came, a torrent, a waterfall. "God, Adam,'' she blubbered childishly, "I love you so much. I can't imagine loving anyone else.''

Adam hugged her. "Ah, Tina, Tina.'' He rubbed her back, massaged the indentation where her neck met her skull. "Don't you know I love you too?''

"I know.''

"It's just too soon. I have nothing, no money, lots of debts. It'll be years before I'm solvent.''

"I don't care about that.''

"Not now, but you would eventually. You'd have to take crumbs.''

Tina stood and faced him. "I've *been* taking crumbs, Adam.''

"I'm sorry. You shouldn't have to. You should have the whole cake.''

She smiled. "A cookie would do.''

"I'm selfish, Tina. I don't want responsibilities. Not now. There are too many things I want to do. I'd be stifled by a wife and family.''

"I'm not talking about having children. Not right away.''

"I know you, know where you've come from. If we married, I'd probably not deny you the children you want, and be miserable about it. Children take time and commitment. I'll never do to my kids what my father did to me.'' Adam rose and stuffed his hands into his pockets. "His career came first and he ignored me. I'm still, to this day, trying for that elusive pat on the back. Maybe that's what drives me, I don't know. But dammit, I won't do it to my own children.''

Tina had heard his diatribes before against his father, an unkind, unaware, selfish man.

"He ignored my mother too, and she went elsewhere for favors, for fulfillment. She thought I didn't know what was going on. I was sixteen when they finally divorced, and I'll never forget the bitterness, the recriminations between them. And the sense of aloneness for me." He took a deep breath. "Maybe I'm self-centered, probably stupid, but it won't work out. What's wrong with leaving things the way they are?"

"Adam, I want more than that." She slipped her arms around his waist.

"You deserve more, sweets." He ran nervous fingers through his hair. "Look, we're getting nowhere with this. Can we talk about it another time? I've got a paper due tomorrow. See, I'm doing it again. Putting other things first.''

"Adam, that would be okay if we were together. I'd help you. I'd type your papers."

He laughed. "You say that now." He kissed her forehead and moved her away. Walking to the door, he said, ''I've got to get busy.''

She stared at him sullenly. "I guess that's the end of the discussion.''

"We'll talk again later, I promise.''

Tina left feeling dismissed. He *had* professed his love. She knew he cared for her. Then why did she feel so let-down? It almost felt like . . . like a kiss-off.

Tina arrived at the Beehive the night before Thanksgiving with Indian corn to decorate the doors and a papier-mâché horn of plenty. She and Marina (in a truce from their undiscussed, yet silently acknowledged war) talked some of the kids into chopping onions and celery for the stuffing, and mixing the ingredients for the pies. Cricket, claiming expertise with crusts, was assigned to pie duty. She was teased when the dough was too sticky, then again when she added too much flour and it fell apart in a crumbly mess. Amid silliness and jokes, they made a unanimous decision to buy ready-made crusts. In the background, the Rolling Stones blared from the radio.

On Thanksgiving Day Adam supervised the cooking and serving. Thankfully, Marina spent the day with her own family.

The pumpkin pies, crusts overdone, slightly dry, the moist cornbread stuffing, the turkey, oozing succulent juices, all combined to give Tina a sense of continuity, of family, albeit this was a pseudo one. The odd assortment of kids, all clean and polished, sat around kibitzing, joking. She watched Adam fondly as he carved the huge golden-brown bird. He slipped easily into his role of father and savior to this brood of misfits. He had talked of being selfish, but she knew of his selflessness in dealing with his kids, knew of his compassion, his acceptance of them. She couldn't help thinking what a fine father he would be to their children.

She and Adam hadn't spoken further about her marriage proposal. But now there was a slender thread of tension between them. She hoped Adam would "come around." They were so right for each other! She was biding her time, waiting for the right opportunity to bring up the subject again.

Now they all linked hands and Adam called on Henry to give a blessing. The boy hung his head, dark stringy hair flopping forward, and thought a moment. "I can't," he said.

Adam quickly turned attention from the awkward boy. "Anyone else?" From shyness, or filled with too much pain, or simply finding little for which to be thankful, none of the runaways came forward. Tina filled the strained silence and said simple words of thanksgiving for being together, for the Beehive, for Adam's comforting protection and goodwill. Amen. Inexplicably, her softly spoken words brought tears to some eyes, and when she noticed, her own grew moist. Not Henry's. He'd suffered much in his few and tender years. "He's going to be hard to salvage," Adam had said earlier, after speaking of the boy's abusive home. It wasn't fair. The kids should all be home, in the bosom of loving families. And so, she thought, should she.

Christmas, mellow Noel, sentimental season, would be the time to talk to Adam. She had planned on his coming to Michigan with her, but his mother was ailing in Florida and he felt duty-bound to visit her. So, tennis racket under his arm, Adam headed for Florida while Tina tearfully packed warm sweaters for her trip back home to Michigan. Tearful because nothing was settled between them; because she was torn between going to Florida with Adam (he *had* asked her) and going home; because . . . well, just because. Did one have to have reasons to cry? Couldn't it be just a general purging?

Michigan. Detroit. Home. Her parents showed signs of aging she had never noticed before—her mother's breathlessness, her father's whitening hair. It was strange to see Ann sans Martin. After her divorce was final, she seemed to be adjusting, though she complained about the boys spending part of the holiday with their father. The twins looked so grown, taller than their mother and still growing. Tina would give them her old Jimi Hendrix and Janis Joplin albums, two rising stars crushed in their prime by drugs. Their songs seemed whining and passé to her, from another era. Tina preferred listening to the classics now.

Louise was the big surprise. She had bloomed, looking stylish in a pantsuit and wearing a bit of makeup. Being in love seemed to have erased the years, and mothering winsome, darling Rachel obviously agreed with her.

In Ann's old bedroom on Christmas Eve day, the girls talked while the children entertained themselves in the basement. Actually, Louise talked about Jonathon while Ann and Tina listened.

"Jonathon's business is thriving. He's a very astute businessman. But that's not the important thing. He's so caring, so kind. Well, you'll see when you meet him."

"He sounds like a dream come true," Tina said. "I can't wait to meet this paragon, this giant among men." She began painting her big toe with red polish. Her leg was angled upward, her heel resting on the dressing table. "Is this too red?"

"Am I being tiresome?" Louise flushed, twisting her one-carat engagement ring around her finger. "Well, I don't care. Jon *is* wonderful. You should see how patient he is with Rachel."

"This is where I came in," Ann said. "But it's all true. He really is a nice man." She hugged her sister. "I don't know anyone who deserves this happiness more than you. Are you excited about the wedding tomorrow?"

"No, I'm strangely calm. I'll probably fall apart at the last minute."

Tina said, "No you won't. Lucky you. Your life is working out."

It was strange, Tina thought, how being together in this bedroom reduced the three of them to teenagers again. In this refuge they could discard their facades, reveal their secrets, be silly, be angry, laugh and cry.

Rachel hobbled into the room on her crutches. "The boys are teasing me," she wailed. "Make them stop."

Louise sprang from the bed to hug the child. "They wouldn't do it if they didn't love you."

"I hate them!"

"You stay put, Louise, I'll handle those brats." Ann

started for the door. "Come on, Rachel. I'll straighten them out."

"Isn't it wonderful?" Louise said. "They're treating her like family."

When Ann returned, she asked, "What's happening with you and Adam, Tina? The truth."

"The truth. I proposed and he declined."

"No!"

Tina tightened the cap on the nail-polish bottle. "Yes. I guess the next step is the big U, the ultimatum. Marry me or else."

"Or else what?" Louise said.

"Sayonara. So long, sucker. *Arrivederci*. The end." Tina sighed. "Actually, I have a plan. Like an alcoholic has to reach rock bottom before he can start his upward journey, so, if Adam has to do without me for a few weeks, he'll change his mind, he'll commit. I'll give him a deadline."

Ann frowned. "It could backfire."

"Then it's not meant to be." Tina propped her chin on her palm. "Oh, God, it *is* meant to be. I love that man. He loves me. Why is he so stubborn?"

"It's a man's birthright," Ann said.

"I don't want to go with him until I'm forty, then have him decide we're not right for each other. Who wants to start over at forty?"

"Some of us are doing it," Ann said.

"Sorry, Ann, yours is a different case. Are you really dating?"

"I've had a few disastrous episodes. I can't say anything in front of Ma. She keeps thinking Martin will 'come to his senses.' "

"Will he?"

"No. It's over between us. But I'm drowning my misery next March in Italy. I should be there now, but I keep postponing it. It's one thing after another in the bridal business."

"Oh, that's terrific," Tina said. "I envy you."

Chiara poked her head into the room. "I finally finished wrapping presents, girls. Next year everyone gets a check instead."

"You always say that," Tina said with a tolerant smile.

"Can I come in, or is this private?"

"Come in, Ma, we're discussing—what else?—men," Tina said.

Chiara entered and the conversation turned to recipes and clothes, in which Tina had little interest.

On Christmas morning Tina trod the stairs quietly, careful not to wake her parents. With a cup of fresh-brewed coffee, she sat in the living room in the soft glow of the Christmas-tree lights. She thought how all her Christmases seemed to be running together in a continuous thread. The tree ornaments and tinsel garlands were treasures from her childhood. Presents were piled high under a tree whose top had been cut off to accommodate the ceiling. When she was a child the gifts were toys and underwear; now they were luxuries—perfume, leather gloves, frilly blouses. She imagined doing the same thing for the next fifty years, same tree, same house. But that was ludicrous. She would have her own house, her own tree, she and Adam.

What was Adam doing this moment? Was he thinking of her? She hadn't told her sisters of the passion, the need, of the bliss when their bodies joined. Just thinking of it tripped her heartbeat. They should be together. It was destined, written in the stars. Was it too early to call Florida? She dialed.

"Merry Christmas, darling. Did I wake you?"

"No, I'm drinking a mug of coffee and thinking of you. I miss you, sweets."

"I miss you, Adam. Wish you were here. Or I there."

"You should be here. The weather's agreeable, sunny. I bought you something nice."

Her heart jumped. A ring? Fool, stop setting yourself up for a fall. "What is it?"

"Can't tell. You'll see."

"Okay, I'll be patient. Tomorrow's Louise's wedding."

A slight hesitation. "Give her my best. Hey, my mother's stirring. I need to help her down the steps."

"Tell your mom hello and Merry Christmas."

They said their good-byes and Tina hung up feeling empty inside. He hadn't said he loved her.

Louise sat in front of the mirror. The ice-blue satin suit complimented her sapphire-blue eyes. She looked and felt serene as her mother pinned the simple headband of pearl clusters in her golden-brown hair. She was marrying Jonathon Wheatly. She'd never known such happiness.

Chiara closed her eyes. "You remind me so much of myself when I was young." She reached down and kissed the top of her daughter's head. "You're the one like me. The others have their father's dark looks." Chiara had never quite understood why Louise had left the convent. Indeed, Louise's explanations were often emotional and not very lucid.

Now Louise wanted her mother's absolution. "Ma, I did the right thing, leaving the convent. I want you to believe that."

"I know, *cara*. I understand." The two hugged for several moments.

Ann entered the bedroom twirling a blue satin garter on her finger. "It's old, borrowed, and blue. I guess everything else is new. You look great."

The garter slid easily over Louise's slender leg to above the knee. "Perfect," Ann said. "Oh, Lou, I'm so happy for you." The sisters hugged and Ann's eyes, suddenly filming over, held a hint of sadness.

She must have bittersweet memories of her own wedding day, Louise thought.

"What are you women doing in there?" Mike boomed from the living room.

"We're ready," Louise said, leading the entourage out of the bedroom.

"You look beautiful," Tina said when her sister emerged.

"Do I look beautiful, Aunt Tina?" Rachel asked, spreading the skirt of her taffeta dress in a little curtsy.

Tina finished tying bows on Rachel's crutches. "More beautifuller than . . . than Cinderella or Snow White." She picked up a camera. "Hold still, hon, I want to take your picture just like that."

Rachel beamed as Tina snapped away.

"She loves her aunts fussing over her," Louise said, proud of the way Rachel had bloomed under the Marcassas' sheltering love.

"Come on, we're late, as usual," Mike grumbled. He picked Rachel up in his strong arms and herded the others toward the door. Outside he called to the boys, who were bouncing a basketball on the driveway concrete, puffs of steam billowing from their mouths into the cold winter air. They picked their way around icy patches to the cars.

At the church, Louise took her father's arm as the familiar *Lohengrin* march boomed from the organ. She smiled at her good friend Father Bernard, who waited at the altar grinning a welcome. He had supported her decision to leave the convent and had met and approved of Jonathon.

Measured steps took her and her father to the front rail. Sensing her father's nervousness, she squeezed his hand. He squeezed back, and as he placed her hand in Jonathon's, there were tears in his eyes. She kissed his cheek and said, "I love you, Pa."

Perfectly calm, perfectly happy, Louise nodded to her friends and family who sat in the cold church, observing the age-old rites with smiles and dewy eyes. Ann and Jonathon's cousin were witnesses and Rachel beamed with pride as a junior bridesmaid.

Louise felt blessed, awash in grace, suffused with love, not only for Jonathon but also for her family, her friends, the city, the universe. It seemed very clear now that this was the reason she had been directed to leave the convent and seek another life.

Father performed the Mass in Latin rather than English, as Louise had requested. The familiar words she'd memorized as a child comforted her, the *glorias* and *Pater nosters* and *pax dominis*, as did the musical cadence.

Finally Father Bernard said the words that joined them.

"Till death us do part," Louise said softly.

"Till death us do part," Jonathon intoned with solemn sincerity.

The final kiss was short and he whispered, "To be continued."

They had dinner at the Top of the Ponch in downtown Detroit and the newlyweds invited everyone to their large new home in suburban Troy, where a caterer set out desserts and drinks. Jon's business prevented a honeymoon, so it was postponed until summer. Which was perfectly all right with Louise. All she needed for happiness was her new husband.

When the last guest left, Jonathon enfolded Louise in his arms. "Now?" he whispered.

"Now," she answered with a crooked smile. Too much champagne. It made one woozy.

Jonathon scooped her up into his arms and wended his way, puffing and panting, up the circular stairs.

She giggled as he undressed her, then wound her arms around him tightly. "I'm petty . . . I mean putty in your hands."

"I'll be damned. You're drunk. This must be a first. Unless you used to nip at the communion wine." He laid her on the bed on silky sheets and kissed her softly.

"Wait," she said, pushing away. "I have a bea-u-tiful new satin nightgown."

"The hell with the nightgown." His kisses were urgent and his hands were all over her, massaging, petting. He spoke sweet, breathless words, then soon he was inside her, but gently, gently, and she felt almost feverish and breathless and suddenly suspended in a bolt of lightning and felt as one with Jonathon, heard his murmured heartfelt "I love you, God how I love you," heard (where did it come from?) a crescendo of Handel's "Hallelujah Chorus," and then, soon, as if from a distance, Jonathon's satisfied moan, felt his weighty collapse, felt her own tears (why tears now?). She wouldn't release her grasp, wouldn't let him move from her. Stay, stay. Stay forever.

Hallelujah, amen.

It had been, she was sure, worth waiting for.

14

The sky was overcast on an early May day in 1973 as Ann boarded the 747 jumbo jet. As the engines roared to life, she took a deep breath in a conscious effort to relax, and unclenched bone-white hands which had been locked together in a viselike grip. She breathed a sigh of relief when they were airborne at last and Manhattan dropped away beneath the wings.

She was bone-weary, tired of being everything to everyone. Her trip to Italy had been postponed twice because of problems in the bridal shops, where a flurry of spring wedding orders caused delays. To top it off, two of her best alteration workers had quit and she'd even pressed her mother into service. The brides-to-be, full of nervous stress, were understandably upset by late orders and had to be handled with kid gloves. Her workers toiled feverishly on alterations to meet their deadlines.

Besides all that, she'd been reluctant to leave because the boys seemed more and more unmanageable. Ten-year-old Theodore's stutter, which had been slight, was now more pronounced, especially in times of stress, and his school progress reports showed falling grades. Brian, at fifteen and in the throes of adolescence, had more serious problems. He seemed to defy her at every turn. One night, after he was forbidden to leave the house, he'd sneaked away and she frantically phoned all his friends. Matthew was no help; he protected his twin fiercely, even when disapproving of his actions. Ann had finally tracked Brian down at a house party where the parents were conveniently away. When she got him on the phone, she insisted he come home or she'd come after him. She smelled beer on his breath, though he denied it. What else was available? she wondered. According to the press, dope was rampant, marijuana was commonplace. Angry and mortified, Brian didn't speak to her for a week, except in sullen grunts and nods. She tried to convince herself his rebelliousness wasn't a serious matter. Most teenagers went through these phases, didn't they?

Martin was no help. "I'll talk to them," he'd say, then give the boys his "stern-father" talk, which seemed to alienate them even further. He never tried for dialogue, never tried to communicate. Those lectures did nothing more than add mortar to the wall between them.

The flight attendant interrupted Ann's reverie. Ann ordered a drink, wanting to blunt her jarring thoughts. Outside her window a solid sea of white cotton-candy clouds floated below. She must try to think of other things, concentrate on this journey. She closed her eyes and rested against the pillow the attendant had handed her. This trip should have been a second honeymoon instead of a quest to find a phantom lover. Despite her declarations to the contrary, she realized she was still angry, still hurt by the divorce, still confused. Unbidden thoughts came of her early days with Martin, when their love was new and urgent. But to be honest, from the beginning her marriage had been less than satisfying, when she realized her husband was moody and tended to insulate himself from problems. Only in the past few years had she admitted her dissatisfaction, when the insights of Friedan and Millett and Bouvier pervaded. For many women a window had been opened in their male-dominated existences, a window that allowed the fresh air of reason and reality into lives blighted by a singular dedication to keeping women in their places. Would the collective consciousness ever change? Not very easily, she thought. Women had always been the keepers of the flame, in the hearth and in the heart, and it would be a long time before men would accept anything less.

She realized that ultimately her own attitude must change. She must take responsibility for her own pleasure and fulfillment. Her happiness mustn't be dependent on a man. Yet . . . yet she wanted, needed a man. The company of women was fine for "sensitivity" sessions, for gossip and jokes, but it didn't satisfy those *other* urges and the deep longing to treasure and be treasured.

But she *was* trying. She *had* done the singles scene. Unfortunately, her brief forays had been unsuccessful, some humorous, some embarrassing. She was well aware that that was partly her own fault. She was unbending, uncommunicative, uncooperative. Mostly, unwilling to meet anyone halfway. Was this a phase? Was she afraid of opening her bruised and calloused heart to new emotions? She only knew that in the silent and numbing hours before dawn, when sleep eluded her, when her mind wasn't occupied with a dozen problems, then she felt vulnerable, alone and lonely. Then the stifled tears would erupt.

A voice intruded into her thoughts. "Have you been to Italy before?"

The man sitting next to her looked youthful in faded jeans and a sweater, yet the faint lines on his brow and at the corners of his eyes were evidence to the contrary. His hair, though receding slightly at the temples, was balanced by long sideburns. He had probing eyes of Prussian blue and a strong chin.

"Yes, when I was seventeen."

"So have I. I was in Florence for several weeks as an art student. It was wonderful. Have you seen Florence?'' Dimples appeared when he smiled. There was something infinitely endearing about dimples.

''No. I plan to go on this trip.''

''You'll love it. A feast for the senses.'' The man droned on about his favorite sights, about sleepy medieval villages in Umbria and Tuscany, about wines he'd known and loved. On and on, while Ann's thoughts scudded about on their own scattered journey.

His hand was in front of her. ''Scott Trayman.''

She collected herself and extended her own hand. ''Ann Norbert.''

Her hesitancy didn't deter Scott. She discovered he was thirty-four years old, unmarried, a designer at General Motors, and a nonstop talker.

''I'll be in Florence at least two weeks. Maybe we could meet for lunch.''

''I'm not sure when I'll be there.''

What was wrong with her? Ann wondered, trying to dispel her nervousness. Scott was a nice-enough man (though she thought of him as boyish) and their meeting was an opportunity for a friendly exchange Yet she demurred. He wasn't her type. (What *was* her type?) He was too young. (Absurd, these days.) He was too slick, too fast. (For lunch in a public place?)

''I'll be staying at the Michelangelo Hotel,'' he said meaningfully.

''How apropos.''

He smiled slightly and his eyes narrowed briefly before Ann excused herself and went to the rest room. When she returned, Scott was gone. He'd found an empty seat beside someone who was undoubtedly more receptive, more forthcoming. Good. She wanted to be alone with her thoughts.

The trip was tedious, but at least faster than the last one in 1951 on a prop plane, which took about twenty-four hours including refueling stops.

At last she was disembarking at Leonardo da Vinci

Airport in Rome, the Eternal City. She'd been too
young to properly enjoy it the first time. Now the sights
seemed more splendid, the very air charged with sig-
nificance. After a brief rest at her hotel, she took a
bus tour that stopped at the Piazza di Spagna, the
Spanish Steps. What should have been an inspiring
setting turned out to be a haven for young hippies with
backpacks and lovers lounging on the ancient steps,
hugging and kissing, oblivious of the tourists who de-
toured around them. Undeterred, Ann walked up the
137 steps to the Trinità dei Monti church perched
above, then took a deep breath and headed back down.

The adjacent Via Condotti housed the high-class rag
trade—Gucci, Valentino. In a spontaneous and un-
characteristic urge to indulge herself, Ann purchased
a scarf for an outrageous sum at Gucci.

Back at the Hotel Beverly Hills (she winced at the
unlikely name), she nursed the charley horse caused
by the steps and fell asleep with thoughts of her trip
to Bari, and after that, her meeting with Dante.

When the plane landed at Bari the next day, Ann felt
a surge of recognition, a sense of homecoming. Her
cousin Vito, whom she knew instantly from the photograph he'd sent, waved his arms wildly as she approached, then kissed her on both cheeks. They
chatted—he in fractured English, she in hesitant Italian—as he drove *lungomare,* along the sea, in a vintage Mercedes. Sea smells and the brilliant aquamarine
of the Adriatic further kindled memories of her earlier
visit twenty-two years ago. Considerable changes had
occurred since then.

It was not the Italy of her mother's youth, but a more
modern Italy. Before Ann left, her mother had spoken
nostalgically of the old days, of simpler times. "We
had little," she'd said. "We were poor, but still I seem
to remember only the good times, the trips to the sea,
the village weddings where everyone danced and ate
all night and into the next day. Ah, the memories, the

memories. A sign of old age, eh?'' She had touched
a handkerchief to her closed eyes, nodding silently,
enjoying the visions that must have passed in her mind
like an enfolding film. Ann wished her mother could
be here now.

At Vito's house the welcoming committee of aunts
and uncles and scores of cousins greeted Ann. They
all seemed familiar and dear. Although rusty, Ann's
Italian served her well enough, she thought, in spite
of occasional obvious mispronunciations that caused
friendly laughter. Dinner was a lengthy multicourse
affair. They exchanged family photos and reminiscences until Ann's yawns drew attention and she was
shown to her room.

Lying under lace-trimmed sheets, she gazed at walls
covered with pictures of saints and let her thoughts
again wash through her mind. Soon she would see
Dante again. What foolish impulse had compelled her
to a reunion? The man, now fifty years old, was surely
married, must have a family. She knew his winery was
successful—better wine shops carried the Ravenna label. She could only ascribe her actions to the ongoing
devastation of her divorce (though she'd assured one
and all that she was over it, healed, stronger), which
seemed to produce a yearning to return to simpler days
and perhaps an innocent love, brief as it had been.

She remembered as if it were yesterday Dante's kiss,
a kiss full of longing and hope and a budding passion.
She remembered her blissful unawareness of the direction her life would take. Had he asked her to run
away with him that night, she would have done it. But
she had been a romantic, an innocent, a vulnerable
seventeen, hardly aware of the world around her.
Probably it was foolishness to think that he would have
wanted to marry her. He was a man, with a man's
passions, and she was a child on the threshold of womanhood. Yet her love had been as real as the cloudless
Italian sky above. When her father hurried them away,

she was enshrouded in misery. After several weeks without word from Dante, Ann had written to him, but her letters went unanswered.

What would Dante look like now? Would he remember her? Finally she drifted off to a dreamless sleep.

Her day was spent in visiting even more relatives (there seemed to be no end) and touring the lovely town and shops that skirted the perimeter of the piazza. The fountain in the center of the piazza, she knew from her mother's stories, was the spot where her parents, strangers until that very day, had become engaged. What anxious thoughts her mother must have had. How can one promise to love a stranger? she wondered. And yet that marriage had endured and thrived, and her own, to a man she thought she knew and understood, had collapsed. What irony.

What changes had transpired in just one generation. Her parents frowned on divorce, and indeed, divorcees were looked down upon. Never mind their reasons, their misery. Life was an endurance contest. Ann realized with a pang the anguish her divorce must have caused her mother. "For better or worse," she had admonished Ann. But this generation wasn't willing to put up with "worse" in hopes that it would get "better."

Those thoughts haunted Ann until the next morning, when Vito delivered her to the train station with sincere urgings that she stay awhile longer. She convinced him that she had a schedule to accommodate. By then she'd been feted with so much food and wine that she despaired of being able to button her skirts.

When the train pulled into Dante's village, she found a cabbie who chattered easily about the area, pointing out places of interest while he skillfully maneuvered the car around narrow inclines on pitted roads. She remembered the vine-covered hills, the olive groves, the lush landscape. An imposing brown fortresslike structure peeped from the surrounding greenery high in the hills. Rectangular turrets jutted into the cloud-dotted sky like brushstrokes in a painting. "An abbey," Ann's driver said, "*vecchia*, very old."

She sat very still, hands clenched in her lap, hardly hearing the cabbie's running commentary, fighting an urge to say, "Turn back." After coming this far, she must continue. She tried to convince herself it was just a visit to an old friend.

When the cab arrived at the gate, it was three-thirty, siesta time. Ann had purposely timed her visit in hopes that Dante would be home then. Now she wondered if it had been a mistake not to have contacted him beforehand.

At the gate a flood of memories returned, a nostalgic *déjà vu* that left her weak. Nothing had changed. Oh, the cypresses and pines lining the green carpet of lawn were larger, taller, the statues more worn and chipped perhaps, but the imposing stone villa with huge wooden double doors and cross-barred windows was the place of her dreams.

Ann alighted and dismissed the cabbie, wondering as she did so if that were wise. If no one was home, she'd be stranded. Surely someone would be there. She passed nervous fingers over her hair and wet her lips. A gangly preadolescent girl skipped down the gravel lane and lifted large brown inquiring eyes, Dante's eyes, toward Ann. "*Buon giorno,*" she said.

"*Buon giorno,*" Ann returned. In her halting Italian she said she was a visitor from America and had known Dante Ravenna many years ago. Was he home now?

"Dante Ravenna is my father. Come along, I'll get him." She led Ann into the foyer, their footsteps noisy on shiny terrazzo floors. "Wait here," she said, disappearing down a dark hallway.

Huge paintings hung on stuccoed walls and two sturdy oak chairs flanked a marble-topped table against the wall. Centered on the table was a large bouquet of spring flowers. Arranged by his wife? Of course he would have a wife, a family, yet she had wanted to believe otherwise.

Moments later she heard footsteps coming from the back of the house, and voices. "Why didn't you ask for a name?"

"I didn't think, Papa."

"Is she a business associate, a wine merchant from New York, or—?"

"No, I don't think so."

The footsteps were close now, and suddenly Ann was face-to-face with Dante. A surge of the old passion stabbed at her heart. The man standing before her was not the man of her dreams, but a middle-aged gentleman with black hair shot with gray, somewhat stout, wearing a worldly, slightly weary expression. Still, he projected that same presence that she'd remembered, a sort of majesty. Here was a man of appetite, of ardor, a man of authority. It was all there, in his face and bearing. A smile slowly lit his countenance, his teeth shone white in a tanned, slightly lined face. His eyes narrowed, then he let out an exclamation of surprise, looking as if he'd seen an apparition.

He threw up his hands. "It can't be. Am I seeing a ghost? Not Anna!"

"Yes, it's me."

He rushed to her and took her hand. Lifting it to his lips, he kissed it in a courtly, old-world gesture.

"I . . . I wasn't sure you'd remember me," she said.

He straightened and leaned back, looking hurt. "How could I not? My dear Anna, how wonderful to see you, and how strange you should come now." He looked away in a momentary reverie. "It's as if you were sent."

"I came to tour and to visit my mother's people, and I thought, as long as I was here . . ."

"But why are we standing here talking? Come, you must meet my wife, Bianca. This one"—he pointed to the young girl—"is my youngest, Adela." He took Ann's hand and pulled her along the hall to the back terrace, while Adela skipped along beside them, asking questions.

"You are from Detroit? Do you know the Supremes? I've saved their records. Do you know Stevie Wonder? How exciting it must be!"

Detroit used to be noted as the Motor City, Ann thought; now it's the home of Motown Records. But the music world with its glitter and excitement was far removed from her life. "No, I'm afraid I don't know them."

The terrace with its exotic flowers and fruity smells and its breathtaking view of the mountains again pricked her recollections. It was here that they'd shared a kiss. A slim open-faced woman rose and smiled in a questioning welcome as they entered.

"Bianca," Dante said, "you remember the friends I told you about in America? The ones who befriended me when I was a prisoner? This is Anna, the lovely daughter. Anna, my wife."

Bianca graciously extended both hands. "How wonderful to meet you. My husband has spoken of your family often." She turned to the child. "Adela, go tell Rose to bring coffee and cakes. And fruit. *Presto.*"

Dante pressed Ann into a chair. "You must tell me about your father. How is he? And your mother and sisters. Tell me everything."

Ann capsuled the past several years, concentrating on her parents and sisters, while Dante nodded. A servant arrived with a laden tray, and Bianca urged coffee and cakes upon her guest.

"But you, *cara,* what about you? You have children? Tell me about yourself."

Ann shrugged. "I graduated from Wayne State University and got married. I manage six bridal salons that my mother founded. I have twin sons, fifteen years old, and another son, ten." She paused and lifted her gaze to the clear blue sky for a moment, seeking composure. "My marriage didn't work out too well. Last year I divorced my husband."

Bianca murmured and clucked in sympathy, then rose. "I have things to attend to in the kitchen. Please excuse me." She and Dante exchanged understanding glances.

"What about your parents?" Ann asked, helping herself to a small almond cake. "I'll never forget their hospitality."

"My father died fifteen years ago and I took over the winery. I have two sons, Giovanni, fourteen, and Carlo, seventeen, who are away at school, and Adela, whom you've met, named after my mother, may she rest in peace. Just a month ago my mother passed away."

"I'm sorry to hear that. You must be still mourning."

Dante nodded, looking distracted. After a moment he said, "I think of your family so often."

"And I assumed you had forgotten all about us. After our visit I wrote to you, but you didn't write back."

"What? No! I answered your letter, and wrote several times more, but never heard from you again." He shook his head. "And now, my dear Anna, after all these years, the mystery has been solved. Your father probably destroyed the letters."

Ann stiffened. "Surely my father wouldn't do such a thing."

"He would if he had sufficient reason."

"Reason?" Ann was puzzled. "What sort of reason?" She remembered their last trip and hasty departure. Something had occurred that day. Something momentous. "Dante, what happened the day we left?"

"I wanted to marry you. Ah, Anna, I was enamored. I told your father that. I suppose you didn't know."

So the tumultuous emotions were not one-sided after all. "No. Was that why we left so abruptly? But I would have thought he'd—"

"He had other reasons for discouraging a marriage. There were things he found out. It was after I'd taken him to visit my Aunt Teresa, a nun, at the abbey in the hills. Do you remember the abbey?

"The cabdriver pointed it out today."

"My aunt died soon after your visit. As I said, my mother died a month ago, and shortly after that the abbess sent for me. She gave me a letter that was written by my aunt. The abbess had instructions to give me the letter after both my parents were dead." Dante frowned and gazed upward, over the trees, toward the mountains. "I don't know how to prepare you for this, so you must simply read the letter." He rose, saying, "Excuse me for a moment while I get it."

Ann walked to the edge of the terrace, drinking in the scenery. What sort of mystery was Dante preparing her for? What did his aunt's letter have to do with her? She strolled down stone steps that led to the secluded shrub-enshrouded area with white wrought-iron settee where she and Dante had talked and kissed.

Hearing Dante's steps, she returned to the terrace. Silently he handed her a letter. She sat at the table and unfolded the ivory sheets, her fingers trembling slightly. Silently she read:

My dear Dante,

Today you brought a visitor to see me. I know it was fate that directed him here at this time and place. And now I must reveal secrets to you, secrets that have been sealed in my heart, and that I swore to keep.

I was present at your birth and adored you from that day on. Now that both your parents are gone, it cannot hurt them if I reveal the facts. The Ravennas have raised you from infancy, but you are not their child.

I will tell it from the beginning.

A young woman appeared at the gate of the abbey one day seeking refuge. She was incoherent and obviously distressed. We fed and harbored her and it became clear that the woman was feeble-minded. Concetta—that was her name—was also pregnant. However, she was cheerful and grateful for our kindness, and was put to work in the kitchen. She died soon after her child was born (and you must have guessed by now, Dante, that child was you) and my sister asked to adopt him. How I hated to see you leave the abbey! But how wonderful to know that you would be well-cared-for. Your parents never wanted you to know that you were not their flesh and blood.

When you brought Michele Marcassa to visit, my heart turned. The young Concetta spoke little, but she did reveal the name of her husband. It was Michele Marcassa. I dismissed you on a pretext that day and spoke to Signore Marcassa. I told him of the woman. He was deeply upset and told me his wife had wandered away and they'd given her up for dead. He understood that the Ravennas did not want their son to know he was not theirs.

So you see, Dante, you are the son of one Michele and Concetta Marcassa. I know that Signore Marcassa has not told you, and probably has told no one, to protect his family from embarrassment and shame.

I hope you forgive both your parents and me for not telling you this earlier, but you must believe it was done with all good intentions.

You have, as always, my total love and affection.

Your loving
Zia Tereza

Heart pounding, Ann dropped her hands to her lap and stared at Dante. Finally she said in a choked whisper, "You are my half-brother."

"Yes." Dante lowered his head.

She continued staring, the thoughts stabbing her brain—the impossible coincidences that had led Dante to his own father; her own long-harbored affection for Dante, her kin; her mother's ignorance of the facts; her father's anguish at not being able to acknowledge his own son, at having to keep this deep, dark secret.

Dante spoke quietly. "You can see that Michele had strong reasons for keeping the secret. Chiara, for one. He wouldn't hurt that wonderful woman for the world. And we mustn't either." He moved his chair beside her and took her hand. "I felt you must know because there were fond feelings between us."

Fond feelings. No, much more than that. A love that might have led to marriage. But it was all so long ago, and she had been so young. Of course, the secret must be kept.

Ann covered her face with her hands, feeling a mixture of pity and shame. "But how can I face my father, knowing all this?"

"You will do it. You will digest this story and put it in proper perspective. No one was really at fault. Perhaps it would be best to say nothing to anyone."

Bianca strode onto the terrace, her lovely countenance wreathed in a sympathetic smile. She placed her hand on Dante's shoulder and he covered it with his. The glance between them spoke more eloquently than words of their bond. Ann felt a stab of jealousy. Obviously Bianca was privy to all Dante's secrets. They had the sort of marriage she had wanted, of understanding and love and sharing. They were *simpatico*.

"You must have supper and stay the night," Bianca said. "I'm sure you'd like to freshen up now, then later we can go to the village—"

"You're very kind. But I leave for Florence tomorrow," Ann said. "I have a hotel room booked in town." There was no reason to stay. Her unformed, unspoken dreams were shattered.

Dante insisted that his handyman drive her back to

town. At the door of his silver Maserati, Ann said, "Dante, for some reason I felt I had to see you; something drove me to come. Who knows what unconscious powers are at work? I suppose I had to know, to . . . to put certain things to rest."

"I understand." Dante took her hand in both of his. "You've had much to digest in a short time. Will you be all right?"

"I think so."

"Now that you know we are related, you must write to me." He kissed her forehead. "Life is strange, is it not? First I thought of you as a little sister, then as a desirable woman, and now I am forced to think of you again as a sister, this time in reality."

"Strange, indeed."

Dante closed the door and the Maserati was off in a swirl of dust. Ann leaned against the soft leather upholstery. Would it have been better if she had never known the truth? No, then perhaps she would have held the image of Dante forever in her mind as the ultimate lover, as a romantic fantasy. She wondered if the phantom of Dante had shadowed her marriage, giving her unrealistic expectations. She would never really know, and now it didn't much matter. It was best put to rest.

She must face reality now, look forward. She was young enough to make a new life for herself. She would put her failed marriage behind her. Perhaps at last she could find in her heart, if not understanding toward Martin, at least forgiveness.

As the car careened around narrow curves, Ann peered from the window. She scanned the hills for a glimpse of the abbey. There it was, majestic and proud, piercing the sky. Closing her eyes, she imagined the old nun, Teresa, scribbling her letter of revelation to Dante. She imagined the spirit of her father's first wife, Concetta, at Teresa's elbow, urging her on. So many things became clear—why her father never mentioned relatives, why he had avoided a visit to his own village. Ann felt a sudden surge of grace, a wash of spiritual energy, and she shivered as she crossed herself.

15

At the Accademia, the line of tourists moved slowly past Michelangelo's *Prisoners,* roughly hewn sculptures of partially formed figures emerging from their prisons of stone. Ann was stunned by the sense of power the statues evoked. At the end of the wide corridor stood the rotunda, housing the statue of David. Proud, luminous, youthful, the image took Ann's breath away. People circled, gazing in awe, whispering as if they were in church, as if it were a religious experience. Ann resisted an impulse to reach out and touch the lifelike hand.

Back on the street, Ann, guidebook in hand, wandered to the Piazza della Signoria. She gazed at the gleaming white statue of Neptune; his disdainful face, his impressive musculature. *Oh, Ammanati, Ammanati, what lovely marble you have ruined!* the Florentines cried. So said her guidebook. She tilted her head this way and that, sorry that she wasn't more of an art connoisseur. Perhaps the old Florentines were right. Neptune *was* awkward. The bronze satyrs and naiads decorating the perimeter of the pool, however, were graceful and lovely. Turning away, she strolled to the Loggia. The sculptures here, though their themes were beatings, beheadings, and rapes, were impressive nonetheless. If art was imitating life, it was a violent life.

After hours of touring Florence, she realized she was hungry and weary. Consulting her map, she wandered away and found herself at a café. She slipped her feet from their loafers and ordered linguine, fruit, and wine. Lifting her face to the afternoon sun, she breathed deeply, smiling, basking in the sense of beauty that had engulfed her since arriving in Florence. The ancient city held almost an embarrassment of riches, Ann thought. In the past few hours she'd had more exposure to art than she'd had in her previous thirty-nine years. Cultural overload, she thought.

She closed her eyes and tried to imagine the Florence of the Medicis, tried to picture the glorious artisans that helped shape this magnificent city, marveled at the concentration of genius in this one area. It might have been nice to share her impressions with someone, a traveling companion.

"*Buon giorno, signora,*" a voice said.

Ann looked up and flashed a smile of recognition at Scott Trayman, the man she'd met on the plane.

"*Permette, signora?*" he asked, pulling out the chair opposite.

Ann laughed. "Of course. Your Italian's pretty good."

He sat, and his long jean-clad legs crowded hers under the table. "I practiced before approaching you."

"You've been watching me?"

"Not exactly. I was having lunch, and fate stepped in and brought you here. You were deep in thought."

"I've had a lot to think about."

"I'm a good listener." There was a certain boyish appeal to his smile.

But Ann hesitated. Did she want to reveal the skeletons in her family closet? On the other hand, it was almost easier to talk to strangers than to close friends. Strangers were neutral.

Scott pushed. "I take it you're not married. Traveling alone, no ring."

"You're right." Ann's right hand went automatically to her ring finger, rubbing the empty place where a wedding band had rested. "I *was* married. I have three children." Better get *that* out of the way.

"A victim of divorce. Me too. But I fortunately don't have children."

"Fortunately? I'm happy I've got them."

He looked abashed. "Of course, I didn't mean . . . what I meant was, it's always messier with children. There's so much more to deal with. I have friends with children, and they're devastated . . . What the hell, I'm not making this any better, am I?"

Ann laughed. "No, but I understand what you're saying. It hasn't been easy."

Somehow she found herself telling Scott of her marriage and divorce. He was an easy listener, making appropriate sympathetic murmurings.

"You're obviously not over it yet," Scott said when she'd finished.

"I guess not. I don't know why I'm telling you all this."

"Maybe it's the fact that you're alone in a foreign city. Besides, telling a virtual stranger isn't risky. When I got a divorce, I talked about it to anyone who would listen. I married right out of college too. It lasted seven years."

"Childhood sweethearts?"

"Not exactly. We were juniors at the University of Michigan when we met and fell in love. As long as we were at school, we had that in common. We realized, after a few years, that the school bond was all we had. She was always more politically inclined than I, even in college. Then she got involved in civil rights, decided to join a group of desegregationists. Eventually she traded in her bouffant hair for a long swingy style, her suits for tie-dyed T-shirts and jeans. Went to Mississippi. She almost got herself killed."

Was Scott's ex-wife's crusading spirit so terrible? Ann wondered, thinking of Tina and the peace march.

"She did what she thought was right, had the courage of her convictions."

"Yeah, she sure did. But *nobody* in our group did that kind of thing. Everyone thought she was crazy, giving up a comfortable life for what? A dream." He bounced a fork, deep in thought. "Now I realize how hard it was for her to go against everyone—me, her parents, our friends. She was sort of a rebel." He laughed cynically. "A rebel with a cause."

Ann couldn't help but defend the errant wife. "It's never easy to stand up for what you think is right."

Scott nodded. "Oh, I give her credit now. But at that time . . . it was just too radical." He looked off into space. "She was a pretty thing, pretty but tough. The divorce wasn't pleasant at first; both families were against it. But we ended up friends. Actually, I eventually understood what she was trying to do. I even admire her. I still hear from her at Christmas. She went on to law school, then moved to LA. She defends underdogs, mostly pro bono cases."

"And you love the bachelor's carefree life," Ann said.

"I did. But now . . . I'm sort of tired of it. There's something to be said for a steady relationship."

"What are you looking for, then?"

"I don't know. Someone who knocks me off my pins, I guess." His flinty blue eyes narrowed and he cocked his head, assessing her. "You know what I mean?"

If it was a line, it was a good one. "Sure. *La passione grande*. That myth."

His eyebrows raised. "Maybe not a myth."

She was navigating dangerous waters. Better pull in her oars. Taking a last draft of wine, she said, "I'm beat. It's way past siesta time."

"Where are you staying?"

"Would you believe the Michelangelo?" Had she

gravitated to his hotel through serendipity or subconscious plan?

"Perfect. Let's find a cab, you can take your rest, then I'll knock on your door for dinner. Eight o'clock?"

Ann hesitated for only a moment. "Eight o'clock is fine."

After a nap, she pampered herself with a luxuriantly oiled bath and picked through her few dresses, finally settling on a plain black sheath. A silver pendant on a long chain and silver dangle earrings completed the outfit. How very long it had been since she'd felt this pleasant anticipation over dinner with a man.

"You're gorgeous," Scott said when she answered his knock.

"So are you." Ann's heart tripped at the sight of him in a dark herringbone sport coat and neatly creased trousers. He smelled invitingly of something musky and masculine.

"The place we're going to is a little out-of-the-way and isn't very touristy. Florentines go there."

"I trust your judgment implicitly." She swung a shawl over her shoulders.

He took her arm proprietarially, making her feel special, desirable. Outside, the air, balmy, velvety, smelling faintly of jasmine, enveloped her, uplifted her.

In the cab, Scott picked up her hand and fitted it to his, palm to palm. Hers was dwarfed. "What a stroke of luck, running into you," he said. "I was getting lonely. It's no fun seeing the sights if you've no one to share them with."

"I know exactly what you mean." When he squeezed her hand it generated a tingle that sent shock waves throughout her body. It had been a long time since a man's touch produced such a reaction.

Cavalierly he helped her from the cab, held open

the door of the family-run trattoria in the Old City, near the Duomo.

When Ann smiled her thanks he said, "I'm never quite sure whether it'll be appreciated or frowned on. So many women make a big thing about being strong enough to open their own doors."

"I guess I still have the fifties mentality."

After scanning the menu, Scott gave the order for both of them in fractured Italian to a pretty young girl, obviously the daughter. An elderly musician with wispy white hair came to their table, picking the strings of his guitar.

"I sing *canzone per amore,*" he said with a wide wink. He strummed and hummed for a bit, then sang a lilting love song in a charming tenor voice.

"He thinks we're lovers," Scott said, reaching for Ann's hand.

She noticed knowing smiles and sly grins from other patrons. Why not? she thought, placing her free hand over their clasped ones.

They ate antipasto from a laden buffet and lemony fish and pasta drenched in a white sauce. They finished one bottle of fruity wine and began another and gazed inanely at one another. She tried to remember what they were talking about. It was witty and intellectual and he seemed to find her fascinating. He was adorable, never mind that he was five years younger than she. She felt exceedingly feminine. And sexy. In the past months she'd wondered if those feminine emotions would ever return, wondered if she had become some sort of unfeeling freak.

Scott's eyes met hers for a few heartbeats. The windows of the soul. Was he reading her soul? If so, it was okay. In fact it was great.

The dinner ended too soon, although her watch read midnight. At her door he kissed her cheek, then moved his lips to her mouth, pulsing gently, tenderly. She responded to his rhythm, letting the warm liquid desire curl through her body, pressing herself closer, wishing he would touch her everywhere, wanting to touch him. This was crazy. Suddenly she moved her hands to his chest and pushed away. Scott was a stranger and she was thinking about sleeping with him.

"Hey, wait," Scott said, trying to draw her close to him. "C'mon, Ann."

"No. It's . . . it's late and I'm tired."

He took a deep breath. His eyes moved over her, then held her gaze. Again she felt the pulse of desire, but she restrained herself.

"Can we do some sightseeing tomorrow?" she asked.

Scott seemed to steady himself and took a step back. "Sure."

The next morning Ann was awakened by the phone.

"Hi," Scott said. "Hope I wasn't too pushy last night."

She stretched in languid grace, warmed by the memory of last night. "No. I had a wonderful time."

"Did I wake you? Sorry, I thought you'd be ready to hit the streets."

"Give me a half-hour."

They spent the morning at the Bargello, the heart of medieval Florence. In the loggia of the Museo Nazionale Ann took pictures of Scott mugging at the bronze animals intended for a Medici garden grotto. After a lunch of pasta they visited the Palazzo Vecchio, where Scott asked an obliging British tourist to take his and Ann's picture together. "Honeymoon, eh?" the Englishman asked with a smarmy grin. Scott nodded and winked, while Ann shook her head, blushing.

Dinner was at a small restaurant with the babble of excited Italian conversation forming a backdrop for their own quiet talk.

"I'm starved and beat," Scott said.

"Me too. My feet will never be the same."

They lingered over wine until Ann felt infused with a pleasant languor. Dusk had descended when they finally hailed a cab. Scott decided they must go to the Piazzale Michelangelo to view the city. From the hilltop they viewed the awesome panorama of Florence spanning the Arno River. The Duomo and spires lifted gracefully into the moon-brightened sky in a spangle of lights.

"I wouldn't have missed this for the world," Ann said.

Scott hugged her close and nuzzled her neck. Purring in response, she turned to kiss him in a moment of spontaneity and delight. She was unprepared for the instantaneous jolt of electricity, and hugged her arms to still the tremble. Arm in arm they walked to their cab, and neither spoke during the ride back.

At the hotel she rested her head on his shoulder while they waited for the elevator.

"You've had a lot of wine," he said.

"So have you. I'm not drunk. I'm merely mellow."

"I'm mellow too. A mellow fellow. A merry mellow fellow. A very merry mellow fellow."

She giggled. "Oh, stop."

He became very serious, and whispered in her ear, "I'm going to make love to you."

"Hmm. I've been thinking about that." She surprised herself by her honesty.

He reared his head back a bit, one eyebrow raised. "So."

Suddenly a wave of insecurity washed over her. Would she be an adequate lover? After all, she had been rejected by Martin after years of thinking their lovemaking was mostly good, always at least adequate. Besides, now that sex had been taken out of the bedroom and into the laboratories for clinical examination, it had become an art and a craft. And she was probably inexpert.

In her room they kissed and all her insecurities disappeared as her knees weakened and her head swam. Was it Scott or the wine, or a combination? He scooped her up into his strong arms and she nipped playfully at his neck. Gently he placed her on the bed and lay beside her, kissing her, touching her. They took turns removing garments from each other in what seemed like slow motion.

She wanted nothing more at that moment than to feel physical pleasure, to surrender to her lust, but her sensuous nature fought with her intellectual side. What was a nice Catholic Italian-American woman doing in bed with a virtual stranger, probably a WASP? The old nay-sayers briefly made their voices heard. *Fornication is a sin.* Look, I'm single. So is Scott. It's not adultery. *Ah, but it's still not acceptable.* No, no, it's okay now. This is the seventies. *Don't you remember* anything *you learned in Catholic school?* Oh, shut up. This feels right.

She drew him close and stroked his skin in easy, fluid movements, willing the rapture to last. It had been so long, so long since she'd even *wanted* a man, or a particular man, that she found herself passionate and insatiable. Scott was wonderful. While the bed creaked beneath them, he moaned, he groaned, he sighed, he murmured. He told her he was falling in love. Ann smiled joyously. In Scott's arms she abandoned her fears and inhibitions, reaching a zenith time and time again.

"This is crazy," she whispered. "I've only slept with my husband—my *ex*-husband—before this."

"It's not crazy. It's the most natural thing in the world." He stroked her cheek. "Are you happy?"

She nodded. "Delirious."

"Then that's all that matters."

They made love several times during the night. She would wake and reach for him or he would wake and reach for her. In the early hours of dawn she slept, cradled in his arms.

She woke to sun streaming in the window, and in the light of day wondered at her wanton, lustful performance of last night. *How could you?* asked the naysayers. Ann gave a mental shrug. It had been natural, inevitable. Last night she had felt loved and loving; womanly, wanted, alive. And why not? She'd lately been lacking a loving relationship that, she realized now, was truly necessary to her well-being; missing that vital component to a full and fulfilled life. She stretched and purred in contentment.

Scott stood naked before the wooden shutters, adjusting them, his muscled arms raised, his compact bottom a white contrast to the rest of his slightly tanned body.

"What are you staring at?" he asked playfully, glancing down at the beginning of an erection.

"You. You're very good-looking, you know, very sensuous."

"Yeah. So are you. We make a good team." He dropped beside her on the bed. "Let's spend the day together."

"Here? In bed?"

He touched her breast and pressed gently. "That's not what I meant, but it's not a bad idea. I'm leaving Florence early tomorrow morning for Rome, then home."

"So soon?" She felt devastated.

"Afraid so." Scott pulled her close to him. "Let's make the most of today."

As Ann meshed her body against him, the nay-sayers once again made a brief appearance, but she banished them peremptorily. *I need this. God, how I need this.*

The next day, when she saw Scott off at the train station, Ann felt both exhausted and exhilarated. Also questioning. Was this one of those summer romances, thrilling but soon forgotten?

"When will I see you again?" he asked.

"I'll be back in Grosse Pointe in three days. Call

me.'' Would he? ''It may be different for us back home, with all our responsibilities, with the daily grind . . .''

Scott looked at her through lowered lids. ''No way. Fate brought us together.''

She touched his cheek. ''You're such a romantic.''

He kissed her soundly while people jostled them, hurrying to get choice seats. They clung to each other until the last moment. On the train he hung out the window as it moved forward and gained momentum, blowing kisses with both hands. *''Non dimenticare,''* he shouted.

No, she wouldn't forget him; how could she? She waved at the train until it was a speck in the distance.

16

Ann exited the plane eager to set foot in her own country and anxious to see her children. She spotted Teddy first, frantically waving, then Matthew, a broad smile splitting his face. Only Brian hung back, looking sullen. Mike and Chiara herded the group forward and they all hugged.

"I missed you!" Ann cried.

They clamored for details of the trip, which Ann supplied on the ride home, skipping over the meeting with Dante. At her house Mike carried in the luggage and Ann distributed the array of gifts—leather gloves, designer shirts, pottery.

After eating the lunch Chiara had prepared, Ann sat talking with her mother over a cup of coffee, feet up on the coffee table.

"We came over every few days, just to check on things," Chiara said. "Flora worries about Brian. He missed school a couple of days because of this pain or that. I'm a little worried too. He's not a happy boy." Ann had been troubled too, though she hadn't mentioned it to her mother. "Adolescence seems harder on him than Matthew. Not to mention all the other trauma he's gone through. He's not handling it very well." Her son's obstreperousness had been slowly surfacing during the past year, since the divorce. His grades were falling and he'd been uncommunicative and uncooperative. Ann had tried to enlist Matt's aid in dealing with Brian, but Matt, ever protective, had shrugged and said, "He's okay, just going through a bad time."

"I hate to see him so unhappy," Chiara said.

"He'll be okay, Ma." Ann didn't want her mother to worry.

Chiara said, "I'll say some prayers."

Later, as Ann unpacked, she tried unsuccessfully to dismiss thoughts of Brian's problems. Always the more sensitive, the more problematic of the twins, since the divorce Brian's attitude had progressively worsened. He blamed Ann as well as Martin for the disintegration of their family. For months now he had been morose and withdrawn. She berated herself for her neglect, for being preoccupied with her own troubles. Life, she thought, was a continuing journey with no resting place; a path full of sudden turns and crevasses and steep inclines. Each step led to new discoveries and new choices. She'd reached a plateau. Her recent emotional earthquakes had settled and she had emerged steady and in control. The trip had been the catalyst she needed. Dante's revelation stunned her even now, when she allowed her thoughts to dwell on it, but it served to end a chapter of her life that had never quite reached a denouement. And her experience in Florence with Scott was as if prescribed by a celestial psychiatrist, better than Valium or a trip to a spa. The problem with Brian was the only disturbing ripple on her sea of contentment.

Maybe the boys needed a change, a trip. School would be out soon. Maybe she could take them to DC. They'd never been there and they could visit with Tina. Her sister hadn't been home since Christmas and Ann missed her. She'd call Tina tonight.

Ann's call last night had left Tina with the pleasant sense that her sister had passed a milestone. Her trip had been wonderful and she'd met a man whom she was sure she'd see again. Though her voice was controlled, Tina caught the undercurrent of excitement. Ann had weathered the trauma of divorce and come away stronger. She deserved whatever happiness she could find. Above all, she had her children to love.

Louise, too, whom Tina had spoken with a few days earlier, was content, and hoping to start a family soon. Tina was the only "unsettled" one, and she supposed the family thought of her as "poor Tina," unfulfilled at the ripe old age of twenty-nine. They probably hated Adam, who was "taking advantage of poor Tina." Actually, she was sure her sisters would like Adam if they ever got the chance to meet him.

She sprinkled granola into a container of yogurt and spooned it leisurely into her mouth. School was out at last and she'd spent her first three days sleeping late and organizing her life, or, to be honest, her mind. There was no longer a need for peace rallies now that the Vietnam war was over and the troops had been withdrawn. Strangely, that goal met, many protesters were left dangling, without a cause, without, so to speak, a job. She'd channeled whatever excess energy she had, after teaching all day, into occasional National Organization for Women meetings, but couldn't seem to rev up much enthusiasm for any of their projects. Adam, her students—those were her priorities.

From the kitchen table she picked up a small notebook, marked with red felt-tipped pen, "Goals and Lists." Opening to the first page, with the day's date, Tina looked over her jottings. She'd become a compulsive listmaker; it helped preserve sanity and order. Frowning, she deciphered the scribblings. Cleaners, PO, vac bdrm, lib, make gyn appt. As she checked off each completed item she realized only the gynecologist remained. She'd have to make an appointment soon. The pill hadn't agreed with her, and after trying different brands, her doctor had suggested discontinuing the pill and using a diaphragm. She would have to be fitted. Placing a circle around the "gyn," she promised to get to it next week for sure.

At the back of the notebook, under "goals," the first item was "clarify situation with Adam." She shook her head. When she returned to Washington after Christmas, Adam had given her, not the ring that she hoped against hope for, but a gold necklace with a gold filigreed heart. "That's my heart," he'd said, "and it belongs to you." So for the past six months she had accepted the status quo, and simply enjoyed whatever he was willing to share of himself. Their time together was precious and pleasurable. So she'd put marriage from her conscious mind; had convinced herself that what she had with Adam on a part-time basis was more than she could get in a lifetime with another man.

Yet here it was in her notebook in black (blue, actually) and white. CLARIFY SITUATION WITH ADAM. Written in a lucid moment of self-awareness. As the school counselor might say, "Just what do you mean by that, Tina?" *I mean I want a commitment.* But he claims he *is* committed. *All right, all right! I want marriage!* There it was again, out in the open, the M word. It was time to trot the subject out once more for Adam's analytical dissemination.

As she placed a letter from Ann in her desk drawer, she realized how much she missed her; missed the entire family, in fact. Family. Adam seemed perfectly satisfied not knowing hers. Was he afraid it would obligate him, bind him further? She, on the other hand, wanted to know all about Adam's family. She'd met his mother briefly when she came from Florida for the funeral of a friend. Winifred Thornberry had seemed a sad and bitter woman and not particularly friendly.

The jangle of the phone interrupted her thoughts. It was Adam.

"My father called. He's coming to town."

"That's a surprise, isn't it?"

"Yeah, I haven't seen him in a couple of years. Want to go to dinner with us?"

"Sure."

"Pick you up at seven."

This was a new wrinkle. She'd finally meet the phantom father. Was there a reason for this visit? Tina wondered.

When Adam came for her, she noticed again his Volkswagen was showing its age, with rusty bits of paint flaking off a fender and new rattles every few weeks. He turned on the ignition and Carol King's voice erupted, singing, "I feel the earth move under my feet." Tina tapped on her knees to the beat.

"I wonder why my father's here," Adam mused.

"To visit you."

"That'll be a first. I wonder if he wants something."

"Tch, tch, so cynical."

A bumper sticker ahead of them read "Help Nixon Out," meaning out of office, referring to the Watergate scandal. How did men become so lacking in ethics? This sort of crookedness was what Adam abhorred. More and more he talked of pursuing a political career when he finished law school. She wondered if he were up to playing the kind of games required. If he had one fault, it was that he was too altruistic. Politics took compromising. It was the nature of the beast. Dirty laundry was beginning to surface even in the case of President Kennedy. Camelot hadn't, after all, been perfect. She felt disillusioned.

Adam's father was waiting for them at the bar. She had expected a big man, pompous, assured, and was surprised by the frail white-haired gentleman. Try as she might, she could see in his features little trace of the son he had sired, except for the smile he flashed on meeting her. He was almost courtly, *Delighted to meet you, my dear,* bowing her ahead of him, holding her chair.

Rich leathers and bronze surrounded them, a harp-ist's melodic renderings, a small dim lamp on each table.

"Making any money at that job yet?" the elder Mr. Thornberry asked Adam when they'd settled in their seats.

Adam sighed, as if they were treading old terrain. "I do it for love, remember?"

"Bull! The only thing you should do for love is make love, ha, ha, ha." His laughter provoked a phlegmy cough, and he hacked for several moments.

He turned his sharp gaze to Tina. "So you're a teacher? A proud profession. Nursing and teaching, excellent professions for women."

She forced a smile. *We can do other things now. We're allowed.* But she couldn't very well argue with this old man, Adam's father.

Adam jumped to the defense of womanhood. "Women are in lots of professions now, Dad. In fact, I'd like to see Tina go to law school. I think she has what it takes."

Tina's eyebrows lifted. "You do?"

"Of course." Adam smiled. "Actually, I was merely making a point. I don't know if you'd even *like* going to law school."

"I think I wouldn't."

"Ha, ha." The old man, recovered from his cough-ing attack, shook his head. "No, no, Tina, it's a tough job for a woman."

Adam glanced at Tina and tacitly decided to drop it. "How's Laurie, Dad?"

"I thought I told you. She went back home to Bliss-field."

Adam had mentioned a "young" wife, only five years older than himself.

"Marry in haste, repent in leisure, ha, ha." His mirthless laugh was getting on Tina's nerves. "Well, Adam, you seem happy in that old wreck of a house.

Who knows, maybe someday you'd have an extra room for me in that old monstrosity, ha, ha.''

Adam was caught by surprise, but, Tina noted, he kept his composure. Now the reason for this visit had become apparent. The old man, finding himself all alone, suddenly realized his mortality. He must be wondering who would care for him in his declining years.

''Well, Dad, I'm thinking of leaving the Beehive when I graduate next semester, or as soon as I get a job. I'm not sure where I'll settle. I may move out west.''

''Out west! Now, son, you don't want to do that. There are lots of crazies out in California, take my word for it, I've been there plenty of times, I know. Of course, it's your life. Ha, ha. And you haven't taken my advice so far.''

''Your ideas and mine have never coincided.''

Mr. Thornberry leaned over the table and nodded. ''You could certainly say that.''

There was clearly an animosity between father and son. But at least Tina had a chance to observe, to fathom some of the genetic ingredients that had shaped Adam, and to piece together the facts of his life that he'd told or leaked. The puzzle pieces of Adam were fitting into place. With the less-than-sterling example he had, it was no wonder he wasn't anxious to become a husband and father.

They got through the meal and dropped Adam's father off at his hotel, declining his invitation to come in and have one for the road. Before he closed the car door, he mumbled, ''I suppose I haven't always been the perfect father. But I always *cared* for you, boy.''

Back in Tina's bedroom, Adam turned on the antique lamp—he called it old—on her dresser. In the dim light he scanned the array of framed photographs of her family. ''Rogues' gallery,'' he said. ''Speaking of rogues, what did you think of the old man?''

"I think he's . . . a bit charming, a bit pathetic."

"Charming and pathetic." Adam snorted. "I haven't seen him in two years, Tina. He's so much older, so much thinner. He may be sick. He hinted about a 'bad liver,' but insists he's fine." He flopped onto the bed, lacing his hands behind his head. "Did you get that left-handed apology? 'I always *cared* for you, boy.' Sure."

"Maybe he did the best he could. He's probably sorry now." Tina sat beside him and rested her hand on his arm. "I think he wants a relationship with you."

"It's too late for that, too late. Where was he when I needed him? Did you see the way he was drinking? Two before dinner, then wine. Now I remember he always had his drink or two before dinner, and probably more later. I suppose he's an alcoholic. All these years, and I never suspected that."

Tina said nothing, let herself be a sounding board.

"I just don't care anymore." He turned to her. "Ah, Tina, that's such a lie. I care. Of course I do. But I just can't give him anything of myself. I can't do it."

Tina rubbed his shoulder, circular movements, a light touch. "Think about forgiving him."

"No." His voice was firm.

"Just think about it."

He turned away and she heard his breath catch. She cupped herself around him, arms around his waist. "It's okay, Adam."

He squeezed her hand hard, hard. "He hates what I'm doing, thinks I'm wasting my time."

"He didn't say that."

"He's said it before, plenty of times."

"He's wrong, Adam. You're doing so much good, helping so many kids. Surely you know that."

"Am I? Yeah, I guess I am. But I wish *he'd* think so. I hate his guts, but I want him to *approve* of me." His voice rose. "Am I being childish?"

"Of course not," she said quietly. "We all want

our parents' approval. Maybe it's more important to some than to others.''

They lay in silence, absorbed in their own thoughts. Tina's gaze went to the picture of her father on the dresser. Though she'd had plenty of disagreements with him, she always felt assured of his love. Because Tina had a "legitimate" job and had eased away from her "goddamn subversive protest activities," the tension had gone out of their relationship. They were friends. In fact, recently the Mighty Mike, who was *never* wrong, had even admitted to her that the Vietnam war might have been a mistake; an admission which, instead of making him appear humble, had actually served to ennoble him. Now she felt another tug of homesickness. She needed a sense of stability. She had had that in Michigan; roots. But lots of people started their own roots in distant places. Her own parents had done it. She could do it in Washington, with Adam. If only he were willing.

Adam's hands wandered idly over her body and they made sweet, urgent love. He seemed to need her tonight more than ever. Tired from the day's events, she soon fell asleep. When she sensed Adam easing himself out of bed, she awakened. She heard him rustle into his jeans. "Where are you going?" she mumbled.

"Can't sleep, sweets. I'm going home."

"If we were married, you wouldn't have to leave. We'd be home together." She hadn't meant to say that. It slipped out.

He ran his fingers through his hair, a weary expression on his face. "Don't start."

Okay. Now wasn't the time. But soon. "I'll see you tomorrow. I promised some of the kids that I'd help with the garden."

He smiled and left Tina to herself. How many times had this happened? Too many to count. *Don't start,* he'd said. There was hardly any point to bringing up marriage again. If he wanted marriage, he'd say so; he certainly knew how she felt.

Tina pulled his pillow to her and hugged it tightly. It was suddenly very clear. There would be no wedding. And she would have to make a decision and this time stick with it. She'd always vacillated in the past, and her resolutions fell by the wayside in the wake of Adam's powerful allure, his proclamations of love. She sobbed into the pillow for several moments, then blew her nose and dried her tears. It was time for resolve. She was almost thirty, *almost thirty!* And still unmarried. While Ann's twins had already passed their fifteenth birthday. Time to move on.

17

As morning sunlight filtered through the bedroom curtains, Brian, wearing only briefs, lit the incense burner on his dresser, then kicked back the decorator spread and lay on his bed. He lit a joint and savored the smoke with a half-open mouth for several seconds. A sombrero and serape, mementos from a family trip to Mexico, were draped on a bentwood clothes stand. Reaching down, he picked up a shoe and tossed it at the straw hat, knocking it off its perch. "Good shot," he said aloud.

He had an algebra test today that he wasn't prepared for. His mother hadn't quite bought his story of an upset stomach. She'd placed a cool hand on his forehead and pursed her lips. He'd turned on his side, averting her scrutiny. She left saying she'd just check out a few problems at one of her shops and return shortly.

He had to be more careful. She'd seen a roach clip on his key chain and wanted to know what it was. "It's just decoration," he'd answered, and fortunately her attention was diverted and the subject was dropped.

Matt warned him to be careful, said he'd get caught, tried to lecture him on the dangers. But his brother wouldn't fink on him. He could be trusted. Maybe. Lately he'd been lecturing and nagging and they'd drifted toward different friends. There was so much shit between them. Brian hated that.

It wasn't that Matt was smarter, or better, it was

that he, Brian, resented the competition, the comparison; he hung back and didn't know why. To avoid failure? His brother succeeded effortlessly at anything he tried, and on the rare occasions when he failed, it didn't seem to matter so much. Matt took setbacks in his stride and ignored his failures, while Brian agonized over his. And yet . . . and yet . . . he loved his brother and was proud of his accomplishments. In some strange way he felt as though Matt's successes were his own.

They were identical—their father's height and build, their grandfather's dark *brooding* (his mother's description) Italian eyes in longish faces. The same, except for, as one of Matt's more poetic girlfriends had observed, an eager optimism in Matt's eyes. To be more precise, Matt saw and expected good in everything and everyone, while Brian was realistic. Life was often shitty.

For a long time he and Matt were a pair, two halves of a whole. But recently Brian had tried to separate and found it wasn't as simple as, say, cutting an apple in half.

Brian took another toke, holding it. He'd have to put it out and open the windows. His mother would be back soon; she was worried about him. He wished he could turn off his thoughts of Matt. They shared the same genes, shouldn't they share the same attitudes? Or was he, Brian, more like his father, Matt more like his mother? What was his father *really* like? Brian remembered camping trips when they were all younger, remembered his father teaching him to swim, to row, to swing on a vine. He smiled, remembering the Tarzan yell. His father, he was well aware, was not perfect, he was often distant, often unavailable, even when he was present. But he was always somewhere in the periphery of their lives. They had been a family back then, a unit. He was generous, too, if not with his

time, at least with his money. Shit. Brian didn't want
his goddamn money.

Everything had changed with the divorce. When it
happened he felt like he'd been hit in the gut. Matt
had warned him it was coming, had sensed their parents were in trouble, but Brian wouldn't believe it. His
mother was different now. So was his father. They used
to have a sort of buddy relationship when he was a
kid, but not anymore. No, really, his father had
changed long before the divorce.

The divorce didn't seem to bother Matt as much.
But Matt was always more of a social guy, busy with
sports and hobbies and, of course, girls. Brian didn't
have Matt's flair. He often settled for his brother's
castoffs, seconds. Like Tricia. She had a thing for
Matt, but he wasn't interested, so she hung around
Brian just to be near Matt.

His world had turned shitty. His father didn't call
very often now, like he did at first. And when he did
call, they didn't have much to say to each other. The
three boys were supposed to spend time with their father, but they often made excuses, excuses which were
intended (at least in Brian's case) as a sort of punish-
ment. *See what you did, you asshole? We wouldn't
have problems if we were all together.*

He wanted things back the way they were. But he
knew that was impossible. Even if his parents reunited
(and his mother vehemently assured him that wouldn't
happen), nothing would be the same. Now he was
hearing his father had a girlfriend. Brian punched his
pillow. His father with a *bimbo!* He couldn't imagine
it, although the old man had tried getting "with it,"
wearing a fringed vest and letting his hair touch his
collar—just barely; he didn't want to step too far out
of his role. At his age he looked ludicrous, like a
banker at a masquerade. Worse, it was embarrassing.
Other than that brief walk on the wild side with his
clothes and hair, his father, and mother too, were to-

tally establishment. Witness the house they lived in, the furniture they bought; conservative, establishment. *Never trust anyone over thirty!*

Carefully he pinched the joint, wrapped it in a tissue, and placed it in a cut-out square of a book. He'd seen that trick in a movie.

He pushed away hair that hung perpetually in front of his eyes. His mother asked politely that he have his hair cut. He agreed, just as politely. But it stayed long. His father, not so politely, said he'd give him twenty bucks if he'd get his hair cut, that he looked like a goddamn hippie. Brian smiled.

He got up and jammed his legs into a pair of Levi's which were ripped at the knees and had a miniature American flag sewn on the seat, another bone of contention. *You have* perfectly *good pants in your closet. Why don't you wear those?* Because they're so conservative, Mom. Because rips and patches are a status symbol. Which, his mother claimed, was evidence of how convoluted the world had become.

He heard the front door open and his mother's tread on the steps. She knocked, then opened the door and peeked in. "Are you better?" Her smile was full of concern.

"Yeah."

"Then you can catch your last two classes, at least. Come on, I'll drive you."

"I'm not feeling *that* good."

She leveled a look at him, then entered the room and sniffed. "What's that smell?"

"Incense."

"It's awful. Brian, what's wrong?" She reached out to touch him, but he moved away and shrugged.

"Look, if something's wrong, I want to know about it."

"Nothing's wrong."

"If you're sick, that's one thing, but—"

"I'm not sick. It was just a stomachache. It's better

now." He took a textbook from his desk. Better to go to class than put up with more of his mother's bull. "Okay, I'm ready."

"Have you eaten?"

"Yeah," he lied.

At the beige-brick school building he hopped out.

"Brian, are you sure you're all right?"

He frowned in annoyance and waved her away.

After classes he jammed books into his locker and twisted the knob.

"Hey, man, where you been?" A tall thin boy with an acned chin punched Brian's shoulder.

"Legs! I skipped this morning. What's happening?"

"Party at my house tonight. The folks are going out." He bent his head and mumbled in the direction of Brian's ear, "I've got some really good stuff. Be there. Eight o'clock." He spun away before Brian could reply.

Good stuff. He'd been talking about getting *good stuff* for several weeks now. Acid? Hash? Speed? Maybe just Acapulco Gold.

Ann had been home a week and Scott hadn't called. Her heart tripped whenever the phone rang, but it was never him. Yet she'd been so sure, *so sure* he'd experienced the same vibrations, the same excitement as she. Now she felt foolish and a bit guilty about her sensual response to him. A man's attitude toward sex was different from a woman's. For her it had been exhilarating and heady, but more than that, her heart was involved. As she recalled *that* night in Florence and the euphoria that it produced, a warm rush invaded her and she wanted Scott at this very moment. She shook her head ruefully. He was very suave. He probably made love to every woman he took out. Wasn't that the way it was these days? Free love. Go with the flow. If it feels good, do it. But perhaps he

had the same thoughts about her, that she was easy.
She hadn't been reluctant; he hadn't exactly seduced
her.

Okay, so it was a holiday romance, best forgotten.
If only forgetting were as easy as saying the words.
She had even seen her gynecologist for a birth-control-
pill prescription. That was how far from the fold she'd
fallen!

When the phone rang after she'd returned from work,
Matt called out, "It's for you, Mom."

"It isn't easy getting hold of you. Your phone's always busy."

Scott! Ann flushed with pleasure. "Teenagers. You
know how they are."

"I've been thinking about you."

"I was hoping you'd call."

"Well . . . I wanted to, but on the other hand, I sort
of wanted to see how long I could hold out."

"That's . . . interesting. Why?"

"I don't know. I guess because it all happened so
quickly. It sort of put me in a tailspin. I had to think
about what was going on in my life. This kind of thing
doesn't happen to me very often."

Ann smiled. "I thought maybe moonlight romances
were a routine thing for you."

"Not hardly." A little laugh. "Can I take you to
dinner? Saturday?"

"Yes, that would be wonderful."

"I'll pick you up at seven."

"Why don't I meet you?" She wasn't ready to spring
a man on the boys, especially a man she cared about.

After dinner Brian told his mother he was going to
Legs's house to study. Matt glared at him but said
nothing. Though his mother seemed to like Legs—that
nice polite boy, she called him—she wore that tight-
lipped look of distrust that he hated. Brian would be
glad when this school year was over. Maybe he'd look

for a job, get some independence, some of his own bread. Next year he'd be sixteen and could get his driver's license.

At Legs's house the stereo in the family room was blasting loud, the way he liked it, with an Alice Cooper record.

Mark was already there, slapping his thighs to the driving beat. Pushing wheat-colored hair from his eyes, he greeted Brian from a wicker chair in the neat plant-filled room. Mark fingered his sparse mustache. Alex, a swarthy-looking seventeen-year-old, came in on Brian's heels. Legs was in the kitchen, mumbling things to himself. Moments later he strolled in with four Cokes.

"Hey, where's the stuff, man?" Mark asked.

"It's here, in the Cokes."

"No shit. What is it?"

"Mesc."

Alex and Mark grinned, pleased, but Brian wasn't sure what mesc was exactly. He thought it was related to LSD. "Far-out, man."

"Try it," Alex urged.

Brian grabbed the Coke bottle and hesitated for a moment.

"You're not chickening out, are you?" Alex said with a sort of sneer.

Brian put the bottle to his mouth and chugged. Before long the olive-green shag carpet began to shift and change into shades of blues and purples and reds. In a psychedelic blur it melted into a field of wildflowers, orange and yellow. He heard a hearty belly laugh and realized it was coming from him, and he couldn't stop. It felt as if he were outside himself. Ideas and wisdom and understanding—perfect profound understanding—of the universe, of the planets, of God, were his. He tried to explain it to Mark, who sat beside him in a blurry liquid outline, but couldn't find the words. Mark's body swayed, slithered, backward and forward, side to side. Brian heard himself babbling, then stopped trying to talk at all. Tears dripped from his eyes. It was too beautiful, too mystical; it was electrifying. The music swirled around him and each note had perfect clarity. He could almost touch and feel the notes as they rippled through the air around his head. He was inventing the music chord by chord, word by word, directing the instruments. He was so happy! So happy! The street sounds of tires against asphalt, a child wailing, seemed inside the room, inside his head. He didn't know how long it went on, whether minutes or hours. His head reeled with new sensations. Slowly his focus returned, the brilliance muted. He began coming down.

"It was like, wow," Legs said, his long limbs wavering in front of Brian's eyes. "It was great."

"Great, man," Alex said, a simpleminded smile on his childish face. "I didn't want to come down."

Only Mark was quiet. His round brown eyes looked fearful.

Legs punched his arm. "Hey, man, what's wrong?"

"I dunno," he mumbled. "It was weird. They were after me."

Brian said, "Who was after you?"

"I dunno. Things." He made a face. "Weird things with tentacles and strange faces."

"A bad trip," Alex said.

Legs looked nervous. He glanced at the Regulator clock above the fireplace. "Christ, it's after midnight. You guys gotta go now. My parents are due home. My old man, he'd kill me—"

"How the hell am I going to get home?" Alex said.

Brian wondered the same. His legs were rubbery, his head mush. He wanted to get home before his mother. If she thought he was into dope she'd kill him and ask questions later. Brian looked at Mark, who seemed to be shrinking into a corner. "You okay?"

"Yeah, yeah." But his voice was unconvincing.

Alex and Brian helped him up. "Maybe we should walk with Mark," Brian said.

Mark shrugged off the boys' hands. "I'm okay." He staggered out the door with Alex and Brian following.

"We're coming with you," Brian said, slurring his words. He nudged Alex and laughed. "Listen to me. Ha, ha, ha, ha." Alex guffawed along with him. The noisy laughter sounded hollow in the still night air as the three boys made their way toward Mark's house.

Brian had no memory of how he got home. The house was dark when he strolled up the walk. He peered into the garage and breathed a sigh of relief. His mother's car wasn't there. She'd gone somewhere with Frieda. His uneven tread was soft on the plush stairway carpeting, both hands clinging for support on the polished handrail. He didn't want to wake Matt. Though he'd love to tell his brother of his fantastic trip, he didn't dare. Head pounding, he dropped into bed and for several moments was trapped between elation and guilt. Now he really knew what "high" meant.

Ann was sorry she'd left the boys tonight. The movie was boring and she couldn't concentrate on Frieda's chatter about the new man she was seeing. Her own thoughts were on her upcoming date with Scott.

Back home her heels tapped noisily on the polished wood foyer floor and she leaned against the wall to slip them off. Upstairs she peeked into Teddy's bedroom. Gently she removed his thumb from his mouth, then leaned down and kissed his pink sleep-warm cheek. He stirred and smiled and she closed the door softly and went to Matt's room, where Matt, in too-short pajamas (they grew so quickly) was sprawled across the bed, the bedclothes in disarray. She tugged the sheet free and lifted it to his shoulders. Brian's room was last. His breathing was deep and noisy and his brow held a frown. He looked so young and innocent in his shorts and T-shirt. Pausing by his bed, she sniffed, then bent closer and sniffed again, hating herself for her suspicion.

She didn't quite trust Brian's friends, although they seemed nice enough, polite and well-mannered. Most of them, like Brian, wore their hair long and managed to look seedy in spite of being from stable families. They were making a statement, she supposed. Against authority, against "the establishment." Hopefully, it was a phase they'd all get over soon. Matt was no aid whatsoever in helping her understand Brian, clamming up whenever she wanted to talk about him. That twin-loyalty thing. But she had other things on her mind. Namely, Scott. She couldn't wait to see him.

On Saturday Scott was waiting at the restaurant and rose to greet her with a warm hug and an electric smile. The restaurant, done in warm woods and exposed brick, had colored glass windows that reminded Ann of church. The waitress, looking bored, spieled off a list of specials.

They spent the early part of the meal tiptoeing around one another. Ann was somewhat chagrined by her actions in Florence. She thought of the accepted dating pattern as consisting of several meetings during which each discovered facets of the other's personality, rather like peeling an onion to find new layer after layer. All the while there would be more advanced kissing and touching, until, when they were finally sure, the ultimate act of love itself. The ritual was like a play in three acts. The unfolding of events with Scott seemed reversionary; their association had practically begun with Act Three. Now Ann wanted to go back and play out the first two acts. The ground rules were different this time. The setting was not a foreign country but home turf. This was not an exotic, carefree night out, but the preliminary move toward a relationship, a fact unstated but perceived. The conversation was a cat-and-mouse game. She was, after all, a mature woman, the mother of three boys, and a successful businesswoman to boot. He was a divorced bachelor, young and vital, with an apparently good position. A desirable catch. She was a Catholic, he was a WASP (like Martin). There were so many *considerations.* Yet floating over all of that there was this astounding *electricity.*

Scott was telling her about his hobby. He loved old cars, collected them, and described a vintage Packard he stored in a friend's barn. "White sidewalls this thick"—spreading thumb and forefinger—"not the little stripe they have nowadays. A real beauty. You could sit close to each other in those old cars, none of this separation stuff."

The waitress placed their food before them. "Enjoy your meal."

Ann barely ate, toyed with her food, sipped some wine. "Tell me about your work," she prodded.

"I told you I'm a designer, but really I'm an ant in an anthill. Someday there'll be computers doing a lot of our work and some people will be cut out of jobs."

"A computer? I can't imagine that."

"Sure. Everyone will have one. Even you."

"Why would I need a computer?"

"For everything. Orders, accounting, everything."

"You must be a visionary."

"No. Just pragmatic."

She wanted the dinner to end so they could be alone together. As he spoke, she imagined his hands on her body, his lips on hers. *How did a nice girl like me get so damn sexy?* Was he thinking what she was thinking? She obviously couldn't invite Scott to her home tonight. Would they go to his apartment?

"Leave your car here," he instructed when they left the restaurant.

As he helped her into his Cadillac, Ann asked, "Where are we going?"

"My place." He grinned. "I'll show you my paintings. A new spin on an old line."

His Bloomfield Hills apartment was modern, glass and chrome, a little impersonal, she thought. He gave her a tour, then went to the kitchenette for wineglasses while she investigated the living area. Interesting pictures—Ansel Adams photographs and other prints and oils she didn't recognize—filled one wall in the dining area.

"These are mine," he said modestly, pointing to a grouping of oils.

She remembered Scott had said he was an artist. "You painted them or you own them?"

"I painted them." He handed her a glass of chardonnay.

She admired the splashes of primary colors in one painting, muted mauves and grays in another. "Very nice. I'm not an art aficionado, but, as the saying goes, I know what I like."

"I know what I like too." His eyes met hers, flustering her, warming her.

She sat on a gray upholstered chair, crossing her legs at the ankles neatly the way nice girls were taught. Scott watched her every move with a smile, then held out his hand. She took it and let him lead her into his bedroom.

"I think we're going to have a relationship," she said.

"At the very least," he said.

So Ann had a boyfriend. Tina smiled, refilled her coffee cup, and finished reading the long letter from her sister, a letter that, judging from the tone and enthusiasm, reflected her complete emotional recovery. Ann had put the divorce behind her and was seeing a man on a regular basis, though she neglected to give many details other than his name, Scott. Most likely she was evading. Openness wasn't her long suit.

The letter triggered Tina's homesickness. She was both pleased for and envious of both her sisters. At least *they* were happy. Two out of three ain't bad.

She straightened the kitchen and left for the Beehive. She'd promised to help weed the garden. Nothing had been resolved between her and Adam since their talk a week ago, but Tina had made a decision.

In the garden she donned oversize sunglasses and a tattered straw hat that Cricket had resurrected from the garage, and pitted her hoe against weeds that threatened the cucumber vines. Cricket herself had abandoned the project after a half-hour, with the excuse of getting some lemonade. Tina didn't mind working alone. There was something inspiring about working the earth.

"Having fun?" Adam appeared, slamming the screen door, grinning.

It had been several days since she'd seen him, and again she experienced a pleasurable rush at the sight of him—neat beard and mustache not quite hiding a bright smile, penetrating brown eyes, muscular physique in cut-off jeans.

"I'm getting blisters." She smiled as she propped the hoe against the fence and sat on the bottom step of the porch.

Adam joined her and draped his arm loosely around her shoulder.

"I got a letter from Ann yesterday," Tina said. "I've decided to go home."

"For a week or two?"

"No, longer."

His dark eyes penetrated hers. "How long?"

"I may not come back."

Adam stared at her for several moments, his features suddenly gone slack. "Are you leaving me?"

She drew off her garden gloves finger by finger. "If I thought there was a chance for us, if I thought we'd eventually get married . . . but I don't think that any-more.''

He turned her to face him. For a few seconds he looked vulnerable. She loved that about him, the sudden little-boy look that came over him in emotional moments. Would she ever be able to stop loving him?

"You still think of marriage as the ultimate goal." His words were accusing.

"Okay, so I'm old-fashioned; in fact, I'm almost establishment. That's me, take it or leave it. The problem with you is, you don't want to grow up. You don't want responsibilities. Or at least the responsibilities that go with marriage. You want to be able to duck out at any time.''

"Maybe. Tina, there just aren't many good marriages around. Look at your sister. You thought *that* was a good marriage.''

"It was, at first. Things went wrong.''

He stuffed his hands into his jeans pockets. "Things usually go wrong.''

"I don't care. Marriage is still better than the alternative.'' She rose and stood squarely in front of him. "Look. Let's stop playing games. Do you love me?''

"Of course I love you. You know that.''

She closed her eyes slowly. Did she know that? She didn't know anything for sure anymore. "Will you marry me? In the near future?''

He gave a disdainful laugh and shook his head, as if she were an obstreperous child. "Look, Tina, we've talked about this before. It's unreasonable to make plans—''

She put her hands to her ears. "Stop, stop, stop! I don't want any more of your rationalization. Either we're going to get married within the next year or we're not. Just yes or no!''

"Tina—''

"Yes or no!''

"You're making this difficult. Maybe when—''

" 'Maybe' isn't one of the choices. Christ, Adam! It's no, then, isn't it?''

"Tina, I love you, I want us to be together.''

Her voice dropped an octave and several decibels. "But you don't want to marry me.''

"I don't want to marry anyone! Not now.''

The next day she arranged for a U-Haul. She dialed her mother. "I'm coming home.''

At long last. Coming home.

"I know, there are plenty of other fish in the sea and all that crap, but I'm crazy about that man. I think about him all the time.'' Tina tore a piece of crust from her pizza and stuffed it into her mouth. Sitting on Ann's patio, with a couple of "loaded'' Little Caesar's pizzas, the three sisters discussed Tina's plight.

A large fan whirred, stirring the sticky July air.

Ann pushed away her paper plate. "Maybe he'll come around.''

"I doubt it. In the month since I've been here, he's called me every couple of days: 'Please come back, I miss you, I love you.' But that's it. On his terms.''

"So, did you quit your job in Washington?'' Louise asked.

"Not yet. I'm waiting until the last minute. Hope springs eternal.'' Tina dropped her chin in her hand. "But I did apply for a job locally, at practically every school district within a fifty-mile radius. No go. I suppose I'll have to substitute teach.''

Louise said, "Too bad you can't have my job. I'm thinking of taking a family-care leave. Jon wants me to stay home, and it would give me more time with Rachel. He says it's up to me. But it's getting to be a grind.''

"Lucky you. You've got a great husband, a beautiful house, and a job that you don't need.''

Louise looked almost apologetic. "Did you find an apartment yet, Tina?''

"I'm holding off for a while. As usual, my money's running out. I'm taking a waitress job, nights, starting next week. That'll free me to sub during the day. I can use the extra money." She shook her head ruefully. "It's time I got my act together, right?"

Louise touched Tina's shoulder. "You'll be fine. The right thing will come along."

Her sisters were supportive and sympathetic, but it didn't help her get to sleep at night. Tina lifted her shoulders. "I'll live. I will survive! I am woman! as the song says." But her heart was doubtful. She couldn't stop thinking negatively about her situation. Damn. Get off the subject of Tina and Adam, star-crossed lovers; talk of other things. "Ann, what about Scott? Are we going to meet him? Is this getting serious?"

"No and maybe."

"Come on!"

"No, you're not going to meet him just yet. And maybe *he's* getting serious. I'm not. I've only gone with him a couple of months."

"Oh, great, here we have the reversal of the Tina-Adam situation. Man is willing, woman holds back." Tina shook her head. "It's bizarre."

Ann said, "This is different. I've *been* married. I have children. And I'm through with all that. I don't need to do the motherhood thing all over again. Scott, on the other hand . . . well, he'd like a family."

"Has he said so?"

"Not in so many words."

"Then you don't know for sure," Tina pointed out.

Ann frowned. "I don't even want to *think* about marriage."

Tina said, "You just want to fool around?"

Coloring, Ann rose and lifted the pitcher from the table. "Anyone want more lemonade? Or pop?"

"Not me," Louise said. "Speaking of babies, we've

been trying, but nothing's happening in that department. I'm going to a fertility clinic.''

Ann sat again. ''I hear lots of people are helped by clinics.''

''I hear that the medication causes multiple births,'' Tina said.

''That's fine with me,'' Louise said. ''I'll have my family in one fell swoop. I'm thirty-six years old. Soon it'll be too late for me.''

''Louise, don't be too sure you want a child,'' Ann said. ''You have Rachel. Kids are great until they turn into teenagers. Then you've got trouble.''

Louise said, ''Oh, Ann, yours are fine. Or are they?''

Ann's eyebrows lifted, but before she could reply, Matthew burst through the gate and did a handspring over the railing.

''What an athlete!'' Tina said. ''Look at this kid's muscles.''

''Hey, Aunt Tina, Aunt Louise.'' Matthew dropped a kiss on each cheek; then his eyes lit on the table. ''Pizza! Great. Any leftovers?''

Ann said, ''Sure. How was tennis practice?''

''Okay.''

''Where's your brother?''

''Bri went to Alex's house.''

''Oh.'' Ann's mouth turned downward at the corners.

''He'll be home soon,'' Matt assured her.

''Don't get too full; Flora left some cannoli.''

The others groaned, ''Oh, no,'' and ''Good-bye, diet.''

With Matt at the table, the conversation turned to sports and school.

Tina touched the phone. Should she call Adam? It had been over a week since he'd called. Was he giving up?

The thing to do was make it a clean break, a surgical cut, one neat slice and it's over. Her eyes welled up with tears. If only it were that easy. *Don't think about him. Think of something else.* She picked up her calendar and made notations for the next day. July had come so quickly. She bit her lower lip. Her period was late. By several days. The last one had been late too, she reassured herself; she'd just come off the pill. But she'd always been irregular before taking the pill. Not to worry. In fact she felt a bit crampy right now. Probably by tomorrow she'd be in the clear.

She hugged the pillow close. *Good night, Adam, wherever you may be. I hope you're thinking of me . . . and kicking yourself for letting the best thing in your life get away.*

18

The living room of Tina's small apartment took only minutes to straighten. She consulted her list. "Buy deterg," "do laund," "gyn at 2." She postponed the "gyn" as long as possible, hoping the welcome red flow would appear. It used to be called "the curse," but not having it was an even worse curse.

Since there wasn't time for a nap, a quick cup of tea would have to do, though nothing seemed to perk her up lately. Another symptom? Her fatigue could be due to the late hours at the restaurant. Since she'd started substitute teaching, she limited her waitressing to weekends, but she was still exhausted.

That afternoon she lay on the hard table in the examining room, hugging the skimpy paper wrapper close around her. She glanced at the baby-blue walls covered haphazardly with pictures of happy cherubic infants. Adorable babies. But Tina didn't want a baby. She *was* a baby. She hated needles and pain and waking up early. She hated the thought of diaper changing and spit-up and endless laundry and sleepless nights—though God knew she'd had plenty of those lately. She remembered her sympathy for Ann when she'd gone through all that.

But undoubtedly her fears would be proved groundless. The queasy tummy was probably the flu; the missed menses, two now, were due to her system's adjustment to withdrawal of the pill. Prior to taking the pill her periods had been erratic, skipping weeks or a month. And nerves could certainly be a factor. Her emotional life had not been too stable of late.

Dr. Iris Marchand, tall and thin with a quick smile and exuding energy, whisked into the room. She swept wispy gray hair behind her ear as she looked at the file, then at Tina, then back.

"You're thirty?"

"Next month, October." Thirty. The watershed year. The age that separates *them* from *us*. Now she would be on the other side.

The doctor asked a few pertinent questions, nodding at answers, then proceeded with the examination.

She listened to Tina's chest, looked down her throat, into her ears, pulled down her lower eyelids, peering. Tina closed her eyes during the rest of it, barely absorbing the doctor's intermittent comments. *Blood pressure's good. Um-hm. Good reflexes. Take a deep breath. Um-hm. Again. This won't hurt, but my hands are cold. Um-hm.*

Just finish, please, get it over with.

Finally the doctor said, "All through," and helped her to a sitting position. "You can get dressed, Tina, and meet me in my office."

Tina blanched. She wanted to ask questions, but her mouth wouldn't form the words: *Just yes or no, please* PLEASE.

The doctor left and Tina's fingers fumbled with her clothing. The brassiere hooks were stubborn. Had her breasts grown larger? *That* wasn't due to nerves, was it?

In the doctor's office she perched on the edge of a leather armchair, gripping the arms, while the doctor jotted information on a chart. Several diplomas hung on the wall behind her, attesting to her credentials. Tina glanced at the desk, overflowing with files and papers and a silver-framed picture of a man and two teenage girls, one of whom looked identical to Dr. Marchand.

The doctor looked up and smiled. "My family." Closing the file, she said, "Our preliminary tests show that you're pregnant, Tina."

Tina's heart stopped beating, her mouth dried up.

"We'll have the results of the other tests in a day or two, but I believe there's little doubt." The doctor tried again for a smile, but failed. "I'd say you're almost twelve weeks."

Tina swallowed and forced the words, "Twelve weeks?"

"Um-hm. You're unmarried, then, Tina?" The doctor remained passive, but Tina imagined her disapproval.

"Yes." Her voice was barely a whisper.

"Well." She steepled her fingers and arched her brows. "Perhaps you plan on getting married?"

Tina shook her head, not trusting her voice.

Dr. Marchand sighed. "I don't know what your intentions are, but maybe you'll want to see a counselor. I can recommend a clinic and—"

Tina shook her head. *I'm falling to pieces inside. Just let me go now so I can collapse. Maybe I'll be lucky and die.*

The doctor's eyes shifted away uncomfortably. "There are alternative measures which I don't perform, which are perfectly legal now. You can see my nurse about that."

Alternative measures. Abortion. Legal, of course, but moral? The doctor spoke on, but Tina didn't hear a word. Finally, obviously finished, the doctor stood and urged a prescription on her. "Are you all right, Tina?"

She nodded. *Please God make it go away maybe she's wrong I don't deserve this I've been stupid sure but not really bad I'll do good works and penance I'll go to church I'll volunteer at the nursing home I'll do anything anything but please please please please make this nightmare go away.*

She pushed herself from the chair, straightened her shoulders, and turned to go.

The doctor put her hand on Tina's arm, saying, "Unless you decide to terminate the pregnancy, I'll see you in a month."

It was all Tina could do to keep from bursting into tears. At the desk she wrote out a check and the nurse handed her a receipt and a list of doctors. Alternative measures. She stuffed the papers in her purse and moved through the waiting room, past women in progressive stages of pregnancy. Were they staring at her? Were they thinking: *There goes an unwed mother.* Unwed mother! She would bring shame and disgrace upon her parents, upon her sisters. How could she possibly tell them?

Safely inside her car, she crossed her arms on the steering wheel and dropped her head heavily. The tears flooded her eyes, ran down her face; her shoulders shuddered and heaved. *Oh, Adam, look what you've done.*

For the next several days Tina felt as though she were operating on automatic pilot, performing all necessary functions while her brain hammered away on this major unsolvable problem of two cells that had interacted successfully to begin a new life. If only there was someone to whom she could talk, to unburden herself, but aside from Adam—and he was out of the question—no one would understand her dilemma. She couldn't tell her sisters or her parents, not yet.

Finally she concluded she was unprepared physically, emotionally, and financially to birth and raise a child. She came to this decision rationally without letting her runaway emotions interfere.

A week later she sat in a soft leather chair across

from Dr. Giles, the first name on the list from Dr. Marchand's nurse. The doctor was thin to the point of gauntness, with black hair hanging to his collar and large glasses that overpowered his narrow face. He kept talking about *the fetus*, as if it were a *thing* and not an organism that was living and growing moment by moment. Tina envisioned the cells forming and shaping and changing, and shook away the thought. Dr. Giles was right. It was only a fetus, shrimp-shaped, unfeatured, unlimbed. Better to think of it in that way. But her thoughts forced themselves upon her: *not a fetus, but a baby, living and growing, composed completely of Adam's and my genes, and including a code from both of our lineages, traced backward from ancestor to ancestor to ancestor, probably to Adam and Eve and even further, to the very first thought-organism.* It was mind-boggling. That meant everyone was connected. It meant she was connected to Dr. Giles, who was looking at her expectantly.

She blinked. "I'm sorry, I wasn't listening."

"I said, for many people, abortion is a viable alternative. Have you thought about it thoroughly? Are you sure you want to consider it?"

Tina swallowed hard. *Just a fetus.* "Yes."

She tried to focus on his words as he described the procedure: ". . . basically a D and C . . . perfectly safe . . . I'll give you Valium, just to make you comfortable . . . a vacuum aspirator . . ." He pointed to a picture in a leaflet on his desk.

Tina's eyes focused on the aspirator, the implement of death. No, not death, it's only a fetus. But *my* fetus, *mine and Adam's.*

"Shall we make an appointment, then?"

"Yes. As soon as possible."

"Next Monday, then, two o'clock? My nurse will make sure that time is available and call you." He rose and extended his hand. "See my nurse for instructions and call if you have any problems."

Have any problems? As if this is not a major problem.

He hadn't smiled, not once. They were strangers, with absolutely no bond to each other, yet they were partners in this . . . this act. Shouldn't they acknowledge that fact in some way?

That night she dreamt. She and her sisters were young and the family was at the seaside. Dark clouds hovered and the sea churned up huge waves. Somehow Ann, though she was only a girl, shepherded her three boys away from the roiling surf. Another child appeared from nowhere and Tina knew it was her job to protect that child from entering the water, but she felt paralyzed and couldn't compel her legs forward, though she ached with the pain of trying. Her parents and sisters urged her to do her duty, and her mother cried out, tears streaming from her eyes, but Tina's legs refused to move. Someone came from out of a shadow, a man, and pulled her upright, pushing her forward, to no avail. She fell back upon the sand. Finally the child, who had entered the water and was about to be engulfed by a huge wave, turned and ran back to the shore, collapsing tearfully in a heap on the wet sand.

Tina awakened in a cold sweat. She hated Adam, *hated* him for putting this burden on her. Yet, what would he say if she confronted him? Out of duty, he'd marry her. Adam, lover of life, lover of children, wouldn't let her proceed with this deed. But Adam was not here and the choice was not his, but hers alone. Meanwhile, this small bunch of cells was multiplying and developing inside her, each day becoming more of what it would ultimately be. She buried her head in the pillow and cried.

Monday dawned befittingly wet and cold. Tina had called on an old school friend, Gena, a nurse, to come with her. They'd kept contact sporadically, mostly by phone, during the past years, yet retained that close connection "best friends" from childhood often have. Gena had been properly sympathetic, nonrecriminatory, and supportive. Now, when Tina joined her in the car, she said, "Are you absolutely sure you want to do this?"

Tina bit her lip. "Did you have to say that?"

"Tina, it's a big step and there's no going back after it's over." She pushed a frond of pale bangs from her forehead and drummed her fingers on the steering wheel.

Tina stared straight ahead. "I'm sure. Drive."

"It's not too late to change your mind. Think of the psychological implications for a nice Catholic girl like you."

"Christ, Gena, I don't need this now. Don't you think I've hashed this all out a million times in my mind?"

"Okay, then. Let's go."

At the hospital she answered questions at the counter and watched horror-stricken as the clerk wrote "unwanted pregnancy." *No, it isn't exactly that I don't want it, it's just that I'm not married and the timing is wrong and . . .*

A thin freckled nurse picked up her chart. "Come this way, Mrs. Marcassa."

"Ms." she said, *"Ms.* Marcassa."

"What?"

"Never mind." It didn't really matter.

She was shown to a small room. "Undress and put on this gown, and I'll be right back."

Tina's stomach heaved. "I . . . I'm going to throw up."

"Quick, here's the bathroom." The nurse pulled her along to a lavatory two rooms down the hall.

She retched up a small amount of bile. There was nothing in her stomach but water.

"Nerves," the nurse said, helping her back to the room. "We'll give you something that will relax you. Get changed and I'll be back in a minute."

Tina removed her sweater, then her shoes. A mounting sense of despair engulfed her. She pressed her hands against her stomach, trying to feel something through the fabric.

"Ready?" the nurse said, opening the door a crack. "Want some help, dear?"

Tina shook her head.

"I'll give you a minute."

Tina sat weakly in the wooden chair, hunched over, mouth dry, hands shaking, recalling her dream, the crying child on the shore.

When the nurse looked in again, Tina was putting on her sweater. "I'm sorry," Tina said. "I changed my mind."

Looking bewildered, the nurse just stared for a moment, then regained her composure. "Many women feel confused and—"

"I'm not confused. Not any longer." Tina slipped into her shoes and moved past the nurse. "Tell the doctor I'm very sorry. Actually, I'm not sorry, but it's too bad he had to waste his time and everything. Goodbye."

She walked to the waiting room with more verve than she'd felt in a long time. Gena, reading a magazine, looked up with a perplexed frown. "What . . . ?"

"I changed my mind. Let's go."

Outside the hospital doors, Tina and Gena hugged, both crying. "I'm glad, Tina, I'm really glad."

"So am I."

Tina loved her mother's kitchen. It always smelled of garlic and spices, and brewing coffee. She pushed back yellow organdy curtains to let in sunlight, then sat at the table. Her mother bustled about, slicing homemade coffee cake, setting out butter. Running her finger around the rim of her coffee cup, Tina said, "Sit down, Ma. I have to tell you something." This would be the most difficult hurdle of all. She bit her lower lip to stop its trembling.

Raising questioning eyebrows, Chiara refilled their cups, then sat.

Tina had chosen a time when her father was absent. She didn't have the courage to tell them both at once. Now she decided on the direct approach. Bam! Get it out and over with. She closed her eyes and blurted, "I'm pregnant."

Her mother stared for a moment, then uttered an agonized sound and lifted her hands into the air. "I knew something was wrong, I knew it! You looked so pale, then you stayed away and hardly talked to me when I called. Oh, Tina, Tina, how could this happen?"

"It happens." Tina had steeled herself for her mother's reaction, but now she couldn't keep her chin from quivering, her eyes from tearing.

"How many months?"

"Four and a half." The baby stirred in corroboration and Tina placed protective hands against her slight swell. She'd waited until the last possible moment—until the small mound was unmistakable—to break the news.

"Oh, my God, I can't believe it. It's that man, that Adam in Washington, isn't it?"

Tina bit her lip and looked away.

"Have you told him?"

"No."

"When are you going to tell him?"

Tina took a deep breath. "I'm not."

"What? You're not going to tell him?"

"No! He's not to know."

"Are you crazy? He's the father! He has a responsibility to take care of you and this child, he—"

"I don't want him to know, and if anyone tries to contact him, I'll . . . I'll . . . well, I don't know what I'll do." She dropped her hands limply in her lap.

Her mother's hand went to her forehead and she lapsed into comforting Italian, moaning, *"Madonna, Madonna, que se fatte?"* She looked up suddenly, as if a thought had struck her.

"You're not thinking of . . . of doing away with . . . ?"

"Of course not." Tina's voice was low, controlled, although her emotional turmoil was almost overwhelming. "I intend to have this child."

"Yes, you must have it. If you do something"—she closed her eyes as if reliving a painful memory— "you'll live with remorse the rest of your life." She went to Tina and took her hand. "Listen to me, Tina. I know what's best. You must tell him."

"Ma, if he cared for me, he would have married me before this."

"He'll do the right thing, give him a chance to decide."

"You don't understand. I asked him to marry me. More than once. He graciously declined. If he found out about the baby, he would marry me; he's an honorable man. But it's as though I planned it, as though I tricked him." She looked down at her tightly clenched hands and bit her lower lip to stop its quivering. "Is that what you want for me? A shotgun wedding?"

"Yes, if that's the way it has to be. It won't be the first time in history. It's better than being an unmarried woman with an illegitimate child."

"I won't have him marry me, then resent it the rest of his life."

"Madre di Dio! How will you support this child?"

"I'll manage."

Her mother put her face in her hands and began

crying, invoking God's help, along with the Blessed Virgin and all the saints and angels. Tina had already tried all that. It didn't work.

Finally Chiara dried her tears, took a deep breath, and rose majestically. "All right. We must make plans."

Tina rested a moment in the restaurant kitchen. The King's Arms was rather posh, with pseudo-English-pub decor and peasant-girl uniforms for the waitresses. Tina had managed to get a uniform two sizes larger than her normal one to accommodate her six-month-pregnant body. She arched her back against a sudden movement of elbow or foot. "Okay, Rebel, settle down," she murmured. She was never alone; always there was this growing child within her whom she'd begun to think of as a miniature Adam. She'd almost adjusted to the notion of motherhood. Ann, after recovering from her shock, was supportive, offering baby equipment she'd stored in her basement. "By the time I have grandchildren, this stuff'll all be obsolete anyway," she'd said. Louise had cried and uncharacteristically said, "Why couldn't it be me?"

Tina's ankles were swollen, her feet hurt, and she was just plain tired. With the added burden of her pregnancy, she wouldn't be able to waitress much longer. It was only a matter of time before she'd be too bulky to get between the tables. At least when she taught, she could sit at her desk part of the time. Fortunately she had a subbing assignment almost every day. She let her coworkers think she was married. Going from school to school as she did, no one knew or cared. Not so long ago a pregnant woman wasn't allowed to teach; even in her own mother's day it was looked upon as a condition to be hidden from public view as much as possible.

Jackson, the short rotund manager, nudged her, saying kindly, "You okay, kid?"

She nodded, grateful for his concern. "Just taking a rest."

"Better get a move on, kid."

A couple had settled at a table in her station. She ambled over and settled her face into a smile. "Are you ready to order?" she said automatically, whipping out her pad.

"Tina!"

She stared for a moment at the attractive man who'd called her name. "Max? Is it you? My God, I hardly recognized you. You look like a . . . a corporate lawyer or something."

He laughed. "Not even close."

"I never thought I'd see you in a suit." She rather liked the new look.

"Yeah, well, we all change. Look at you. Last I heard, you were in Washington, teaching."

"I was. I came back last June. Now I'm substitute-teaching and working here part-time."

"It's just great seeing you." He kept nodding and smiling.

The woman opposite, looking annoyed, cleared her throat.

"Sorry," Max said. "Clare Treadwell, this is an old friend, Tina Marcassa."

"Nice to meet you, Clare. Max and I fought a war together."

Clare smiled archly. "I'm famished. Let's order, Max."

Max kept his eyes on Tina while she took their orders. She smiled, remembering the crush he'd had on her. But that was another century. It was hard to believe he'd changed so drastically, hair shorn, conservative suit, neat tie. But the grin that almost closed his gray eyes, the energy, the self-containment—that was all still in evidence. When she returned a little later to place steaming plates before them, she kept chatter to a minimum, aware of Clare's icy glare.

An hour later Tina was standing in back by the kitchen totaling a bill, when Max sidled up next to her.

"God, it was great seeing you again, Tina. You look wonderful. Different, but wonderful."

Did "different" mean he'd noticed the bulge under her loose uniform? How would he feel about that?

"We should get together sometime. Soon." Max pressed a card into her hand. "Will you call me?"

"Sure." She wouldn't call. What was the point?

Finally the restaurant emptied out. As she put on her coat, Jackson stopped her, handing her a pay envelope. "Next week'll be your last, Tina. I hate to do it, you've been a good worker, but . . ." He ran nervous fingers through his thinning hair.

"It's okay, I understand. I was going to throw in the towel soon anyway."

"After it's all over"—his eyes slid uneasily over her abdomen—"and you're recovered, you know you're welcome to come back. Just give me a call. I'll fire someone and put you on."

She laughed. "You don't want to do that." She kissed his cheek and pressed an index finger to his chest. "I'll keep in touch."

A few days later Max called, sounding slightly remonstrative. "I thought you'd call me."

"I've been busy, Max. So, how've you been? Your card said you work for Noble, Gordon, and Fitzpatrick."

"Yeah, NGF, an advertising firm. We're small but mighty. I'm in the creative department."

"Who would've thought. Still, I suppose that suits you. We all kind of finked out, didn't we?"

"Or grew up."

"It was fun, though, while it lasted."

"It was great. What memories we'll have when we

get old." Max laughed. "You're not married or anything, are you? I didn't notice a ring."

"No, I'm single. And alone." Might as well be clear.

"Let me take you to dinner tonight and we'll reminisce."

This was the third day of a two-week subbing stint, and after correcting a stack of math papers, she longed for a bath and bed. "I'm awfully tired." She massaged the back of her neck.

"Then I'll come over for an hour or so, how's that?"

She hesitated for a moment. "Sure, why not?"

A large loose sweater camouflaged her "condition" somewhat. She searched for old records, the Doors, early Stones, Jefferson Airplane.

When Max arrived, they hugged for a long moment. "This is more like the old Max," she said, pointing to his jeans.

He tugged at a lock of Tina's hair. "This used to hang way past your shoulders."

"Ah, what time has wrought." She hung his leather jacket in the closet. "But I suspect we're pretty much the same on the inside."

Max laughed. "I doubt it. Remember how we put down materialism? Well, I sort of like it now. I've become a consumer."

She laughed too, thinking of the baby growing within her. *She'd* certainly changed on the inside. "I know what you mean."

She set out cheese and crackers, and as she poured wine they began catching each other up on their lives since 1970, three and a half years ago. Tina talked about her job in Washington, but skimped on the details of Adam.

Max popped a cracker into his mouth. "I knew something was brewing with you and that guy. I was so jealous."

Better not dwell on Adam. "Tell me about the job. How long have you been with, what is it, NGF?"

"Yeah, that's it. I've been there two years. Got tired of being broke. My father set up some interviews for me—he's not without influence, you may recall—and voilà, I'm an eight-hour-a-day man, mapping out advertising strategy. I kind of like it."

Tina went to the kitchenette and plugged in a popcorn popper. Max followed her, saying, "Popcorn instead of pot. We've come a long way."

"Yeah. And I'm watching my weight."

"I noticed you put on a little."

Okay, Tina, don't pull any punches. Out with it. "I'm pregnant."

"Ah." Max looked into her eyes, unflinching. "So I suspected. Want to talk about it?"

"No."

"You're not planning to get married or anything?"

"No."

"Want to tell me about the father?"

"No."

"Okay, what is this, Twenty Questions? We're old friends, remember? We've shared a lot." He dropped his eyes. "I used to care about you. Still do."

Unexpectedly, Tina's eyes filled with tears. And she had thought she was through with the weeping and gnashing of teeth. Max pulled her close and hugged her, patting her back, smoothing her hair. It felt good to let the emotions spill out, to be comforted. After she felt calmed, they spent another hour talking, but Tina steadfastly avoided mentioning Adam. Other than her immediate family, no one would know he was the father of her child.

As Max left, he kissed the top of her head. "I'll call you tomorrow."

"Max, I'll soon be an unwed mother. I'll have an illegitimate child. Even in this enlightened age, it's not a great situation. You don't want to get involved with me."

"Too late. I already am."

The next day Adam called, the first time in several weeks. The ever-lingering tears sprang forth at the sound of his voice. She swallowed hard and steeled herself. "Adam, please don't call me again. It's over."

"You know you don't mean that. You're thinking about me all the time, just like I'm thinking about you."

"No," she lied, fingering the glass beads around her neck, the ones he'd given her. "I don't even remember what you look like." *Chocolate-brown eyes, full of love and lust, sloping muscular shoulders . . .* Stop it!

"Tina, I'm thinking of taking a few days off, coming to Michigan—"

"No! I don't want to see you. Not ever again."

"You don't mean that."

"I do. There's someone else."

There was a pause. "Someone else?"

"Yes. Don't you get it? It's over!"

She slammed the phone down hard and imagined his hurt, bewildered look. Well, he'd get over it. Marina would be there to offer him aid and comfort. Lifting the beads from her neck, she stared at them, then threw them in a wastebasket. Moments later she fished them out and tossed them into a drawer. She picked up the photograph in an old-fashioned bronze frame of her and Adam standing in the doorway of the Beehive. Her tears splattered on the glass and she wiped them away with her sleeve. Sliding the glass away, she lifted the picture and tore it into small pieces. The next day she had her number changed to an unlisted one.

She missed the jangle of the phone, his teasing, confident voice. A hundred times a day she reminded herself: *It's over.* The next week a letter arrived with his unmistakable hurried scrawl. With a black marker she wrote, "Return to sender," and jammed it halfway in the mailbox.

"It's over," she said aloud. The baby squirmed and rolled, as if objecting. "So, okay, Rebel. It's not quite over."

19

Louise brushed snow-flakes from her alpaca coat as she entered the fertility clinic. The waiting room—aptly named in more ways than one—was crowded with women who, for one reason or another, could not conceive. The majority, the doctor assured her, could be helped. But it didn't appear that she would be in that fortunate group. She'd had tests and pills and injections and examinations; had been pried, picked, and poked until she felt like a specimen. In addition, she'd prayed. Rosaries and novenas and quiet pleadings as she knelt beside her bed. *If it's your will—and please let it be your will—let me have a baby.* At thirty-six years old, she hadn't much time left. She briefly wondered if a vengeful God was punishing her for leaving his service, but discarded that notion as unworthy of a just and loving Father.

Jonathon too had gone, not uncomplaining, for his tortures, and found there were certainly enough wiggly, microscopic tadpolelike sperm anxious to swim upstream and do battle for the mighty ovum, as he put it. He'd been visibly relieved—it seemed such a macho thing.

Her mother, bewildered by the problem that rarely seemed to have troubled her own generation, wondered if it were due to the fluoridated water, the atom bomb, or, and this seemed most likely, the polio that had stricken Louise as a child.

Louise thought of Tina having a baby she didn't even want, and fought the bitterness that welled up inside her. What sort of perverse Puck meddled in their lives to complicate and entangle them?

She noticed one of the patients wore an I've-got-a-special-secret smile as she chatted with the woman seated beside her. Eavesdropping, Louise understood that the woman, after months of treatment, was finally pregnant. Others who had heard brightened visibly. Hope. A light at the end of the tunnel. Louise smiled. Maybe this time the doctor would have good news. Picking up a wrinkled year-old copy of *Newsweek,* she read without concentration until she was finally escorted into the examination room.

Enveloped in the skimpy paper wrapper, she shivered. A glance in the mirror revealed a comely face, like her mother's at the same age, she thought, with softly waving light brown hair, vivid blue eyes, healthy pink coloring. Who would guess that beneath the calm facade, this one failure tortured her? She hugged her arms to her chest and studied the anatomy pictures on the wall. Fallopian tubes, uterus, cervix. Why weren't her parts working properly? Dr. Taroum bustled in, asked questions, examined her. He took her blood pressure a second time, saying, "You seem a little nervous. Relax."

Afterward he jammed his large hands into the pockets of his white coat and asked more questions. "Let's stay with Clomid. We'll increase the dosage." Noting Louise's discouragement, he added, "Now, don't give up, Mrs. Wheatly. We're not through with our magic potions yet."

That's what they seemed to Louise. Magic potions. She might as well try witchcraft for all the good the medications did. She imagined the doctor rattling bones and doing a dance.

As he opened the door to leave, Dr. Taroum turned. "It may not be a bad idea to put your name in at an adoption agency, if you haven't already done so. Just as a precaution, mind you. It can take years, you know.''

Thank you for that note of confidence, Doctor. She dressed slowly, methodically, and left, not wanting to go home just yet. Jonathon had promised to pick up Rachel from school, so that wasn't a problem. Tina's apartment was only minutes away. She consulted her watch. Four-fifteen. Her sister would be home by now.

Tina answered the door in a housecoat and hugged Louise. ''I just got home a few minutes ago. First thing I do is get comfortable.''

In the kitchen, dishes were piled in the sink and crumbs spotted the floor. ''You need a dishwasher,'' Louise said.

''Among other things. Tea or coffee?''

''Tea's fine. Or whatever you're having. How are you doing?''

''I'm managing. I went to Ma's on Sunday. She's sort of adjusted, but she shakes her head and tears up whenever I go there. Pa hasn't spoken to me. He leaves the house when I arrive. I know this has hurt them pretty bad.''

''Pa will come around,'' Louise said. ''You were always his favorite.''

''Not anymore.'' Tina placed her hand at the small of her back and arched her shoulders. ''I was just going to make myself a grilled cheese. Want one?''

''Yes, but let me do it. You sit down. You look awfully tired.'' Louise took a box of Velveeta and a loaf of rye bread from the refrigerator. She sniffed the bread and decided it was still fresh.

''I am tired,'' Tina said, moving scattered student papers into a stack on the kitchen table. ''I've been getting long-term subbing jobs. It's better to have the continuity, but it means lots of extra work in preparation and checking papers. It's report-card time too, which makes it all the harder.''

"I'm glad to be finished with all of that. I invested too much emotion in my students, and now with Jonathon and Rachel, I want to give them all my attention." Louise had given up teaching a few months ago. Money wasn't a problem, and Rachel needed her. Her life would be complete if only, if only . . .

Tina said, "Have you been to the doctor?"

"Yes. Nothing new. I'm beginning to give up hope."

Tina set plates and glasses on the table. "Give it a chance. How long have you been going?"

"Nine months. Long enough to have had a baby. I used to believe God answered our prayers. I don't think that anymore. Tina, do you believe in God?"

"I guess I do."

"If there's a God, does he care about me? I used to be so sure. Now I don't know."

"Louise, don't lose faith. It will all work out." Tina placed her hands on her hips. "Aren't we a pair? I'm having one I don't want and you want one you can't have." She shook her head. "I finally went to a counselor last week. My doctor kept badgering me to go."

"And?"

"She wasn't much help, really. She was clearly accustomed to working with teenagers, and her routine advice is to give up the child for adoption."

"It's advice worth considering. You don't have money or a husband. Look at this place. It's hardly big enough for you, much less a baby."

Tina tipped her chin defensively. "Babies don't take up much room, not at first. And I know I'll have to work; that or go on welfare."

Thinking she'd hurt her sister's feelings, Louise was sorry she'd spoken so harshly.

"Look, I don't want to talk about it. I'm really bummed out." Tina sliced up a large dill pickle. "I was just thinking about you, Louise, wondering what to get you for Christmas. You have everything. Of course it won't be much, a token, really. Money's tight.'' She laughed. ''So what else is new?''

A startling thought had just occurred to Louise. She took a deep breath. ''I know what you could give me.''

''What?''

She slid the sandwiches from the skillet to the plates, yellow cheese bubbling from the edges. ''A baby.''

Tina stared. ''You can't be serious.''

Louise sat beside her and clutched her arm. ''I am serious. Jonathon and I could give him everything. Oh, Tina, I'd be such a good mother.'' She made a choking sound. ''I want a baby.''

''Louise.'' Tina cried as she nuzzled her head against her sister's. ''I don't know. I just don't know.''

''It's done all the time. In the old days girls would go off to a distant relative and come back with a baby, all hush-hush of course, then the grandmother or aunt would take over.''

''But think of the problems. I'd see you raising *my* child. He'd *have* to know. Someone would let the truth slip out. How would he feel?''

''He wouldn't have to know. We'd tell everyone to keep it a secret. And after a while it would seem as if he was ours. People forget.''

Forget? Tina would never be able to forget the child was hers and Adam's. But what could she offer besides love? She wiped the moisture from her cheek. Yet Louise's proposal wasn't so unusual she supposed. There were probably many children who grew up mistakenly thinking their grandparents or aunts and uncles were their real birth parents. Besides that, Tina would have a hardscrabble life, whereas Louise could give the child everything. ''I don't know what to do. I *just don't know.*''

''It would be perfect for me. We would at least share some of the same genes. Promise me you'll think about it.'' Louise stood and locked her hands together as if in supplication. ''I'd better get going, Tina.''

"Your sandwich." Tina pointed to the plate.

"I'm not hungry. Call me soon."

After Louise left, Tina sat scraping hardened circles of cheese around the plate with her thumbnail. For a change, she wasn't hungry.

Tina stood before the Christmas tree fingering an ornament she'd fashioned years before with a Styrofoam ball, sequins, and glitter. Cheerful chatter from her mother and sisters as they moved about the kitchen putting the final touches on the holiday dinner reached her through strains of carols from the stereo. This was the same Christmas scene she'd been part of for as long as she could remember: the same carols, the same furniture, standing in the same places, even the tree could have been preserved from year to year—there was only the addition of new tinsel. "I'm old-fashioned," her mother had said. "I don't like letting go of all the old decorations. They comfort me some way." Tina wished she could conjure up the excitement of her childhood Christmases with all their expectations and joy.

But this Christmas her sisters, as well as she, had some personal unhappiness to deal with. Louise and Jonathon wanted, more than anything, a child of their own. Barring that, Louise wanted to adopt Tina's child, though she'd said nothing about it since their conversation over a week ago. And Ann had problems with Brian, though she steadfastly refused to talk about them. As for herself, she carried her "love child," and couldn't make the decision to keep it or to give it up for adoption to Louise or to an agency. She sensed an attitude from her family of almost resentment toward her, because it was she rather than Louise having the baby. At least Louise and Jonathon had each other, and Ann spoke of a wonderful relationship with Scott, the "mystery man" whom the family still hadn't met. He'd given her a lovely bracelet for Christmas. But Tina? Without Adam she had no one.

Her misery was compounded by the knowledge of the pain she'd inflicted on her parents. Her father hadn't spoken to her since her *secret shame* was revealed. Feeling like a coward, she'd left the disclosure to her mother. Mike had been understandably angry but more than that, he'd been hurt, Chiara reported. His girls were all virtuous, he'd thought, even in this permissive, self-indulgent decade. Well, so be it. She'd have to accept the woolly mantle of the black sheep in this family.

Her eyes filmed over and the tree lights shimmered in a festive rainbow. A soft footfall sounded on the carpet and Tina turned to see her father. He stood for a moment gazing at her.

"Hello, Pa." She looked into his eyes, then down at the floor.

Mike came to her and put his arm around her shoulder, squeezing hard. "Ah, Tina. My baby."

His peace offering. Tina—self-proclaimed feminist, peace activist, tough cookie—dissolved into tears and buried her head in her father's chest while he patted her hair clumsily, lovingly. "It's okay, baby, it's okay." Mike handed her his handkerchief. "Have you decided to keep the child?"

"I don't know. My head is reeling with advice and options and decisions."

He patted her stomach. "You're being a damn fool, you know, not telling the father. He deserves to know. It's his child as much as it is yours."

Painful memories of Adam's negative comments on the responsibility of marriage and children made Tina's face close up. "You don't understand. I don't want him to know. And that's final."

Mike shook his head. "It's wrong, Tina. And you may not want any more advice, but I'll give it anyway. Keep the baby. A baby belongs with its mother. If you don't, you'll always wonder if you made the right choice.''

She snuffled into the handkerchief. ''I can't even imagine how hard that would be. Pa, I know . . . how I've disappointed you.''

His voice was gruff. ''Don't worry about that. And don't worry what people will think. Do what's right, now.''

''Thanks, Pa, for the advice . . . and everything.''

''Your mother and me, we'll help you all we can.''

''I know, but I'm a big girl. I'll do this on my own.''

She noted the mixture of dismay and pride in her father's eyes. He gave her another hug.

Ann, intending to call them to the table, had walked in on the tail end of the conversation. Her father had advised Tina to tell the baby's father. Was he thinking of his own child, Dante, of whom he'd been unaware until the boy was a grown man? History seemed to be repeating itself. Ann longed to go to her father and tell him that Dante *knew;* that he'd discovered the circumstances of his birth. Father and son could reunite now and mend fences. But that would mean telling her mother and her sisters, and that decision was Mike's. Oh, what a tangled web we weave . . . Ann's heart went out to her father. And to Tina. She put her arms around the two of them and said softly, ''Dinner's ready.'' None of them moved for several seconds, each wearing a bittersweet smile, all immersed in their own thoughts.

Dinner was more subdued than usual. The children were on their best behavior and refrained from bickering and teasing.

''Flora is thinking of quitting me,'' Ann announced, passing a bowl of creamy yellow *risotto*. ''She says she's not so useful anymore now that the boys are growing up.''

Tina said, ''Doesn't she need the money?''

''She has some social security.''

"What about you?" Tina popped a wrinkled olive into her mouth. "You'll still need help with the house, won't you?"

"I'll get a cleaning woman once a week, and the boys will just have to help more. Zi' Flora was never that big on housecleaning, anyway. That house is too darn big." Ann looked pointedly at Tina. "She said she needs a baby to cuddle again."

After dinner Rachel and the boys went to the basement, where Chiara had stocked an old bookcase with games and books. The twins played pool to a background of blaring rock music, while Teddy's and Rachel's squabbles over a card game occasionally wafted upstairs. Ann sat in the easy chair next to the fireplace, where a fire roared and spit. With cups of coffee laced with anisette, and a plate of *pizzelle* and *castagnelli* on the coffee table, this Christmas Day seemed almost normal. Ann had almost asked Scott to come by to meet the family after dinner, but thought better of it. Meeting the family put an official stamp on their relationship, something that she wasn't ready to acknowledge just yet. Uneasy at the relationship, which had solidified more quickly than she was prepared for, she tried to pull back. But in Scott's arms she came alive, when they were apart she longed for him. Scott, too, admitted the same sort of magnetism.

Her father's voice brought her back to the present. "Do you ever talk to Martin?"

"Rarely. Only if there's something we need to discuss about the boys. Usually I relay information through them."

He shook his head. "I hate to see the boys go through this . . . this hostility."

"So do I. But there's nothing I can do about it now."

"Does he want to come back? Does he say he's sorry?"

"Pa, you don't understand. He made the choice. I don't care if he's sorry or not. It's finished."

"Ann, don't you think for the children's sake—?"

"Please! I don't want to talk about it." Rising, Ann set her coffee cup down, spilling a few drops on the coffee table, and left the room.

In her old bedroom she tried to regain a sense of peace, but it eluded her. She turned on the small Motorola radio, now probably a collector's item, that her father had given her on her tenth birthday. Christmas carols wafted through the room. Her parents couldn't abide the idea of divorce. In their minds it was sinful, no matter the reason. And they wouldn't let her escape the residual guilt that the divorce had left. What would they think if they knew she was sleeping with Scott? After a few minutes she returned to the living room, where they all smiled at her lovingly. She had probably been the subject of discussion. Soon afterward, she collected her sons and prepared to leave. The goodbye hugs were long, tight ones, consoling, conciliatory.

A few days later, when Ann went into each room to say good night, Brian's bed was empty. He'd been grounded for a week for coming home at twelve-thirty on a school night. Ann realized that sixteen was the age when peers were everything and parents were hopelessly old-fashioned; when children had to cut away from authority figures. But Brian was using a saw to make his escape, and leaving open, painful wounds.

She went to Matthew's room. "Where's your brother?"

"Isn't he in bed?"

"No. What's wrong with him, Matthew? Why is he doing this?"

"I don't know. Maybe it's his friends. They're burnouts."

"Burnouts? What does that mean?

Matthew hesitated. "Losers, zeros."

"Then that's what he'll become. Birds of a feather."
She turned pleading eyes to her son. "Matthew, you're
closer to him than anyone. Talk to him."

"I have. He's okay. Don't get on him so much."

She could see it in his face, that loyalty. He wouldn't
betray his twin. If he had to make a choice between
his mother and his brother, brother would win out. "If
you want to help him, talk to him."

Matthew nodded halfheartedly.

A few minutes later the front door creaked open,
giving Brian away. He'd probably hoped his mother
would be in the family room at the back of the house,
allowing him to sneak in unnoticed.

Ann waylaid him as he reached the first step.
"Brian!"

He mumbled, "Shit."

"Where were you?"

"I was just at Alex's for a few minutes."

"You know you're grounded. This is the last straw!"

Brian's eyes flared with anger. "You can't keep me
a prisoner forever."

"Not forever. Just until you learn to live by the rules
around here."

He mimicked her, "Live by the rules. I'm sick of
your rules!"

Angered beyond control, Ann slapped him across
the face, hard, then instantly regretted her loss of composure. His eyes glared at her with hatred.

"I didn't mean to do that, Brian. You just make me
so damn mad!"

Brian ran up the steps and slammed his bedroom
door while Ann pressed her fingertips to her throbbing
temples. She had to regain some control, had to *reach*
him somehow, before it was too late to bridge the span
that kept widening between them. She wanted to talk
to him again, but knew her anger would get the better
of her. She took a sleeping pill that night.

The next morning Brian hurried off to school before

Ann could bring up his transgressions once again. She had hoped for an apology, or at least an opening so they could try for a discussion. But their discussions always ended in her lecturing, then angry recriminations on both sides. She'd have to try again later. After she saw Teddy off to school, she tackled a load of laundry. Her shops didn't open until ten, which gave her time to accomplish some household tasks. Fortunately her managers were competent and reliable. She carried a basket of clean folded laundry up the stairs and entered Brian's bedroom.

For a teenager, Brian kept his room relatively neat, except for shoes scattered about and books strewn on his desk. Usually Ann let the boys fold and put away their own clothing. But this time she methodically, neatly, went through Brian's closet and his chest, even as she mentally rebuked herself. Did the end justify the means? she wondered, tugging open the last drawer. Under a pile of socks she found a package of Zigzags. They looked like cigarette papers. She remembered seeing them on a film during one of the PTA meetings. She stiffened. Tonight she would have to deal with this. She wasn't looking forward to it.

Most of the remainder of her day she spent at the Redford shop. Talking to Frieda soothed her somewhat. "You'll work it out," she assured Ann. "Kids, nowadays! They'll make you crazy. My sister went through that phase, smoking pot and heaven knows what, but she's fine now."

By the time Ann returned home, she felt calmer. Teddy, head bent over a math textbook, greeted her with a preoccupied smile. He'd been working hard to pull up his grades. Matt, she knew, was at basketball practice. Brian, complaining that he rarely got to play, had quit. From Brian's room the roar of rock music unnerved her, the drumbeat rattling through her very bones. She knocked on his door, and receiving no answer, opened it. "Turn it down," she shouted over the ruckus. "I want to talk to you."

Brian sat at his desk, chair tilted back, feet on the desk, hands rapping his thighs to the beat. He made a face, then took his time walking to the stereo. After he'd turned the volume to low, he turned to face her, arms crossed, head tilted in an arrogant manner. "What do you want to talk about?"

"I was putting away your clean clothing and found this." She held out the packet of thin papers.

"You're spying on me! You have no right!"

"I have every right, when it concerns your welfare!"

"Okay, okay! You know what they are. I smoke pot. Big wow."

"Oh, God, Brian—"

"Quit making a big deal out of it." He turned away in disgust. "Everybody does it. It's not worse than cigarettes, and everybody does that, adults, I mean."

"Everybody doesn't. I don't."

He flopped onto his bed and draped his arms over his bony knees. "What do you want from me?"

She could almost see the dividing wall emerge, brick by brick. "I want you to stop smoking pot. I want you to get good grades, the way you're capable of doing." Her voice broke. "I want us to be friends again."

Brian looked away and tapped his foot impatiently on the bright striped bedspread. Joseph's coat of many colors, she'd called it when he'd chosen it. That was when they *liked* one another, a lifetime ago, it seemed.

He stared out the window. "Okay, I'll do whatever you want. Now, leave me alone."

She swallowed. Go easy, don't alienate him. "Brian, please, if there's a problem . . ."

"You don't understand. You don't understand anything."

"Try me. I want to understand, but how can I if you won't talk to me?"

He shook his head silently, and when Ann touched his head, he shrugged away.

As she closed his door behind her, the music swelled to an ear-splitting clamor. Teddy hovered outside the room looking woebegone. "What's wrong, Mom?"

"Nothing, sweetie. Just a little fuss with Brian."

He hugged her around the waist. "Nobody's happy around here anymore."

Oh, God, what was happening to her family, her happy little family? They'd once had everything, *everything*. And now . . . "We'll be happy again." She forced a smile. "How about helping me make some brownies?"

She'd have to call Martin, enlist his help with Brian. Whatever faults Martin had, he *did* love his children. And lately she'd been able to talk to him without rancor. Through the boys she'd discovered that he wasn't dating Janet any longer; and through Frieda, who'd heard "through the grapevine," learned that Janet had begun pushing for marriage but Martin had decided he didn't need and couldn't afford another family. "I'm not interested in his love affairs," Ann lied. "I'm sure he won't have any trouble finding another girlfriend." Her life had turned into a soap opera, she thought wryly.

When she called Martin that night, she found it surprisingly easy to talk to him. He was sympathetic and understanding; after all, he was emotionally involved with his children just as she was.

"I'm handling it all wrong, but I don't know what to do. I thought I was so smart about kids; I thought I could manage anything. But it's simply beyond me. I just cannot reach Brian. I don't want to hate him, or to have him hate me. I can hardly force myself to be civil to him, he's so angry, so sarcastic."

"I'll try to talk to him," Martin promised. "But I don't know what good it'll do. I take them to a hockey game and Brian doesn't say two words. But I'll try."

"I think we should see a psychiatrist or someone about him. Maybe I should make an appointment with the school counselor."

"Good idea. Set it up and I'll come too."

"You don't need to do that."

"I want to."

Ann hung up feeling that she'd accomplished something. At least she'd made a decision.

Brian was still on Ann's mind the following Saturday when she went out with Scott. The comedy at Meadowbrook Theater failed to divert her thoughts, and afterward, in Scott's apartment, he chided her.

"We only go out on Saturday nights and an occasional lunch, and half the time your mind's a million miles away."

Ann straightened a silver-framed abstract painting on the wall. "Sorry. I'm preoccupied tonight."

"As usual." He went to the kitchen and returned with a beer for himself and wine for Ann.

His apartment was neat, probably because he had a cleaning woman and didn't spend a lot of time there. She kicked off her shoes and stretched out on the tan leather sofa. "Scott, I told you about Brian. You're not a parent, so you don't understand."

Scott sat on the floor next to Ann. "I understand. I was a kid once. Not so long ago." He took her hand and traced around each finger. "Isn't it time I met your family? Are you protecting me or them?"

"Neither. It's just that . . . well, I told you how traumatic the divorce was for the boys. They know their father's dating, and it upsets them, so I hate to throw another curve at them. Teddy, especially, hopes and prays his father and I will get back together again. 'Be a family again' is how he puts it." She touched Scott's head, riffling her hand through his thick hair. "But Teddy isn't the one I worry about. It's Brian. He's sullen and distant and I can hardly keep track of him. Comes home late, with lame excuses. We can't even talk to each other without anger.''

"I was like that with my parents, I remember. It's a phase.''

Ann rubbed a knuckle over the faint stubble on his firm jawline. "I hope so. I can't take it much longer.'' She was silent for a few minutes. "Maybe I shouldn't have gotten a divorce. Maybe we could have lived together with a permanent truce.''

"That's not very realistic.''

"I know. I'm not thinking straight. It wouldn't have worked. I could never hide my anger.''

"Don't tell me you still love him.''

"No, that's long gone. I'm just thinking about a sense of stability for the children.'' She sighed. "It's funny, but when I was young I thought marriage was the be-all and end-all. The pot of gold at the end of the rainbow. Silly. But that was every girl's dream. I wonder if this new generation feels the same way.''

"Probably not. What do you want now, now that you're older and wiser?''

Ann screwed up her face. "Um . . . companionship, for one. Satisfying work. Loving children. Um, that's it for starters.''

"Nice. Where do I fit in?''

"You're squeezed in between companionship and . . .''

"And sex?''

"Well, there is *that.* ''

"What's wrong with sex and companionship on a steady basis? That's what marriage is.''

"There's one problem with that, Scott. I have a family. How many times have I heard you say you'd like to have a child someday? That's what you want, and deserve to have. Don't deny it.''

"I guess so. But it's not the most important thing . . .''

"Maybe not now. But later on. And no matter how nice you are, my children will never think of you as a father. They already have one of those.''

"Ann. You're not too old to have another one." He turned to nuzzle her neck, and his voice was playful. "Think of it; with your looks and my brains . . ."

"No. No way. I've *done* that. I couldn't bear to think of starting it all over again."

He gently tugged her off the couch and onto his lap and kissed away her protestations. They went silently to his black-and-chrome bedroom, where she had remarked the first time she saw it, "This room screams out *bachelor.*" By now she felt completely comfortable in his room, his bed, his arms. On cool sheets she stretched out against him, opened her mouth for his kisses, and was enveloped in an aura of passion. While in the act of lovemaking, in the giving and taking of pleasure, she was sure any problems between them would dissolve. Because she needed this man. He adored her, he stabilized her, he took her as she was, with foibles, with family. Nothing mattered now but being together. She moaned her pleasure, inciting him, and they rocked together in a cocoon of happiness.

Afterward he massaged her back. "We're so completely compatible." He nibbled her shoulder.

Reluctantly she curled to a sitting position and moved languidly to the edge of the bed. "I'd better get going."

He drew her back to him. "Come on, spend the night."

"I wish I could. It's almost twelve."

"What are you, Cinderella?"

"I have to check on the boys. You know that."

He sighed and leveled icy blue eyes on her. "They can't take up your entire life."

"Yes. Yes, they can. If I can't do *this* right, mothering . . ." She shrugged.

Scott shook his head imperceptibly and Ann wondered how long they could go on like this, being close but not bound. She cared for Scott, and though she hadn't said the words, she loved him. He'd made her feel beautiful again, and desirable. The early passionate blaze hadn't abated after almost a year together, and they had talked *around* marriage, not really saying the words, but tiptoeing cautiously. Before long, he'd push for a wedding. Was that what she wanted? A day-in-and-day-out relationship? She'd had that and it didn't work out. Could he put up with the problems inherent in being a parent? And would he try to convince her to have another baby? Would he resent it when she wouldn't? One day there'd be a showdown, she knew. And that day seemed to be coming closer.

20

March 2. It was too early, Tina thought, false alarm. She brewed a pot of tea and spread crackers with peanut butter. She wasn't due for another couple of weeks. But there it was again, and no mistaking it, that clutching feeling, just the way the film described it. It had begun only a couple of hours ago and now the contractions were eight minutes apart. But first-child labor took a long time, so said the experts.

Oh, God, she wasn't ready. There was so much to think about, like what was she going to *do* with this child. She had promised Louise she'd make a decision about the adoption by last week, but her brain wasn't working properly. She weighed every pro, every con, but came to no conclusion. She asked for a sign from heaven, a dream, a vision, anything, but no miraculous answers materialized.

At least it was evening, and if she had to get a ride to the hospital, her family would be home and available. She set to work packing an overnight bag. Folding a tiny yellow sleeper and knit wrapper in tissue paper brought the reality home to her. This is a happening, an event! A baby is on its way!

Consulting her watch again, she made a notation. Seven minutes now. Her heart pounded in a panic. She'd better call someone. Her mother. She dialed with an unsteady finger and let it ring a dozen times, then remembered. It was bingo night. Her parents wouldn't be home until ten or later. Louise, then. She'd accompanied Tina to Lamaze class and had agreed to be her coach.

Jonathon answered. "Sorry, Tina, she's at an oil-painting class. I'll have her call."

"Oh, hell."

"Any problem?"

"A minor one. I'm in labor."

"Oh, man." His voice was excited. "That's great, I mean, it's early, isn't it? Look, I'll drop Rachel at my mother's and get Louise and we'll be right over."

"No, it's okay, Jonathon, I'll try Ann."

"Well, if there's any problem, call right back, hear?"

"I will."

"Tina? We love you, sweetheart. Everything's going to be fine."

Easy for you to say, she thought as another contraction swept over her tight mound. "Thanks, Jonathon," she managed to croak just before hanging up.

Good Lord, she'd forgotten to call the doctor. She felt suddenly panicky, and twice dialed the wrong number. Taking a deep breath, she scolded herself: *Get a grip on yourself, girl.* Finally she reached the doctor's answering service and was assured the doctor would be contacted immediately.

She called Ann.

"Ma had to go to the shop," Teddy reported. "There's a big sale going on. But she said she'd be home by nine."

"Tell her to call me as soon as she gets home. It's urgent. Is she at the Mack Avenue branch?"

"Yeah. Are you okay, Aunt Tina?"

"I'm wonderful. You may be an uncle before long, Teddy."

"Like, wow! That's terrific."

She hung up and dialed the bridal shop. Busy. Damn, damn, damn.

Again she looked at her notations. Six minutes apart. Good grief, this child was in a hurry. She moaned audibly. The contractions were getting stronger. She dialed the bridal shop again, and again it was busy.

Max, you're my last hope, she thought as she dialed his number. *Answer, answer, dammit.* He'd become a constant in her life, her security blanket. He was unflappable and durable, putting up with her moods, making her laugh, helping her with grocery shopping and laundry. A few nights ago he had rubbed her back and then her feet.

"Max," she'd said, "do yourself a favor and get a regular girlfriend."

"You're pretty regular," he said.

"No," she said, "I'm a mess." She worried about where their relationship would go after the baby. He'd want more from her physically, he'd want intimacy, and she wasn't sure how much she was willing to give. So far, he'd been patient.

Finally, after many rings, he picked up his phone. Thank God. His cheery voice barely got through the "hel" of "hello" when she blurted, "I'm in labor, Max. Can you come?"

"Hey, sure, let me throw some clothes on. I just got out of the shower."

"Hurry. The pains are—" She gasped as another spasm began. "Look, meet me at St. John's Hospital," she said breathlessly. "I'm leaving now."

"No, you can't drive. Wait for me!"

"I'll get a cab. Oh, God, the pain is awful. See you at the hospital."

FIVE MINUTES APART. *I need a cab. Call a cab.* The cab-company dispatcher was pleasant. "It'll be forty-five minutes before we can get a car out to you."

Forty-five minutes! She felt a trickle of fluid run down her legs. "Never mind."

She cleaned up the puddle and changed her underwear, then grabbed her car keys and bag and a couple of towels. Throwing on a jacket that didn't come near meeting in the middle, she waddled out the door. Rain pelted down, but she didn't bother going back for an umbrella. With the car seat pushed as far back as possible, her feet barely reached the pedals. *I don't think I can do this; I've changed my mind about the baby thing. It's really not my bag.* She turned the key in the ignition. Nothing happened. *Dammit. Don't fail me now, ol' Paint.* She tried again and the engine turned over, but another contraction began and she laid her head back on the headrest, willing it to be over, panting, trying not to moan too loudly. She looked at her watch. FOUR MINUTES.

Shifting into gear, she steered the car onto the slick, rain-soaked street, hugging the right side of the road. The windshield wipers squeaked furiously in their arcing journey but couldn't keep up with the splatters of water.

"Oh, God, don't let me have this baby on Moross Road," she pleaded as another contraction began nudging her belly. Groaning, she pulled over until it was over, her face breaking out in perspiration. As she eased back into traffic, a passing motorist swerved and honked at her, making an obscene gesture.

"Same to you, fella," she said. "I'm having a baby, you jerk!" Having a baby. She began crying, and could hardly see through the haze her tears formed. *Just like you to screw this up, Tina.* Her hands, gripping the steering wheel, were trembling and the towels beneath her were soaked. Just ahead loomed the massive hospital complex. If she could just hold on. But no, another pain gripped her and she barely made the turn into the emergency driveway. Just a little farther, just a bit, another turn . . . At the emergency entrance she braked and lay on the horn, panting. She looked at her watch as the gurney appeared beside the door. TWO

MINUTES. Strong, capable hands lifted her. "I'm having a baby," she explained inanely.

"Yeah, lady, we figured that." A man in a green cotton jacket smiled at her. "Relax, you're in good hands."

"She looks ready," said the other one. "Get her to Labor and Delivery stat."

Past the doors, through a short corridor, into a larger room. Someone yanked curtains around the bed, making a tiny cubicle. A nurse helped her undress while another asked questions, questions, questions. She could barely answer through a curtain of pain. *Tina Marcassa. Dr. Marchand's my doctor. Water broke about a half-hour ago.* A new contraction (or was it part of the old one?) engulfed her as a nurse snapped on rubber gloves, eased Tina's knees up and out, and examined her. "Oh, my," she said, and stuck her head out of the cloth cubicle. "Get her to the delivery room. Now."

She felt a prick as someone punched a needle into her arm. "This will take the edge off the pain, hon." Then she was wheeled out into the corridor. Suddenly Max was at her side, squeezing her hand, while the gurney speeded forward, its wheels making a *sheesh, sheesh* sound.

"Husband?" the nurse inquired.

"Ah, sort of," he answered. "You okay, Tina?"

"Piece of cake." She winced.

His kind gray eyes were full of concern. "You should have called me earlier."

"It *was* earlier." She twisted her head away and propped up awkwardly onto her elbows in anticipation of another contraction.

"Deep breaths, honey, deep breaths," the nurse said. "Don't push, hon. Just hold on a couple of minutes." She dismissed Max, saying, "The waiting room's at the end of the hall."

He squeezed Tina's shoulder and kissed her forehead before turning away and down the hall.

The pain subsided momentarily. She closed her eyes and heard doors open and close behind her, and when she opened her eyes she was in the delivery room, where a white light engulfed her and people garbed in moss green moved around her on soft-soled shoes. Moments later Dr. Marchand's green-capped head and smiling face appeared at the foot of the table. Thank God she'd gotten the message.

"You don't fool around, do you?" the doctor said, gloved hands probing. The pain had returned and now continued in a steady, aching crescendo.

"Aagh," Tina moaned, pushing, pushing, unable to cease the pushing.

"Go ahead and push, Tina. I can see the head. Now, easy, easy. A couple of good ones and we're home-free."

Tina had hold of someone's hand and squeezed tight. She closed her eyes and let nature dictate her actions. Pushing, crying, panting. Her breath came fast, as if she'd run a marathon. Rivulets of perspiration ran into her eyes. Moments later a thin wail sounded.

Over? Already? What was all this fuss about childbirth?

Someone blotted her damp forehead. "A girl. All ten fingers and toes, Mama. Welcome to our world, little one. Do you have a name?"

"No. I want my baby," Tina croaked.

"In a minute. We'll just clean her up a bit and weigh her."

"Give her to me."

"I'm going to press down for the afterbirth," Dr. Marchand said in a calm, even voice.

She felt the pressure and a sloughing away.

"This is some kind of record, Tina. You're a natural. You ought to think about having babies as a profession."

"No, thanks, it wasn't *that* much fun."

A nurse placed a small bundle on her chest. "Here she is for just one minute. Seven pounds, three ounces. Hold tight, hon."

Tina forced her head up. For a moment she gazed, speechless, at the tiny miracle in her arms. "Oh, God, *look* at her."

The infant's slitted eyes opened wide in a pink pudgy-cheeked face and connected with Tina's. Tina's heart turned to mush and she started to cry. "Oh, sweetie, you're adorable."

The doctor continued to work, murmuring, "A few stitches and we'll be finished. A good day's work."

A nurse took the baby from her and another wiped her face with a sponge. "Go ahead and cry, hon. You've had a big day."

When she was wheeled into her room, the first thing she saw was a giant spray of red roses. From Max, the card said. Her parents entered as soon as she was settled.

Her mother kissed her and stroked her cheek. "Max called us. Are you all right? Why didn't you call us? The baby's beautiful."

"I'm fine. And I did call, but nobody was home. It happened so fast, I couldn't believe it."

Her father patted her head. "She's a pretty baby, Tina. Now what? What are you going to do?"

"I don't know."

"You have to make up your mind. Pretty quick."

"I know."

"Whatever you decide, if you need any help, any money . . ."

"Thanks, Pa."

Ann bustled in with Louise close behind.

"Will you look at her?" Ann said. "You sure don't look like you just had a baby."

When Louise hugged her, Tina whispered, "Louise, come early tomorrow. We'll talk then."

They all talked at once, wanting details, commiserating, congratulating, comforting. Max peeked into the room, waving a stuffed brown teddy bear, and Tina beckoned him in and introduced him. He made small talk and left soon after, saying he'd call tomorrow, leaving the family clustered around Tina.

"Family," Tina said. "Thanks for being my family."

A nurse strode in, saying, "What's going on in here? Only two at a time; that's the rule."

The visitors trooped out and Tina, spent, emotionally and physically, soon fell asleep. When she was awakened by a cry, she stirred, then sat bolt upright. The activity on the floor had died down, and besides the cry, only a few voices from the nurses' station could be heard. Now footsteps proceeded toward her bed and the cry became louder.

A nurse whispered, "Someone's very hungry," and handed her the baby. "I'll help you nurse the first few times. You'll need a nursing bra."

"But . . ." She had told a nurse earlier she wasn't sure about breast feeding. If she wasn't keeping the baby, she surely shouldn't be nursing her. But the child was obviously hungry and she couldn't deny her. Maybe just this time. The baby latched on to her nipple quickly and sucked hungrily for a few minutes, then fell fast asleep, obviously exhausted by the effort.

"You're doin' fine, Tina. Now move her to the other breast. Touch her cheek or flick her feet to wake her up. Keep trying for a few minutes." She turned to go, and Tina felt a bit panicky. "Just ring when you're finished and I'll put her back in her bassinet. We'll keep it in your room for a while."

The baby stirred and began sucking again. What a smart little thing, Tina thought, she knows just what to do. A warmth suffused her as she watched the infant's lips move. Oh, God, she loved this tiny warm bundle. This baby *needed* her mother. And Tina needed her baby. Adam's baby. This was the sign, this feeling of love and connection and responsibility. Tears welled up and spilled over again and she knew she couldn't let this baby go. Her thoughts veered to Adam again and she was suffused with the desire to see him, touch him, share this wonder with him. *Oh, Adam, damn you, you should be here. You'd love this little one. And I need you.*

Tina had finished breakfast when Louise stole in quietly and handed her a gift. After removing sheets of tissue, Tina saw an exquisite pale blue satin robe. "It's gorgeous, Lou. I wish I could give you news that would make you happy, but . . ."

"You're keeping her, aren't you?"

"Yes."

"I guess I knew all along. I really didn't think you could give her up." Louise's eyes welled up as the baby began stirring in her crib. "Can I hold her?"

"Of course."

Louise gently eased the baby from the crib and held her close to her heart. "I've given up hoping for one of my own."

"Don't say that, Lou. There's always hope."

Louise shook her head. "Some things are just not meant to be." The baby began crying and rooting toward her breast. "You'd better take her. I hope you won't mind a doting aunt."

"We'll take all the doting we can get."

Tina's living-room window caught the evening sun and tonight the pink-and-lavender sky was filled with tomorrow's promise. The apartment, which had been merely adequate for one, was now crowded with baby paraphernalia. Tina rocked month-old Elena as she nursed, singing nursery rhymes: "Ding dong bell, pussy's in the well." Having a baby in March was lovely; spring was in the air and she strolled Elena

every day, singing to her, talking to her, basking in
the delights of motherhood, dreading the day she'd
have to return to work. It was remarkable how her
entire life had altered since Elena's birth. So much of
her existence prior to her daughter's coming now
seemed inconsequential. Caring and loving her child
were the only important occupations in the entire universe now. Although her days were often chaotic, her
sleep disrupted, her social life nil, and though she suffered occasional panic attacks, overall she experienced a sense of peace, of pleasure in caring for her
child.

She released the baby's firm hold on her breast with
a little finger, then burped and changed her. After she
put Elena down, Max entered, heralding his arrival
with a whistle and carrying two sacks full of groceries.
Since the baby arrived, he'd been a regular visitor,
conferring the title of godfather on himself.

Tina relieved him of a bag. "Max, you shouldn't do
this."

"Don't want you to starve." He began emptying the
bags onto the table, vitamins, oranges, cereal, vegetables.

"I won't starve. I have the magical food stamps,
remember?"

Reluctantly she'd swallowed her pride and applied
for Aid to Dependent Children. Between that and what
her father generously gave her (with her fervent promises to repay), she managed. Picking up a jar, she said,
"What the hell is this?"

"Wheat germ. It's good for you." He shoved things,
helter-skelter, into the refrigerator.

She rolled her eyes. "Want some dinner? I've got
vegetable soup my mom brought over."

"Sure. Is Elena sleeping?"

"Um-hm. But you can see her." She led him into
the bedroom, where the slumbering child lay in an
eyelet-covered bassinet. "Isn't she adorable?"

Max grinned down at the baby. "She's absolutely gorgeous."

"Hey, I did something right, Max."

"Yeah." Elena opened her round dark eyes and Max cooed to her, placing his large index finger into her little fist. "She likes me."

"Of course she likes Uncle Max."

He put his arm around Tina. "Almost five weeks old."

"I'll have to get back to work soon. I hate being on welfare, but I also can't bear the thought of leaving Elena. Dilemma, dilemma." She tiptoed out and Max followed.

In the kitchen she turned the heat on under a saucepan. "The first time I used food stamps, I felt like everyone was looking at me critically, like I was the dregs of the earth or something. I suppose I was projecting my own attitude on the situation."

"Hey, you made some mistakes, that's all." Max poured coffee into a large mug with his name imprinted in red block letters, a gift from Tina.

"I can't even think of Elena as a mistake, Max. She's blessed my life. But I never imagined how much work a baby could be. I never seem to get enough sleep. I hardly have time to take a shower." While the soup heated, she set the table.

"Wait till she's a teenager, then you'll see trouble."

"That's what Ann says. She wants me to talk to Brian. From one rebel to another." She ladled soup into crockery bowls.

Max pulled a chair to the table and sat down. "Will you go back to subbing?"

"I hate to. School's out in June, then I'd be out of work. I'm thirty years old. If I'm going to be an old maid, I need a *career!* But I don't know what else to do. I don't want to wait tables again. *That's* certainly not a career."

"Why don't you try my company? I'm the golden-haired boy at Noble, Gordon, and Fitzpatrick. Get together a résumé and I'll get you an interview. I'll give you the big buildup.''

"Oh, Max, I have no background in advertising, or communications, or whatever's required.'' She buttered a roll and urged the basket toward him.

"Sure you do. You have a minor in journalism. You wrote leaflets for the peace movement. You told me you wrote a couple of plays for your students.''

"Does that count?''

"Sure, it all counts. You'd probably have to start as an intern. But you're bright, you'd catch on fast. I'll help you with your résumé.''

"Well. That's something to think about. But I want three months at least with the baby.'' She felt like crying whenever she faced the thought of *abandoning* her child to return to work. "Flora wants to babysit. At least I'll know she's in good, loving hands.''

After she and Max tidied the kitchen, they sat in the living room and watched Walter Cronkite. Tina, a basket of laundry at her feet, folded miniature clothing, remarking, "Isn't this cute? Don't you love this one?''

Max alternately laughed at her and shushed her. "Why don't you take a break for a few minutes? Sit by me,'' he said, patting the sofa.

Tina complied and lay down, resting her head in his lap. "I'm wiped out. I'd give anything for a full night's sleep.'' She hadn't realized how consuming and exhausting a baby could be. Her every waking moment seemed to revolve around Elena.

Max pulled away the band holding her hair into a ponytail and with soothing fingers raked back her heavy dark hair from the temples. Tina closed her eyes and dozed. She awakened to the touch of his lips grazing hers. After a few seconds she moved her head aside.

"What's wrong?'' Max asked.

"Nothing." And everything. She closed her eyes again.

His hand slid over her breast, swollen with milk. "It's time we made love, Tina."

Tina opened one eye and observed him. She had put him off all during the pregnancy, using that as an excuse. Max was one of the nicest and kindest people she'd ever known, offering her emotional support at a time when she needed it badly. She had no doubt that he cared for her. And she cared for him. But she didn't love him. And she didn't want to lead him on.

"Not now, Max. Not yet."

"It's safe. I checked with a nurse friend." He twirled a lock of her hair around his finger.

"That's not it."

"What is it, then?" He tugged the twist of curl and released it.

Tina searched for a reply. This wasn't the time to be cute or evasive. She sat up and took his hand. "Max, how can I explain what you've meant to me? You've helped me keep my sanity through all this. You . . . you're my best friend."

He shook his head. "That's not the description I was hoping for. Try again?"

She lowered her head and tears rushed forward. Oh, God, damn the hormones. When would they settle down? "The feeling I have for you, Max, it's here." She touched her heart. "But not in some other vital organs."

He shook his head disparagingly. "Come on."

"No, it's true. I wish I could have the same feeling as you." She snuffled and wiped her nose with the edge of her blouse.

Max said, "Maybe it's too soon after the baby."

No, that wasn't it. But she mumbled, "Maybe."

"Tina, are you still carrying the torch for that guy in Washington?" Early on Max had guessed Adam was Elena's father, but Tina would neither confirm nor deny or even discuss it. Max had nothing but contempt for Adam, unaware that Adam knew nothing of Elena's existence.

Tina shrugged. "Max, I've told you before. Find yourself a nice girl, someone who deserves you."

"You mean you don't want me hanging around."

"No, I love having you hang around. But it isn't going to lead anywhere. You're a desirable guy, a good catch. You're funny and kind and nice and . . . dammit, why can't I be in love with you?"

"Yeah, why?"

"Look, I'll introduce you to some nice young teachers I know."

"Thanks a lot." He snorted and rose from the sofa, dropping her hand. "Just forget it."

"Don't be mad."

Silently he reached for his jacket.

"Are you leaving?"

Max hesitated with his hand on the doorknob, then said, "Yeah, I'm leaving, as if you care. And I won't be back."

"Max . . ."

The door slammed before she could finish, and she stared at it for several minutes. The noise woke Elena and she began howling. Suddenly the knowledge that she might never again see her dear friend, her companion, struck her. *What is your problem, Tina? You're acting like an idiot, hurting the people you care for most.* The problem, she knew, was Adam. He still visited her dreams, and she saw him in Elena's smile, in her eyes that were already changing from deep blue to Adam's soft brown. She loved him still. Pressing her lips together, she willed herself not to cry, but cry she did, silently, profusely. "I've become a regular Niagara," she said as she hurried to answer her child's insistent howls.

* * *

A week later Max came by with a pizza and some beer. "I hear beer's good for nursing mothers."

"Pizza's even better," Tina said. "I've missed you, Uncle Max." She was surprised to realize it was true.

"This is nice," he said, nibbling on pizza crust.

"Um-hmm," she agreed, enjoying the pleasant warmth he always brought with him.

After settling Elena in bed, Tina began washing up the few dishes and Max put an Eydie Gorme record, "I'll Take Romance," on the stereo. Max sidled up behind Tina, placing his arms tightly around her, stilling her movements.

"Max, let me finish." She wondered if she could deflect his romantic overtures this time. Or if she wanted to.

His voice was husky. "You can finish later." His hands lifted her T-shirt and wriggled under her bra.

She turned to face him, locking sudsy hands behind his head. He danced her into the living room, humming softly in her ear.

"I'm not ready for this, Max."

"Sure you are."

But she wasn't; not mentally. Still, her body obeyed the age-old signals and she let him ease her to the sofa. Aroused and eager, he kissed her and she returned his kisses with ardor, thinking: The sofa is too narrow for lovemaking and I would really like to stop. But if I stop, I'll lose him once and for all, and on the other hand . . . it's too late, too late to turn back. Relax and enjoy.

So she responded to his passion and let the instinctual rhythms take hold.

Afterward he said, "Well worth waiting for," and she murmured her agreement.

And it *was* fine. But different. Max was not Adam.

And why, why, couldn't she exorcise the memory of Adam once and for all?

When Max left, she realized he hadn't said he loved her. Nor had she uttered those all-important words.

21

On a warm mid-April night Brian hesitated at the ornate double door to Legs's house, debating whether or not to go in. He'd turned on three times now, but tripping wasn't a steady thing with him and he could take it or leave it. He should probably cool it. He didn't want to get hooked. He'd heard of guys who couldn't quit; a couple of them had dropped out of school. But that wouldn't happen to him and, what the hell, it felt so damn good, it made him a part of something special. He would quit after this. One more time wouldn't hurt.

Legs let him in and the heavy door closed firmly behind him.

"I called Alex, but he didn't think he could get away," Brian said. "Maybe his old man is onto him."

Mark, a beer in his hand, appeared from the kitchen. "Naw, his family's going to a show, you know, doing the *buddy* thing."

Brian helped himself to a beer in the refrigerator and joined the other two in the family room, folding his long form into a chair. "Have you got the stuff?"

"Just some pot. Jonesy wouldn't give me anything else." Legs turned the stereo on full blast.

"Isn't there someone else from Wayne State who'd supply us?" Mark asked.

"I don't think so. I'm in deep shit with Jonesy. Everybody owes me for stuff. I promised I'd collect and pay him tomorrow. Maybe I can put him off for a couple of days. I owe him a hundred and fifty bucks. You guys have to come through for me.''

Brian frowned. ''You're pushing? Jesus, Legs, how could you get in so deep?''

''You don't complain when I give you some of my stash, do you?'' Legs tapped some grass onto a paper and rolled it expertly.

''I didn't know you owed so much!'' Brian said.

''You never said nothing about paying.'' Mark looked petulant.

''Yeah, well now I am.'' Legs lit the joint and took a deep drag, holding it for a long moment. He passed the weed to Mark.

''I've got about twenty bucks at home,'' Mark said, taking a toke.

''I don't have any money,'' Brian said. ''Six bucks, that's all.''

''Christ, come on, you guys.'' Legs's voice turned whiny.

''Okay, cool it.'' Mark gave the joint to Brian. ''We'll think of something.''

Brian said, ''I'll get some from my mom for clothes.''

''Sure, she'll give you a bill and never ask what you bought?''

Brian laid his head back. He was feeling mellow. ''Then you think of something.''

Mark fingered his mustache with a sly look. ''I know where we can get some money.''

''Where?''

''Alex's house. No one's home and I know where they keep a key.''

''Jesus,'' Brian said, ''he's our *friend.*''

''We wouldn't be taking it from *him!* His father's a doctor, he probably has plenty of dough just lying around. He wouldn't even miss a hundred bucks.'' Mark drummed his hands on the coffee table in beat with the music.

Brian stood and shoved his hands into his pockets. "I don't know, you guys, we could get caught."

"How?" Mark asked. "We'll just let ourselves in with the key, real quiet, search in desks and drawers and stuff for money, then get out. They might not even discover anything's gone."

"Okay, we have to have a plan." Legs slapped his thighs in a nervous rhythm, frowning. "Mark, you got a car, so you drive and stay in the car for a quick getaway . . ."

"Christ, you've seen too many old movies," Brian drawled. He was feeling relaxed, cool.

"Just listen, will ya?" Legs said. "Mark'll keep the motor running. In case there's a problem, we can get out fast. Brian, you know the inside of his house, don't you? You been there a lot, right?"

"Yeah, I guess so." Brian's voice wavered.

"Don't chicken out on us!"

A nerve twitched in his cheek. "I'm not!" But this was breaking and entering. What if something went wrong?

"So you and Brian make a quick run through the place," Mark said, getting into the adventure. "Just take money, no jewelry or anything."

They jostled each other as they got into the Camaro. When Mark turned on the ignition the music jumped out at them.

Legs said, "Keep the radio down, dummy, we don't want anyone to hear us."

"Like someone can hear blocks away," Mark said.

They argued about that in jittery banter, releasing some tension, until they reached Alex's street, where the homes, two and three stories high, loomed large on the tree-shrouded lots.

Brian clenched his hands between his knees. His stomach turned over. "It's that one."

Mark pulled up in the circular drive, parked, and cut the lights.

"Christ, the house is all lit up!" Legs said.

"We always leave lights on when we go out, to discourage burglars." Brian laughed uneasily. "Let's ring the bell, then if no one answers, we'll get in with the key."

Mark said, "Leave the car doors open."

As he left the car, Brian's lean body cast a shadow in the moon's bright illumination and his heart pounded with fear and excitement. He punched the bell button and faintly heard a responding musical gong. Shifting uneasily from one foot to the other, he said, "I don't know about this. Maybe we ought to forget the whole deal."

"No!" Legs said in a loud whisper. "We started, now we'll finish."

The several rings went unanswered.

"Mark said the key's on the patio, underneath the biggest flowerpot, the one on the far side." Legs hurried off the porch and toward the back, with Brian following.

Brian jumped as a branch brushed the top of his head. In the backyard several clay flowerpots of various sizes lined the edges of the patio. Both boys searched beneath them, unsuccessfully, until finally Legs whispered, "Whoa, here it is." He held the key aloft and headed for the door.

Brian held the unlocked screen door open while Legs fumbled to get the key into the lock. "C'mon, c'mon."

"Shut up! You're making me nervous." Legs wiggled the key. "The damn thing won't turn. You try it. No, wait, here it goes."

He flashed a victorious grin and turned the knob. A moment after he swung the door open, a shrill alarm sounded. For a split second both boys stood rooted in the spot, then, swearing, dashed to the car, tripping over each other.

"Go, go, go, Mark," Brian screamed. The tires

burned against concrete as the car backed to the street and roared away.

"Christ, I didn't think of an alarm!" Legs said.

Don't let them catch us, please, don't let them catch us. Brian repeated the litany in his head.

"You and your bright ideas, Legs," Mark sputtered, turning a corner on screeching tires.

"Me! It was your idea!"

"Well, I wasn't serious."

Brian expected to hear a siren any moment, expected a squad car to roar up behind them.

Minutes later they huddled in Legs's kitchen, passing a joint, worrying, discussing what they would say if questioned.

"We have to have our stories straight," Legs said. "We were here all night, right?"

"Yeah, playing cards."

"Euchre! And I won," Mark said.

Brian went home early. Looking up, his mother closed a book on her finger and smiled, saying, "You're home early, Brian. Did you have a good time?"

For once she wasn't on him. "Yeah, we just played cards." He didn't want to get too close, in case the smell of pot lingered on his clothes. But he would be cordial. "What are you reading?"

She looked pleased at his interest. *"Jonathan Livingston Seagull.* About a bird. You'd enjoy it."

He nodded. "G'night, Mom. I'm going to bed."

"Is everything all right, Brian?"

"Yeah, I'm just tired."

In bed, he tossed, unable to sleep. What if someone saw them taking off and got the license number? No, it was too dark for that. But maybe someone got the make of the car, or glimpsed the boys and got a description of them. He finally dropped off to a troubled, nightmarish sleep.

After a few days went by without repercussions, he relaxed a bit.

Not long after the attempted break-in incident, Brian stood on a corner adjacent to the junior high school. A light drizzle fell, coating his sandy hair with a misty aura. This was the third time he'd been here. He had just made a fast twenty-five bucks selling pot to the kids. Legs got the supply from Jonesy, who assured him that selling was the easiest way to get money. The last two kids wandered off, a baby-faced blond girl who flirted with him and a pimply, scowly boy. Shit, he felt really slimy, doing this, but he had no choice. If no one else showed up in a few minutes, he'd leave. He'd hiked over to a school in another neighborhood; he couldn't risk seeing Teddy. Besides, he didn't want his kid brother involved in drugs. If he didn't need the bread so bad he wouldn't be selling, but he'd conned and stolen as much as he could from his family.

A woman, some kid's mother probably, began walking toward him. "You! You, boy, stop!" she shouted. Stuffing the bills into his pocket, Brian sprinted away, across one street, down another, breathing hard, his shoes slapping the pavement.

He found himself near Mark's street, and decided to go there. At his knock, Mark came outside, his brown cocker spaniel at his heels. The rain had stopped so they proceeded to the back of the lot, where forsythia and spirea lined the edges of the lawn.

Brian said, "I was selling pot at the junior high and some old lady comes after me. I shot out of there so damn fast!"

"Christ! I'd like to get out of this burg." Mark took a joint from his pocket and lit it. "My old man's always on me, about my grades, about staying out late. I can't do anything to please him."

"My mother's the same." Brian sat on the bottom step of the deck leading to the pool and took a deep drag from the weed Mark handed him. His mother nagged him all the time; his father was no better. The last time he'd seen his father, he talked about taking Brian to a counselor. So far he'd been able to avoid it. If they thought he was on drugs, he might end up in military school. It was only a matter of time before his mother discovered he'd swiped some bread from her "secret" hiding place, an old silver evening bag in her closet. What a dumb spot to hide something in. Any thief would look there first. He'd conned Matthew out of half his allowance, his father out of extra money for a "new jacket," had even rifled through Teddy's bank. A niggling sense of guilt pricked his conscience, but he shrugged it away. He'd pay the money back. And he'd get off the stuff soon. Meanwhile, as long as it was so available, so easy to get, what the hell.

Mark's voice broke into his thoughts. "What we oughta do is hitchhike to San Francisco, Haight-Ashbury, that's where the action is." His foot kicked the loamy dirt of a flowerbed.

"Yeah." It was a tempting idea, to finally be on his own, free of the restrictions his parents placed on him, free of his mother's nagging and his father's lectures that were always "for your own good." Yet leaving home was scary too.

Mark said, "Maybe when school's out. That's two more months." He bent to one knee and scratched the dog under his chin. "Hey, you wanna go over to Legs's? I can get the car."

"No, I should go home. I don't want any more heat from my mother. Matt's been on me too."

"Well, tomorrow after school. He says he'll have some acid, as long as we got the money."

The next day, after the last bell rang, Tricia walked toward Brian as he slammed his locker door. He tried to avoid her serious green eyes. Plain bell-bottoms and a silky blouse outlined her curves.

"What's happening, Bri?"

"Nothing much."

She tossed long honey-colored hair over her shoulder, studying him for a moment. He wanted to touch her hair.

"I don't like what I'm hearing."

His chin went up imperceptibly. "What?"

She hesitated. "I hear you're doing drugs."

"Shit." He reddened. "It's none of your business, even if I was."

"Yeah, well, I like you a lot and I hate to see you get into trouble."

He pushed past her. "Just mind your own business, okay?"

Mark was waiting for him in the Camaro. "What's bugging you, Bri?"

"Nothing. Tricia. Now *she's* on me about drugs. Why doesn't everyone leave me alone?"

When they got to Legs's he said, "Good timing. I got some stuff."

"What?" Brian asked.

"Angel dust, what else? The drug of choice."

"I don't know," Mark said. "The first time I had a bummer, the next time was great, then the last time I freaked out again."

Legs led the way to the family room. "This time will be great. It's good stuff. I guarantee it."

He unwrapped a piece of white paper to reveal three sugar cubes. Brian took one and lay out on the floor, pulling a pillow behind him, sucking slowly, thoughtfully. A silver candelabrum on the mantel above the fireplace caught his eye and moments later it seemed to waver and dance. He looked around the room. Somehow it all turned into a whirlpool of colors, first soft-hued baby colors, then fierce brilliant colors, then sounds, first soft sounds that built into humming, then droning, then howling, then a crescendo of beautiful sounds, harps and flutes, and an orchestra, and the smells, so strong, like a huge flower garden with a fragrance so potent it rose in swirls—breathing it in hurt his head—and then the colors again, indescribably vivid colors, whirling, curling, and the strident sounds, and his flesh yearning for something, something more, some superior sensation, a higher plane. Now a sense of weightlessness: he could do anything, he could part the waters, he could fly, he was a God of the universe. He knew everything now, all the world's secrets, all its beauty, all its pain; he must explain it to his father. He would see his father and explain it all to him, maybe he would understand, maybe they could be buddies again, pals. He was moving out of the house, onto the street, heading toward Mack Avenue. He walked a long time. He watched his feet and they were moving, moving, but it still took a long time. He would hitch a ride to his father's office. "Hey, you crazy kid," he heard, "get outta the street." Brian laughed, it was so funny, so hilarious, so . . . so . . . He'd have to quit laughing if he expected to hitch a ride. Laughing wasn't allowed. The cars were all moving so slowly. Where was he now? In a car, a white Buick, a young hip black driver, a cool guy. This was the building. How did he get here? My father, I'm visiting my father, he explained very slowly to the guard, enunciating each word, being careful not to laugh. The elevator moved too fast. How did he get on the elevator? Open, close, open, close, the elevator door moved smoothly. In slow motion he let himself out on the fourth floor. But now his head hurt. His father's office was down this hall. He had been six or seven when he'd gone to his father's office and sat in the swivel chair and his father had let him buy a candy bar from the machine, and had said, my son, proudly, both my sons, my boys, so proudly, and given him a yellow pad of paper to draw on. Daddy, Daddy, Daddy, I love you, where did you go? Wait, wait, wait, where was the office? Had he gone past it? No, it was down this corridor. Daddy, Daddy, Daddy. The carpet was lavender, then blue, then pink, so vivid, so lovely. Maybe on another floor, but wait, wait, wait, there at the end of the hallway, a huge window, and beyond it, a sky, a huge blue cloud-dotted sky, so blue, I have to see it closer, and quickly. I must run, run, run like the wind to the sky—so beautiful, the creamy pudding clouds, the lavender-blue swirling, swirling, a whirlpool of color, run to the window, race before it disappears, touch it, touch the sky . . .

"Hold it, kid, what the hell . . ."

That was all he heard before the crash—a tinkling, shattering, melodious crackling; a body, his body, hurtling through thick plate glass.

Ann had left work early for once. The phone was ringing when she opened the door. Teddy picked it up and handed it to her as she shrugged out of her jacket. Martin's secretary's voice, a voice she hadn't heard in a long time, came through. "Mrs. Norbert?" It used to be friendly, chummy even, now it was shrill, frightened. "There's been an accident, a serious accident. Your son Brian. He . . . he fell from a fourth-story window. Mr. Norbert is riding in the ambulance. They're taking him to Henry Ford Hospital."

A high-pitched siren went off in Ann's head as she dropped the receiver and leaned weakly against the wall. She pressed both hands against the sides of her head to still the noise. Then she went into action, screaming to Teddy that Brian had been in an accident, to stay by the phone, and she'd call as soon as she could. How she arrived at the hospital was a mystery. She vaguely remembered cursing the traffic, skidding through stop streets and yield signs and red lights, her stomach clutched in a spasm of terror, her entire body enveloped in a shuddering chill.

At the hospital the receptionist patiently, slowly directed her with a pink-tipped finger and Ann ran to the elevator, where she punched the button and watched a dial charting its leisurely descent. Once she got inside, the elevator made its sluggish way upward, with three earnest-looking doctors discussing a technique and two elderly sad-faced visitors remaining starkly silent. Then doors, doors, so many doors to go through. In a waiting room she saw Martin.

Through a haze she heard him explain, his voice ragged and dry. "They're operating on him. Cracked skull, crushed pelvis, I don't know what else. The guard called and said Brian was heading up to see me. Five minutes later the floor was buzzing with the horror story that someone had crashed through the window. I knew at that moment . . ." he sobbed into his hands. "Somehow I knew. Oh, God . . ." They held each other, both crying in their pain and anguish. A few moments later Martin sat Ann down and brought coffee.

She tried to ferret out reasons. "Did he call you? Did he say he was coming?"

"No, I had no idea."

"Why did he want to see you?"

"I wish I knew."

"How could such a thing happen?" Ann's eyes bore into Martin's.

He ran his hand over his face and shook his head. Reluctantly he said, "Maybe drugs."

"No! He wasn't on drugs!" Even as she denied it, she knew it was true. She remembered the cigarette papers she'd found in Brian's drawer, his admission that he'd smoked marijuana. Marijuana led to other drugs, didn't it?

Martin calmed her. "Maybe. No one knows. It doesn't matter right now. What's important is that he survive."

"What are they doing in the operating room so long?" Ann asked. How would they piece together his shattered body? Silently she uttered tortured prayers, making deals with God as she moved tensely from standing to sitting and back again. Martin urged her to settle on the cracked red vinyl couch and tried to say comforting words, but they sounded hollow to her ears. It seemed hours later when a doctor came out, sad-eyed, weary. He shook Martin's hand. "I'm Dr. Tarpin, Mr. Norbert. We've done all we could to patch your son." He lapsed into medical jargon. Ann heard the words, but they didn't make sense to her. She clutched at the doctor's sleeve, her eyes imploring him to tell her good news.

"Will he be all right?" Martin asked, a desperate edge to his voice.

"He's critical. We did our best. Now . . ." The surgeon shrugged.

In the intensive-care unit, machines hummed and beeped, tubes and wires dangled from a steel stand. Clear plastic pinched the inside of Brian's puffy nose. His face, white as . . . as death, except for the bruises and cuts, looked so childish, so frail.

Ann bent down to his ear and whispered, "I'm here, Brian. Your father's here. We love you. You're going to be fine." Her voice broke. *He'll live. He must live!*

The little green line on the monitor darted up and down in an erratic journey, then settled evenly for a spell. A nurse rehung the plastic bags and made adjustments to the valves that dripped fluid into his inert body. The doctor, rubbing his forehead, gravely shook his head. "A pity, a real pity."

This child . . . this baby nursing and gurgling at her breast, solemn little thing, bright, walking at ten months, talking in short sentences at eighteen months, at six reading the comic strips out loud, inquisitive and sweet and loving and . . .

What happened? What did I do wrong? What did I neglect? Did I start back to work too early? Did it start way back then, when he was a toddler? Did I simply lose touch? The boys he hung out with, were they bad, delinquent? Was it simply the permissive, uncertain times we live in? And what about the school? The teachers, they should have seen and known, *someone should have known*. The divorce. He was all right before that. We shattered his life, Martin and I. *Mea culpa, mea culpa*. Why? Why? Why?

Gently the nurse tugged Ann away. "You can come back in a half-hour. Go get some coffee."

Martin, hovering behind Ann, urged her to leave. "You're like ice," he said, taking her hand. "We'll get something to eat."

"No. I'm staying here." She was adamant, stiff. "Calls. I've got to call people. Teddy and Matthew. Matt'll be home by now. My parents. Louise, Tina."

"You sit. I'll call them."

"I want to tell the boys. You call the others."

She broke down completely on the phone to Matthew.

"We're coming," he said.

When Matt and Teddy arrived, she pulled them to her and they cried quietly together, Teddy resting his head in the curve of her neck. Her innate mother's voice tried to calm their fears, and her own as well. "He'll be all right. Shh, darlings. He'll make it."

Martin returned with a sandwich for Ann and hugged the boys clumsily. They talked quietly, Martin explaining what the doctor had told them.

Every half-hour they all trooped in for a few minutes and Ann spoke in Brian's ear, telling him they were there, they loved him, he was going to be fine.

Back out in the hall, Matt broke down. "I knew what was going on, he was into drugs, getting high, but I didn't think it had gotten that serious. I should have stopped him." He punched a fist into his hand. "I talked to him. I tried telling him it was crazy, but all I got was 'Yeah, I'm quitting the stuff.' I should have *done* something. It's my fault. I knew where he was headed; I should have stopped him. But, Mom, I didn't know how bad it was, how far he'd gone."

Ann grabbed his hands. "Why didn't you tell me?"

He hung his head, shaking it helplessly. "I don't know. I didn't want to rat on him. I was sure he'd quit on his own. I don't know."

Ann cupped his chin, tipping his head upward. "It wasn't your fault. Don't blame yourself." She looked into his stricken eyes. "Hear me?"

"Yeah."

They sat silently, both boys leaning into Ann, Martin a seat removed.

After they trooped in for another look, the nurse said, "Why don't you all go home for a rest? I'll call immediately if there's a change."

"Yes, Ann, please go home," Martin said. "There's nothing you can do."

"No, I have to be with him when he wakes up."

"Please."

She shook her head. "You go. Stay at my house with the boys."

"I'll be back early in the morning." He gave her shoulder a comforting squeeze.

She nodded.

A coffeepot dripped noisily on a table in the corner. Ann poured some into a Styrofoam cup and tried to drink it. Making a pillow of her jacket, she curled up on the Naugahyde two-seater and let the thoughts surface.

Brian was the quiet twin, Matthew the loquacious one, the smiling one, even from babyhood. "Brian's always so serious," she'd say when they were toddlers, a bit regretfully, as if it were somehow her fault. As a teenager he was earnest, dissecting rather than enjoying music and movies, jokes, and stories. He didn't collect friends as Matthew did, didn't have a real girl, though he talked to Tricia on the phone and they'd gone out a few times. Ann twisted, trying to find a position that wouldn't pain her back, and finally dozed fitfully.

When she looked at her watch again it read one

o'clock. Sitting up, she rubbed her eyes and straightened her hair, then went into Brian's room. He was still, grayish. A slight gurgle came from his throat. A nurse walked in. Ann held her breath. Something was wrong. The green line jumped erratically, then lengthened. A red light flashing. A beeper screaming.

"Get the doctor! Do something!"

Within seconds medical personnel converged upon the slight figure on the bed. A nurse firmly pushed Ann out the door, where she hovered, her fist pressed to her mouth. It seemed like an eternity before Dr. Tarpin came from the room slowly, shaking his head. "There was nothing we could do." Ann staggered forward and the doctor grabbed her, but she wrenched away and into the room. She threw herself across the bed, screaming, "No! No! Brian, no!"

Screams. Ann heard a series of screams, so loud they hurt her eardrums. She finally realized they were coming from her. She didn't remember dropping in a heap.

Muted shades of blue lent a sense of serenity to the large room where Brian lay in his casket. Flowers fanned out around him, the traditional gladioli, roses, carnations. He loved daisies, Ann remembered. Matthew and Teddy, her remaining sons, their faces grave, greeted friends and made simple unsatisfactory explanations. *He pushed hard against the window,* they guessed, *and it gave way.*

Ann watched Matthew, worried for him, knowing that his loss was almost as great as her own. His hands were clasped before him, his head tilted, his demeanor solemn, nodding at a white-haired neighbor's condolences.

You boys were always so close, too, weren't you? So young, such a good-looking boy.

Yes, just sixteen.

So sorry, so very sorry.

Yes, thank you.

You'll have to help your parents hold up.

Of course.

Matthew wished she would stop talking. His brain was on fast forward and he couldn't stop it. He hadn't been able to sleep since it happened.

They'd been a duo, a team, a matched set. Until they rebelled at eight or nine, they wore the same outfits in different colors. Often their parents would call out to them, "Twins!" rather than by their names. Inseparable. Bri used to say, "When you get an itch, I scratch." Now Matthew was half of a whole. Would he ever get over the feeling that part of him was missing?

He went over in his mind all the clues he'd chosen to ignore. A lot of the guys smoked pot, and he did himself occasionally. But with Brian it had escalated to the hard stuff. Matt wasn't sure how or when, but he had sensed the change. And he *had* tried to talk sense to his brother a few times, but Bri shrugged it off. *No big wow; I know what I'm doing.* And Matt trusted that he *did* know what he was doing, that he could and would stop short of getting hooked.

Ann sat on the brocade sofa or stood talking to people, making proper responses, wanting to glean from them some kernel of comfort, but finding none. The words they said didn't matter, meant nothing. *He's in a better place.* No. This was his place. *God wanted him.* I wanted him. Spotting Legs, Mark, and Alex, she remembered that she wanted to talk to them, sort out the facts and events of his last day. But it didn't matter now.

Scott was there, in the background, careful not to intrude in the family's suffering. She felt his presence, his abiding love. He called her each morning and each night, and though he was not a religious man, promised his prayers.

For the two evenings and during the requiem mass she bore up, and even afterward at the cemetery under a fittingly gray sky, she endured. But after the priest gave a final blessing, she looked around and saw his friends wearing devastated expressions, but vital, breathing. Why her son? Why Brian? Why? Why? Her legs gave way and strong male arms helped her to the limousine. She sat in a crumpled heap in the corner of the funeral car, inconsolable.

Afterward, at her house, she accepted some small comfort from her parents, who shared her sorrow in bewildered angst, from her sisters, whose tears almost matched her own, from her own remaining children, whose sorrow she couldn't even begin to ameliorate, and even from Martin, whose misery was equally deep.

Ann reached for Tina's baby and hugged her tightly. Elena sank her tiny fingers in Ann's hair, pulling, and cooed, gurgled, and smiled, unmindful of the suffering around her.

22

Louise lifted Elena from her crib and nuzzled her neck, eliciting a wide gummy smile. Since the baby's birth she had visited Tina often and offered to babysit while Tina went shopping or just took a break. Playing with the baby somewhat assuaged Louise's hunger for mothering. Now that school was out, Rachel often accompanied her on visits to Tina's house and spent hours playing patty-cake, ponyboy, or just smiling at Elena, who was now a fat, happy four-month-old.

Tina flitted about the kitchen, preparing food. "I made brownies," she whispered conspiratorially to Rachel.

Louise was delighted at the special relationship between Rachel and her favorite aunt.

Rachel asked, "Are we having chili dogs, Aunt Tina?"

"Of course, that was your request, right?" Tina stirred the chili sauce. "Check the buns in the oven, hon. I don't want to burn them." She began tearing lettuce for a salad.

"You can have Elena back," Louise said. "She needs a change."

"You know the rule: the first one to smell her changes her." Nevertheless Tina took the baby and laid her on the sofa. Elena kicked and gurgled and tried to get her foot into her mouth, while Tina tickled and cooed. "Did I tell you? Ann's coming after work."

"Good. I talk to her almost every day," Louise said. "She seems a bit better, I think. I've urged her to go for counseling." By July, Ann's wounds were still raw but at least beginning to heal. They'd traced Brian's actions on that fatal day and discovered what had happened, but Ann steadfastly refused to talk about it. "I'll never recover from this," she'd said. "There's no greater tragedy than losing a child."

"Let me have Elena, please," Rachel pleaded.

Tina put a rattle in the baby's hand and left her in Rachel's charge while she and Louise finished dinner preparations.

Ann knocked and entered and the sisters hugged. She looked haggard and thinner than ever.

"Are you all right, Ann?" Tina asked.

Ann nodded, but Louise noted that her older sister's eyes filmed over for a moment.

"Here," Tina said, handing Ann an onion. "You can chop."

"Swell, my favorite job," Ann said sarcastically. "I can't stay too long. I took your advice and made an appointment with a counselor. Poor Matt is beating himself up over Brian's death. I guess we all are. Scott has been great, so supportive, but he's never had a child. He doesn't know what it's like."

When they all sat down to eat, Louise said, "I've put my name on three adoption lists."

"Louise, you already have your hands full. Are you sure you can handle a baby too?" Tina asked. "This kid of mine is a handful of work. And you've got Rachel to deal with, taking her to school, doing therapy—"

"Tina, I've never been more sure of anything." Louise glanced at the baby, lying contentedly on the olive shag carpet.

"Well, in that case," Tina said, "I've got some information for you. I waited for Ann to come to tell you."

"What?" Ann and Louise said in unison.

"You know the doctor who delivered Elena, Dr. Marchand?"

Louise nodded.

"Well, I had told her how you wanted to adopt my baby." Juice dribbled down her chin as she took a bite of the chili dog.

"Wipe your chin," Ann said, smiling at her younger sister.

"And . . . ?" Louise urged her.

"And"—Tina strung out the word for dramatic effect—"she thinks she may have a baby for you."

"Oh, Lord." Louise's heart raced. "You mean now?"

"No. One of her patients is a pregnant girl who wants to give her child up for adoption. But she's very particular about the couple that adopts. She wants to choose."

"What else?"

"I don't know too much. You'll have to talk first to Dr. Marchand, and she'll put you in touch."

"What's the girl like? Tell me about her."

"All I know is that she comes from a fairly well-to-do family, nice and proper people, and wants to go to college and just be a kid, not a mother."

"What about the father?"

"She won't talk about him. Apparently he just dropped out of the picture, flew the coop, so to speak."

Louise clutched her heart. "When is she due?"

"September, I think."

"Oh, Lord, just a couple of months."

When she left Tina's, Louise was filled with renewed hope. A baby, finally, a baby, to kiss and dress and cuddle and love. Mentally she began outfitting a nursery, yellow maybe, neutral enough for boy or girl, a rocking chair, a changing table, everything brand, spanking new, no hand-me-downs for her baby.

Jonathon, on the other hand, when he heard the good news, cautioned her, "Sweetheart, don't get your hopes up too much."

"They are up. This is what I've been praying for."

"A dozen things could go wrong with this kind of situation."

"Oh, Jon, I have a feeling this is meant to be."

In her conversation with Dr. Marchand the next day, Louise tried to curb her excitement.

"She's a very nice young lady," the doctor said. "Her name is Marissa Casaday, and while she wants to give her child up for adoption, she also wants some control. She wants to screen and choose the couple who will take the baby."

"Do you have other people you'll suggest to her, Doctor?"

"There are several names I could give her, but yours came to me first. She will probably want to interview others."

"How is her health?"

"She's in excellent condition and should have a normal birth."

Marissa Casaday's phone call a few days later resulted in a dinner date the following night.

Louise fidgeted in the spacious booth, twisted her napkin, glanced at the entrance, sipped water, looked at her watch. Jonathon stilled her fingers with his large square hands, squeezing.

"Settle down. I've never seen you so jittery."

"I'm nervous."

"So am I."

"What if she doesn't like us?"

"What? How could she not? A charming couple like the Wheatlys? We're Barbie and Ken, Romeo and Juliet, Ozzie and Harriet, Bonnie and Clyde—"

She slapped playfully at his arm. "Don't get carried

away. I'll invite her to the house soon. Perhaps for dinner. Do you think that would be appropriate?''

''Sure.''

''I wonder if we should try to meet her parents, sort of check out her background. She sounded very nice on the phone. Young, unsure, but nice.''

He nodded.

''She just wants a good home for her baby. That's what everyone wants, isn't it?''

Again he nodded.

''But she wants a chance for herself too. She's just too young to be a mother. Seventeen.''

Jonathon stopped bothering to nod. A toddler in the next booth caught his attention and he waved and winked, to the child's delight.

''Look, Jon, just coming in. It must be her. Just a kid, really. Oh, Jonathon, she's so pretty.''

The girl flicked straight long blond hair from her shoulder, looked uncertainly about, and said something to the hostess. Louise smiled and beckoned to her.

Jonathon rose as she clumped toward them in platform shoes.

''I'm Marissa,'' she said a bit shyly. ''You must be the Wheatlys.'' The simple peasant-style maternity dress that stopped just above her knees billowed as she slipped into the booth next to Louise.

Jonathon returned to his seat across from them. ''Yes, I'm Jonathon.''

Louise shook her hand. ''Call me Louise, please.'' They all smiled at the rhyme.

''Why don't we order first?'' Jonathon suggested. ''Then we can talk.''

They busied themselves studying the huge menus, but Louise couldn't help glancing at the girl.

''The red snapper is excellent here,'' Jonathon said.

''I think I'll just have soup and salad.'' Marissa's voice was soft and childlike. ''Watching my calories.''

After they'd ordered, Jonathon said, "So you plan to go to college, Marissa?"

"Yes, University of Michigan."

"Have you picked a major?"

"I think I want to be a commercial artist."

Good, thought Louise, some creative genes. She longed to reach over and move the blond bangs that stopped just below the girl's eyelids, to get a good look at the eyes in that round baby face.

"Um," Marissa said, folding her hands on the table, "I have some questions."

"Shoot," Jonathon said.

"Do you have other children?"

"One daughter, Rachel. She's ten and also adopted. She's handicapped. She's a bright girl but has cerebral palsy."

"Will you have time for a baby too?"

"Rachel doesn't require much, and I can always hire help if I need it."

Marissa chewed her lip. "Well, I think it's good to have siblings. I'm an only child." She thought for a moment, frowning slightly. "I'm assuming you have a good income?"

"Yes," Louise said. "I don't work and don't plan to in the near future. We'd like you to visit our home."

"Um. Yes, if this part goes okay, then I'd like to come. Do you plan to have any other children?"

"It doesn't seem likely," Louise said. "I'm thirty-seven. At that age it's hard to adopt, and the good Lord hasn't seen fit to send a baby by the normal route."

"Oh. That's too bad." Marissa sighed. "What do you plan for my baby's future? I mean, what kind of work would you like for him? Or her."

Jonathon said, "That would depend on what sort of talents he has. We would give him every opportunity for the best schools. I may as well tell you that I'd be a bit strict and my wife might be, well, a little over-protective. That's her nature."

"I kind of like that." Marissa smiled wistfully. "Do you go to church?"

"Yes. I'm a Catholic. Jonathon comes with me sometimes. He's out of town quite a bit."

They were all silent for a few moments; then Louise asked, "Do you want to talk about the child's father?"

"No, not really."

"Do you mind just telling us a bit about him—what he looks like, what his interests are?"

Marissa thought for a moment. "Okay. He's interested in music. Rock. He's got kind of hazel eyes and um, dark blond hair."

Ah, musical genes, thought Louise, delighted. They would have to arrange for lessons, piano or violin perhaps. "How old is he?"

"Twenty-one."

Marissa spoke of her father, an engineer, and her mother, a boutique owner, and asked about Louise's and Jonathon's backgrounds. At the meal's end Louise invited Marissa to dinner the following week. On the way home Louise bubbled over with happiness. "Oh, Jon, it feels so right. I'm sure it's going to happen."

Jon was about to say something, but thought better of it and just squeezed her hand.

Louise rearranged vases of fresh flowers and punched up sofa pillows. Jonathon had gone to drop Rachel off at Tina's, because they'd decided it wasn't wise to have her involved in any of the discussions until the adoption was a *fait accompli*. It would be unfair to Rachel to raise her hopes, then to have them suddenly dashed.

Jonathon returned, kissed Louise, and cupped a few cashews from a dish on the low teak cocktail table.

"Now, don't make a mess, Jon," Louise said, whisking her hand over a crumb.

"We're not entertaining Queen Elizabeth, Lou. Try to relax."

"But I want her to like us. I want us to be irresistible. Do you think she'll like veal parmigiana?"

Jonathon kissed the back of her neck and sat her down. "She'll love it."

Popping up again, Louise straightened the edge of the Persian rug, then jumped when the doorbell chimed. Marissa appeared with her hair pulled into a ponytail and a bouquet of daisies.

During dinner the talk was impersonal and inconsequential. "Let's have dessert on the patio," Louise suggested when they'd finished. She led them through French doors to the enclosed patio, which housed white wicker furniture. The garden itself spread into a wide pie shape edged in trees and shrubbery. Small black-sheathed spotlights illuminated Louise's roses and annuals. In the rock garden, where Louise spent part of every morning battling weeds, black-eyed Susans nodded in the evening breeze alongside pansies, larkspurs, and sweet Williams.

"It's nice here. A nice place for a kid," Marissa said, easing her awkward body onto a redwood chaise.

"I have a small vegetable garden the other side of the pool," Louise said. "Gardening is a hobby with me."

"That's a nice hobby. Mine's photography." Marissa seemed to relax as she opened up more about her life and her former boyfriend as well.

"He's a musician and I was so crazy about him. I thought he was crazy about me too. But I guess I didn't really love him after all, and I knew he'd be rotten to me and especially to a baby. He acts like a spoiled baby himself. And he knocked me around a few times. That was before this." She pointed to her bulging abdomen. Scraping the last bit of raspberry sherbet from the bowl, she said, "I sure didn't expect this to happen. But he got stoned one night and, well, it just happened. When I told him about the baby, he disappeared for a couple of weeks. Then I heard he was back, and he finally called but we just argued. I haven't heard from him since.'' She chewed nervously on a fingernail. ''Now I just hate him and I hope I never see him again.''

''So you don't think there would be any problem with him in the future?'' Jonathon asked.

''No way. He probably wants to forget he ever knew me.''

Jonathon sat forward in his chair. ''I think you should know we've been in contact with our lawyer. There are papers you'd have to sign, relinquishing all rights to the child and promising not to try to see her or enter into our lives. How do you feel about that?''

''Well, um, I guess it has to be that way. A kid can't really have two mothers.'' There was the hint of a tear, the first crack in her armor.

Louise went to Marissa and hugged her. ''Marissa, I hope you realize what this means to us.''

Marissa held herself stiffly. ''Well, I haven't decided absolutely, yet.''

''I understand.''

''I did meet with another couple. They're nice too.''

Louise's heart dropped to the region of her stomach. Competition.

Jon patted Marissa's shoulder. ''This is an important decision for you. Take your time.''

''Well, I don't have too much time left. I'll decide in the next week or so. I'll call you.''

''Can we come to the hospital when you deliver?'' Louise asked. ''That is, if we are the ones?''

''Um, I haven't thought about that. Maybe.''

Jonathon stood and walked toward her with a legal-size folder. ''I'd like you to take home a copy of the papers the lawyer gave us. You'll want to read them and then maybe have your own lawyer go over them. The baby's father will have to sign also.''

''That won't be a problem. If I can find him.'' Her mouth turned down at the corners.

"And, Marissa, we'd also like you to see a coun- selor in the next few weeks. We'll pay all expenses, of course."

Marissa pondered, then said, "I guess that's okay."

After Marissa left, Louise said, "I have such a pos- itive feeling about this. Don't you, Jon?"

He took her hand and pressed it to his cheek. "I'm trying to. I just don't know."

"Oh, darling, please be optimistic with me. It's go- ing to work out, I know it is." After all the praying and hoping, it *had* to work out. God was answering her prayers after all.

Louise marked a small heart on the calendar as each day passed. One day, two, then a week dragged by. September 15 was marked with a large "B-day."

On September 7 she got a call from Marissa. "I made my decision, Louise. You can have the baby."

For a moment Louise, overwhelmed with joy, couldn't answer. Finally she blurted, "Oh, Marissa, thank you. Your child will have the very best life we can manage. We'll have to get together with the law- yer. Will you try to find the baby's father so he can also sign the papers? That'll make everything legal."

Marissa sighed. "Okay, I'll call you."

Four days later, just after the yellow bus had picked Rachel up for school, a call came, not from Marissa, but from her mother. "Marissa asked me to tell you she's going into labor, Mrs. Wheatly. I'll call as soon as she delivers."

Louise had wanted to be there, but that was all right, she would still see the baby minutes after it was born, and could take her home, God willing, a few days later. She made arrangements for Tina to pick up Ra- chel from school, just in case, then called Jonathon, who was out of town. "I'll fly back as soon as I can," he promised.

Louise went to the nursery and gave it a cursory inspection. Neat and orderly, yellow organdy curtains, white furniture, teddy bears resting on the dresser next to the Mother Goose lamp. Perfect. She sat quietly in the rocking chair and prayed. She envisioned the baby—blue-eyed like Marissa and herself, chubby, peaceful—lying in her arms. Tears of excitement, gratitude, and just a touch of fear rose up and spilled down her cheeks.

By three o'clock, when she'd had no word from Marissa's mother and the hospital gave only terse reports that Marissa was in labor, Louise could stand it no longer and drove to the suburban hospital. She searched the maternity waiting room. A young man smoked nervously while an older couple, eating from a package of potato chips, smiled encouragingly at him. The other occupant was a tall well-dressed woman who sat uneasily at the edge of a chair, thin legs crossed, flipping through a magazine. She looked about Louise's age, but bore a striking resemblance to Marissa. It seemed ironic to Louise that Marissa's mother was expecting a grandchild, while she herself, at about the same age, was waiting for a child of her own. Beginnings and endings.

"Mrs. Casaday?" Louise said, approaching the woman.

She turned worried eyes toward Louise and closed the magazine with a snap. "Yes."

"I'm Louise Wheatly. I was too nervous to wait for your call."

Mrs. Casaday assessed Louise, then nodded. "Call me Gladys. They just took her into delivery."

"How is she doing?"

"She's fine. Hurting, upset, miserable, but all in all, fine. I must tell you, I'm not happy about her decision to give up her baby, but it's her choice and I can't do anything about it." She shook her head as if in a silent reproach against her daughter.

Louise sat beside the woman on a turquoise mock-leather chair. "Would you have helped raise her?"

"No. I've done my child-rearing; I don't want to start that all over again. Marissa made her bed, let her lie in it."

"How would she have managed?" Louise thought of Tina, who managed by dint of determination and courage, but Tina was older and wiser than Marissa.

"I don't know, I just don't know. Perhaps this is the best way."

"Does Mr. Casaday feel the same?"

"He won't even discuss it. My husband is very active in the church, and he feels that this is a reflection on him. He's been very upset, and chose not to be here today. We all do what we think is right." She dropped her head and looked at the floor. "I don't know how this could have happened. I always thought she was smarter than this, thought she knew about birth control, even though we never discussed it. But she's always been headstrong, always done whatever she wanted. Our own fault, I suppose. We raised her to be independent. That was important to us. And the times we live in seem to foster a kind of wildness, don't they? 'Do your own thing' and all of that." She shook her head. "I wonder . . . I wonder what the right way is, or if there is a right way."

Empathizing with Gladys' dilemma, Louise wished she could hug her, but the woman remained rigid, forbidding.

"In some ways we were indulgent, in other ways . . ." Gladys rummaged through a large leather bag for a tissue, then dabbed at the lone tear that overran the edge of her eyes. "You must excuse me. This thing has thrown me terribly off-balance."

A nurse came into the room and said, "Mr. Donaldson? You have a baby girl. The doctor will see you out here." The other three, who had been talking quietly, rose as one and hurried out, jabbering with excitement. The door closed softly behind them; then moments later it opened again and a young man wearing a denim jacket, cowboy boots, and jeans faded to a soft white at the knees flew into the room.

"Ross!" Gladys said.

The man planted himself before Gladys, hands stuffed into his pockets, stringy hair hanging forward from his bent head. "How's she doin'?"

"What are you doing here?"

"I came to see Marissa and my baby."

Louise clutched at her heart. His baby.

"How do you expect she's doing? She's having a baby, thanks to you."

The man's gaze didn't waver. "I know I been a jerk. But I . . . I love Marissa. I want to marry her."

"No!" Louise jumped up. "You can't!"

Gladys and Ross turned toward her simultaneously. "Who's she?" asked Ross, jerking his thumb toward Louise.

"Marissa's giving the baby up for adoption. She tried to contact you. This is Mrs. Wheatly. She's taking the baby. Everything's been arranged; it's final and it's all legal."

Ross looked stricken for a moment, then glared at Louise. "You're not taking the baby, okay? I'm sorry. I've thought about it and it ain't right. I know I've done wrong, but now, well, I'm sorry, but I won't let you take my baby."

"You've no right!" Louise said. "Marissa's already made the decision."

"Wait a minute, lady. I got rights, okay? I'm the father."

"No, it's all arranged." Louise began to cry. "It's all arranged."

"Ross, listen," Gladys said. "We've got to talk about this."

He turned toward Gladys with angry eyes. "There's nothing to talk about."

A pink-cheeked nurse entered. "Looks like a run on girls today, Mrs. Casaday. Seven and a half pounds.

Mom and baby are fine. Doctor will see you in a minute, and we'll have Mom in her room in five, ten minutes.''

"I gotta see Marissa," Ross said, rushing out past the nurse. "I'm the father."

Gladys rose and stood before Louise, patting her arm nervously. "Louise, I can't tell you how sorry . . . Perhaps it's for the best . . . I just don't know. I'm not even sure that Marissa will marry him, after the way . . . I'm so sorry . . ."

Louise clutched Gladys' hand. "Don't let him do it, please, please."

Gladys took a deep breath. "It's up to Marissa. She has to decide." She went through the door, leaving Louise standing there white, stricken.

Louise wanted to follow, wanted to see the baby (not *her* baby any longer), but couldn't bear the thought of gazing at the child she had come *this* close to having, the child she'd lost in a grim twist of fate.

She walked slowly down the hall, her shoes clacking loudly, holding back the tears. On the drive home in the shadowy twilight she tried to reconcile all that had happened, tried to convince herself it was all for the best. Perhaps when she got home there'd be a phone call saying, "It was all a mistake. Come and get your baby."

As she drove up, Jonathon was pulling into the circular driveway. Through her tears she blurted, brokenly, the tragic story. Collapsing against his shoulder, she sobbed, "I'll never have a baby. Never."

23

"There'll be another baby for us, honey." Jonathon knelt at the edge of the lawn and spaded several small holes in the moist dirt next to the patio. He'd stopped off after work to buy three pots of purple asters in an effort to buoy Louise's spirits, though they'd hardly have time to enjoy them this late in the season. Louise had been inconsolable since yesterday, when she "lost my baby," as she dramatically put it. "One of the agencies will come through for us," he said. "Have a little faith."

Louise loved Jonathon, but he didn't understand. He didn't have this aching hollow within him that yearned and hungered for a child. "We're at the bottom of the agencies' lists. We're too old, they say."

Rachel joined them. "Let me plant some." She'd been disappointed as well, after having resurrected her old stuffed toys and shopped for a special plate and silver spoon.

Jonathon handed her the spade. "Here, sweetie, dig a hole. A little deeper than the roots. That's it."

They worked in silence for a few moments, then Jonathon said, "Maybe Marissa will convince Ross that it's best for all concerned to let the baby go."

Louise said, "No. He was adamant."

"Look at the other side of this. Mother, father, and baby are reunited, a family. That's how it should be, the natural way of things." He took one of the plants from Louise and held it firmly while she tossed loose dirt around it.

"Some family. He plays in a rock band."

Jonathon tamped the dirt around the plants and brought the hose around from the side of the house.

"I'll water them," Rachel said, taking the hose.

The garden, a profusion of color, usually afforded Louise a sense of peace and consolation. In a last burst of September glory, the roses, pink, yellow, cream, and red, were especially breathtaking. But today the garden failed to cheer her. Distractedly she pulled a few weeds from the verbena border. "You should have seen him, Jon," she said. "He wouldn't know the first thing about being a father; he didn't even look clean."

"He's young. Maybe he'll change. Fatherhood has a way of doing that sometimes."

"When I left I saw a motorcycle parked near my car. I'm sure it was his. A motorcycle! Even if they marry, they'll probably be divorced in a year or two. They're both such *children.*"

"We'll keep up the search, honey. You remember my friend Dr. Morton? We play golf together. I'll talk to him."

Louise gazed after a brown squirrel scampering across the back lawn and up a butternut tree. "Dr. Morton's a podiatrist."

"It's worth a try. He may know someone who knows someone, and so on. And Dr. Marchand will keep us in mind. And there are still the agencies." He washed his hands under the hose's spray.

"Oh, Jonathon, it's hopeless. We may as well admit it. The agencies haven't even contacted us."

"Where's that old optimism?" Jonathon wiped a dirt smudge from her cheek and kissed her forehead.

She shook her head. "I'm just so depressed."

The phone sounded and Rachel ran to answer it. Moments later she poked her head out the patio door and said, "Telephone, Louise. It's Marissa."

When Louise picked up the phone Marissa's thin voice sounded faraway and sad. "Louise, I don't know what to say, except that I'm very, very sorry."

Louise fought for control. "Then you're going to keep the baby?"

"Yes. Ross wants to get married right away. I don't know what changed him, and I don't care. I really love him. He loves me."

"What about college?"

"Maybe I can take some night classes."

Louise's innate sense of correctness, of compassion, took hold. "Well, I wish you the best, Marissa. Enjoy your baby."

She saw herself in years to come, a lover of other people's babies, crocheting sweaters and booties, giving showers, full of envy and sadness. Picking up a Dr. Spock book from the kitchen table, she riffled through the pages. She'd read it from end to end. Twice. She tossed it across the table.

Max had finally arranged for Tina's interview at the advertising firm where he worked, and with both excitement and trepidation Tina dressed in her new navy pantsuit with flared legs, purchased with money borrowed from Louise. She fussed over her hair, which clearly needed styling. Impetuously she snipped an inch off the bottom and coaxed it to turn under. Somehow, she didn't feel up to the challenge of tackling a new job, something for which she didn't have a clear concept. Chiding herself for lack of confidence, she kissed Elena, gave Flora last-minute instructions, and was off.

The huge modern building with its wall of gray glass intimidated her. Stylishly coiffed and dressed women moved about with airs of confidence and purpose. Should she have worn a skirt, had her hair done?

An indifferent receptionist gave her a sheaf of forms. "Fill them out at the table over there and bring them back.'' Looking bored, she gazed down her nose at Tina. Tina filled out a questionnaire and a personality profile, and lingered over each of the thinly veiled questions. Should she come across as aggressive, passive, passive-aggressive? a leader or a team player? an independent thinker? The questions became more and more confusing. In the end she tried to answer honestly.

Afterward a secretary took her into the office of Mr. Slade Billingsley. Was his real name Slade? she wondered. He looked at some notes and asked several questions, while Tina focused on his many large white teeth, which seemed to take over half his face. Tina asked a few questions of her own, and listened attentively to his answers. He told her something about the company and she made pertinent remarks to indicate that she'd done her homework.

''It's an entry-level position and the pay isn't spectacular to begin with, but there's room for growth, especially for someone bright and enthusiastic,'' he said.

Was she coming across as bright and enthusiastic? she wondered, sitting up a bit straighter and stretching her mouth into a smile. The interview was proceeding fairly well, Tina thought. And yet on some level she wasn't quite selling herself. And she didn't quite know why. The firm was solid, the job interesting and challenging. Mr. Billingsley rose and took her on a short tour of the offices—well-appointed with the latest equipment—which covered two floors. ''And we're growing every day,'' he said with unmasked pride, his teeth gleaming.

At the conclusion of the interview she shook his hand, firmly but not too firmly, and said, ''It's been a pleasure.''

She and Max had arranged to meet afterward for lunch at a restaurant close by. While she waited at a checked-cloth-covered table, she replayed the interview in her mind. It had gone well, she decided. She would have to write him a note tonight. *Dear Mr. Happytooth, thanks for the interview and, by the by, what kind of toothpaste do you use?*

She giggled inwardly.

What if she actually got the job? She closed her eyes and felt a sudden rush of clarity, felt as if she were listening to a conch shell spill out the sounds of the sea. *Is this what you really want to do, Tina?* Vivid scenes from her teaching days in Washington paraded through her mind. She remembered the sense of satisfaction and pride she had received from her work, and realized she loved touching small minds, loved seeing faces light up when a new concept was received and understood, loved the sense of worth when lessons went well. She didn't want a job in advertising. She wanted to be a teacher.

Max joined her with a kiss on the cheek. "I didn't get a chance to talk to Billingsley, but I did pass him in the hall and he gave me a thumbs-up sign. Looks good, kid."

Tina smiled. "Whether I get it or not, it's okay either way."

"Hey, think positive. I think you'll get it. I went to bat for you."

"Max, I really appreciate you setting this up, going to all the trouble . . ."

"Oh, I just took Billingsley out to lunch and put in a few good words." He grinned modestly.

"I know, and it means a lot to me. But I've been thinking." She stirred her coffee. "Would I really fit into this sort of business?"

"Of course you would. You'd be great. You *will* be great."

She took a deep breath. "You know, I've told you how I enjoy teaching, how gratifying it is for me—"

"Yeah, Tina, but this is a great career move."

"What I'm trying to say is, well, teaching is what I really want to do."

Max's eyes widened. "You're just subbing. There's no money in that."

"True, but I'll get a permanent job; I'm sure of it."

He shook his head. "You're not going to throw this opportunity away, are you, after I've set it up?"

"Max, the truth of the matter is, I don't really care whether people smoke one brand of cigarettes over another, use one brand of toothpaste over another, eat one brand of cereal over another." She pulled back, not wanting to hurt Max's feelings. "I mean, it sounds creative and exciting—I can see how your adrenaline can get moving—but for me, well, I keep thinking of a few special kids I taught in Washington, kids that I may have made a small difference with. One of them sent me a note the other day. I tutored him after school, against his will, and now he's doing well. He may not end up president, but at least he'll probably stay out of the gutter. I need to do something that, well, that touches my heart." She lowered her eyes. "That sounds hopelessly corny, doesn't it?"

"No. It sounds stupid. Tina, think about the future. You could move right up in this industry. Where's the growth in teaching? How high can you go? You can become a principal, maybe, if you keep going to school and piling on degrees."

"I don't want to move ahead; I just want to teach. Advertising can chew you up and spit you out too. I'm not naive. You're only as good as your last good idea."

"It's a challenge."

"So is teaching; much more so."

"Tina, it would be different if you had a permanent job. You might be subbing for years before you get permanent."

"I'll get something soon."

"Think about the money."

"Maybe I don't care about that."

He gave an exasperated sigh and looked away, shaking his head. "I can't believe this."

With a stubborn lift of her chin Tina said, "Well, that's the way I feel."

He threw some bills on the table. "Let's get out of here. I've got work to do."

Later the next day Tina got a phone call from Mr. Billingsley. He was pleased to inform her she had the job.

Tina cleared her throat. "I'm so, *so* sorry, Mr. Billingsley, but something else has come up. I'm afraid I must decline. I really appreciate everything."

After a moment's silence on the other end he politely but coldly said he was sorry too and hung up.

Tina wondered fleetingly if she were being a fool.

Later that evening, with Elena propped in the curve of her arm, she arrived at Louise's to commiserate about Marissa's baby.

"Louise," she said, turning Elena over to Rachel, "you're going to get a baby. I had a dream and in it we both had babies. I've got a strong feeling about this."

"I wish I felt that way. Right now I think it's hopeless."

"Come on, Lou, I hate to see you this way," Tina said. "Go back to the fertility clinic."

"No. It doesn't do a bit of good. God just doesn't mean for me to have a baby. If there *is* a God, and if he cares."

"Lou, don't give up like this. Have a little trust. My dream was so vivid. Both babies were dressed in pink." Tina followed her sister to the family room with milk (for the nursing mom with the big bazooms, as Tina said) and cookies.

"I don't want to talk about it." Louise fluffed a pillow and sat, glumly crossing her arms over her chest. "Tell me about the job interview."

"It went really well. They offered me the job, but I

didn't take it. Max is furious with me. But I've decided I want to teach.''

"I always loved teaching too. When Rachel's a little older, I'll probably go back to it."

"So I start subbing again tomorrow, the sixteenth."

"Is Flora going to babysit?" Louise asked, ignoring Walter Cronkite reciting the news in the background.

"Yes, she's in seventh heaven. But I'm a mess. I hate to leave the baby." Tina shot a wistful glance in Elena's direction.

Taking a sip of ginger ale, Louise sneezed when the bubbles drifted to her nose. "Wait a minute. This is the fifteenth? Tina, I should have had my period two days ago."

Tina's eyes widened. "Your emotions can screw it up. Mine are never regular."

"But mine are. Like clockwork. Like the seasons of the moon."

"You don't think . . . ?"

Louise closed her eyes and said fervently, "I'm afraid to think."

"Oh, God. What if? Please, Lou, don't get your hopes up too soon."

Louise's heart did a dance. "I won't." But she did. This had never happened before. Maybe, maybe, maybe her prayers were being answered at long, agonizing last.

When her flow didn't start after another week, she went to Dr. Marchand, who said it was a bit early, but nevertheless examined her and took a test.

A few days later, with thumping heart and Jonathon at her side, Louise called the doctor. At the last minute she handed the phone to Jonathon. If it was bad news, she couldn't bear it. Jon's face revealed nothing as he listened and nodded. Finally he said, "Would you repeat that for my wife, Doctor?"

Louise took the receiver with a trembling hand.

"The test came back positive, Louise. You are pregnant."

Too overcome to speak, Louise handed the receiver back to Jonathon and grabbed him around the neck.

The heavens had parted and the angels sang. It was a miracle.

Ann didn't encourage Martin to visit, but she didn't discourage him either. After all, besides herself, no one was more affected by the tragedy of Brian's death, no one more concerned about Matthew and Teddy, than Martin. He called often and usually stopped by on Saturday mornings. They found some small solace in talking together, in discussing the boys' lives and futures.

On this particular Saturday he called to say he'd be over to take both boys shopping—Teddy had his heart set on Earth shoes, whatever they were—and why didn't Ann come along?

Eleven-year-old Teddy, like a scarecrow whose clothing shrank in a rainstorm, outgrew his clothes at an alarming rate. Thin wrists showed below his shirt cuffs, scrawny neck emerged from his collar even though she'd bought clothes before school started a month ago. At the mall, he wore a perpetual grin from the pleasure of having his parents together.

Matt, on the other hand, was taciturn, his usual state during the past several months. Ann's heart ached for him, knowing the pain he tried valiantly to hide. She nudged him with her elbow, and made a frowning face, trying to draw a smile, but he merely glanced at her with a disparaging look that said: *Mothers—who can figure them?*

After two hours of prowling the mall for just the "right" thing, Ann threw in the towel. "I've had it. You two shop on your own."

Martin said, "Let's you and me have coffee, Ann. The guys can meet us at the Big Boy in an hour." As the boys walked away, a passing bevy of adolescent girls turned to ogle them.

At the restaurant Martin slid into a booth. "Matt's having a hard time, isn't he?"

"He's getting better. His girlfriend, Diane, helps; she's very sweet, very understanding."

"I blame myself for Brian's death." He put his head in his hands. "God, how I blame myself."

"Stop that, Martin, it doesn't help. I know. I've been doing the same thing." It seemed to Ann he'd aged overnight. Gray merged with brown in his newly grown mustache, and worry lines permanently creased his forehead.

He dumped sugar into his coffee. "I've been so damn miserable. And lonely. I've been lonely."

Ann didn't answer. From the boys' reports she knew that he was dating a variety of women, but not seriously.

"Maybe we should get back together, for the kids' sake." He kept his eyes down, intently stirring his coffee.

Ann watched him in silence. She hadn't expected this, wasn't prepared for it. "For the kids. Not a very good reason."

"Not only for the kids, then, for us too."

Ann shook her head. "Don't you remember all the problems?"

He finally met her gaze. "There weren't so many problems. Everyone has a few. There are no marriages made in heaven."

"You had an affair, remember? That's a problem. And there were things going wrong long before that."

He looked surprised. "That's not true. For years we got along fine."

"We got along. That's all. We weren't *together*, a team. We just shared a house and children. Did we ever talk, really talk?"

"You know me, I don't like discussing and dissecting every little thing." He toyed with a packet of sugar.

Ann observed him for a moment, head tilted. "Yes, I know you. And you're not likely to change. And I'm not likely to either. So I guess that's that."

"We could try again. Do things differently this time."

"If nothing's changed inside of us, then we'll have more of whatever we had—or, actually, didn't have—before."

"Was that so bad, really? I mean, before I started goofing off."

"Martin, I can't just dismiss the 'goofing off,' as you so cavalierly put it. I don't know if I can ever forgive that, or trust that it won't happen again. Can you guarantee it won't?"

His mouth tightened. "Jesus, Ann, don't keep beating a dead horse. I just thought . . . maybe we should just *consider* it. *Consider* getting together again." He took a deep breath. "Why don't we go to a show this evening?"

"I have a date."

He nodded. Ann thought the boys must have mentioned Scott to Martin. Scott had finally badgered her into introducing him to the boys a few weeks earlier.

"Is it serious?" Martin asked.

"It could be."

They both fell silent.

"You know," Ann said, "I was unhappy a lot of the time during our marriage, but didn't really let you know about it. Now I think I should have screamed and yelled. Instead, I bottled up a lot of resentment. Mostly, I put up with things, didn't want to rock the boat or make you mad."

"We could both change, both try to communicate more." He reached for her hand. "We've been to hell and back, haven't we?"

Tears welled up in Ann's eyes, but she remained

silent. Martin hadn't met her needs and probably she hadn't met his. But he was the one who had strayed, who had broken their marriage vows. The fabric of their marriage had torn in many places. Was it too late to mend the frayed edges? Moments later, when the boys rushed up to their booth, she pasted a hasty smile on her face.

"Well, just think about it," Martin said under his breath.

Ann aimed the dryer at her short dark hair, bemoaning the fact that she hadn't quite acquired the knack for blow-drying. She gave up and used her fingers and a bit of hair spray, then made up her face carefully, smoothing extra concealer under her clear dark eyes. At forty, the telltale creases were just beginning to surface. The idea of aging never really bothered her, and in fact with the passing years she felt increasingly more comfortable in her skin. Scott, younger by five years, looked deceptively more youthful than thirty-five. "I am what I am," she said defiantly to her mirror image.

Martin's proposal monopolized her thoughts. What had prompted it? Was he just getting tired of "baching it," fending for himself, making his own meals or eating out? His apartment was small, the boys said. He used to love sprawling out in their large home, puttering in the basement or garage. Probably he missed that as well as the patio and garden on summer evenings. And the child-support payments must be restricting his spending. There was little doubt that a remarriage would be best for the children. But what about her? And what about the years together after the children were grown and gone?

Martin minimized his affair, and in truth, Ann could even understand how it had happened. The era of flower children and free love, the notion of instant gratification, permeated every area of their lives.

"Love the one you're with," said Stephen Stills. "Do your own thing," was the battle cry, along with, "If it feels good, do it." That consciousness flowed from newspapers, movies, books. Drugs proliferated, marijuana use was common, crime was rising. Scandal had reached the White House with the Watergate wiretapping toppling President Nixon, who'd recently proclaimed, "I am not a crook." Some good had evolved from the social changes—women were taking more responsibility for the direction of their lives. Armed with new awareness, they had ceased being passive participants in the sex act.

Contrarily, Ann worried for the world, the planet, wondered if the new sexual freedom would perpetuate more diseases despite the Red Cross prediction that, "In twenty years' time there may well be a permissive society that is relatively free from venereal diseases." Perhaps. She wondered if this decade would be a small blip on the time line of history, or if its effects would be felt for many years to come. But none of her ruminations answered her doubts about Martin.

He was still, in many ways, an enigma. He needed her—that was evident. Or he thought he did. But he hadn't said he loved her. Was an affirmation of love a requirement, or was she seeking her own version of romantic love? And most important, did she love him? There was no doubt she felt a connection; he had been a major part of her life, the father of her children. She'd forgiven much. But love? What was that, anyway? she wondered. There should be a wider choice of vocabulary to describe the different kinds of caring. The sort of intoxicating need she felt for Scott was entirely different from the sort of caring she now felt for Martin, which had evolved into a mixture of sympathy and empathy.

Her parents would probably advise her to remarry him, having always liked Martin while recognizing his emotional limitations. But her parents, steeped in old traditions, weren't in her shoes and their moral and religious strictures were no longer hers.

And what about Scott? She loved him and had come to depend on him emotionally and physically. He had listened to her self-recriminations during the aftermath of Brian's death and tolerated her tears, offering a quiet comfort, an acceptance, while remaining in the background. He'd called every day and sent missives and flowers often. But he had never *known* Brian, hadn't had children, so he couldn't possibly fathom the deep wounds that she knew would never totally heal. She should tell Scott about Martin's proposal. They always tried to be honest with one another.

When Scott called for her, she hugged him tightly and lingered over his kiss, letting the passion surface to reassure herself it was still there, still strong, still important.

"In due time," he said, laughing, pleased with her reaction. He held her at arm's length. "You look gorgeous."

She knew she looked good in a classic beige silk suit and turquoise blouse. Their destination was a wedding, a second one for both bride and groom, at the home of one of Scott's good friends. Second marriages seemed almost the norm lately.

The simple ceremony was held in the large living room and the reception took place outside, where servers circled with huge platters of food. A three-piece band played while guests mingled on the three decks overlooking a North Oakland County lake. The moon shed a dazzling spangle of lights on the dark water.

Ann and Scott were recognized as a couple by their friends, who made jokes about marriage. A matter of time, they obviously thought, before the decision would be made, the date set. Scott laughed off the teasing remarks, but Ann felt uncomfortable with the chiding. They kissed in the romantic moonlight and danced until very late. Early on in their relationship, Scott, an expert dancer, had taught Ann the cha-cha when she had protested that all she knew was the twist.

"It's time to go," Ann said finally, after most of the guests had gone. "And I'm driving. You've had too much to drink."

"I have not. I'm not drunk, just a little sleepy," Scott said, but he offered little resistance. Back at his apartment he fell onto the sofa and dropped off to sleep. An unruly lock of hair had fallen to his eyes, giving him an innocent-little-boy expression and bringing a smile to Ann's lips.

She kissed his cheek and shook his shoulder. "Wake up, Scotty, I'm going to take your car and go home."

Opening one eye, he aimed a lopsided grin in her direction and promptly fell back to sleep.

She'd never seen him like this, so vulnerable. Smiling, she untied his shoes and wiggled them off, then laid a quilt over him. "I'm taking your car home, Scott," she said loudly.

Rousing, he made a grab for her hand and missed. "Stay," he urged. "Call the boys and say you're with me."

"I can't."

"They probably figure we're sleeping together anyway."

"No, they don't." Ann felt unreasonably upset by that notion.

"Do they think you're a nun? They weren't born yesterday."

Ann yanked her hand away. "I'm going. I'll take your car. Get a good night's sleep and I'll come by tomorrow after church. You can take me to brunch and drive me home."

"You always evade," he mumbled. "We have to talk, Ann."

She shook her head, knowing Scott was beyond talk.

"Not now." She paused at the door. "I'll call you in the morning."

When she saw Scott the next day, she fully expected him to bring up the subject of marriage, but surprisingly he didn't. Nor did he during the next several weeks. Was he waiting for her to bring it up? She knew she should mention to Scott that she was occasionally seeing Martin, who continued to be attentive without being intrusive. Twice Martin had taken the family to dinner and once he and Ann went alone. He didn't mention remarriage again, but the question hovered around them, just below the surface. In his own low-keyed manner, Martin was courting her. Ann felt as though she was caught in a vise pressing tighter and tighter. Just before Thanksgiving Martin asked if he could spend the day with them. "You're all I have," he said, "my family."

Despite the stirring of sympathy—which he'd certainly counted on—Ann said, "It's out of the question. We're having dinner with my parents and sisters." He was trying hard to wiggle his way back into favor. He seemed so alone.

A few weeks before Christmas Scott came for dinner and stayed to help decorate the tree. The boys had picked out the largest Scotch pine in the lot and as usual a foot had to be cut from the bottom. Together Scott and the boys sawed inexpertly and finally secured the tree in its wobbly stand, amid directions from Ann, "To the left . . . just a smidgen . . . too much . . . turn it a bit. Ah, perfect."

Scott circled the tree with strings of lights and the boys, unusually subdued as they decorated, didn't even yell insults to one another. Other years they would have been tossing tinsel, choking one another with golden garlands. Other years Brian would have been there. Though no one spoke of him, his ghost seemed to haunt the room.

"The best tree ever," Ann said as she served their traditional hot chocolate and Christmas cookies.

"I'd like to propose a toast," Scott said, raising his mug. "To the missing family member, Brian, whose spirit is surely in this room, who must be smiling, who must have loved you all very much."

Ann shot a surprised look at Scott, then dropped her chin to her chest and said through a film of tears, "To Brian. I love you so and I miss you. Merry Christmas."

Teddy laid his head on Ann's shoulder. "I love you, Bri. I think of you all the time and pray for you."

Matt, sitting at the edge of the coffee table, stared into the fire. In a tortured voice he began to talk softly. "Brian was like my right arm. I always knew what he was thinking. That's why it's so damn hard for me, because I *knew* he was in trouble. He quit talking to me, he dropped out of sports, so I knew. But I thought he'd come out of it, and he would have, I know he would have, if that . . . the accident hadn't happened." He banged his fist on the table. "Dammit! Damn you, Brian! Damn you!" Again and again he hit the table, crying a torrent of tears.

Ann and Teddy huddled beside him, hugging, crying together, comforting one another. Finally Teddy said, "Hey, Matt, remember when we were rowing at Pine Lake and Bri pretended he'd fallen in? We thought he'd drowned. You were so mad you wouldn't let him in the boat and he had to swim to shore. Man, was he mad."

"Yeah. And then he tried to dry his sneakers by the fire and they just shriveled up." Matt laughed. "We took a picture of them."

Stories seemed to bubble up from them and they vied with each other to recall incidents, funny and poignant and sad, that brought Brian back for a short time. Finally they all fell into a somber and peaceful silence. Matt went to the piano and began playing, not

Christmas carols, as Ann expected, but a favorite of Brian's, "Let It Be." Afterward he sat hunched over the keys for several moments, then slowly rose. "I think I'll turn in."

Teddy said, "Me too."

They each kissed their mother, then Matt shook Scott's hand. "Thanks, Scott."

Teddy held out his hand to Scott, but Scott waved it aside and hugged him instead. "Merry Christmas," Teddy said, his voice gruff with emotion.

After the boys left, Scott coaxed the fire into life and added a couple of logs, then sat staring into it.

Ann brought them each a Scotch. "Cocoa didn't quite do it." She sat beside him, resting her head on his shoulder. "You took a calculated risk, you know."

"It was waiting to be said. Was it okay?"

"Yes. We needed that. We haven't cried together since the funeral."

The fire, along with the multicolored tree lights, lent a cheery warmth to the large room.

Scott bounced Ann's hand in his. "I like your boys, Ann."

"You would've liked Brian too." Her eyes teared up again despite her efforts at control.

He pressed her hand to his cheek. "I know."

"I think Teddy and Matthew like you too."

"Shall I take you all to midnight mass Christmas Eve?"

"Martin wants to take the boys on Christmas morning. Scott, I need to be honest with you. Martin's been coming around. We went to dinner a couple of times."

A vein jumped in Scott's temple. "Why did you go out with him?"

"We had things to discuss. About the boys."

"What's wrong with the telephone?"

She took Scott's hand. "It's easier to talk in person."

Scott was silent for a moment. "Do you still love him?"

"Not in the same sense that I love you. I'm concerned for him. And he's concerned about me and his children. He makes a good argument about the cohesiveness of the family."

The muscles below Scott's eyes grew taut. "Forget about the family for just a while. What does Ann want?"

She shook her head. "I don't know."

"Well, you're going to have to decide. It's him or me. I give you until January 1. That's it."

"Scott—"

"This isn't open for argument, Ann. I know you've been through hell, but I'm tired of being patient." He turned and retrieved his coat from the hall closet.

She followed him to the door. "Will you call me tomorrow?"

He shrugged and opened the door, letting a drift of snowflakes float in on a cold wind.

He didn't even kiss her good-bye. The door slammed behind him.

Ann wrenched the door open. "Scott, wait, please."

He hesitated for a moment, looking both forlorn and angry, his coat collar up against his ears. Then he hurried to his car and shot out of the driveway on screeching tires.

When he didn't call in two days, Ann called him. There was no answer at seven o'clock, nine, or eleven. Her heart did a flip. Where could he be? She went to bed but couldn't sleep, imagining him with a voluptuous blonde in red satin who fawned and flirted. The next afternoon she went to his condominium. He opened the door and let her in without a word.

"I tried calling you last night," Ann said. "There was no answer."

"I was out."

She walked past him into the living room. "I guess you're still mad."

"Don't I have a right to be?" Scott glared at her, arms crossed over his chest.

Ann stepped toward him. "Yes, but you don't understand. Martin and I will always have a connection through the boys. But that's all."

"All I want to know is, do you love him?"

"No. That's over and done with. Whatever feeling I have for him is dead." She put her arms around his waist. "I love you, Scott."

He drew her close and kissed her eyelids. "Ah, Annie. I need you. You don't know what it did to me, thinking of you with that bastard Martin. I was so afraid he had some sort of hold on you. God, I need you in my life. I love you." His hips thrust forward, rolling against her.

Hungrily her mouth met his, her desire, ever-present, escalating with each movement. He swept her up into his strong arms, nuzzling her neck, nibbling her ear, and released her onto his rumpled bed, the king-size bed of which she'd grown so fond, become so familiar. They made love urgently, then after a while again, this time in leisure, exploring each other, delighting one another.

"Where were you last night?" she asked, her head resting in its place against his shoulder.

"Were you worried?"

"Yes."

"I was just out with the guys. Drowning my troubles." He ran his fingers through her hair. "I was miserable. I can't go without you for more than two days. You're my sustenance. I need you so."

She smiled, content, and placed butterfly kisses across his chest.

Afterward, wearing Scott's pajama top, she made omelets while he made toast and coffee.

"I feel like we're on a honeymoon," she said when they'd eaten. "I hate to leave."

"You don't have to." He reached up under the pajama top and brushed her breast, arousing her once again.

"One more time?" she asked as he unbuttoned the top and drew it from her shoulders.

"At least."

It was after three o'clock in the morning when she let herself into her house, feeling exhilarated and blissful. Thank God the boys slept like logs.

She couldn't sleep thinking of Scott. Although she loved him, she was content with her existence just as it was. They saw each other several times a week, but neither interfered in the other's daily lives. Ann wasn't responsible for his food or laundry or dental appointments or charge cards. Especially, she wasn't responsible for his moodiness (which was rare) or his happiness (which was not). If she happened to work late, she needn't apologize for disrupting the routine. If she wanted to sleep late on weekends, she was accountable to no one. It seemed a shame to disturb such a perfect setup. Her only real concern was that if she didn't marry Scott, they had no solid commitment. Might he be tempted someday to look elsewhere?

The next weekend Scott suggested they go Christmas shopping.

"I thought you hated shopping as much as I do."

"Indulge me. I'd like to get you a Christmas gift."

"Surprise me. You know I love surprises."

"You're no fun. Most women would jump at the chance to pick out a gift. My charge cards are burning a hole in my pocket and you aren't even interested."

"Okay, I'm convinced."

At Eastland Mall Scott stopped before a jewelry store. She squeezed his arm. She didn't wear a great deal of jewelry, but loved to have a few extravagant pieces, keepsakes. She wished fleetingly for a daughter to inherit her few mementos.

Inside, when Scott reached the ring display, he stopped. "That one." He pointed to a large solitaire, glistening in its black velvet background.

"It's gorgeous." She searched for his hand and squeezed it. "An engagement ring, isn't it?"

He nodded. "It's time."

"I . . . I don't know what to say."

His eyes grew very serious. "Say yes."

She took a deep breath. "Yes," she whispered.

24

Chiara and her daughters nibbled and chattered in the kitchen as they put the finishing touches on Christmas dinner. Tina ducked an elbow, then escaped the steamy heat and the voices for the cooler air of the dining room. As she placed red napkins around the table, strains of Perry Como singing "I'll Be Home for Christmas" wafted from the living room along with the men's voices discussing sports, politics, the state of the nation and the state, in short, man-talk.

All in all, 1974 had been a strange year, Tina thought. The year's news reviews were filled with stories from ridiculous to tragic. Mooning (baring backsides to surprised spectators) was out, streaking (running naked through public places) was in. The Vietnam war, against which she'd protested, was now just a bad dream, but at home there was unrest. Violence went unchecked. The mother of slain civil-rights leader Martin Luther King was shot in a church. A Sarasota television commentator shot herself on the air, in living color, and later died. The nation was rocked when President Richard Nixon resigned and was replaced by Gerald Ford of Michigan. A nation of violence, Tina thought. Her reverie was disturbed by a pat on the shoulder.

"It's been quite a year, hasn't it?" Ann said.

"That's what I was thinking. So much has happened. Last Christmas I was pregnant with Elena and oblivious of the struggles of a single working mother. Now look at me! I wouldn't give up a minute of my life with Elena, but damn, I'd give anything to bask in a bubble bath for an hour or read the paper without interruption. Or, most of all, to sleep until nine!''

"Welcome to the real world.'' Ann placed gleaming silver at each plate. "By the way, where's Max?''

"He's spending Christmas with his sister and her family in Traverse City. His parents are coming up from Florida.''

"You ought to marry that man.''

Tina pondered that statement. She hadn't really thought about marrying Max, yet he *had* burrowed into her life.

Ann said, "Did you hear me, or do you choose to ignore the statement?''

"I was just thinking about that situation. I'm not sure where we stand. We don't actually date much, but he comes around, surprises me with a deli meal, or he'll offer to shop or pick up cleaning. And he loves Elena.''

"He's got my vote. Do you love him?''

"Good question. We never talk about love. I like him and care for him. But, I don't know . . .''

"You need to think about Elena too. She needs a father.''

"Elena and I get along just fine. We're quite self-sufficient.''

"Tina, are you still carrying a torch for Adam?''

Tina shrugged away the question. She had tried, unsuccessfully, to put thoughts of Adam behind her.

"If so, give it up. Get on with your life.''

Tina lifted her chin. "I think I'm doing okay. Speaking of marriage, have you set the date?''

Ann's finger toyed with her engagement ring. "Not yet.''

"What's stopping you?'' Tina had noticed the easy

rapport between Scott and Ann as well as the physical spark. Although the specter of her recent tragedy still hovered over Ann, she wore a new air of serenity.

Ann occupied herself with the table setting. "We're both so busy."

"Oh, Ann, what an excuse. He's obviously good for you, and I know he's anxious. Look at him, ingratiating himself with the family."

Scott was making small talk with Jonathon and her father. Earlier, he'd tossed Elena in the air, teased Matthew and Teddy, and complimented all the women. They'd all met him before, briefly, but a family holiday was the acid test. He'd pass, Tina decided.

Ann smiled possessively. "He's quite a guy."

"Don't let him get away."

Tina felt a tugging at her ankles. Elena had crawled to her and was pulling upright unsteadily and babbling for attention. Tina settled her in the high chair Chiara had resurrected from the basement and put a cracker in her pudgy hand. Two tiny, shiny white nubs of teeth peeped through her pink gums.

"What are you two gossiping about?" Louise set a bread basket on the table. "Am I missing anything?" Although she was barely showing, Louise wore maternity clothes and looked like a Madonna. In contrast, Tina had tried to conceal her belly until the last possible moment, desperate to keep the unsavory secret.

"We were talking about—what else?—men," Tina said. "We'd probably bore you, with your perfect marriage." She couldn't help a niggling kernel of envy. Her sister was spared money worries; her child would have a stable two-parent home with a kind and loving dad.

"Oh, Jon has his moments. Actually he's become tiresome now that he's a child-care expert. He's read every book."

Ann said, "He's the proverbial cock of the walk, now that fatherhood is impending."

From the kitchen Chiara called. "Girls, enough of the talk, I need some help here."

They bustled back to the kitchen and shortly the meal was ready. The table, stretched to its limit, almost groaned under the weight of food. Afterward, leftovers would accompany the guests home. They bowed heads and Mike said the standard grace, "Bless us, O Lord, and these, thy gifts . . ." then added a few moments of silent prayer for Brian. Somehow, Tina thought, his spirit was among them. Mike ended with a special welcome for Scott. Apparently he'd passed. Tina felt saddened to see that her father, at seventy-four, born with the century, showed signs of aging—bent shoulders, totally white hair, which still lay in neat waves. Lately he had asked "What?" repeatedly, though he vehemently denied a hearing loss.

Elena rattled her spoon against the tray, smiling and cooing in delight to one and all. Tina planted a kiss on her cheek, suddenly buoyed by this small representation of the next generation. Elena laughed and pumped chubby arms up and down with the pleasure of being well-loved.

They were all part of a couple today, all but Tina. One more Christmas dinner in the photo album of her mind. A lump formed in her throat. She had her own family of two, a lopsided family that was missing a most important figure, the father, that one person that had always been a solid element in her own growth and maturation, despite (or maybe because of) the disagreements. Perhaps Ann was right. Elena needed a father.

A few days later, Tina folded the bedclothes from the sofa bed, and muttering, shoved the mattress back into place while Elena crawled about looking for dust particles she could ingest. The worst feature about the apartment was its single bedroom, which Tina had turned into a nursery. She'd searched for a two-bedroom apartment, but couldn't afford the increase in rent.

Since Christmas she'd been thinking about Max and their relationship. Although she'd been a feminist proponent, sure that "making it on your own" was possible and that a meaningful life could be had sans marriage, still there was much to be said for sharing the domestic load. All her energies seemed to go into the trials of daily living, feeding and clothing herself and her baby, laundry, shopping. There was little strength for anything else. She was grateful for her parents and sisters, who often offered to sit, and for Max, who offered companionship.

Tina thought about her conversation with Ann. Despite the pro-women movements of the sixties and seventies, the myriad of articles and books written about the strength and independence of women (*I am woman, hear me roar,* Helen Reddy sang), the world still revolved around couples. She wanted a helpmeet, a man in her bed, a father for her daughter, and—she must be perfectly honest—financial support. In short, she wanted a husband. And the only candidate on the horizon, though he had shortcomings of which she was well aware, was Max.

She had floated naturally into a steady sort of relationship with Max. He had become a constant in her life, her best friend. From the time they'd made up and made love, they drifted into a satisfying sexual relationship. She enjoyed his lovemaking, entering into it wholeheartedly. Yet, though Max didn't seem to notice, something was missing—that particular unity, a total involvement of the senses, a communion of body and soul. The way it had been with Adam. Moisture filmed her eyes as she thought again of Adam. With a mental shake she said aloud through gritted teeth, "Forget him."

She lived for vacations now, two weeks at Christmas and a glorious ten weeks next summer. Money, however, would be tight and she might have to waitress during the summer months. She carried a burden of guilt, knowing she owed her father money, although he never mentioned it. At thirty she should at least be self-supporting. A ray of hope had appeared recently, when the principal of the school she subbed in on a semiregular basis told her he was losing two teachers to retirement next year. He promised Tina he'd do everything in his power to get her hired. With so many schools closing because of the trend to ZPG, zero population growth, and laid-off teachers abounding, she knew getting the job meant he'd have to pull strings. She prayed he had the political clout to carry it off.

Elena made a choking sound and Tina scooped her up and retrieved a minuscule speck of paper from her throat, then sat her in a walker, where she proceeded to careen into furniture. Tina sighed. The small apartment wore her down. It became more and more impossible to find inventive ways of stacking the accumulation of baby things, not to mention her own necessary *stuff*. But the worst of it was the one bedroom, and the blasted, stubborn sofa, which had to be pulled out each night and returned to its position each morning. She, who had always had a room of her own, her own space, was now stuck in a barless cafe.

Her thoughts returned to her dilemma, and to Max. She and Max had never spoken of love. But there were caring and concern and a genuine liking between them. And perhaps this was the basis for many successful unions that were not encumbered with heart-soul-mind complications as well as sexual intensity. Couldn't one have a happy marriage without that intense and totally involving angst that often accompanies mindless passion?

She longed to go to all her married friends and acquaintances and ask what their marriages were based on; about sexual attraction versus simple affection. Males, she felt sure, were mainly guided by their hormones. Women, despite the new theories, seemed always to lead with their hearts and were destined to enjoy sex while desiring intimacy of another sort. The feminists would argue that not every woman needed a man for fulfillment. Oh, really? Then why this gnawing need? Well, she had followed her heart once to an unsatisfactory ending; this time she'd use her intellect.

Her mother arrived that afternoon with a pot of *gnocci*. She helped Tina put away the ornaments from the miniature Christmas tree she'd set on the kitchen table.

Tina rolled a golden garland into a ball and stored it in a plastic bag. "Ma, were you and Pa in love when you got married?"

Her mother shrugged and continued wrapping a delicate ornament in tissue. "Love. What a word. It was different then, in 1928, in Italy; a different world. We had an arranged marriage and everything was so . . . so backward, so primitive." She grew pensive. "I'll never forget the first time I saw your father. Oh, he was handsome and had that"—she threw her shoulders back—"that energy and strength. I knew he was a good man."

"But what about . . . well, sexual attraction?"

"Ah, you young people make such a big thing about that. At my age we don't think about sex so much."

"You're not old! Sixty-five isn't old! Don't you remember what it was like when you were young?"

Chiara nodded. "Oh, sure, sure I remember. At first I was just scared, scared to death of him, of sex, of all the things that were a mystery to me. No one ever spoke of personal things like sex. It was like a sin to talk about it, not like now, when you can't turn around without seeing undressed women in the newspapers, on television, in movies. Sex is everywhere." She shook her head disdainfully. "Then, right after we got married, off we went to a new country, and I was still scared." She laughed. "I'm older and wiser and don't scare so easily anymore. But after a while, yes, there was lots of love between us." She looked off into the distance in a glassy stare and Tina didn't want to intrude in her memories. Besides, how did one ask one's mother to describe her innermost feelings about the most personal act in which two people can engage?

Early on New Year's morning Tina took a fresh notepad, wrote "1975" in large figures across the cover, and made her lists, this time in the form of resolutions. Number one was "Stabilize my life." And that meant exorcising from her consciousness, once and for all, all thoughts of Adam, and concentrating on finding a suitable husband. Max was the obvious choice. He had a good job and adored Elena and her. She had known him since they were freshmen at Wayne State. He'd settled down since those early days, when he seemed always to have a string of girlfriends and had already been engaged twice by the time they graduated. Chewing the end of her pencil, Tina pondered how to change their relationship to one of courtship. As usual, she would take the direct course.

That evening she took care to look glamorous, twisting her long glossy hair off her face with escaping tendrils kissing cheeks and forehead. She'd updated an old black dress with sequin edging at the low neckline. The mirror told her she was meeting her thirties quite nicely, with an unlined, still-youthful face and trim figure that had returned quickly to the soft curves of her pre-Elena days.

Unfortunately, at the last moment Flora called to say she couldn't baby-sit because of a cold. Max cheerfully insisted on taking Elena along and was excited to show her the downtown Christmas-lights display. Afterward he took them to dinner at the Laikon in Greek Town. Elena squealed at the blaze of light from a flaming saganaki at the next table and the shouts of "Opa!"

Tina ordered stuffed grape leaves, then folded her hands demurely before her. "Let's talk, Max."

He tied a bib around wiggling Elena's neck. "This sounds serious."

"It is serious. Are you seeing anyone else besides me?"

"Not really."

"That didn't sound very positive."

"Well, I did see Clare a couple of times, but not recently. You remember her, don't you? She was the girl you met at the restaurant." He chewed on a wrinkled olive from his salad.

Tina recalled the slim, attractive woman who had been distinctly cool toward her. "I remember."

"She called me and we went out." He sipped some of his retsina and set the glass down carefully. "That was a few months ago."

Tina supposed she shouldn't have been too surprised. "Is there anything going on there? I mean, are you still interested? Are you going to see her again?"

"No. I told her you and I were pretty steady. An item."

Tina was silent for a long moment. "We're an item, eh?"

"Sure. Aren't we? I spend a couple of days a week at your place. We go out a lot."

"We've been going together for about a year."

"That long?" He smiled. "We've known each other forever."

"Max, do you love me?"

He looked startled, then gave a small embarrassed laugh. "Yeah, I guess I do."

"You guess?"

"No, I mean I do. I really do."

It sounded awkward; not a glorious and spontaneous expression of undying love and devotion.

"What about you, Tina? Do you love me?"

She smiled. "I guess I do." She reached for his hand. "Max, for a long time I told you to go out and get a real girlfriend. I'm not saying that anymore. It's time we talked about our future."

Max frowned. "What brought this on?"

"I don't know. Lots of things. We're both more mature now. I want a sense of security, I think."

"I thought you were satisfied, Tina."

"Well, I was. But, Max, we're not getting any younger. I have to think about Elena. She needs some stability. I don't want her to grow up with a series of 'uncles' coming to visit for a time, then leaving." Her voice grew soft. "We've come to depend on you."

"You can depend on me. Uncle Maxie."

"I guess what I mean is, where is this relationship heading?"

"Does it have to head someplace? What's wrong with just going together?"

She took a deep breath and stifled her annoyance. "People don't just 'go together' forever."

"Some do."

"Well, I don't."

Max cocked his head and stared at her. "Tina, is this a proposal?"

She bristled. This was not going well at all. "No! I just want to know . . . well, where we stand." Now that he seemed to be slipping slyly from the hook, she couldn't admit to having cast her line.

He looked perplexed. "What is it about women?

Can't you just enjoy the moment, the day, the month? Why do you always have to look for some kind of permanency? Here I thought we were happy just the way we were, and you have to go and spoil it.''

Tina bit her lip to keep from shouting. "Spoil it?''

"Yes, spoil it. This is the seventies, Tina. Not everybody gets married anymore. Some of us are free spirits.''

"I've been a free spirit! Now I'd like to try for companionship and security.''

Max made a settling gesture with his hands. "Okay, relax. Look, do you want to live together? Because that's okay by me. We could get a condo together and—''

Elena, sensing the tension, let out a howl.

"No, I don't want to live together,'' Tina said through tight lips. She scooped Elena out of her chair. "Let's go. I'm finished.''

They drove home in an awkward silence. At her apartment Max started to leave the car to help Tina with the baby, but she snapped, "Don't bother. I can manage.''

So he sat while Tina struggled to get Elena and the baby seat out of the back, the wintry wind slicing through her coat.

"I'll call you,'' he called after her. The car door slammed on his words.

In the warmth of the apartment Tina cuddled Elena close around her and cried. What was it about her that distanced men? Was she wearing some sort of invisible sign that said "Love me and leave me''? Or was it that she was destined to care for immature and irresponsible men all her life? Max was just using her and Elena as his pseudo family, getting comfort as well as sex without involvement.

But wasn't she using him as well, trying to convince herself she was in love, when what she wanted was merely a marriage of convenience? Perhaps Max was smarter than she, after all. Perhaps he intuitively saw behind her reasons.

Elena pulled at her hair, tugging it away from its mooring.

Tina kissed the baby's fingers. "I know, love, you need a change."

After that Max's visits were less and less frequent, and when they talked, he seemed to smell orange blossoms behind her every remark. She told herself it didn't matter. But truly it did matter, for he'd been there for her when she needed him and he was funny and generous and entertaining, a nice guy and good company. And now they were somewhat awkward with one another.

In June, after she hadn't heard from him in several weeks, he came over unexpectedly with a dozen yellow roses, wine, and a sack full of small white Chinese food cartons.

"Max! How nice. It's not my birthday. And I know it's not the Chinese New Year. To what do I owe this pleasant surprise?"

"Hey, I'm just a nice guy, remember?"

Elena, now fifteen months old, lit up at the sight of him. He produced from his pocket a small wind-up puppy who performed somersaults that sent Elena into paroxysms of giggles.

"I've missed you, toots," Max said, chucking Elena under the chin. "I've missed your mother too."

Tina wondered fleetingly if he'd had a change of heart.

After they'd finished the food and read the fortunes enclosed in stale cookies (ironically, hers said she should "follow her heart"), Max drained the wine bottle.

"Are we celebrating something I don't know about?" Tina asked, spooning leftovers back into the cartons.

"Not exactly celebrating."

"What, then? Come on, Max, we've always been honest. Or tried to be. What's going on?"

He evaded her stare. "Well, I . . . ah, sort of thought it was only fair to put a proper end to our relationship or whatever it was."

Tina's smile was a bit sad, a bit wistful. "Please don't tell me you've met someone and you're engaged to be married."

"Close. I've met someone and we're going to live together."

Tina sighed. "Well, that's what you wanted, isn't it?"

He rubbed his forehead. "I'm not sure. It's what *she* wants."

"Well. Well, well, well."

"I'm sorry, Tina."

"Don't be sorry. It wasn't meant to be for us." She rose and went to him, then kissed him tenderly. "Funny thing, Max. I think we'll always love one another. But just not enough."

"Yeah. It's kind of too bad, isn't it?"

"Yeah. If this were twenty years ago, when people got married the minute their hormones started jumping, you and I might have ended up together."

He nodded. "So it goes." He stood and hugged her and they held hands for a few moments.

She leaned into him, enjoying the masculine smell and feel of him, savoring a few last regrets.

"Hey," he murmured, "we couldn't sort of fool around for old times' sake? One for the road?"

Tina pushed away with a wry look.

"I didn't think so." He looked a little sheepish. "Well, I guess I'll be on my way."

"Keep in touch," she said, hugging him before he left.

She closed the door and leaned against it, wishing she could at least cry. But she didn't feel like crying, felt only a bittersweet sadness at the way life kept dealing her such frustrating hands. Max was not the man for her, but it was he who had ended it. And that hurt.

When Tina went to bed that night, she lay awake a long time thinking. She had made the best of her single life. But that wasn't really what she wanted. She'd like to meet someone, fall in love, get married, and live happily ever after, just like in the romance novels. Unfortunately, there was little opportunity to meet men while working in elementary schools, where mostly women worked and the few men were already married. And she had little inclination, time, or energy to look elsewhere, particularly in bars, where most alliances seemed to be made. Sleep came slowly and fitfully.

She slept late the next morning and had to rush to work, always a bad way to start. An unruly boy in her class pushed her to the limit and she reluctantly resorted to sending him to the principal's office. Before the final bell, the principal sent word to her classroom that he wanted her to stop at his office before she left. It would be about today's problem or the run-in she'd had earlier in the week with the parent of a troubled child.

She entered the office and sat while Mr. Tyler removed his glasses and took several moments to clean them. Finally he said, "Good news, Tina. You have a teaching contract for the next school year."

Tina was speechless for a moment. He'd promised to try getting her a spot, but she'd been afraid to hope. Rising, she shook his hand. "Thank you, Mr. Tyler. I really appreciate this."

"See Jean Benson at the board office for an interview. Just a formality, actually. It's in the bag."

"You won't be sorry."

"Glad to have you on board," he said, walking her to the door.

She gave a thumbs-up sign to the secretary, who'd become her friend. Hallelujah! At long last she would be completely self-supporting. Perhaps life did have a way of working out.

25

In mid-June Louise went into labor and little Susan Chiara made her appearance into the world, not without trauma. After twenty hours of steady but ineffectual contractions, when Louise hadn't dilated past five centimeters, the doctor considered performing a cesarean section. At that point, even stoic Louise pleaded, "Yes, yes, do it, please."

Always a pillar of composure in the past, Jonathon was now totally unraveled and readily agreed. A short time later the sleepy pink baby was laid in his arms and he and Louise both cried with joy and exhaustion. They held hands and said a prayer of thanksgiving. Louise's faith had been justified and rewarded.

The next morning, when Ann visited Louise in the hospital, she was struck by the baby's resemblance to an infant picture of Louise herself, with pale skin, an even layer of light hair, and alert round eyes. Ann suddenly remembered Louise's own birth, which she'd greeted with a mixture of curiosity and awe. Later, she'd considered her sister an intrusion and a pest. Ann's charge was to "watch over" her little sister. It was years before they became friends.

Now, holding tiny Susan evoked in Ann the old maternal urgings that had been dormant and unrousable even with Tina's baby, Elena. She inhaled the sweet milky, powdery baby smells and murmured throaty "mother" sounds.

Louise managed a colorless smile and said, as if

from a great distance, "I've never been happier, Ann, but I never imagined it would be so hard. I wanted a natural delivery and expected it would be like Tina's, swift and easy."

The baby whimpered and Ann returned her into the crook of Louise's arm and arranged pillows around for comfort. "I tried to warn you. Tina's delivery was unusual." She stroked her sister's hair. "You'll be great in a day or two."

Louise put the baby to her breast, where she sucked halfheartedly, then fell fast asleep. "I thought you were hungry, Susan," she said, patting her cheek.

Jonathon strode in with a fresh bouquet of flowers and two more stuffed animals. "Isn't she great? I think she knows my voice. Watch this." He put his mouth close to the baby's ear and said, "Susan. Susan. Susan." The baby slumbered on, unmindful of her expected performance. "Well, she's asleep now, but I'm sure she knows my voice."

"I'm sure she does," Ann said indulgently.

"Look at those long fingers." He slid his index finger under the baby's hand and she reflexively curled her fingers around it. "She'll be a pianist, or maybe a surgeon. At first I thought law school. Maybe out East. But now I don't know."

Louise managed a small laugh, pressing a hand against her stitches, while Ann said, "Isn't this a little premature, Jon?"

Noticing her sister's eyes were closing, Ann said, "You're tired, Lou. I'll come back day after tomorrow."

When Ann returned, Louise's color was back and she looked as if she'd been born to motherhood. Ann picked the baby up and kissed her downy cheek.

Louise said, "Doesn't it make you want to have one of your—?"

"Don't even think it," Ann said, feeling uncomfortable under Louise's studied gaze.

Louise shifted awkwardly on the bed. "Doesn't Scott ever talk about having a child?"

"He's mentioned it. But he knows I don't want children."

"And that's agreeable with him?"

Ann hesitated. "Yes, I guess."

"Not a wholehearted concurrence."

Ann laid the baby in her bed, and when the infant objected, stroked her cheek. "Scott knows how I feel and he hasn't made any waves. I think he hopes I may change my mind."

Louise rearranged a spray of white and red carnations in a pottery vase on her tray table. "And you don't feel that it may be a problem?"

"Oh, God, Louise." Ann sat heavily in the single chair at the foot of the bed. "Why are you doing this to me?"

"Because you need to confront it. You've been engaged since Christmas, six months. And because I think that's the reason you haven't set a date yet."

"That's not it at all. We're both busy."

Louise said nothing, but her look was chiding.

Shortly Ann left the happy family, and driving home, she thought about Louise's perceptive remarks. Ann *was* uneasy about the wedding, about Scott's attitude toward having children. But she had other reservations as well. Teddy, on the brink of adolescence, might present a behavior problem. Ann knew how difficult and intractable teenagers could be. She imagined him shouting, "You can't tell me what to do; you're not my father." Then again, Scott and Teddy *did* seem to get on well, and it was foolish to anticipate trouble. Perhaps Teddy would be perfectly agreeable and Scott would be considerate and understanding. Matt, on the other hand, wouldn't be around much longer. Next year he'd be leaving for Ann Arbor and the University of Michigan. He'd only be home summers, if that. He'd announced that he wanted to become a doctor, a psychiatrist. Ann knew that Brian's problems and premature death had precipitated his decision. Meanwhile, between school, sports, and a part-time job, he was rarely home.

Scott urged her incessantly to name a date, but she had made one excuse after another. Finally, she said it would be autumn, her favorite season, but hadn't pinpointed a day. Probably she should talk to both boys, include them in their plans. The Catholic Church wouldn't perform the ceremony unless she had her previous marriage annulled, which she refused to consider. She couldn't, after all, simply eradicate so many years of marriage to Martin as if they hadn't existed. The church laws exasperated her. Therefore the wedding would be a simple civil ceremony.

She kept hedging, she knew, because she loved her existence just as it was. She saw Scott several times a week, but neither interfered in the other's daily life. Yet she couldn't risk losing him.

Arriving home, Ann heard tinkering noises and voices, Scott's and Teddy's, coming from the garage. She had agreed to let Scott store a 1956 Thunderbird in her roomy three-car garage. Scott had a passion for old cars that Teddy was increasingly drawn to almost against his will, probably because of a sense of loyalty to Martin. Ann stopped at the kitchen for snacks and soft drinks, then, balancing a tray, traversed the small distance from house to garage.

In the yard next door, teenagers, swimming in the rectangular pool, shouted and frolicked in high spirits. A ball, carelessly tossed, flew into a bed of marigolds. Ann retrieved it and heaved it back, amid cries of "Sorry" and "Thanks." "Hey," one lad shouted, "tell Teddy to come over. We need one more."

"Okay," she said. Matt and Brian used to join the youths occasionally, other summers, a lifetime ago, it seemed. Now Matt was too busy and Brian was gone.

She brushed past a bank of hollyhocks blooming

against the garage and kneed open the door, calling, "Can I interest anyone in food?"

Teddy relieved her of her burden, while Scott mumbled, his head under the hood, his hands smudged with grease. Ann's heart jumped at the sight of him, muscles straining against his shirt, sandy hair tumbling down his forehead.

"How's Aunt Louise?" Teddy asked.

"Wonderful. The baby's a joy. You'd think she and Jonathon invented parenthood."

Scott emerged, kissed her cheek, and rubbed his hands on a grease-covered cloth. Ann pushed back a lock of sandy hair that had fallen to his eyes. He looked so appealing, his sky-blue eyes full of affection.

"So," he said. "Did seeing the baby give you any ideas?"

Ann frowned and blushed slightly as she glanced at Teddy for his reaction. He seemed not to hear. "The guys next door want you to go swimming with them."

Teddy stuffed a couple of cookies into his mouth. "Maybe I will. See ya later." He ran out, whistling.

"You didn't answer my question, Ann." Scott rubbed a smudge from the car's glossy red finish.

Ann popped the tab on a can of Vernor's ginger ale. "We've talked about it before, Scott, and I've thought about it. A lot. I don't want to have a baby."

"Would it be so awful?"

"No. But it wouldn't be so wonderful either. I don't have the stamina for another baby now. I'd be almost sixty when the child graduated from high school."

"Quit thinking you're old. My mother was forty-six when she had my sister."

"I know it happens. I just don't want it to happen to me." She bit a cracker and chewed thoughtfully. "Scott, how important is this to you?"

Scott leaned against the wall, crossing his arms. "Right now, not very. I'm just thinking about the future. I'm not sure how I'll feel later on."

Ann went to him and twined her arms around his waist. "I'm not going to change my mind."

He rested his chin on Ann's head. "And I'm not willing to give you up just for that. I can enjoy your sisters' babies. Love 'em and leave 'em. No diapers to change, no whining to put up with. That's not all bad." He brushed a kiss on her forehead.

"Scott, are you absolutely sure?"

"As sure as I can be right now. Nothing in life is certain, Ann. I just know one thing. I want you in my life."

She nestled her head against his shoulder. He wanted her. That was the important thing. Babies didn't matter, nothing mattered but that they were together. With that thought, a rush of pure joy penetrated her heart.

"Let's get married right away," he said. "I know a judge who'll do it. We can have a reception for friends and family later on."

"Oh, Scott, be serious."

"I *am* serious."

She hesitated, thinking of what her parents would say, and decided that it wasn't important. "All right. If that's what you really want."

"Tomorrow?"

"Make it next Saturday and you have a deal."

He let out a yell. "All right! Next Saturday I'll be a married man!" He hugged her. "But right now I'm a mess. I need a shower. Take one with me." The last was delivered in a sensuous growl.

Ann couldn't suppress a giggle. "You're so crazy. Teddy might come back."

"Lock the doors."

She hoped he would never lose that sense of fun, of spontaneity, of passion. "Let's go."

They rushed to the house laughing, and in the bathroom they undressed each other in a rush, leaving their clothing in heaps on the black-and-white-tile floor. Ann had never felt so carefree. This was what she loved, the air of youthful exuberance he generated, a playfulness she'd never experienced with Martin. Would it disappear in the mundane everydayness of marriage? Scott spread suds over her body in a slow, meandering way. "We'll do this every Saturday," he murmured. She melted against him in a squish of lather. She knew with certainty she'd made the right decision.

When they emerged the phone was ringing. Ann answered, clutching an oversize towel around her chest.

"Ann," her mother's urgent voice called out. "Your father's had a heart attack. I'm at St. John's."

"Oh, God. How is he?"

"I think he's going to be all right." Chiara's voice faltered, then regained strength. "The doctor says it's a good thing I made him come. Mike kept saying it was just indigestion."

"Oh, God. I'll be right there." Ann felt faint. Her father had never even had a cold. He was invincible. Now, imagining him at death's door, she couldn't fathom life without him. Scott offered to drive her, but she preferred he stay and tell the boys when they returned.

Ann fought tears as she drove to the hospital. As she remembered that other frantic drive to a hospital, her heart thudded against her ribs. If her father should die, she didn't think she could stand it, not on the heels of all the other trauma in her recent life. At one time she'd had an unwavering faith that God or *someone* was looking out for her interests, that everything would turn out for the best. When Martin left, so did that illusion. After meeting Scott, though, she again had felt she could exert some control in her life, garner some happiness. Then Brian's accident occurred. Though she projected an outward calm, inside she had unraveled. Yet her wounds had slowly begun to knit and she felt almost whole again. Now the realization that her father was possibly on the brink of death threw her once again into a panic, making her feel like so much driftwood, tossed from one crashing wave to another. She was totally helpless against the events in her life. She told herself that her father at the age of seventy-five had lived a reasonably long life, that almost everyone loses her parents sometime, that their death, probably in her lifetime, was inevitable. But that was scant consolation.

In the intensive-care unit two nurses hovered and Chiara stood aside frowning, her hands in a tight knot, her mouth drawn down. Tubes dangled from a stand to Mike's arm, dispensing their magic potion, their hope. A plastic tube supplied oxygen through his nose. He looked old and tired, his skin loose. "Only a few minutes," a young nurse in white pants and tunic said sternly.

Ann kissed her mother. "He looks so pale." Mike opened his eyes and managed a wan smile, but it looked as if the old fight was gone.

"The doctor says you're going to be fine, Pa."

He nodded, his eyes unfocused. On the monitor above his head, an erratic green line journeyed endlessly, jumping and dipping. Her mother continuously fussed over him, patting his shoulder, straightening his hair, touching his hand. Finally he moved his head, annoyed.

The nurse said, "It's time to go now."

Her mother dropped a kiss on his forehead and turned to go. Ann hesitated for a moment, observing her father. His eyes were closed. Ann thought he was asleep. His mouth formed a word that emerged slowly, barely a whisper.

"What did he say?" Chiara asked.

Ann shrugged. But she knew the word. He had said, "Dante."

Tina was outside the door, trying to convince the nurse to let her in. They all hugged, mother and daughters, clinging tearfully.

"I know he'll be all right. I just know it," Tina said.

They decided to postpone telling Louise for the time being, and stayed at the hospital until very late, seeing Mike for short periods every hour. Together they spoke to the doctor, who returned to check on him. Most likely, he told them, Mike would make it. He was in good physical shape otherwise and the heart had recuperative powers, sometimes making its own bypass. If he was careful, he should live several more years. "My father was a union buddy of Mr. Marcassa's," the doctor said. "They were in several skirmishes together, including the big strike in Flint. I'll keep a special eye on him."

Several more years, Ann thought. They should be satisfying years, quality years. He'd whispered the name Dante, his only son. Did he want to make a declaration, a confession after all these years, to settle his accounts? He was unaware that Dante knew the circumstances of his birth. Was it up to Ann to tell her father? Then what? Would he want to see Dante and Dante's children? Would he want to tell his wife and daughters the truth?

Back home Scott and the boys pressed her with questions. Her sons adored their grandfather, who in turn adored them. She assured them the prognosis looked good. When the boys went to bed, she cuddled against Scott on the big easy chair and cried softly into his shoulder while he comforted her, smoothed her hair.

"Family secrets, skeletons in the closet," she said.

"Hm?"

"I have a half-brother in Italy."

He sat up straighter, jarring her. "What are you talking about?"

She began the story of the family trip to Italy when she was seventeen, and her adolescent crush on Dante. She described her momentous meeting with Dante a few years ago, just before chancing on Scott in Florence.

"In the hospital he said, 'Dante.' I'm sure of it. I think he would like to see his son again. Now what do I do?"

Scott mulled it over. "It's not your decision. Talk to your father. Tell him you know."

"I knew you'd say that." She rested against Scott's sturdy chest and ran her knuckles softly against his cheek. "Let's hold off a bit on the wedding. Until my father's well."

Scott groaned. "Not too long, Annie. I'm getting impatient."

The third day after his heart attack, Mike was joking with the nurses, demanding more food, and insisting they let him go home. In a week he was home, with instructions to take it easy for eight weeks, then slowly introduce walking exercise. His diet would have to change too—less fat, less meat. Mike grudgingly agreed. "I'll go back to the Italian style," he said. "Plenty of greens and pasta."

Toward the end of July, on a perfect sunshiny day, the sort of day that inspired courage, Ann went to see her father. She'd practiced what she would say, but now, as she entered the house, she couldn't remember any of it.

Her mother greeted her. "Your father's out in the back. I was just going to bring him some orange juice."

"You're spoiling him, Ma. How's he doing?"

"Good. But he gets sad and cries sometimes."

The nurse warned that he might be depressed and easily moved to tears.

"Here, let me have that." Ann reached for the tray with orange juice and crackers. "I want to talk to him alone for a few minutes, okay?"

Ann avoided her mother's sharp look and took the tray to the yard. Her father sat in a canvas chair beneath a fig tree, the one he'd planted when they first moved to this house. He faced his beloved vegetable garden, where a hose trailed a trickle of water to a tomato plant. He moved the hose to the next plant, and Ann heard him speaking softly.

When he saw Ann approach, his eyes lit up. She handed him the glass, then took a chair from the patio and drew close.

"Who were you talking to? The plant?"

He looked embarrassed, then said defensively, "They grow better when you talk to them. I read that in the paper."

"How do you feel?"

"Good as new, but your mother babies me all the time." He glanced behind him, as though looking for spies, and whispered conspiratorially, "Next time you come, bring me a cannoli. She won't let me have those. She made me cut back on my wine too."

Ann laughed. "I'll bring one cannoli and we'll share it."

He pointed to the front page of the *Free Press* lying on the ground. "Did you see that? Hoffa's disappeared. From the Machus Red Fox Restaurant. I remember when he was just a kid." He shook his head disparagingly. "Union's not the same as when I was in it. It got crooked. People get greedy, power-hungry. When we started the UAW we worked for nothing, me and the Reuthers. Nothing."

Ann had heard his stories many times. She looked at the paper, then tossed it aside. "Pa, I want to talk to you."

He eyed her warily, one eyebrow cocked. "Go ahead, talk."

She took a deep breath and held her hands tightly to still their tremor. "When I went to Italy, I visited Dante."

Mike's eyes widened; then he lowered his gaze to his hands, which were clenched together on his knees.

"He has a lovely wife and three children. He told me that before his Zia Teresa died, she had left a letter." She paused, watching her father's reaction. A vein jumped in his temple. "She left him a letter, explaining the circumstances of his birth. She also told him that she told you."

Her father's head dropped, his chin bouncing on his chest. He made mewling noises while tears squeezed from his closed lids. Ann pulled his head against her shoulder, feeling like a mother to her own father. Had she gone too far? Was he too weak to confront this news?

"Are you upset that I know?"

He shook his head slowly, then lifted it and met her gaze. "Do you think I'm a terrible man?"

She reached for his hands and held them tightly. "No. You're only human."

They were silent for several minutes. Only the chirping of birds and faraway traffic sounds were heard.

Finally Ann said, "I think Dante would like to hear from you."

Mike shook his head.

"Yes," Ann persisted. "He has always admired you and is proud that you're his father. I'm sure that he would like his children to know their grandfather."

Mike muttered, "What about Don Ravello, the father who raised him?"

"Both his parents have died."

He passed his hand over his face. "How can I tell your mother? What would she say, after all these years? I kept that lie, that secret. I was so young, just a boy . . ." He cried anew, his tears smearing in grooves down his cheeks.

"I think Ma would understand, especially when you explain it. Do you want me to tell her with you?"

"No. It's my business."

They remained silent for a few moments.

"I want to write to Dante, tell him of your heart attack. Unless you want to do that."

"No. You do it."

The patio door opened and Chiara approached, frowning. *"Che succede?"* she said in soft Italian. "What's happening?"

Mike said, "Sit down, wife. I want to tell you something."

Ann left feeling as though a great burden had lifted from her heart.

26

Ann hesitated at the door of Louise's house, nervous about her self-imposed mission of telling her sisters about Dante, yet relieved at finally being able to share the secret. As she knocked and walked in, cinnamon and other spices assailed her. "Smells good," she said, going to the kitchen.

"Oh, I made cookies," Louise said while Susan suckled contentedly at her breast. "That's what I missed so much in the convent, home cooking."

Tina was already settled in a chair with Elena on her lap. "Louise's house always smells so *homey*." She untwined Elena's fingers from her necklace and set her on the floor. "I can't stay long. I have lots of papers to correct. So, what's this big conference about? The wedding? It's on? It's off?"

Ann poured coffee and helped herself to a cookie. "It's not about the wedding, which is definitely on. This is about our father." Pausing, she looked at each sister. "And about his son."

She had their rapt attention. She began explaining, beginning with her enlightening trip to see Dante and ending with her encounter with her father a few days earlier. Louise and Tina took the news first with stunned surprise, then a calm acceptance.

"It sounds like some sort of medieval drama," Louise said after a moment's silence. "Our own father."

"Our own father," Tina repeated with a reproachful

frown. "You've known for a couple of years and never said a word?"

"How could I? It was Father's secret to keep or to tell, not mine."

"But we're your sisters."

"I could hardly tell you and not Mother. The pivotal question was, did Father want to tell Mother? Oh, I suppose eventually I would have told, after our parents were both gone. But I'm glad to have it out in the open now."

Louise chewed her lower lip. "I wonder if it was wise to do this so soon after his heart attack?"

"I worried about that too," Ann said. "But when I heard him whisper Dante's name in the hospital, I felt we had to talk about it. I think Pa's relieved to have it out too. It must have been quite a burden to bear that secret for so many years."

"What about Ma? How did she take it?"

"I don't know. She hasn't even called me. Maybe she's mad at all of us. I'm going over there tomorrow."

"But how about you, Ann?" Tina asked. "You had a thing for Dante; don't deny it. I think you had some idea of reviving that spark when you went back. How did you feel when you found out?"

"In the first place, I met his devoted wife and one of his three children. That sort of put the damper on any ill-conceived ideas of romance. When I read the letter from his aunt, I was just stunned." She reflected, almost to herself. "How nicely things worked out. Right after that I ran into Scott in Florence. And the rest, as they say, is history."

"Will Pa and Dante get together? Does Pa want to?" Tina asked.

"I don't know what he wants. But I'm planning to write to Dante and tell him the rest of you know."

There were more questions, more discussing, more second-guessing about that long-ago marriage between Mike and Concetta. Finally Ann wearily begged off. It had been an emotional few days.

The next day Ann parked the Lincoln in her parents' driveway and ducked raindrops on her way to the door. Her mother was unusually subdued as Ann walked in. Mike, watching television, looked up and smiled. Ann went to him and kissed his cheek. "How are you, Pa?"

He squeezed her hand. "I'm great. I walked around the block this morning."

"Wonderful." She followed her mother to the kitchen and waited for an opening. Her mother said nothing as she poured coffee and filled a plate with amaretti.

Finally Ann said, "Ma, don't you want to talk about it?"

"What is there to talk about?"

"You know, Dante. Were you angry? Shocked? What?"

Chiara sighed and sat, smoothing her dress over her thighs. "At first I cried and screamed at him. It seemed our marriage had begun with a lie. 'Miserable liar,' I said. Then I wouldn't talk to him. After a while I calmed down. I decided it wasn't so terrible after all. It wasn't as though he deserted his first wife. She was the one who left. He didn't know she was with child. He didn't know for sure if she were dead or alive. It was all a big confusion. Then he did try his best to find her."

Ann should have known her mother would search her heart and find compassion. "It was one of those twists of fate that happen despite all good intentions." She put her arms around Chiara.

Her mother shook her head slowly, sadly. "I feel very sorry for the poor woman. But in the end, it turned out well for Dante. He was adopted by wonderful people who loved him as their own." She looked pensive. "What hurt is that your father never told me. All those years, he never told me." She pressed her hands to her face. "I remember when we were first married I used to think he had deep, dark secrets when he would get moody and quiet and wouldn't answer my questions. Then, as time went on, he stopped acting like that."

Ann asked, "If he had told you when you first met him, would you have married him?"

"No, I don't think so."

"I'm sure he knew that; that's why he couldn't tell." Ann's sympathies were split between both parents. "I don't suppose he could have gotten a divorce."

Chiara made a disparaging face. "In Italy? Never."

"It seems to me there's something in the law about after a disappearance of seven years, it's considered death and the remaining partner is free."

"That may be so in America, but I'm sure he didn't know about it. He says he always meant to tell me, but as the years passed, it got harder and harder, until it was impossible."

"Don't you think it's time for Pa and Dante to get together? Maybe you two could take a trip to Italy."

"No, I'm sure he wouldn't go, not after that heart attack. He worries about having another one. When we talked about going to Italy a few years ago, even then he said he was too old, and besides, there was no one he wanted to see."

"Has he written to Dante?"

"Not yet. He keeps saying he's going to, but . . . it's hard for him, hard to talk about his feelings. You know your father." She wrapped her fingers around her cup. "At first I thought he'd have another heart attack, but now I think getting this secret off his chest was good for him. He's getting stronger every day."

"I think I'll write to Dante. Do you think that would be okay?"

"I don't know, Ann. I just don't know. It's really your father's place."

Ann left feeling buoyed and hopeful, as if the threads in the fabric of her life were beginning to weave together into a pleasing pattern. There remained the one thread with Scott which still dangled uncertainly.

When she left, she went directly to Scott's place.

When he opened the door, she hugged him and asked, "Still want to marry me?"

"God, you know I do."

Her heart swelled with love. "Then let's set the date."

Scott parked the shiny, softly purring Thunderbird beside the courthouse. The ignition key stuck and he swore under his breath.

"Relax." Ann smiled reassuringly, although her own insides churned.

"It's not like we get married every day." Scott grinned nervously.

Louise and Jonathon pulled up beside them with Ann's sons. The others would meet them at the restaurant.

Scott, handsome in his new navy suit, squeezed Ann's hand as he helped her from the car. "I never thought this would actually happen," he whispered.

"You chased me until I caught you."

"Did I tell you you're the most beautiful bride in the world?"

"Only twice." She pressed his hand to still her own slight tremor.

"It's a perfect day," Louise said, pacing alongside Ann.

Autumn of 1975 was coming to a spectacular close, with balmy days, cool nights, and vivid blooms. A perfect day to pledge one's troth, Ann thought, lifting her small bouquet of white roses to her nose and breathing deeply. She felt gloriously young and lovely in a pale peach dress and matching tunic. In her ears glittered the diamond earrings Scott had given her. At forty-one she felt as though her life were just beginning.

She smiled at her boys, who looked uncomfortable in their suits. They liked and respected Scott but were still somewhat uncomfortable with him. It would take time and patience, both of which Scott had, to form bonds of love.

The small entourage walked up the steps of the redbrick building. Inside a bustling wrenlike secretary assured them the judge would arrive shortly. "We haven't had a wedding in ages," she trilled. "Just wait in his office, and he'll be right along."

The room, somber and dignified as befitted a judge's chamber, smelled of old leather and cigars. Scott paced impatiently, grumbling at the delay, while Jonathon teased him about losing his freedom.

The judge, a grizzled bushy-haired octogenarian, bustled in and shook Scott's hand while clapping him on the shoulder. "Well, well, well, Scott, 'bout time you got married. Haven't done this in a while." He consulted a blue-leather-bound book, and after flipping through several pages, looked up and smiled. "Okay, I think I'm ready." He recited simple instructions and positioned them, Ann and Scott in front of his desk, the others grouped slightly behind.

A tape that Louise had brought—an old family favorite of Mario Lanza singing "Ave Maria"—played softly in the background.

Scott, his square jaw determined, stumbled over the few words he and Ann had written and rehearsed, so Ann cued him a few times and they ended up saying both his words and hers together. Which was fine with Ann. They were partners now, helpmates, the way it should be, the way she'd always wanted.

Then Scott fumbled for the ring and finally placed it with shaking hands on Ann's finger. A surge of love and affection bubbled over and tears sprang to her eyes. This was a far cry from the hoopla of her first marriage. Perhaps, she thought, the simpler the ceremony, the stronger the bond. Until this very moment she had felt a sliver of uncertainty that she was doing the right thing. Now that evaporated and all she felt was elation and joy.

After they'd spoken, the judge intoned, "Do you, Scott Trayman, take this woman to be your lawfully wedded wife?"

In a strong but solemn voice Scott said, "I do."

"And do you, Anna Cecilia Norbert, take this man to be your lawfully wedded husband?"

"I do."

"Then, by the authority vested in me under the laws of the State of Michigan, I declare you wedded as man and wife."

They kissed lightly and turned to hug the others.

As they trooped out of the building, Ann teased Scott about his memory loss. "For a man so anxious to get married, you're acting like a reluctant bridegroom."

"That's because until the last minute I was afraid you'd back out."

Such a brave man, she thought, taking on a ready-made family as well as a woman who bore the scars of an unhappy marriage and the loss of a child. She squeezed his arm. "I really love you, Scott."

Family and a few friends gathered for dinner at Little Harry's, where toasts were made and champagne drunk, and Rachel carried out the Italian custom of passing out small packets of *convetti*. Later, only family members returned to Ann's house, hers and Scott's now, for wedding cake. Fresh golden fall flowers filled the house and a caterer had prepared hors d'oeuvres and sliced fruit arranged in colorful patterns. Scott's father, in Europe on business, couldn't get away for the wedding but sent them a generous check. Scott's mother had died when he was a teenager.

Tina nibbled fresh pineapple and gave Elena a strawberry. Standing apart, she looked at Scott and Ann. Happiness oozed from their very pores. Even Teddy and Matthew looked pleased. It's going to work, Tina thought with a burst of pure pleasure. If anyone deserved happiness, it was Ann. Tina felt singularly unenvious. The pattern of her life with Elena was now measured and even. She didn't allow herself to think ahead to when her child would ask, "Where's my daddy?" When that time came, would she be able to tell the truth or would she fabricate a story?

Louise strode to her side. "It's wonderful, isn't it? They're so in love."

Tina nodded. "You're reading my thoughts."

"Your turn next. We've got to find you a Mr. Wonderful."

Tina made a face. "This is the seventies, Lou. Plenty of people manage fine alone. Besides, we both know this idyllic moment won't last forever. Marriage has a way of leveling romance."

"Since when did you become such a cynic?"

"Admit it, Louise. Even you and Jonathon must have your fights."

Louise smiled. "Disagreements. And they don't last. Never more than a week."

They both laughed.

"Look at our parents," Louise continued. "Married forty-seven years."

"I remember plenty of fights, don't you? And I always got the feeling there were things we didn't know about. Dante was one; are there more?"

"You have quite an imagination. Maybe you should write a novel."

Ann approached and asked Tina, "Would you mind slicing up the cake after Scott and I make the first cut?"

"Of course not. Anything else I can do?"

"No, I have a sort of surprise coming soon." She bit her lip.

"A surprise? What's up?"

"I said it's a surprise." Ann moved away, then turned back and whispered, "Keep your fingers crossed that everything works out."

Ann crossed the room and said something to Matthew, who nodded and left. Tina, consumed with curiosity, stopped him at the door and said, "Where are you going, Matt?"

"Can't tell. See you soon." The door closed behind him.

"C'mon, Ann," Tina said when her sister breezed by. "No secrets between sisters. What the hell's going on?"

Ann laughed. "You'll know soon enough. Just pray it's okay."

During the next hour she looked anxiously at her watch.

Finally Matt made an entrance, leaving the door open. "We're here!"

"Oh, God." Ann pressed her hand to her mouth. "Wait a minute, Matt." She called to her father, who was telling Scott stories about the "old days" in the UAW, and to her mother, who was rocking Susan to sleep. She wondered fleetingly if Scott would grow tired of the old stories.

"Sit down, over here," she ordered pointing to the sofa and taking the baby from her mother. She handed the baby to Louise and said to her parents, "I wanted this to be a surprise, but now I think I'd better prepare you." She took a deep breath. "Someone came a long way to see you. From Italy, in fact. Someone who loves you, and whom, I'm sure, you love too." She paused, letting this sink in.

Her father frowned, then gasped. "Oh, no . . ."

"Ann, what is this?" her mother said, her hand flying to her heart.

"Ta-da!" Matthew shouted, opening the door wide.

Dante entered, tall, handsome, a presence, his tanned face spreading into a huge smile. Ann went to him. "I'm so happy you're here."

He hugged her and kissed her cheek. "Anna. Beautiful, as always. Thank you for arranging this."

Her father held out his trembling hands. His mouth worked, but no words came forth.

Dante went to him and bent a knee to the floor. "Father."

Mike reached up and took Dante's face in both his hands, crying openly now. Brokenly he said, "My son."

"I knew there was a bond between us when we first met. There was something here"—Dante thumped his chest—"in my heart."

"I wanted to talk about it after I found out," Mike said in a whisper, "but I couldn't . . . I just couldn't. You understand?"

"Yes. Yes, of course."

The room was silent as Tina and the others watched the drama unfold. Tears ran down the cheeks of both men. Finally Chiara broke the tension, saying quietly, "I think of you as my son too."

Dante hugged, then kissed her on each cheek. "You were like a mother to me, all those years ago when I was a prisoner. I've never forgotten your kindness. You are a warm and generous-hearted woman."

Chiara dabbed at her eyes while Dante stood.

"Now. Where are the others?" Dante looked at the group, then pointed to Tina. "You must be Cristina, and you"—pointing to Louise—"you are Luisa. My sisters." He put an arm possessively around each of them, and asked to be introduced to the assorted husbands and children.

Soon all were talking and asking questions. Why

hadn't Dante brought his family? How long could he stay? What was his home like, the vineyards? His children?

Dante could stay in Michigan for only three days, as he had business in New York. His children were in school and his wife not up to travel. He showed them photographs of the family, pointing out each child. "This one, Giovanni, reminds me of you, Father, strong and determined. Carlo, he's more like his mother. And Adela, ah, she's sweet and gentle."

"My grandchildren," Mike said, repeating their names. "Giovanni, Carlo, and Adela. Now all of a sudden I have eight grandchildren." He looked overwhelmed.

"Be thankful you don't have to feed them all," Chiara said, laughing.

Dante was to have stayed with Ann, but Mike and Chiara insisted that he come to their home. They had much catching up to do. Mike bubbled with plans to show Dante the city. "It's changed since 1945," he said. "It's a different Detroit."

Before they left, Mike took Ann's hand. "Thank you for this reunion. Now I can die happy."

When the guests left and the boys had gone to bed, Ann turned out the lights and sat on Scott's lap. "It went well, didn't it? I was so worried my father might have a relapse or something."

Scott rubbed the back of her neck. "It was wonderful, a wedding and a reunion all at once. But I'm glad everyone's gone. After all, this is our honeymoon."

"Not really." Neither had been able to leave work on short notice and decided on a trip in January to a tropical island. "Do you mind postponing for a few months?"

He plucked a rose from a vase beside him and tucked it in her hair. "Yes, but you can console me."

As they made their way up the stairs, hip to hip, to

get their luggage for the overnight stay at the St. Clair Inn, he hummed, "Here Comes the Bride."

Teddy's door opened and he stood in his pajamas and giggled uncomfortably at them. "You kids!" he said. Then he kissed his mother good night and shook Scott's hand.

Scott grabbed him as he turned away, saying, "Hold it, kid," and gave him a bear hug. Teddy didn't return the hug, but didn't resist either.

"I think everything's going to be fine," Ann said fervently as she dabbed on fresh makeup.

Scott lifted her hair and kissed the back of her neck. "It's going to be perfect."

27

In the spring of 1976 Tina, with her steadily increasing salary, found a larger, ground-floor, sun-filled apartment in a building mostly populated, she soon discovered, by other single parents. The kitchen was small and narrow, but both the dining room and living room were ample. A doorway opened to a small patio beyond which was a general play area scattered with toys—wooden animals on springs, swings, slides, and teeter-totters.

"At long last, a room of my own again," she said when she moved her considerable belongings into one of the two bedrooms. Chiara kept Elena out of trouble while Mike, apologizing for not being more help, insisted on moving small boxes.

"I told you I'd lend you a down payment on one of those new condominiums that are sprouting up all over," her father said.

"No, Pa, you've helped me enough. I'm going to start paying you back now."

"I'm not worried. I know you're good for the money."

"You didn't give like this to the others."

"They didn't need it. If you want, I'll leave you less in my will." His eyes teased.

She kissed his cheek and put a pizza into the oven to warm.

When they all paused to eat, Chiara said, "Now what, Tina? What about your life?"

"What do you mean, my life?"

"You need to get married. You don't even date, how are you going to find a husband? Elena needs a father. Comare Lena has a nephew just your age—"

"Please. Spare me the blind dates." She stacked plates in the cupboard. She hadn't bothered to describe the few unrewarding dates she'd allowed friends to arrange, or the equally dispiriting trips to Parents Without Partners. "Ma, I told you before, I don't want to get married. Women can manage without marriage just fine. Let's face it, I'll probably be single the rest of my life."

"Don't say that!"

"Ma, you're so old-fashioned! There's no stigma to being a single parent nowadays."

"Tina, I didn't raise you to be like this. It isn't right. You have a child and no husband to help take care of the two of you."

Tina held her annoyance in check. "I'm doing great."

"Great." Chiara glanced heavenward, then spread her arms. "This is great? You need a home of your own."

"This apartment suits me for now. Eventually I'll buy a house or maybe a condo."

"You could have stayed with us for a while, saved some money."

"I'm doing my own thing in my own way."

"But you could save more if you—"

"Ma, stop."

Her mother threw her hands in the air. "All right. Be stubborn."

"I am. And I'm not changing."

Even as she said it, Tina realized she *had* changed. After her parents left, she put Elena to bed and sat in quiet exhaustion, comtemplating the altered direction of her life. A few years ago she would have disdained someone like herself who was content to work at an ordinary job and live in a rented apartment with no sense of adventure. A few years ago she had thought pompously that she could direct her life. Now she was dubious. Had she unconsciously *planned* to get pregnant? Surely not. Yet, who could say what unseen, unknown forces were at work within?

Possibly she could once again veer away from the usual, safe path and pursue an active role in feminist activities. In her own school district, for instance, the great majority of principals were male, while most of the teachers were female. It wasn't that women were less qualified.

Yet she didn't feel pushed to right wrongs, not now. Her goals were simple now: put in a good day's work, collect her just payment, and care for Elena, who was endlessly entertaining with chatter and songs. Was she copping out? she wondered a bit guiltily. What would have happened if she hadn't had Elena? Where would she be mentally, physically? Despite all the satisfaction she derived from motherhood, from her independence, a nostalgic wistfulness rose for the younger, carefree Tina.

That summer she made inquiries into joining a local chapter of the National Organization for Women, but didn't have the energy to pursue it further. None of the issues seemed strong enough for her to make a commitment of time. She felt many of the women's issues were actually divisive, serving to alienate men rather than recognizing that they could be included in seeking solutions.

She also considered taking classes in school administration, but in the end she decided not to erode what little time she had with Elena. When September rolled around, she learned she would be teaching a first-grade class, just what she wanted.

School had been in session one week, and Tina, unused to the long hours after a relaxing summer off, was pleased at the prospect of having an entire week-end to herself. In the cool of the evening she dusted off a plastic chair on her small patio, stretched out her slim tanned legs, and sat watching Elena chase after their neighbor's chocolate-colored mutt.

"Doggie, doggie," Elena cried, tearing after the puppy. When they finally collided, she tumbled to the ground with him in shrieks of laughter. A hunger of love overcame Tina as she watched her daughter's antics.

A neighbor joined her, with her little boy following. "Go play with Elena, Jason," she said, nudging him forward. Sandra, newly divorced, had introduced herself soon after Tina moved in. They had since become fast friends and their children often played together. The women chatted as the children tugged toys away from each other with shouts of "Mine!"

Tina smiled, contented, listening to Sandra's gossip and admiring her new "mood" ring, which changed colors according to her emotional state.

After Sandra and Jason left, Tina basked in the evening sun as it filtered through a lone beech tree. She relished these last delicious days of summer.

She started at the sound of a car pulling up in the space by her apartment. A car door slammed, foot-steps sounded, and moments later her bell rang.

Expecting a visit from Louise, Tina yelled, "I'm out back."

The front screen door squeaked then slammed, and footsteps sounded across the kitchen floor. The door opened behind her.

"Hello, Tina," a voice said softly.

She gasped inaudibly, her heart lurching in her chest. Adam! Caught unaware, she could only stare. The sight of him brought a rush of emotions and memories, memories she thought she'd buried.

Rising awkwardly, she said, "Adam . . ."

For a moment he seemed wary, as though waiting

for permission to smile. "I'm surprised you recognized me." His hand rubbed the chin that had once sprouted a beard. "A few changes."

"More than a few." The mustache was gone too, his dark waving hair neatly trimmed to the edge of his neck. He was without the signature jeans and wore, instead, a knit shirt and dark pants.

Now he did smile, and the well-remembered grin tugged at her heart. "I, uh, I was in town and thought—"

"How did you find me? I'm not in the book."

"It was easy. I called your parents' house and said I had some tax information to mail you and needed your current address. Your mother was happy to oblige."

"My mother always was too gullible." She felt a niggling annoyance with her mother.

"So, how are you?" His soulful eyes, dark as sable, penetrated hers until she looked away.

"I'm great." She spread her mouth into a wide smile and willed her heart to stop its frantic pounding. "How are you? I heard you made it through law school."

"Yeah. I'm working in the prosecutor's office."

"Great. Congratulations. What about the Beehive?"

"It's still functioning. A woman is director now."

"Someone I know?"

"No, someone new."

"Mama," Elena shouted. Running to her mother, she half-hid behind Tina's legs, thrusting her thumb in her mouth, as she always did when she felt insecure.

"This is my daughter." Tina watched closely for Adam's reaction. Would he notice the long lashes over dark eyes, the shape of the chin, the easy grin, all genetic imprints from his seed?

The smile slowly left his face. "I, uh, didn't know you were married."

Tina lifted her chin. "I'm not."

"Oh." He shifted uncomfortably and tried to look noncommittal. "She's cute. How old is she?"

"Two." She nudged Elena from behind her. "Say hello, darling. This is Adam."

Elena peered at him from lowered lashes.

Adam knelt to her level. "You're a little sweetheart, aren't you? What's your name?"

Elena hid her face behind her mother.

"It's Elena," Tina supplied.

"Ah, that's nice. Italian."

"Yes."

Neither seemed to know what else to say; then both began at once, and stopped and laughed.

"You first," Adam said.

"Would you like some cola? Or wine?"

"No, don't go to any bother."

"It's no bother, really." Why was he here? She wanted him to leave. Yet something inside her, some contradictory emotion she'd thought long obliterated, wanted him to stay.

The air had turned cool and thunder rumbled in the distance. Tina gathered Elena up and all three went into the apartment. Adam's eyes were on her as she poured wine into two stemmed glasses and apple juice for her daughter.

Elena took a sip and began singing "This Old Man."

"She's only two?" Adam asked. "She's bright for her age."

"Well, two and a half, actually." She handed Elena a cracker. "Adam, what are you doing here, really?"

"I just wanted to see you. I never felt it was completely finished between us."

"It was finished."

"I tried to get in touch with you. My letters were returned. Your number was changed and unlisted. At first I didn't think you meant it when you said it was over."

"You were the one who ended it, really. The relationship was going nowhere."

"That's not true. We were good for each other."

She met his eyes, earnest, imploring eyes. "But not good enough to make it permanent. Look, it's all been said before." She looked out the window at the rain that had started to fall, then remembered Louise. "My sister is coming over soon."

"I'd like a chance to talk to you. Call her and tell her not to come."

Tina hesitated. Elena, sensing the tension, began to whine.

"Please," Adam said.

The appeal in his voice was too much to resist and she made the call, then whisked Elena from her chair. "I have to get her to bed. You can watch TV or something."

As Tina wrestled Elena's pajamas on her wiggling form, the child said, "A-dam." *Daddy,* Tina wanted to say. *He's your daddy.* Why had he come back? To reopen old wounds? She had adjusted well without him. She was sure he didn't recognize Elena as his child. Why should he? She would ask him to leave before he starting figuring things out. She could never forgive him for allowing her to walk out of his life. And yet . . . and yet. Just looking at him brought back the desire to touch him. She could hardly force her eyes to meet his, for fear he would see the naked longing to be in his arms, to kiss his dear face.

She gave herself a mental shake. Remember, he didn't want you. Not then and not now. The persistent voice in her head questioned: *Then why is he here?*

When she came from the bedroom, Adam was sitting with his head resting back on the chair and his eyes closed. She thought he was asleep.

"Adam?" she said quietly.

He opened his eyes and looked at her intently.

"Why are you here?"

"I needed to see you. Why don't you sit down?"

She sat on the sofa across from him.

"Tina, when you left, I realized what a fool I'd been. I knew I'd let go of the best thing that ever happened to me. I wanted another chance. But you made it clear it was all over and you'd found someone else."

Tina grew uncomfortably warm. "Yes. I did. Find someone else."

"Who is it?"

"Just someone."

"Elena's father?"

Tina began to shake her head, then thought better of it and said, "Yes."

"Where is he now?"

She shifted uncomfortably. "Why do you care?"

"Tina, something's not fitting together. It's not like you to fall in love and get yourself pregnant in such short order."

She said quietly, "I fell for you pretty quickly. The first time I saw you, in fact. It was in jail, remember?"

"Of course I remember." He leaned forward, resting his arms on his knees. "Okay. So you left Washington, came to Michigan, and immediately met this guy and got pregnant."

Her jaw tightened. "Yes." She didn't like the direction this conversation was taking.

"Someone you just met?"

"Yes. No, actually, someone I knew from school. We used to date and . . . well, one thing led to another."

"So where is this lover boy?"

"He . . . he died soon after that in a car accident." She gave a small sad smile, pleased with the invention.

He shook his head wryly. "And you can't even dredge up one tear for this poor sucker?"

Tina's smile evaporated into indignation. "That was a long time ago. My tears are all used up."

"But your daughter's father!"

"Even so. The past is over and done with. Get on with your life, I always say." She shifted a pillow behind her back. "Look, Adam, maybe you'd better go. It's getting late. Elena wakes up early, and I'm pretty tired."

Adam moved swiftly from the chair to Tina's side and gripped her arm. "I've been doing some figuring. When was Elena born?"

"Let go of me, Adam. That hurts."

"When!"

She wrenched away and yelled, "March 2."

Adam wet his lips and shook his head. "You were pregnant when you left Washington, weren't you?"

She started crying.

"Tina, answer me!"

"All right, yes! I didn't know I was. Not until later."

"I'm Elena's father." He said it quietly, as a statement rather than a question, and dropped back against the sofa.

Tina, sobbing now, went to the kitchen in search of a tissue, and finding one, blew noisily into it.

"How could you do this?" Adam asked, following her.

"How could *I* do this?" She spun around to face him. "It took the two of us. And you're the one who didn't want marriage."

Adam paced in front of her. "I mean not telling me. It never occurred to you how deceitful it was? It never occurred to you I should have had the privilege, the pleasure, of watching this . . . this event unfold?"

Tina stood an inch from him and yelled, "You didn't want a family. No encumbrances, you said. You were a free spirit, you said."

"But I didn't know *then* about the baby!" He closed his eyes and shook his head. "Tina, Tina," he said softly. "I didn't know what I wanted. I was stupid.

You should have given me the opportunity to make a choice when you found out you were pregnant.''

"How could I? You'd have married me out of a sense of duty or a sense of pity.''

Again he shook his head and said in a flat voice, "I'd have married you out of a sense of love.''

Love? She looked up and met his intense gaze, then looked away. Would he have married her, wholeheartedly, with no regrets?

The only sound was of the rain falling in great splatters against the windows, and a low, far-off crack of thunder. Elena called out, frightened at the noise. Tina hurried to her, comforting her, kissing her.

Adam followed Tina into the small bedroom. He stood beside her and ran his hand over Elena's hair and down her cheek. "She's so beautiful,'' he said, his voice cracking. Tina turned and saw the glitter of tears in his eyes.

Elena, calm now, lay quietly, her blanket against her cheek and her thumb firmly in her mouth.

Back in the living room, Adam said, "I don't even know what to say. I'm so . . . *overwhelmed.*''

"There's nothing to say. I have a good life. Elena's my joy.''

"We have to settle some things.''

"It's all settled. You have your life, I have mine.''

"But—''

"Adam, I want you to go. This has been . . . too much . . . too sudden, for both of us.''

He nodded numbly as she led him to the door. Outside, the rain slashed down from the porch roof in a liquid curtain.

"Better take my umbrella,'' Tina said, reaching into the hall closet.

Adam accepted the umbrella and looked as if he wanted to say something more, but he stood silently for a moment, piercing her with his eyes. Then he turned and sprinted to the car.

Tina closed the door and stood against it, pressing her head into the cool wood. She pounded it with both fists. "Damn you! Damn you! Damn you! Why did you have to come back? Why do you have to torture me like this? Why, why? What do you want?"

Automatically she went through the motions of preparing for bed, her mind racing, racing, seeking answers. Until the moment he'd appeared at her door, she'd been pleased with her adjustment to single parenthood. Her life was moving in an orderly direction; she was content, loved her work, had as much social activity as she wanted. And now Adam had to show up and disrupt her existence. The bastard! Hadn't he done enough? She hated him!

No. She loved him. It was as simple as that. The look of him, the cut of him, his gentleness and his strength. All her protestations to the contrary, she loved him as she'd loved no other, had been magnetically drawn to him from the very first time she saw him. Though she'd tried to forget him, the constant reminder in the face of her child often triggered waves of desire and need.

And he had loved her, she was sure of it. But not enough. Not enough to make that final major commitment.

How dare he return now and fault her for not telling him about their child? He'd had the opportunity for marriage and had made the choice against it.

She creamed lotion on her arms and legs and lay down stiffly on the bed. She knew sleep would be impossible.

Well, she wasn't subjecting herself to any more of Adam's games. If he showed up tomorrow, she wouldn't be home. She'd pack up Elena and go to Louise's. She wouldn't let him creep back into her heart just to tear it open again. She had let him mess up her life once; she wasn't going to do it again.

* * *

In his motel room, Adam turned on the television and flopped onto the bed, but the late news made no impression. He tried reading, to no avail; the words blurred into a senseless jumble. If he were a drinking man, he'd go out and get good and drunk. He might anyway. He slid into his pants and opened the door. To his disappointment, the rain had ceased. It would have been a welcome catharsis to let the healing rain pound down on him, purge him, cleanse his thoughts, clarify his emotions.

He strode quickly down one street, up another, trying to make sense of things. Why had he come? Just because he happened to be in Michigan for his uncle's funeral? No, he had been compelled to see Tina again. Whenever he'd thought of her with another man, he'd been consumed with jealousy. He was fired with the need to see for himself if she was married, happy, or if, like himself, she still hungered for a lost love.

He was a father. He had a daughter. Now what? There was no question but that he would provide for his child. But what about Tina?

Tina. His face crumbled and he leaned against a building and cried, until someone passed with a frightened scare. He walked on, sloshing through puddles, unmindful of the water seeping in his shoes, thinking of Tina's dilemma in finding herself pregnant, imagining her anxiety, her fear. What sort of pregnancy was it? Was the delivery hard? What did Elena look like as an infant? Suddenly he was angry. How dare she have so little faith in him, after what they'd meant to one another? How dare she dismiss his role in all this so lightly. Yet he had made it abundantly clear that he didn't want marriage. In a convoluted way, she *did* have reason to sever their ties.

He'd been with other women in the past three years, but none had pleased him. He found himself constantly comparing them with Tina. And they all fell short. And he was tiring of the game.

The lights of a family restaurant flashed in the darkness, beckoning him inside. He sat in a booth and ordered coffee. His feet were wet and cold, his clothing damp. When the waitress brought his coffee, he clutched it as though it were precious nectar, then took a long draft of the dark, steaming brew.

So now what? He wanted Tina still, had never stopped loving her. When she ended it by saying she was seeing someone else, he was tortured for months, yet he wasn't able to contact her; she'd changed her number and sent his letters back unopened. He had finally caught on. She had dumped him. Royally. She wasn't willing to wait for the "right" time, whatever that meant for him.

Last night, when he'd seen her sitting on her patio, as beautiful as ever, a Madonna, his emotions had almost overpowered him. His love and lust and need were as strong as ever, stronger even. But did she still care for him, or had her embittered emotions destroyed what they'd had? Probably she had a man in her life. She was, after all, beautiful, desirable.

The teenage waitress refilled his cup and flashed a smile, flirting. "Anything else I can get you?"

"No." He threw a bill on the table and left.

Back at the motel, sleep eluded him until the sky turned a gunmetal gray and a hazy sun appeared. He awakened after a fitful few hours of sleep, determined to see Tina, to penetrate her defenses, to make her talk to him.

The next morning the sun beat down, making steam of the previous night's rainstorm. Tina chased down Elena and dressed her over protests, feeling a sense of desperation rising. "Come on, we're going to Aunt Louise's. We'll see Susan and Rachel."

"An' Lulu?"

"Yes, Aunt Lulu. Hurry, now." Tina didn't want a confrontation with Adam, especially now, with her

head groggy from too little sleep and her mind mud-
dled from too much thinking. She collected her child's
paraphernalia into a shopping bag and headed out the
door, Elena in tow.

As she closed the door, a white Chrysler pulled up
at the curb before her door. Adam. Damn.

"Going somewhere?" he asked from the lowered
window, with an ingratiating smile.

"Yes." She headed toward her car. "I don't want
to talk to you."

He hopped out of the car. "There are things we
need to discuss."

"I've nothing to say." Elena scampered from her
grasp and down the sidewalk toward Adam. She stood
a foot away from him and stared.

"Hello, darlin'," Adam said, bending to one knee.

Elena ran back to the protection of her mother's
skirt. Don't be afraid, Tina wanted to say, he wouldn't
hurt you. He's your father.

Adam stood. "We have to talk about our child. I'm
entitled to see her on a regular basis."

Tina's look was disdainful. "I'm sure. You'll com-
mute every weekend from Washington?"

"If I have to."

"You can't claim her as yours, Adam. I'll deny it."
Why did he want to complicate her life?

"I could in a court of law. There are blood tests,
you know."

"You wouldn't." A cold anger glinted in her eyes.

"Try me."

Tina sputtered. "You're being impossible."

"Can we talk now?" Adam asked.

Reluctantly, with lips compressed in anger, Tina unlocked the door. Inside, she took Elena's hand and led
her to the bedroom. "Why don't you play in your room
for a little while, sweetie? You can play with Mama's
old jewelry." That, she knew, would occupy Elena for
hours. She took the box from a shelf in the closet and

sat the child down with her treasures. Returning to the living room, she faced Adam, who sat on the edge of the recliner.

Hands on hips, she said, "Just what is it you want, Adam?"

"Let's quit sparring. I want . . ." He stood and reached for her hand, but she yanked out of range. "I want you."

"How dare you! You come back into my life and expect that nothing's changed. Well, everything's changed. Me! I've changed. Get out of my life and—"

He sprang to his feet. "You're going to marry me."

"What?"

"You're going to marry me. Right away."

"You're crazy."

"Me? You're the one who's crazy. I thought that's what you wanted."

"Then. Not now. My life's great just the way it is."

"I'm not asking you to marry me. I'm telling you."

"You . . . you bastard! You think you can waltz in here—"

He grabbed her and pulled her hard against him. "Yes, I think I can waltz in here and make you love me again. The way I love you." His lips were hard and bruising against hers. She wanted to pull away, but the sorcery of his touch wound invisible tendrils around her heart. She gave in to his searching mouth, to the sensual heat from his body so close against hers. How easily she succumbed to his potent intensity. Angry again, she tried to push away, unwilling to become a slave to his seduction, but he held her fast. He had no right to expect her to crumble the moment he beckoned. She beat her fists against his muscular arms until finally he released her.

He moved back a step and observed her through slitted eyes. "Sorry. But you wanted me to kiss you, didn't you?"

"Yes, damn you."

"Who do you know who can marry us in a hurry?"

"I'm not marrying you."

"Why not? Give me one good reason."

"Because you're unreliable."

"Where's your evidence?"

"Oh, play the counselor, eh?"

"Yes. In fact, *you're* unreliable. You withheld the truth. But I won't hold that against you."

"Adam, what do you really want?"

"I told you, I want you."

She stared at him, hard. His eyes held depths of love. Was it possible she had within her grasp that ineffable something that had been sorely missing in her life, that had left great empty gaps in her heart? But she was afraid. Afraid to trust, afraid to believe. Tears sprang to her eyes.

She didn't resist when Adam gathered her in his arms. "Tina, listen," he murmured. "I never wanted to hurt you and I never stopped loving you. When you said it was over, I was devastated. I'd been sure you'd hang around and wait for me to grow up." He brushed away a tear from her cheek with his fingertip. "Please don't cry. If you say you don't love me, I'll leave you alone. Say it."

She shook her head.

"Say you don't love me and I'll leave now."

She couldn't commit once again and leave herself vulnerable. "I . . . I don't love you."

The animation left his face. The energy dissipated. Slowly he turned away. With his back to her he said quietly, "You'll be hearing from a lawyer, a colleague, about support payments and visitation rights."

What was she doing? Sending him away with the lie that she didn't love him, when he was all she'd ever wanted. She felt overcome with a sense of time running out. If she didn't reach out and seize this moment, she wouldn't have it again.

Adam turned with his hand on the doorknob.

"Wait," she said. "I . . . I do love you." She stared at the floor. "I don't know why, but I do. I can't help myself. I tried so hard to forget you, but it was no good . . ."

He rushed to her side and held her close. "I know, I know. Listen, baby. I'm not letting you go, no matter what. We're getting married and you're coming back to Washington with me."

She moved to his arms and he enclosed her gently, patting her. "Whither thou goest," she said, her face wreathed in a joyous smile.

He caressed her back, her arms. With slow movements he unbuttoned her blouse and fondled her breasts. His eyes sought and locked with hers. "I've dreamt of making love to you."

"So have I."

They pulled apart as light footsteps sounded from the hall. "Mama! Want juice," Elena said.

"Oh, God, I forgot about her." Tina hastily buttoned her blouse as she went to the kitchen. She poured apple juice into a plastic glass and fitted a lid to it, taking a moment to allow the flush to drain from her face. The need for Adam filled her, enveloped her.

She went to the phone and dialed Sandra. "Could Elena come there to play with Jason for a while?"

Sandra agreed readily.

"A friend in need," Tina said to Adam, who'd come up behind her to nuzzle her neck. "Hold the thought. Be right back."

She pushed an errant lock of hair from her eyes and took Elena, clutching a container of animal crackers and her juice, to Sandra's apartment.

When she returned, Adam took her into his arms again and rocked her as he kissed her forehead, her cheek, her lips.

She loosened the knit shirt from his waist and slipped her hands underneath, feeling the taut flesh of his back. His caresses were downy soft, his kisses light and airy. Curling her arms around his neck, she pulled him close, arching her body against his.

"Oh, my love." He scooped her up into his arms and carried her to the bedroom.

She slithered to the bed, opening her arms to him. "I've wanted you for so long, so long." An urgency filled her to mesh every part of her body to his. She wound her arms and legs around him as he fitted himself within her. Feeling the flat mole on his right shoulder, the crisp hair on his chest, breathing the well-remembered smell of him, all that banished the emptiness of the past three years, melted it away as a spring sun melts the snow. Outside noises of water spraying, of traffic, of children playing, all receded, and nothing was important but their rhythmic movements, their oneness, their love.

Later, lying in the crook of his arm, she said, "It's as if we were never apart."

"Ah, Tina. When I thought I'd lost you, I was shattered."

"I thought you were tired of me, tired of the relationship."

"How could you? I kept trying to convince you to come back." He rubbed his thumb over her knuckles. "Will you hold all this against me? That I wasn't there for you?"

"No. You didn't know."

"Last night I kept thinking about how you went through this alone, how hard it must have been."

She tapped a tune on his chest with her fingers. "It was. I even considered abortion. But I couldn't go through with it."

"No, of course you couldn't, not you. Thank God you didn't."

She sat upright and gazed into his eyes. "Are you sure you want marriage? Is this the right thing for us now?"

"I've never been more sure of anything in my life."

"I don't know, Adam. There are a lot of things to consider. My job, for one."

"You can work in Washington. Or I can support you. Maybe not in the lap of luxury for a while, but adequately."

She put his hand to her cheek. "I think I'm dreaming. Pinch me."

"You're not dreaming, baby."

"If I am, I don't ever want to wake." She moved from the bed. "I'd better get dressed. I don't want Sandra to walk in and catch me in bed with a perfect stranger."

"Who's a stranger?" He watched as she slipped lean legs into jeans. "Let's decide about the wedding right now. Do you want the whole shebang or a quiet ceremony?"

"Under the circumstances, a quiet ceremony."

"When?"

"I don't know. When?"

"You make all the preparations and I'll be back in a week. I'll sweep you and Elena up on my white stallion and take you back to Washington."

Adam left for Metro Airport in a hurry to catch a plane, and Tina sat in a daze for a long while, feeling a glow of happiness that spread through her body, reflecting through her every pore.

When Sandra brought Elena in, she took one look and asked, "Is something wrong?"

"No, something's right. I'm getting married."

"Isn't this rather sudden?"

"No, actually, it's been coming on for several years."

Sandra left looking confused. Tina held Elena on her lap and said, "That nice man, Adam, is your daddy. We're going to live with your daddy. Won't that be nice?"

Elena screwed up her face in puzzlement. "Daddy."

Tina roused from her state of inactivity and made a

flurry of calls. Her first was to her mother. "I'm getting married."

"Married? Have you gone crazy?"

"Crazy with happiness."

"You don't even have a boyfriend. Who wants to marry you?"

"Adam Thornberry, Elena's father."

There were a few moments of silence at the other end. "Tell me what happened."

At the end of Tina's explanation, her mother was still skeptical, still disbelieving.

The calls to her sisters were met first with amazement, then with cautious happiness.

But their reaction didn't matter. What mattered was that she was in love with a man who loved her. She was finally getting the happy ending she'd longed for and that she thought would always elude her.

Tina did something she hadn't done in a long, long time. She dropped to her knees and said a prayer of thanksgiving.

Epilogue

It hardly seemed possible to Tina that a year had elapsed since she had married and left Michigan. Now she sat on the floor of Ann's old bedroom sorting through the contents of a flowered hat box. She'd flown in from Washington for a long weekend on this glorious May day to join her sisters in helping her parents move. They had at last consented to sell the house and move into a small condominium, admitting finally that the upkeep—the garden in summer, the snow in winter—all of it was more than they could handle. Mike was seventy-seven and Chiara sixty-eight.

Tomorrow they would hold an estate sale. The girls had combed through a lifetime worth of memories, a slow and sometimes painful process, especially in Ann's room, where they'd sat so many times before, sharing dreams, arguing, making up.

"I hate to see that old dressing table go," Ann said. "Many's the night we sat in front of it primping. Maybe I'll take it. With a coat of paint it'll be good as new."

Tina sat on the floor, rummaging through a box. "I didn't know you were so sentimental. It's not exactly a family heirloom."

Ann said, "I'm attached. This room brings back memories. Remember our first television in 1950? We watched *Roller Derby* and *Broadway Open House*."

Tina said, "I was only six. I remember Ed Sullivan and Dave Garroway."

"Frank Sinatra seventy-eights, proms, wrist corsages," Ann said dreamily.

"Ponytails, Bermuda shorts, crinolines, Pat Boone," Louise said.

"Howdy Doody, sock hops, James Dean, Hootenanies, the twist." Tina leaned back, gazing at the ceiling, remembering. "The Mouseketeers."

The three of them began the refrain, "M-i-c-k-e-y M-o-u-s-e," and giggled like kids.

Tina unfurled a Wayne State University pennant and suddenly started crying. "Excuse me, but I'm suffering from an excess of emotion today. I hate being so far away. I keep thinking I should be around in case my parents need me." She was supremely happy with Adam, who had settled them in a lovely home in Arlington, Virginia, with her work in a nursery school, with life in general.

Ann said quietly, "Lou and I keep an eye on them."

"It's a quick flight from Washington." Louise patted her hand. "And they're both doing so well."

"What I hate most is that Elena hardly gets to see her grandparents." Tina sniffed into a tissue.

Louise said, "Why don't we pool our resources and send them to Washington for a week?"

Tina said, "Do you think they'd come?"

"We'll convince them. September or October, when the weather cools." Ann rummaged through a cardboard carton. "Hey, remember my Shirley Temple doll?" She rested on her haunches and cradled the doll in her arm, amidst scattered toys from another era.

Louise lifted a limp curl from the doll's head. "A little the worse for wear."

"I think I'll keep it."

"Why? It's not in good enough shape to be worth anything."

"For my progeny. I may have a little girl."

Louise and Tina stared. Finally Tina broke the silence. "Don't tell us you're pregnant."

"I won't tell you; I'll let you guess." Ann flopped onto the bed and massaged her legs. "Whew, I'm tired."

Tina said, "You are! You're pregnant! Ann, you're forty-three!"

Ann snapped, "I know how old I am."

"Whose idea was this?" Louise asked. "Scott's?"

"Mine, really. It suddenly seemed important that we have a child together. It's not unheard-of, you know." Ann looked from one to the other. "How about a little support here? It *is* a little scary."

Louise hugged her. "Oh, Ann, it was just a surprise, that's all. I'm delighted for you. I wish it were me. Did you tell Ma and Pa?"

"Yes. They feel like I do—elated and scared at the same time. Scott is in seventh heaven. I dearly love that man."

Their mother's voice floated upward and her slow tread sounded on the stairs. "What are you girls doing up there? You're supposed to be cleaning things out." She appeared in the doorway and Mike came up behind her."

"At this rate we won't move till Christmas," Mike said.

"We're just talking and remembering," Louise said. "Do you feel awful about leaving this house, Ma?"

"Yes and no. There's a time for everything, and this is the time to move on. But this morning I cried when I talked about it to your Aunt Flora. We started talking about the old days, remembering how she met me and your father at the train when I came to America in 1928. A long time ago."

"Ma, you've seen a lot in your life, you and Pa. You should write your story."

Their mother was silent for a moment, then said,

"Yes, we've seen a lot. But so have you. When you think about it, everyone has a story."

The scent of lilacs wafted in the open window as they all fell silent, thinking of the years that had passed, the joys, the sorrows.

Tina rested her head on her mother's shoulder. "I was feeling sad about being so far away. I miss everyone." She could remember how desperately she had wanted to get away from family when she was young, to be free from her parents' restrictions, to be independent. It seemed an important rite of passage then. Now their love and caring was a constant element in her life. She hated saying good-bye to this place. This was home. A haven. The place one returns to for love and shelter from the buffeting of the world. Yet wasn't home really a place in the heart?

"It doesn't matter, you know, how far away you are," Ann said softly, seeming to read Tina's thoughts. "We're all still here for you. We're bound by a powerful cord. We're family."